Praise for *Where'd*

The *New York*
Shortlisted for the 2
A Waterstones Book Club p

'Extremely funny, often laugh-out-loud so . . . with her penchant for unexpected twists and smart jet-propelled dialogue, Semple has a way of combining a technologically savvy, ice-cool wit with a stealthy ability to show gradually a character's warmer side'

Tom Cox, *Sunday Times*

'As sharp as lemon juice' Wendy Holden, *Daily Mail*

'Semple's epistolary novel satirizes Seattle, Microsoft, helicopter parents, the elite, and the overeducated – while revealing truths about family, genius, ambition, and resilience'

Gillian Flynn, *GQ*

'In what is at times a sad and painful tale about family dysfunction, black comedy waylays sentimentality. Semple's second novel is a witty, thrilling adventure about creation, destruction, the Antarctic – and the maternal bond' Anna Trench, *Observer*

'I have hardly stopped raving about this since I read it, back in the spring . . . Funny poignant and pointed, think Jennifer Egan's Goon Squad rewritten by Tina Fey and you get the picture. Without doubt, my book of the year' Sam Baker, *Red*

'[A] heart-warming, life-affirming novel of the year'

Polly Vernon, *The Times*

'A clever, witty page-turner with sparkling dialogue, some hilarious e

Sunday

'An invigorating, hilarious, addictive ride of a novel'

Maggie O'Farrell

'A funny, flamboyant portrait of a floored heroine's attempts to fit in'   *Marie Claire*

'The characters in Bernadette may be in real emotional pain, but Semple has the wit and perspective and imagination to make their story hilarious. I tore through this book with heedless pleasure'   Jonathan Franzen

'Fresh and funny and accomplished, but the best thing about it was that I never had any idea what was going to happen next. It was a wild ride'   Kate Atkinson

'I've been devouring the savagely funny *Where'd You Go, Bernadette* by Maria Semple. A TV comedy writer, Semple's wide array of targets include parenting, over-achievement, schoolgates rivalry, creativity, Seattle, Canadians, Microsoft, Antarctica and marital love . . . Semple is funny, smart and deeply touching'

Rowan Pelling, *Daily Telegraph*

'A dazzling comic novel about a misunderstood architect. It's an eccentric and brilliantly accomplished story with a real screenplay quality to it'   Viv Groskop, *Observer*

'My happy summer holiday book was the funny, quirky and surprisingly moving *Where'd You Go, Bernadette* by Maria Semple. It's the kind of book you read and want to buy for friends'

Alison Starling, *Guardian*

'My favourite novel of the year so far . . . It's funnier than a season's worth of *Modern Family*, *Curb Your Enthusiasm* and *Justified* episodes; it's also the most original and imaginative fiction I've read since *The Invention of Hugo Cabret*'

James Patterson, *New York Times*

'Semple's exuberant tale is buoyed up by deft plotting and pitch-perfect characters, whose idiosyncrasies and wrong-headed interactions are by turns comic, tender and craven. Excellent stuff'
James Urquhart, *Financial Times*

'Semple is a TV comedy writer, and the pleasures of *Where'd You Go, Bernadette* are the pleasures of the best American TV: plot, wit and heart. It's refreshing to find a female misunderstood genius at the heart of the book, and a mother-daughter relationship characterised by unadulterated mutual affection'   Justine Jordan, *Guardian*

Praise for *This One Is Mine*

'A fresh, flamboyantly witty new voice'   Helen Fielding

'A sharp, funny first novel . . . *This One Is Mine* is a delight'
Boston Globe

'Maria Semple beautifully renders the twists and turns an overburdened heart can take'   Mary McNamara, *Los Angeles Times*

'*This One Is Mine* is an uncompromising and trenchantly funny portrait of Los Angeles life that rings uncomfortably true'
Darren Star, creator of *Sex and the City*

'Maria Semple delves unafraid, with a sharp eye and sharper hand, into the big issues: Love, Happiness, Life, and Death, and emerges with a Los Angeles we never knew, but always suspected. A triumphant debut'
Gigi Levangie Grazer, author of *The Starter Wife*

'This delightful novel gives pleasure on every page. Deftly satiric, wickedly hilarious, brilliantly plotted to ensure maximum mayhem, it also sustains a sweet, triumphant tenderness toward characters who act so appallingly'

Phillip Loparte, author of *The Art of the Personal Essay*

'Once I started this book, I couldn't put it down. It is funny, carefully observed, beautifully written, very knowing, and in general a real treat. Stop wondering which book to buy. Buy this one'

Merrill Markoe, author of *Walking in Circles Before Lying Down*

'Maria Semple's remarkable first novel isn't just a witty, sharp-edged satire about adultery, social climbing, and the absurdities of L.A. On a deeper level, *This One Is Mine* is a complex, unexpectedly moving story about the risks and rewards of love, in all its irrational glory'

Tom Perrotta, author of *Election* and *Little Children*

THIS ONE IS MINE

Maria Semple was a television writer in Los Angeles for fifteen years, working on hit shows including *Ellen*, *Saturday Night Live*, *Mad About You* and *Arrested Development*. Her second novel, *Where'd You Go, Bernadette*, was shortlisted for the 2013 Women's Prize and was a critical and commercial success on both sides of the Atlantic. She lives in Seattle.

www.mariasemple.com

By Maria Semple

This One Is Mine
Where'd You Go, Bernadette

THIS ONE IS MINE

Maria Semple

PHOENIX

A PHOENIX PAPERBACK

First published in Great Britain in 2014
by Phoenix,
an imprint of Orion Books Ltd,
Orion House, 5 Upper St Martin's Lane,
London WC2H 9EA

An Hachette UK company

1 3 5 7 9 10 8 6 4 2

A CIP catalogue record for this book
is available from the British Library.

ISBN 978-1-7802-2193-9

Printed and bound in Great Britain by
Clays Ltd, St Ives plc

The Orion Publishing Group's policy is to use papers that
are natural, renewable and recyclable products and
made from wood grown in sustainable forests. The logging
and manufacturing processes are expected to conform to
the environmental regulations of the country of origin.

www.orionbooks.co.uk

For my little family

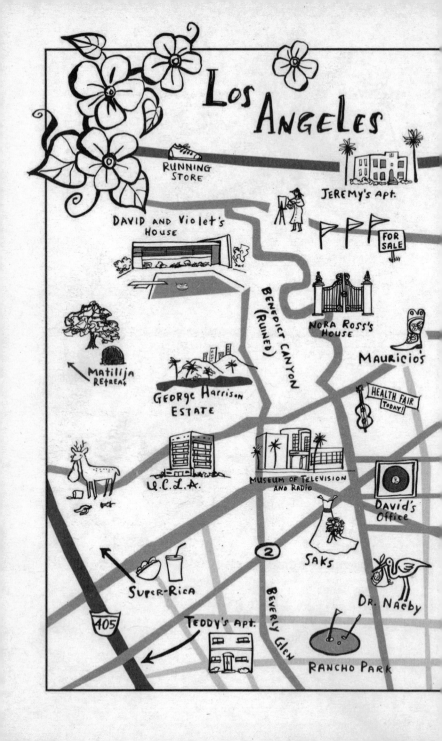

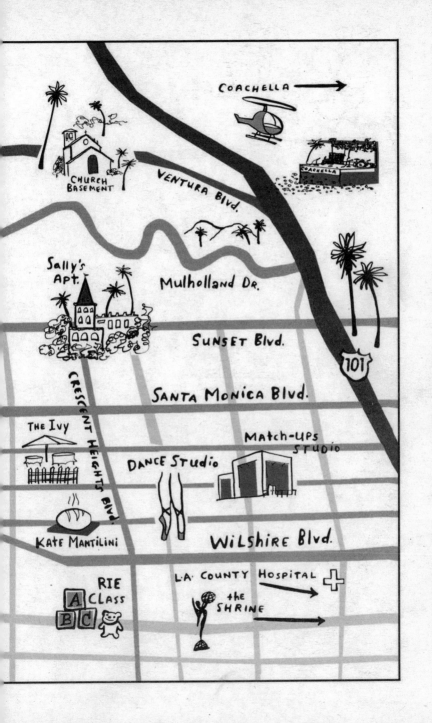

Someone put
You on a slave block
And the unreal bought
You

Now I keep coming to your owner
Saying,
"This one is mine."
You often overhear us talking
And this can make your heart leap
With excitement.

Don't worry,
I will not let sadness
Possess you.

I will gladly borrow all the gold
I need

To get you
Back.

— Hafiz

THIS ONE IS MINE

CHAPTER ONE

DAVID STOOD AT THE SINK, A PINE FOREST TO HIS LEFT, THE PACIFIC OCEAN to his right, and cursed the morning sun. It beat through the skylight and smashed into the mirror, making it all but impossible to shave without squinting. He had lived in Los Angeles long enough to lose track of the seasons, so it took glancing up at CNBC and seeing live images of people snowshoeing down Madison Avenue for it to register: it was the middle of winter. And he determined that all day, no matter how bad things got, at least he'd be grateful for the weather.

His pool shimmered. Stone Canyon Reservoir shimmered. The ocean shimmered. He cocked his head and flicked his wrist, skipping an imaginary stone from the pool to the reservoir. It split some Westwood high-rises, then landed in the Santa Monica Bay. He wound up again—this time to clear Catalina—then stopped.

There was a furry…brown…*thing* floating in the Jacuzzi.

"Honey!" He walked into the bedroom. "There's something in the Jacuzzi." He paused, waiting for the daylight in his eyes to fade.

His wife was in bed, her back to him, her hair seeping from under the pillow she'd taken to putting over her head at night.

"Ma-ma, Ma-ma." A squawk erupted from the baby monitor. There was a cough, then a bleat.

But Violet didn't move. What was her plan? Who did she think was going to get the baby? Was a standoff really so necessary that Violet would let Dot cry like this? *Jesus Christ.* David marched by the bed, skirting the rug so his bare heels struck the hardwood.

"Aggh." Violet pulled the pillow off her head. And there they were, the reason he fell in love with her almost twenty years ago in front of the Murray Hill Cinema: the violets tattooed behind her ear.

David's dog walker, a friend of Violet's from Barnard, had set them up. David managed two bands at the time—big ones, but still, only two. He'd been told Violet worked for a legendary theater producer and was the daughter of some obscure intellectual he'd never heard of. The plan was to meet half an hour before *Full Metal Jacket.* David arrived on time, but the movie had already sold out. He spotted Violet—she had said she'd be the one wearing red plastic sandals—sitting on the sidewalk in the ticket holders' line, engrossed in the *New York Times,* and listening to a Walkman. Two movie tickets were tucked under her leg. She wasn't a knockout, but wasn't fat either, and had a face you wanted to look into. She turned the page of the business section and folded it, then folded it again. An artsy chick who read the business section? Who was responsible enough to have arrived early and bought tickets? With enough Ivy League pluck to sit on a dirty sidewalk and not care who saw her? It was done and done. He had to have her. As he stepped forward, she absentmindedly twisted her long hair off her neck. That's when he first glimpsed the tattoo behind her ear, teasing him from the edge of her hairline. He found it wildly sexy. But something inside him sank. He knew then there'd be a part of her he'd never possess.

"I'll get her, I'll get her, I'll get her." Violet threw off the covers and trudged to Dot's room without looking up.

The violets. *Those fucking violets.*

DAVID headed to the kitchen, comforted by the sounds of the morning: babbling Dot, the hiss of brewing coffee, the crunch of Rice Krispies underfoot. These days, there were two kinds of Rice Krispies, those waiting to be stepped on and those that already had been.

Pffft. He landed on some Krispy dust.

"Dada!" Dot shouted. She sat with perfect posture at her miniature wooden table, covered head to toe in croissant flakes, a darling, crusty monster.

"Aww, good morning!" David said, stepping on some Krispy virgins. "That's what I like to see, my girls!" A carafe of coffee and his newspaper awaited. "Honey," he said to Violet, "there's something floating in the Jacuzzi."

Violet opened the fridge. "What?"

He walked to the window. "It looks like a dead gopher."

"Then it's probably a dead gopher." She rooted around in the fridge. "Ah! There it is." She tore white butcher paper from a hunk of cheese. At least she still did that for him, got him the good cheese.

"How long has it been there?" David asked.

"Mama, what's dat?" said Dot.

"It's cheese, sweetie." Violet sliced some off.

"Want dat."

"I'll get you some. First, I'm making Dada his breakfast."

"How long has the gopher been there?" David repeated.

"I don't know. This is the first I've heard of it." Violet placed

David's breakfast on the counter: wheat toast, sheep's-milk cheese, sliced apples sprinkled with lemon juice and freshly grated nutmeg. "Are we good?"

"You didn't notice it when you looked out the window this morning?"

"Apparently not," Violet said. "Oh! Your milk." She removed a small pitcher from the microwave, set it next to the coffee, and surveyed David's domain. "Okay, that's everything."

"It doesn't upset you that there's a dead animal in our Jacuzzi?"

"I guess it does, a little. For the gopher."

"What gopher?" asked Dot.

"That water could have dysentery in it." David sat down. "What if Marta took Dot in there to swim?" To underscore the seriousness of his point, he had called their nanny by her real name, Marta, not their nickname for her, LadyGo.

"Mama! Want cheese," said Dot.

"I'm getting you some." Violet walked a piece of cheese over to Dot, then sat down on a tiny stool beside her and looked up at David. "Marcelino is coming today. I'll have him fish out the gopher, drain the Jacuzzi, and disinfect it." There was no discernible edge to her voice. This was one of Violet's most bedeviling tactics, acting as if she was being completely reasonable and it was David who was hell-bent on ruining a perfectly fine morning.

"Thank you," he said. "Look, I'm sorry. Today's big. KROQ is debuting the Hanging with Yoko single at nine. I've got tickets going on sale at the Troubadour at ten— Shit."

"What, Dada?"

"Yesterday was my sister's birthday," he said to Violet. "I totally spaced it. That must have been why she kept calling the office."

"I'll get her something and have it messengered over," Violet said. "I'll make sure it's expensive enough so she can't complain."

"Really? Thanks." David was heartened. This was the Violet he loved, the Violet who took care of business. He jiggled the mouse on his laptop and clicked open his brokerage account. Up from yesterday, and the Dow was down eighty points. The hard part wasn't *making* the money, it was *keeping* the money. And he had his gold stocks, his little fighters, to thank for that. He opened the chart for Nightingale Mining and sang its theme song. (After all, what would a stock be without its own theme song?) For Nightingale Mining—symbol XNI—he sang Metallica's "Enter Sandman." "X-N-I. X-N-I. Take my hand. Off to never-never land."

Plunk. Something landed on the newspaper. David ignored it and clicked the chart for Wheaton River Minerals. "Now, that's what you want a chart to look like." To the tune of "Whiskey River," David sang, "Wheaton River, take my mind. Don't let memories torture me. Wheaton River, don't run dry. You're all I got, take care of me."

"Good morning, *Meester* David." It was LadyGo, sliding open the back door. She carried clippers and a canvas gardening bag.

"Good morning," he said, then resumed singing. "I'm drowning in a Wheaton River—"

Plunk. David looked over. The *Los Angeles Times* was covered in something sticky. "Violet? What is this?"

"What is what?" She was lost in thought, staring at the floor.

"What's all over the newspaper?"

Violet blinked, then got up. She stuck her finger in the goo, smelled it, then raised it to her mouth.

"Don't eat it—"

Too late. "It's honey," she said. "That's weird. I didn't put any honey out." She looked up. "There must be a beehive in the crawl space." There was, in fact, a dark stain between two cedar ceiling planks.

"What do you mean, There must be a beehive in the crawl space?"

"Well, I don't know."

"You act like that's something that always happens."

"Want honey," said Dot.

"No, sweetie," Violet said. "This honey is not for you." She turned to David. "Perhaps because it's been so unseasonably hot, the honey melted and dripped through the ceiling." She shrugged and returned to the little stool. "But I don't know anything."

The only reason Violet dared say something so self-pitying and provocative was that she knew David wouldn't get into it in front of LadyGo. LadyGo, the human shield! David glared at Violet, but she wouldn't look at him.

"*Meesuz,* look," the nanny said to Violet, a glint in her eye. "The animals. They eat all the vegetables." LadyGo held out a handful of sugar snap peas. Each pod had tiny holes bored in it. "I ask Javier. LadyGo, What animal is it? LadyGo, I spray next time."

"No," said Violet. "I don't want Javier spraying the vegetables."

"What animals?" asked Dot.

"Maybe *las ratas*. All the carrots? *No mas*."

"That's probably gophers," Violet mused. "Oh well. I'll just have to get carrots and peas at the farmers' market tomorrow." She got up. "Okay, I'm going to take a shower."

David stared at the floor, took a long breath, and clenched his jaw. What the fuck was going on around here? Was this his house or a goddamned wild-animal sanctuary?

"I'll call the gopher guy and the bee guy at nine," Violet said. "There's nothing I can do but deal with it, right?"

"Those are your vegetables. You planted them from seeds. They're ruined. Why doesn't that upset you? I don't understand you sometimes."

"I'll try to be more upset, then."

"What kind of a thing is that to say?"

"David," Violet said. "Please, I can't."

"Where *las ratas*?" squeaked Dot.

"You can't *what*?" David asked.

"I can't," Violet said. "I can't…nothing."

"You can't *nothing!* Great. Thanks for the fucking insight."

"Why Dada sad?" asked Dot.

"Dada's happy," Violet said quickly.

David got up. At the sound of the stool skidding, Violet flinched. LadyGo swooped up Dot and carried her away. *For fuck's sake.*

A drop of honey landed on David's shoulder. He pinched it off and grabbed his car keys. "I'm going to fucking Starbucks."

SALLY awoke to the rising sound of the "babbling brook" feature on her alarm clock, which, like "bamboo waterfall" and "ocean waves," just sounded like an airplane flying overhead. She hit the snooze button and braced herself. It wasn't yesterday, her birthday, that had worried her. That was filled with phone calls, funny cards, a cake at work, and margaritas at El Coyote. It was today she feared, the day *after:* when everyone's attention drifted elsewhere and she woke up in her same one-bedroom apartment on a noisy street, one year older. She took a breath, then another, then smiled. Thirty-six she could manage.

Moving on to today. Sally was teaching back-to-back ballet until Maryam picked her up for the party where Sally would finally be introduced to Jeremy White. Her husband to be. Since today was so jam-packed, Sally had done her bring-a-new-guy-home sweep of the apartment last night. She went over the list in her head one last time.

> Waste baskets: empty
> Box of tampons: off the toilet
> Dishes: washed and put away
> Floors: vacuumed
> Medicine: tucked away in the fridge
> Credit card bills: in the back of the desk drawer
> Candles: everywhere

Sally sprang up. The gossip magazines she had plucked from the studio's recycling basket were still visible on the coffee table. She didn't want Jeremy White to think she was shallow, so she'd bought a *New Yorker* to place on top of them. She got out of bed, then tripped on something.

A wisteria vine from the balcony had crept under the door, across the carpet, and under Sally's bed. She had noticed it last night when she was vacuuming. Thinking it a carefree touch—a thing Holly Golightly might have let grow wild in *her* first apartment—Sally had vacuumed around it. Now something terrible occurred to her. As of eleven o'clock last night, she'd been able to pick up the whole branch; this morning it was stuck to something. She dropped to her hands and knees and traced the vine under the Laura Ashley dust ruffle. A lime green tendril was coiled around the leg of her bed. That meant the vine had snaked around it *while she was sleeping*.

Sally shuddered. She yanked the wisteria, but that only tightened its grip on the metal rod. She clawed off the wet young growth with her fingernails, then threw open the door and hurled the awful branch off the balcony. But the door wouldn't close. The stupid knob had been painted over too many times. She kicked the wood frame until the lock clicked. Her hands trembled as she checked to make sure her manicure wasn't wrecked.

The *tap, tap, tapping* of tangled backstage passes hanging from the doorknob slowed until there was silence. Def Leppard, the Rolling Stones, Commonhouse, the Red Hot Chili Peppers. All bands managed by David at some point. All more important than his little sister's birthday.

The babbling brook started up again. *The New Yorker*. She couldn't forget *The New Yorker*.

TUESDAYS in Los Angeles made Violet sad. It always caught her by surprise, the sadness, like today, as she was driving, safe and alone

in her car after another revolting morning with David. Then she'd
see the open-house signs and would remember: Tuesday, open-
house day.

She stopped at the light at Beverly Glen and watched Gwen
Gold struggle to haul a sign from her white Lexus SUV and place
it strategically to block the other signs. (Who cared if a dozen cars
saw her, she had a house to sell, baby!) Gwen stuck several eye-
catching GWEN GOLD flags in the hard earth, careful not to muss
her Chanel knockoff pantsuit. She wore a grimace, and unlaced
hiking boots over her hose, saving her smiles and good heels
for later, when she'd be all poise as she presented the peekaboo
city views and granite countertops, trying to concentrate on the
client and not the math in her head—*listed at 1.65, half of 3 percent
of 1.5 is 30,000, if I can get five of these a year, that's 150 before taxes, I
could pay off the face-lift and put ten down on a condo. That's good, that's
enough.*...

Violet knew the type, and they made her sad. Those divorcées
who had staked it all on being the perfect wife and mother. Nothing evil in that, nothing that everyone else wasn't doing, nothing to be punished for. But something had gone awry, and now
these women were single, fifty, and forced to earn a living without
any discernible skills. So they became realtors. How had Gwen
played her cards wrong? Had she let herself go after giving birth to
four boys? Had that driven her husband into the arms of his hard-
bodied young secretary? Had the pressures of a disabled child
been too much for even a solid marriage? Or had Gwen had the
affair? A desperately needed fling with a young green-eyed man
who worked at J. Crew? And her husband, Stan—Violet thought
Gwen would be married to a Stan—Stan had caught them and
thrown Gwen out, just when her preppy lover got scared away by
her need. Whatever Gwen had done, she didn't deserve the indig-
nity of this; of that Violet was certain.

The light turned green. Just past Deep Canyon, a woman

wearing a puffy straw hat and a billowy white linen dress painted a picture of the valley, taking advantage of this especially crisp day. Violet caught a glimpse of the oil as she drove past. It wasn't very good. It would never sell. How sad for this woman, who obviously imagined herself on Nantucket the way she was dressed, not choking on fumes overlooking Sherman Oaks. Would she try to get into a group art show with her series of unremarkable landscapes? Would a friend buy a few to make her feel good? Violet had an impulse to turn around and buy the painting on the spot, but she'd never make the U-turn. The traffic on Mulholland had gotten so relentless. She always felt as though someone was about to ram into her while she snaked along the only street in LA she had ever lived, the spine of the city.

Floating past the gatehouse guarding the swollen mansions of Beverly Park, Violet remembered words spoken by her father at this same spot, decades before the mansions. "When you get older," he had said, "you will learn there are two kinds of people. Those who grew up listening to Sondheim on Mulholland, and those who didn't." Years later, he'd lose control of the convertible Jaguar on another part of Mulholland and sail to his death. A drunk-driving accident? A final attempt to make a splash—any splash would do—after never fulfilling the promise of his youth? It was unclear. Violet had hardly spoken to him toward the end.

She flowed with traffic down Coldwater Canyon. A cement truck was backing out of a driveway up ahead. Violet stopped for it, making the driver tailgating her slam on his brakes and hit his horn for a good ten seconds. But he didn't know Violet had nowhere to go. A little shopping. Sally's present. A movie by herself, perhaps. The New York Times at a sushi bar. Dot needed socks.

At the weird, long park along Santa Monica Boulevard, some workers had just raised a banner that read BEVERLY HILLS HEALTH FAIR. A dozen card tables anchored bunches of colorful balloons. But there were no people! How sad for the organizers, who had no doubt spent months planning this event. Violet wanted to reassure them that the crowds would come, just wait until lunchtime. A band was setting up on the grass. A brown-skinned man wearing a black suit sound-checked his upright bass. Poor dear. He probably had no idea how hot it was expected to be when he got dressed this February morning.

David had always accused Violet of feeling sorry for the wrong people. She could cry at the mere thought of Buzz Aldrin's having to endure a lifetime of being known as merely the *second* man on the moon. "Ultra," David would say—it was the nickname he gave her on their first date, as in Ultra Violet—"you really don't need to feel sorry for Buzz Aldrin." But once Violet saw the inherent sadness in one thing, she couldn't stop.

That is why, when she walked into the French chocolate shop on Little Santa Monica, the tiny one that was always empty, the one that sold the gorgeous, bitter truffles, she couldn't help it. She felt unbearably sad. The heaviness filled Violet's stomach, then her chest. She grabbed a small wooden crate of truffles and placed it on the counter. At thirty-five dollars, no wonder there were no customers! The saleslady, her hair pulled severely back and tied with a silk scarf, looked up from her Sudoku book. Her sevens and ones were unmistakably French. This made Violet even sadder. She grabbed two giant crates and placed them on the counter. Perhaps this act of charity would stanch the sadness rising in her chest and prevent it from spilling out her eyes.

"*Bonjour, madame,*" Violet managed to say.

"*Bonjour, madame,*" answered the woman in that curt way of the French.

A pregnant woman announced her entrance with a singsong "Hi!"

Violet could tell she was eager to talk about her pregnancy, and obliged. "Is it your first?" she asked.

"Yes." The woman touched her stomach. "Cody. A boy."

This poor woman. She had no idea how hard it was going to be, even if she loved her baby as much as Violet did Dot. And how Violet did love Dot, was possessed by her. Not a night went by without Violet uttering her name, Dot, just before slipping off. Even if Cody was this woman's blood and heart and every thought, did she know that love wouldn't be enough? Love wouldn't make being a mother any less boring or draining or bewildering. Love wouldn't prevent her from, some mornings, standing at the bottom of the driveway, like Popeye, a wailing Swee'Pea dangling from stiff arms, waiting for the arrival of the nanny.

For too many years, Violet had identified with the comic-book lady on that eighties T-shirt — the one everyone thought was a Lichtenstein but wasn't — who realizes, to her horror, OH NO, I FORGOT TO HAVE CHILDREN! But these first years of motherhood made Violet think there should be a follow-up T-shirt. On it, the same woman is finally cradling her prized baby. But she's still stricken, and her thought bubble now reads IT'S ALL ADDING UP TO NOTHING! There was no reward, no thank-you, no sense of accomplishment, no sustaining happiness. Often, Violet would find herself standing in a room, having no idea what she had gone in to do. It reminded her of the great Stephen Sondheim line…

> *Sometimes I stand in the middle of the floor*
> *Not going left. Not going right.*

Then she'd realize that Dot was back in the other room. And Violet's only purpose in leaving had been to *get out of the same room as her baby*. It was truly astonishing that something as unremarkable as having a kid would be the thing that had finally felled Violet Grace Parry.

"Congratulations," Violet told the expectant mother.

"Et voilà." The saleswoman handed Violet a sales slip.

"Merci, madame."

There was a sticker on the French lady's black cardigan. It was of a bear with a Band-Aid on its arm. I GAVE BLOOD, it read. That did it. Violet was about to start crying. She signed the sales slip without really looking at the amount. It began with a three.

SALLY was sitting on the edge of the tub inspecting her feet when the phone rang. It was her best friend. "Hi, Maryam, I don't have much time." Her toes looked good, no cuts, no blisters.

"I just want to give you directions to the party," said her friend.

"I thought you were going to pick me up." Sally admired her naked body in the mirror. How many thirty-six-year-olds could say there was *nothing* they'd want to change about their body? Heart-shaped ass, delts to die for, not a whisper of ab flab.

"But the party's in Marina del Rey," Maryam started in. "And I am, too, so it doesn't make sense for me to drive all the way to West Hollywood at rush hour to pick you up, then have to drive you back after the party."

Sally knew all this. But she needed Maryam to drive. That way, after Sally captivated Jeremy White at the party, she could tell him that Maryam had left without her, then innocently ask him for a ride home. She'd invite him up, tease him with the best kiss of his life, and abruptly send him on his way. Always leave them wanting more.

"Then I just won't go," Sally said.

"You can't not go!" Maryam cried. "Jeremy never goes to parties. The only reason he's coming tonight is to meet *you*. And my boss invited a bunch of people to impress them. If Jeremy shows up and you're not there, he'll turn around and go home, then I'll look like an idiot."

"You know I hate going to parties alone—" Sally practically dropped the phone: there was a red bump on her bikini line. Please, she prayed, not an ingrown hair. She took a closer look. It was. *Fudge*. If she didn't get the hair out, it would get all gross and infected.

"I *would* pick you up," Maryam said, "but I'm on location in the desert and I need to shower and change when I get home."

"Unlike you, I'd never make *my* best friend do something she's not comfortable with, so I just won't go." Sally squeezed the bump. Nothing came out. She pinched it between her fingernails. Blood collected under the purplish crescent indentations. What a freaking disaster! "Have a nice day," she said. "Good-bye."

"No, Sally—"

Sally hung up. Ice might keep it from getting infected. She went to the kitchen and popped an ice cube out of the tray, then placed it on the splotch.

When Sally moved into this delightful one-bedroom on Crescent Heights Boulevard, she had discovered a bunch of baskets that the previous tenant had left behind in a closet. Full of confidence and whimsy, she hung the baskets from her new kitchen ceiling. But the whole Shabby Chic craze came and went; still, there were the baskets. Except for the two or three she had to throw away because they got infested with those horrible moths that got into her cereal, too. She'd arrived in LA feeling so full of promise. Her career as a dancer hadn't worked out, but that was okay. She invented a ballet-inspired workout, named it Core-de-Ballet, and within a month was teaching classes. All without any help from David.

David. She couldn't believe he forgot her birthday yesterday. She had called to remind him, for his sake. Three times. A snooty secretary answered. "May I tell Mr. Parry your last name?" she asked. "It's the same as his," Sally said. "I'm his *sister*." David still didn't take her call! When she had returned home from her birthday dinner, there was a message on her machine. "I have David Parry returning," said the witch. David always used to remember Sally's birthday. But now he was too busy up there in his zillion-dollar house with that baby of his, who'd won the lottery of the universe just by being born. And Violet, always throwing dinner parties for rock stars, most of them single, and not inviting Sally. Sally knew David way before Violet did, and now Violet acted like she owned him.

Sally's phone rang. "Hello?" It would have been cruel to answer, Hello, Maryam.

"I'll pick you up at six," said her defeated friend.

"Oh, Maryam!" Sally gushed. "You're the best!"

"But I'm going to be wearing hiking boots, and my hair will be caked with dust. Just so you know, my cat will probably pee on my pillow again to punish me for not coming home to feed her—"

Sally jumped in before the subject of the cat could take hold. "Thanks sooo much," she said. Sally loved Maryam but wished she'd change her name to something less Persian. *Maryam* practically begged to be *Marianne*. She was, after all, born in LA and completely American. Sally had brought it up several times, but Maryam got all touchy because her name meant "sweet-smelling flower" or something. Sally wouldn't have been so hung up on it if it weren't for Maryam's surliness and disregard for her personal appearance. She had a nice face and a good body. A little makeup and better clothes could kick her up to a whole other level. Sally herself didn't care one way or the other. She was only thinking of Maryam. As the pretty friend, Sally felt it her obligation.

She checked the ingrown hair. The ice seemed to be working.

Violet walked as fast as she could down Little Santa Monica. If she ran, she'd feel her ass jiggle, and that in itself might let loose the tears. She turned down Beverly Drive, then stopped. She was parked back on Camden. But she couldn't just turn around. Someone she knew might see her flailing. Her heart was full-blown in her chest, fluttering, double and triple beating. The tingling bled down her inner arms to her hands, then got trapped in her fingertips, which felt as if they might burst. The heat prickled in her jaw and rose up her cheeks. Oh God, she had to get off the street.

The Museum of Television and Radio was right there. Violet flung open the heavy glass door and entered the hushed travertine lobby. An elderly docent didn't look up from her knitting. Violet remembered her from a few years back.

It was when *Mann About Town* was being inducted. During the screening of an episode—it was one Violet had written—she had stepped out to read the paper but ended up stuck in a conversation with the excitable docent, who recounted all the famous TV people she'd met. Violet acted impressed, but TV never really interested her. She had always considered her destiny to be more noble, like writing plays or teaching English. But a one-act she had written in college had gotten noticed by a TV writer who quickly hired her. She and David hadn't even been dating a year, but he could manage bands from LA just the same as from New York, so he was happy to relocate. One thing led to another, and there she had found herself, almost twenty years later, being honored at a museum for crap.

But today, even the most innocuous conversation with this docent might cause Violet to collapse, or scream, or die, even. She nestled her face in her shoulder and made a break for the bathroom.

The antechamber was softly lit, with beige walls and comfy carpet. Violet crumpled onto a tufted Knoll bench and allowed the tears to flow. *Why don't you get the baby—you're already awake! I was up all night because of your snoring. If you're so upset about the gopher, get it out of the Jacuzzi yourself! I'm making breakfast for you and Dot. Why don't you figure out what the sticky stuff is in the ceiling? The gophers and rats already ate the damn vegetables—bitching about it isn't going to bring them back. You're not the only one living in this house. Have some consideration before you ruin everybody's morning. See! It's not just me. Dot and LadyGo are scared of you, too!* These were all things Violet would never actually say to David. It was easier to nod.

Violet wiped her nose on her sleeve. There was some pink Play-

Doh on the lapel of her corduroy jacket. She scraped it off with her front teeth; the salt tasted good. A crack of light on the carpet widened into a wedge. A silhouette stepped into it. Violet raised her eyes. A man stood in the door that led to the bathroom proper. Behind him were urinals.

"Oh God," she said. "I'm in the men's room."

"I'm sorry," he said.

"No, it's my fault. I didn't look."

The man wore black, had brown skin and moppish black hair. "Hey," she said. "You're the one playing bass at the health fair."

"Are they looking for me?" Fear danced in his eyes. "They said we were on a fifteen-minute break."

"No, I noticed you when I drove by, that's all." It was rather dear, how worried he was. Violet figured he didn't frequent Beverly Hills and might be intimidated. She felt an odd responsibility to put him at ease. "Are you having fun?" she asked.

"What are you, the ambassador of Beverly Hills?"

"No," she said with a laugh, startled by his acuity, or her transparency, she didn't know which.

"Since you asked," he said, "my answer is no. The Jew bandleader won't give me gas money. It's my fault because I wrote it down wrong. And I show up and see it's a fucking blood drive so there's no tip jar. Not to mention the shit going on with my car, which probably won't start. So here I am, a one-man charity event for a bunch of Beverly Hills receptionists raking in sixty G's a year."

"Jew bandleader, huh?" Violet couldn't tell if he was Jewish himself or some other kind of ethnicity.

"What," he said. "Are you Jewish?"

"No, but I could be."

"Come on, I was just saying that. You seemed cool."

"I am cool."

"Anyway, he's a nigger. I just called him a Jew because he's so cheap."

"My God," she said. "Did you miss the memo? These aren't words people use anymore. Who raised you?"

"Wolves." He sat down beside her. He had bloodshot eyes and lint in his hair. It was hard to tell if it was full of gel or in need of a shampoo. His clothes smelled like a Goodwill. "Really, though," he said. "Are you okay? I'm a good listener."

"I'm fine."

"Nigger, please. What kind of future can we expect when you lie to me like that?"

"Future?" She felt mortified by how besotted she sounded and lowered her voice a register. "I mean it. I have a car that starts. That's something to be grateful for, right?"

"Amen to that." His pants were shiny and polyester. Neat rows of staples held up the hems. On his feet were stiff black-and-white shoes. He must have bought golf shoes without knowing it, probably at a thrift store. "My tires are the thickness of rolling paper, and when I turn on the engine, there's a weird chugging. I think the axle is bent, because it pulls to the left. The whole thing's about to die, I can feel it."

Violet's tunic was twisted so it exposed the elastic panel of her pants. She quickly yanked down her shirt. Jesus, Dot was almost two and Violet was still wearing maternity jeans. Last night, during the Clippers-Nuggets game, a horrifying fact had flashed on the screen: Allen Iverson weighed 165 pounds. In other words, Violet was one pound heavier than the NBA's star point guard. She was completely disgusting.

"And if my car dies," he continued, "I'm dead. I have no cash to fix it. I'd have to leave it on the street. No more gigs, because I can't haul my upright around on a fucking bus. Then I'd lose my apartment, so I might as well be back in Palm Springs." He ran his fingers forcefully through his hair. "Okay," he said, talking himself down, "I have to stop thinking like that. I've got to have faith that God will take care of me."

"Aren't we full of contradictions?" Violet said. "Talking about God now."

He gnawed at a cuticle.

"Stop biting your nails."

"I know, thanks." He leaned back and turned so he could get a square look at her. "So. Are your problems worse than mine?"

"My problems." Violet stared at the three hundred dollars' worth of chocolate nestled between her four-hundred-dollar loafers. "My problems are all problems I'm lucky to have. And I know it, so therein lies the rub."

"You know what we say. If you're alive, all problems are quality problems."

"We say that, do we?"

"How about you and me trade? Your problems for my problems."

"No, thanks," she said.

"You didn't even think about it!" he said. "You bitch!"

Violet laughed loudly.

"Wow, there's a laugh," he said. "Am I good or am I good?"

"You're good." Violet handed him the bag. "I can pay you for your services in chocolate."

"I don't eat chocolate."

"It cost three hundred dollars."

"Are you fucking high?" He rifled through the bag. "How do you blow three Benjamins on chocolate?"

"I got it for this salesman at Hermès. Ten years ago, I bought a hat at Hermès in Paris, which I absolutely cherished. But it blew off when I was flying in a small plane over the Pantanal. We were looking for tapirs. Anyway, I went to the Hermès here in Beverly Hills to replace it, but it had been discontinued. So ever since, the salesman, Daniel, calls me any time a similar hat comes in. Resulting in me not only buying hats that I never wear, but also feeling an insane obligation to get him this ridiculously overpriced chocolate that ironically only a salesman at Hermès would appreciate. And he's not even French, but *Australian*, if you can believe it."

"Okay," said the bass player. "My price just went up for having the shit bored out of me."

Violet gave him a shove. "Good-bye. We wouldn't want you to be tardy for the light-headed secretaries."

He laughed. One of his teeth was missing, not a front tooth, or the one over, but the one beside that. Still, it was a shock. Violet had never been this close to a grown person with a missing tooth. He stood up and looked in the mirror. Violet expected a gasp when he beheld the state of his hair. Instead, he gave himself a churlish smile. Then, without warning, he dropped to one knee and took her hand. "It was a pleasure to meet you, milady."

His skin was so rough. Violet turned her hand up so his rested in it. His nails were savaged, the cuticles stained black. "Do you garden?" she asked.

"Listen to you. Do I garden."

There was a calm in his face, an invitation to linger. She lowered her eyes. His hand, scarred with worry. Hers, plump from herbal-infused creams. The only way people like them were meant to meet was across a counter. She wasn't supposed to be alone with him in a lavishly appointed men's room, a black American Express card in her wallet, a month's rent worth of artisan truffles at her feet. If the chatty docent came upon them and caught the foul-mouthed bass player from Palm Springs holding Violet Parry's hand, it would be within reason for her to call security.

Violet placed her other hand on top of his, cupping it as she would a cricket that had made its way inside the house and she had to return to the safety of the wild. The bass player looked up. She met his green eyes, daring him to do something. But he looked down. She quickly let go of his hand. "Blood," she said.

"What?"

"There, where you were biting your nails." A poppy seed of

blood rested on his cuticle. Violet went to wipe it off, but he jerked his hand away before she could touch it. Violet was momentarily confused, then it occurred to her: he must have just noticed her five-carat diamond ring. "I'm married," she said.

He rose to his feet. "Stay happy," he said. "You twinkle when you're happy." A blast of sunlight blinded her, and the bass player was gone.

SALLY pulled up to the gate off Mandeville Canyon, early for her one o'clock, a private ballet class for three-year-old twins. She got out of her Toyota RAV4—her "truck" as she liked to call it—with the CORE-DE-BALLET placard in the window and picked up the newspaper. She had made sure to arrive early because Jeremy White's column ran Tuesdays in the *Los Angeles Times* and she wanted to appear informed when she finally met him tonight. Sally scooched the paper out of its plastic so she'd be able to return it undetected. The parents were super-nice and would have let her read it if she had asked, but one of the things that made Sally so successful as a private instructor was knowing her boundaries.

She opened the sports section and found "Just the Stats" by Jeremy White. Jeremy's column had started running last fall, and since then he'd predicted the winner of some amazing number of football games. So amazing, apparently, that Maryam, a producer for ESPN, was giving him a segment on their Sunday-morning show beginning next month. That's why tonight was so important. Sally had to get a ring on her finger *before* Jeremy became famous and started earning the big bucks. That's how they never leave you. Because no matter what happens, they know you loved them for them and not for their money.

Her phone rang. She recognized the number as David's office and wasn't thrilled at the prospect of another unpleasant exchange with his secretary. "Hello."

"Hey, Sal, it's me!"

"Oh—David—Hi!"

"Happy birthday. I'm sorry we didn't connect yesterday."

"That's okay," Sally said, unable to resist the surge of love her brother's voice always triggered. "I know how super-busy you are."

"Thirty-six," he said. "That's a big one."

"Yeah, I went out with friends. How are you—"

"You're good?" he asked. It was more of a statement than a question. "Health's good? Work's good?"

"Yeah, fine. What are you up to?"

"Same old—Violet, Dot, my bands. Hey, I saw the Bolshoi is coming. I thought you'd like to go."

"Wow, I'd love to. When is it?"

"April something," he said. "I'll be out of town, but I'll get you tickets—"

Caw! Caw! A screech echoed through the breezy canyon. Sally covered her free ear.

"Well, sounds like you're busy," David said with a laugh.

"No, I'm not, it's just—"

"Call if you need anything."

Then—*splat!* And another *splat.* Out of nowhere, the hood of Sally's truck was freckled with white. And in the tree overhead, parrots! A whole flock of them! "Aaaah!" Sally shut her phone and shielded her hair with the *LA Times. Splat-splat. Splat-splat. Splat-splat-splat.* Wet bird poop machine-gunned the flimsy newsprint. She jumped into her truck, turned on the engine, and drove into the clear. She opened the door and ditched the gross newspaper on the driveway. Always one to learn from her mistakes, Sally resolved to never again park under a tree without first looking for parrots.

OVER the past several hours, Violet had found many excuses to wander the streets of Beverly Hills, the jazz music beckoning her through the mash of traffic. At one point, she had stood across from the park and watched him. The song was "My Funny Valentine," whose lyrics always broke Violet's heart.

> Your looks are laughable,
> Unphotographable,
> Yet you're my fav'rite work of art.

The bass loomed over the bass player. His stance was wide, aggressive, and his arms snaked around the instrument's neck as if trying to wrestle it to its death. But the bass was surely older than the musician who slapped it. It would survive long after he was dust. Between songs, the wizened black drummer said something to the bassist, who in turn laughed. His same laugh from the bathroom. Violet had felt jealousy, stacked with the preposterousness of such jealousy. She had shaken it off and headed to her car.

Yet here she was again, an hour later, pulled toward the park and the dismantled health fair. She didn't realize it until her heart quickened. There he was, getting into a car across Santa Monica Boulevard. Violet hustled through traffic, then flat-out ran up the block to the fenderless Mazda hatchback.

"Fuck! Fuck!" He pounded the wheel with both hands.

Violet tapped on the window. Still looking down, he smiled, then cocked his head and met Violet's eyes. He nodded, as if he'd been expecting her. She motioned for him to roll down the window. He turned the crank with one hand and hooked his finger over the top of the glass.

"Push down," his muffled voice instructed Violet. She flattened both hands against the window and pushed. Their combined effort lowered it six inches. "Did I fucking predict this?" he said with a great big laugh. "My car won't start."

"Can I give you a ride home?" she asked. The passenger seat was fully reclined. On it rested the upright bass in a black bag.

Violet imagined him tenderly laying the instrument on the tattered seat, and blushed.

"I need this fucking car," he said. "I have a champagne brunch gig in Agoura Hills on Sunday, and the rest of the band lives in Ventura, so if someone comes to pick me up, I'll have to give them gas money, and I'm only making fifty bucks for the gig."

"Oh my God. It's like every other word out of your mouth is gas money."

"Excuse me if my biggest concern in life isn't chocolate and hats."

"I have a great mechanic," she said. "I can have your car towed there. He'll arrange for a rental and make sure your car is fixed in time for your gig."

"Really?" he asked.

"Really."

"That's the way it's going to happen?"

"That's the way it's going to happen," Violet said, "because I'm going to pay for it." She felt as though she had just hurled herself off a cliff. He looked away, unable to see she was falling, falling. He started chewing his nails. "Stop that," she said, eager to change the subject.

"Thanks." He pulled his finger out of his mouth. "Why are you doing this?"

"Noblesse oblige?"

"Heh?"

"Never mind. It was—it's just my way of saying thank you. For cheering me up in the men's room."

"Don't let your rich husband hear you say that."

"Whatever it's going to cost, it's an insignificant amount of money."

"Say that again."

"What?"

"Insignificant amount of money."

Violet did. The bass player looked off and thought about it. "I might never be able to pay you back," he said.

"Think of it as me *miracling* you."

"*Miracling* me?"

"It's a Deadhead thing," Violet said. "At Grateful Dead shows, there'd be all these nasty hippies walking around holding up one finger, saying, I need a miracle, which was meant to take the form of someone giving them a free ticket."

"You're a Deadhead?" he asked skeptically.

"I was."

"I feel less guilty accepting your money knowing you have such shitty taste in music."

"I'll call our car service to pick you up," she said. "The mechanic will take care of you."

"Do you think one day *I'll* ever say, Our car service?"

"Most likely no."

"Man, as hippie chicks go, you have one hell of a mean streak."

"The best ones always do."

He got out of the car. His black shirt was wet and stuck to his back. Violet resisted the urge to peel it off.

"You do know how to get shit done," he said. "Are you sure you're not a cokehead, too?" He had changed into flimsy flip-flops. His feet were small and delicate, with black hairs sprouting from the tops of his toes.

Violet fumbled for her cell phone. "What's your name?"

He pulled out a stiff leather wallet chained to his belt loop and removed a business card.

TEDDY REYES
BASS PLAYER
11838 Venice Blvd.
Los Angeles, CA 90066
(310) 555-0199

Reyes. It meant "kings" in Spanish. That answered it; he must be Mexican. Violet pictured Venice Boulevard but could see only oil-change places, strip malls, and junk shops. She didn't know people actually lived on Venice. The zip code—90066—meant nothing to her. Bordering the card were colorful dancing pharmaceutical pills. "What are you, some kind of pill freak?"

"I was," he said. "Among other things. I've been clean almost three years."

"So that's the royal we? AA?"

"I'm Teddy and I'm an alcoholic."

"I'm Violet," she said. "And I'm…I'm happy to meet you."

Teddy gave a big laugh. There it was, his laugh: her laugh. "Of course you're a Violet," he said. "Nice to meet you, too, Violet. I need a miracle."

SALLY followed Maryam into her boss's Marina del Rey condo. It was packed, loud and overlit with twenty-dollar halogen torch lamps you could get at any drugstore. Sally couldn't believe that after all these years in LA, she was still stuck at the level of party where they served baby carrots and Trader Joe's hummus. Since she had the best arms in the room, Sally took off her coat and pushed it into Maryam. "Could you put this somewhere?"

Maryam dutifully did as told and disappeared into the crowd.

"You must be Maryam's friend," a voice called, "the beautiful Sally."

"And you must be our gracious host!" Sally handed the sweaty man two crates of chocolate. She couldn't figure out why Violet had sent over seven pounds of chocolate for her birthday. (The card had read "Love, David and Violet," but Sally knew Violet's writing.) It was a thoughtless, bizarre choice. Sally was about to chuck the bag in the trash, but then saw the round orange box.

In it was a gorgeous Hermès belt. She could forgive Violet the chocolate.

"May I get you a drink?" asked the host.

"No, thanks. I'll just wander." Sally scanned the crowd for Jeremy White. Not wanting to appear too eager, she had never pumped Maryam about Jeremy's looks. All Maryam had said was "He's actually kind of cute." *Actually* kind of cute. Sally wondered, Why the *actually*?

"Hey! Look who it is!" Maryam had reappeared and was spinning Sally around by her shoulders. "Jeremy! This is my friend Sally." Sally found herself, without ceremony, face-to-face with Jeremy White. He was pressed against a wall, a beer high to his chest.

He stuck out his hand. "Nice to meet you, Sally."

Sally shook it. Clammy. "Likewise," she said.

"I can't believe you came to a party," Maryam said, and punched Jeremy in the shoulder.

"You told me I had no choice." He shot a glance at Sally, but before she could engineer a seductive smile, he looked down.

The tension that had been building in Sally's neck and shoulders all day swooshed down her spine and disappeared. Tonight would be easy-peasy-lemon-squeezy. "I'm a big fan of your column," she said. "I don't know how you do it."

"I have a secret system," Jeremy said.

Sally pantomimed pointing a gun at him. "We have ways of making you talk."

"I'm scared," he replied to her left cheek. She worried a zit had sprung up.

Maryam laughed. "You guys are totally made for each other."

Sally felt a flush of excitement that what she was thinking had just been spoken aloud. "Maryam, look! They have five-layer dip." Sally gave her a little wave. *"Your favorite."* Maryam glowered and walked off.

"It involves finding the value in a spread," Jeremy was saying. "Even a half-point discrepancy—especially if it's a valuable half point from three to three and a half—can be statistically significant." It took Sally a second to realize he was still talking about his betting system.

For a geek. That's what Maryam must have meant: he's actually kind of cute *for a geek.* Jeremy had perfect posture. His chin was tucked in, as if to create an extra half-inch distance between himself and the world. He had pale skin and lots of sandy hair, with no signs of balding. He looked slender under a crumply button-down and wide-wale cords. It was a good start, something Sally could work with. "I think it's so amazing you work at the *LA Times,*" she said.

"I work at home. I've only been to Spring Street once."

"Even better! Working at home!"

"Gee. Everything makes you happy," he said.

"I guess I'm just one of those types of people."

"I've never heard of the type who is happy one hundred percent of the time."

"Try me."

"That would require spending every day and night with you."

A joyous "Aah—" was all that came out.

A dumpy, unattractive woman in sweatpants butted in. "Let me know when you're ready to go," she said to Jeremy.

Sally waited for an introduction, but there was none. "Hi, I'm Sally Parry," she had to say.

"I'm Jeremy's neighbor." She had a big mole on her cheek.

"Jennifer drove me here," Jeremy said. "I don't drive."

Jeremy didn't drive here? What about Sally's plan? If he didn't drive her home, she couldn't bring him upstairs. If she couldn't bring him upstairs, she couldn't tease him. If she couldn't tease him, she couldn't send him away, flummoxed and erect. This was a four-alarm disaster! "That's so fascinating!" Sally squealed. "I wish I had a neighbor to chauffeur me!"

"There you go again," he said. "Happy about everything."

"Whatever," Jennifer said. "I'm ready when you are."

"I'm having fun," he said to Jennifer. "Do you mind staying?"

The neighbor girl looked Sally up and down. Sally stood her ground with confidence. Jennifer turned to Jeremy. "Let me know when you're ready. I have to get up early."

Sally had to think fast. Jeremy was totally flirting with her, but were just five minutes face-to-face enough for him to ask her out? This blind date had taken three whole months to maneuver. Sally had only six weeks before Jeremy became a TV star. She grabbed his hand. "Come with me."

VIOLET found David in the bathroom, flossing his teeth in his boxers. At forty-six, his physique was as good as when Violet had first met him.

"Pick a number," he said. Floss hung from either side of his mouth, like a brontosaurus. "From one to five."

"Why?"

"Just pick one and I'll tell you if you're right."

"I don't know...."

"One to five. It isn't hard."

Violet stiffened. She had an eighty percent chance of saying the wrong thing. "Two."

"Five! That's the number of nights we sold out at the Troubadour. They played the single on KROQ. It was massive. By noon we sold out five nights."

"No kidding!" Violet said. David was legendary when it came to breaking new bands, but with the music business imploding, all the old methods were being challenged. "You're the greatest, baby!"

"You better believe it."

Violet removed her hat from the Hermès bag and cut off the

tag. Six hundred dollars. Daniel had seen it in the spring *chapeaux* catalogue and declared a "shopping emergency"—those words were actually preprinted on a slip of paper. The hat was Fed-Exed from Paris to Beverly Hills for Violet's perusal, "no obligation to buy, of course." It wasn't a great hat. But, trapped in a friendship with scented Daniel, Violet gave him the small crate of chocolates and bought it anyway.

"I met the sweetest guy today," Violet said. "A bass player."

All day Violet had been analyzing what had happened between her and Teddy. All day she had reached the same conclusion: nothing. Their meeting was purely accidental. She had made it clear she was married. She'd probably never see him again. But paying to have his car fixed was trickier to rationalize. Technically, it was David's money. But he had just given a bunch to a charity for struggling musicians. And if he did happen across the mechanic's bill—which he wouldn't, as all the bills went straight to the accountant—Violet would say she'd helped a struggling musician.

Still, as Violet kept combing over the details of her strange encounter—Teddy's soulful eyes, the way he kept repeating what she said as if she were the most mesmerizing person in the world, how safe she felt when he took her hand, how their banter made her twinkle, how she practically dared him to kiss her, the desperation she felt offering to fix his car, and the insanity as she tried to play it down—her shame intensified. She kept having to remind herself that nothing illicit had happened. No self-exculpation was necessary. If it were, would she be telling her husband?

"He was playing at a health fair," she added. "I helped him get his car fixed."

"I'm going to get Tara McPherson to do some artwork for the Troubadour shows," David said. He shot antiplaque rinse into his mouth and swished it around.

"That's a great idea." Violet stepped into the closet. She quickly changed into her pajamas while David was occupied with his teeth, to ensure he wouldn't see her naked. "Oh," she said, emerging from the closet, "I sent Sally a belt from Hermès. One of those orange ones with the H buckles. It's a bit arriviste for me, but she likes that kind of thing."

"I'll get Tara to do some T-shirts for the guys at KROQ," David said. "They did me a real solid playing that single."

Violet felt a pang every time David ignored what she said. In a college psych book, she once read that conversations were like contracts between people. Everyone would prefer to talk *all* the time, but if they did, the person they were talking to would lose interest and end the conversation. Therefore, in order to keep talking, a person had to stop talking and listen to the other person. Then, and only then, could they continue talking themselves. At the time, Violet had found it cynical. But after sixteen years of marriage, what she would give! She didn't expect David to genuinely care about a person she'd helped, or a present she'd bought for his sister, but he could at least act as if he cared. One time, as an experiment, Violet had decided to only listen to what he said and never bring anything up about herself. After a couple of days, he grew depressed and became hostile toward her. Still, he had never asked a single question about her day or how she was. Violet had secured her proof that he was a selfish asshole, but she felt terrible to have been responsible for any strife. The whole thing taught her to every day volunteer something about herself. Even knowing it would be met with indifference.

Violet put on her new hat.

"Hey, look at you in that hat," David said. "What a cutie you are." He blew her a kiss in the mirror and headed off to bed.

JEREMY didn't protest as Sally led him to the bedroom and shut the door. "Do you have to use the restroom?" he asked.

That's what was so weird about the way he spoke, Sally realized.

His voice had no inflection. She was about to change that, and how. She took the beer out of his hand and set it on the dresser.

"Forgive me," she said, "but there's something I have to do." She kissed him. He stood there with frozen eyes. She kissed him again.

This time he puckered back with a loud "Mmwwaa." *Mmwwaa* was the sound your grandmother made when she kissed you. Sally tickled his lips with her tongue, caught an opening between his teeth, and wedged them apart. She went in for a slow, sensual kiss. His tongue flapped wildly in her mouth. "Mmwwaa." He pulled his head back and wiped the saliva off his face. "What?" He was breathing heavily. "What do you have to do?"

"Make love." Sally kissed him again and undid his top button.

"Here?" His voice cracked.

"That's right." She walked him to the foot of the bed and pushed him onto the mountain of purses and coats. She straddled him with straight legs to showcase her flexibility. He grabbed her ass. She gave him a few seconds to register the firmness of her glutes. She slalomed her tongue up his cheek to his ear, then recoiled when she hit something synthetic. Weird, he had earplugs in. "Take off your pants," she whispered. She climbed off the bed and locked the door. When she turned around, his tighty-whiteys were nestled in his cords at his ankles. Everything about him was reedy and pale: his dick, his thighs, his pubic hair.

Sally unwrapped her dress, appreciating how sexy it must look as it poured onto the floor. Because of her firm, small breasts, she could get away with going braless. In thong and heels, she sashayed toward Jeremy in big pronounced steps. (It was a walk she had learned at a bridal shower years ago, where a stripper had been hired to give the girls lessons.) In one move, Sally slipped one leg out of her underwear and raised her turned-out leg so her foot was next to Jeremy's waist. Not something he got the pleasure of seeing every day, she was sure of that. He grabbed a breast in each hand and pulsed them. She smiled once, then again to mask a wince. The last thing Sally needed was for Jeremy to come before they made love, which she knew was a serious possibility. Therefore, she couldn't risk licking or even touching his penis. She wanted them to come together this time, their first time, for the romance.

"You turn me on so much," she said. "I swear, I think I might come as soon as you stick it in me." She picked up his dick, now thick and vanilla, like a Twinkie, and lowered herself onto it. Jeremy's eyes rolled back in his head. She knew it—he was coming! She let out a yelp and faked it, "Jeremy! Jeremy!" He closed his eyes and gulped. "Oh God," she said. "Did you come, too?"

"Yes." His eyes were still closed.

Sally rolled onto her side and covered her face with her hands. "I'm so embarrassed."

His eyes flew open, but he didn't look over.

"I've never done that before," she said. "I bet you do that to all the girls, naughty boy."

"Do what?" His eyes moved across the ceiling, as if he were counting the white cork tiles.

"Drive the girls crazy with your statistics."

"No girl has ever done that to me." Jeremy pulled his pants up and shuddered, as if the cheapness of what happened had just penetrated him. He fixed his eyes on the floor.

Sally could tell she was losing him. They had both partaken in the desperate act of a middle-aged woman in a Marina del Rey condo. She was lying naked, a stranger's sperm dripping out of her onto someone's jean jacket. All because she had played it wrong too many times before. The married travel agent who didn't leave his wife for her like he had promised; the Pepperdine law student who had moved in with her for two years, then dumped her the day he passed the bar for some paralegal who "was a better fit intellectually"; the would-be garment king who had talked her into bankrolling his leather jacket business, then dumped her, along with twenty-six grand of credit card debt in her name.

This one Sally would play right. She pulled her knee into her chest, then twisted so her back was arched and her breasts were well showcased. A classic sexy pose, like those early shots of Marilyn Monroe, only Sally wasn't so fat. "Well, did you like it?" she purred.

"Yes."

"Don't make me do it again," she said with a tease. She didn't want a big wet spot on her dress. She grabbed something from the bed and cleaned herself off. Whoops. It was Maryam's scarf. Sally kicked it under the bed and got dressed.

There was a knock on the door. The knob rattled. Sally ignored it. "Would you like to do it again sometime?" she asked.

"Yes." Jeremy patted his pockets. Sally could relax: he wanted a pen to write down her number.

"Sally! Jeremy! Are you in there?" It was Maryam, of course.

"Maybe we could go on a date." Sally fixed Jeremy's collar. "You could send a car to pick me up."

"That could happen." Jeremy had a sweet submissiveness that was starting to grow on her. Sally's type was usually hot guys with hot cars. Like Kurt and his white Jeep Wrangler. How she had loved driving around LA with him, her hair flapping in the wind, a Starbucks *venti* in one hand, the other clinging to the roll bar for dear life. If Don Henley had ever seen them, she was convinced he would have starred them in his next music video. Sally smiled now just remembering it.

"Sally! Are you in there?" Maryam again.

Sally grabbed her coat and swung open the door. "There you are!" she said. "Jeremy had to pee and I was just getting my coat." Sally turned. Jeremy stood in the dim light, flipping a quarter in the air, slapping it on his hand, then doing it again. He must have not found that pen after all....

"If you want a ride home," Maryam said, "we have to leave now. I'm sure my cat is peeing all over my comforter as we speak."

"God, okay. I'm ready." Sally tossed Maryam her jacket. "Here you go."

"Where's my scarf?"

"You didn't have it on when you came in," said Sally.

"But—"

"It's in the car," Sally snapped. She reached into her pocket and found the single business card she'd tucked in especially for this occasion. She slipped it to Jeremy. "Call me." She gave him a peck on the cheek.

"Mmwwaa," he said.

CHAPTER TWO

From One to Ten

THE SPLASH OF COLD WATER HELPED. AT LEAST IT WOULD MASK THE TEARS
streaming down her cheeks. Violet opened her eyes and stared at
herself in the mirror, something she normally took great pains to
avoid. She obviously wasn't beautiful, or people would have said
so. But was one feature in particular the culprit? She had big eyes,
long lashes, high cheekbones, a nice-enough nose. Maybe it was
her mouth. Her mouth might be too small, her lips too thin. Or
was it her chin? In some pictures it looked pointy and witch-like.
Violet had always wanted to know what number she'd be on a
scale from one to ten. She once asked David. "Whoooaaa," he had
said, "there's no right answer to that question." She promised not
to get all weird on him. He relented and told her she was an eight.
She thanked him for the compliment but secretly went wild with

insecurity. Why just an eight? Was she really a six, and he added two to keep the peace? Would he someday leave her for a nine? God knows he was surrounded by them. Years back, when one of his bands was playing the Coliseum, Violet went to find David in his makeshift office, the production trailer. In the tiny bathroom, she saw a *Perfect Ten* magazine. It made her want to collapse.

Thump. Thump. Thump. The swift pounding of David's heels heralded a confrontation. This one promised to be a doozy. An hour ago, in the middle of their private yoga class, David had spotted the dead gopher at the bottom of the Jacuzzi. The one Violet had completely forgotten to take care of. David castigated her in front of the yoga teacher. Ten minutes later, Violet excused herself to the bathroom, and had been here ever since.

"Honey!" David entered, sweaty from yoga. "What happened? Why didn't you come back?"

"I couldn't deal with yoga today." Violet blotted her face.

David took a breath. She knew he was trying to control his temper. All she could do was wait and hope. "Shiva wanted to confirm our place at the yoga retreat next month," he said.

"I'll call her about it later." Violet opened the shower door and turned on the steam.

"Wait a second," he said. "Are you crying?"

"No, I'm fine."

"Is it the gopher?"

"No, it's—"

"What the fuck else am I supposed to do? I'm standing there trying to balance on one leg, and Shiva says pick a spot to focus on. So I look into the Jacuzzi and I see the *same dead gopher* that was there—what—two weeks ago?"

"You were right to yell," Violet said, instantly regretting it.

"Yell? I would hardly call that yelling."

"I know, I know."

"Really. Let's get Shiva on the phone and ask her if I *yelled* at you.

I was merely expressing my very authentic and justifiable shock. You said you'd take care of it *two weeks ago*. Come on, Violet, what's going on? I used to be able to rely on you."

"I'll go fish it out now." Violet headed out.

"Violet, stop." She froze in place, as if playing red-light-green-light. "Every time I come home," he said, "there's some truck in the driveway and a Mexican I've never seen before walking around scowling. Have one of *them* get the gopher out of the Jacuzzi."

Violet couldn't stand him looking at her fat ass anymore. She turned around and walked toward the shower. "Okay, I will."

David intercepted her and gave her a big hug. She stood on her tiptoes and looked into his eyes. They were so gorgeous and mournful, even when he was angry. "It's just that I trust you," he said. "When you say you're going to do something, you usually do it. I've grown to expect it from you. Remember, you're UV-A, not UV-B."

UV-B: Violet despised being called that. David's first nickname for her, Ultraviolet, was endearing. Ultraviolet had morphed into Ultra, and then UV-A. One day, many years ago, when she accidentally locked her keys in her car, Violet had jokingly referred to herself as UV-B. Even though it had originated with her, UV-B struck her as unspeakably cruel coming from her husband.

David got undressed and stepped into the steam. The door sealed shut behind him.

Violet knew she deserved this. She hadn't worked in five years. She didn't *have* to quit her job, but the hours were brutal and she had grown to despise the executives with their idiotic notes. As David had put it, she was too rich to let people dumber than she was have power over her. Plus, it was time to get serious about getting pregnant. She'd been off the pill for a year and nothing had happened. Before she resorted to in vitro, Violet decided to quit her job. A week later, driving down Mulholland, she saw an open-house sign at the bottom of a long driveway she'd always wondered about. On a lark, she went up. She got out of the car and found herself pulled up the exposed aggregate stepping-stones, through the Aleppo pines, and into a glass box on five acres overlooking Stone Canyon Reservoir. The realtor was in the yard talking to a client, so Violet walked through the house alone. It was as if a benevolent force guided her from room to room. Violet had been in a few Richard Neutra houses before and knew instinctively that this was his and arguably one of his best. The place had been neglected since the sixties and needed a ton of work. Still, she raced down the hill to David's office, alive with images of David and her living in the house, entertaining in the house, bringing their elusive baby home from the hospital to the house. Without removing his headset, David had said that if she really wanted it, she could offer full asking price. He didn't need to see it. He trusted her. She was UV-A.

How could she have foreseen that the house would be her undoing? The restoration and addition cost four times the estimate and took three times as long. Overnight, Violet shape-shifted from in-demand, Emmy-winning writer to resident dunce. Every day David pummeled her with questions she couldn't know the answers to. Why didn't the electrician show up? Who scratched the brand-new floors? Why did the decorator charge twenty grand for a throw rug? How did that window get broken? Why did they deliver the wrong tile? But the house was Violet's big idea, so she stoically accepted her role as human bucket for David to vomit into. In addition to the daily drubbings, she was paying for the remodel with her own money and ended up burning through her entire savings. When they finally moved in, Violet was pregnant and, for the first time in her life, unemployed and without a penny to her name. David had no reaction to the news that she'd need to start sending her bills to his accountant. She knew it was a fair trade. Lots of women would gladly get called a dumb fuck a couple times a week in exchange for not having to work.

Steam hissed from the cracked shower door. "Ultra?" David stuck his head out. "Aren't you coming in?"

"One second." Violet opened the medicine cabinet and lifted the colorful Venetian glass votive they'd gotten on their honeymoon, crammed tight with Q-tips. Underneath was the business card she couldn't throw away but hadn't dared touch.

TEDDY REYES
BASS PLAYER

Violet closed the cabinet door and gave her face a hard look. Her skin was holding up well. From one to ten, she'd give herself a seven, with room for improvement.

CHAPTER THREE

SALLY WAS FOUR BLOCKS FROM JEREMY'S BUILDING WHEN SHE STARTED LOOKING for a parking space. His street was nothing but apartments, which meant there was never any place to park. It made Sally want to scream. She trolled the endless stretch of crammed cars and had to remind herself: when Jeremy became a giant TV star and they were married and living in Beverly Hills, she'd be *nostalgic* for the days she fretted over finding a parking space in the valley.

A car pulled out—smack in front of Jeremy's building! Sally gunned it and waved to the exiting Cadillac. The old boat had left so much room that Sally was able to glide right in, headfirst, without having to go into reverse even once. She turned off the ignition, then thought of something: if this was her one allotment of good luck for the day, did she really want to waste it on a parking space? Maybe she should park somewhere else. A car pulled up alongside her. The driver gave Sally an exasperated are-you-staying-or-are-you-going look and threw up her hands. That settled it. No way was Sally going to gift this biotch with a primo parking space. She pulled the key out of the ignition.

In Jeremy's courtyard, she came upon the mailman sorting mail. "Apartment Two G?" she asked. "I'll take that." She plucked Jeremy's bundle and rolled off the rubber band. Bulk mail coupons, a reminder from his dentist, a Visa bill—Sally felt a pang at the mere sight of a boyfriend's Visa bill.

Once, during the final throes of her relationship with Kurt, she had steamed open his Visa bill. Orders for the leather jackets weren't coming in as expected, and Sally had been forced to take out a second credit card to pay off the first. Then one day, lo and behold, Kurt—whose signature look was vintage Hawaiian shirts—traipsed out of the bedroom wearing a new one. "Where did that come from?" she asked. "I've had it forever," he said, rattling the pen cup for the black Sharpie he used to paint his gray hairs. "Well, why haven't I seen it before?" "Maybe you weren't looking." After Kurt left for work, Sally ransacked their waste-baskets and even the big cans in back to find proof he'd recently bought the shirt, but came up empty. Then his Visa bill appeared in the mail. She steamed it open and discovered an eighty-five-dollar charge from Wasteland, his favorite vintage-clothing store. She drove to the boot shop where he worked and confronted him. But he totally turned it around and used this "invasion of privacy" as his basis to dump her!

Sally tucked Jeremy's Visa bill into his other mail and knocked on 2G.

Jeremy opened the door. "You don't have to knock," he said. "You have a key."

"I know." She gave him a big kiss. "I just don't want to barge in on anything."

"There's nothing to barge in on. You've already seen me naked."

Sally laughed. "You're so sweet. Here's the mail."

"How was your class this morning?"

"I had forty-five people," Sally said. "They were spilling next door into the hip-hop class. My manager couldn't believe it."

"That's really great," he said. He tried to shut the door, but it caught on his shoe. Sally wished he'd get rid of those clunky docksiders with the gigantic gummy soles. But he had resisted her attempts to make him over. She finally had to resort to stuffing his *really* geeky clothes between his mattress and box spring. Unfortunately, the dumb shoes were too bulky to hide. Maybe if they went to a shoe store together, Sally could innocently suggest he try on some cross-trainers....

"Hey, I need some new sneakers," she said. "After lunch maybe we could drive to that running store."

"I write my column after lunch."

As if she hadn't noticed! Every day, Jeremy woke up, read two newspapers, ate his breakfast, checked his sports websites, walked to Hamburger Hamlet for lunch, came home, wrote his column, then walked to El Torito and watched sports at a corner table while he ate a cheese quesadilla. Yes, it was boring. On the upside, Sally didn't have to spend her whole life driving around to check if he really was where he said he was.

"Of course *after* you write your column, silly."

There was a knock. It was Jeremy's friend Vance, who joined them for lunch every Wednesday.

"Surprise, surprise," she said.

Vance had been Jeremy's roommate at Cal Poly Pomona. An inveterate gambler, Vance would drag Jeremy to Santa Anita, where he had discovered Jeremy's genius at handicapping horses. It was

Vance who had persuaded a friend at the *LA Times* to give Jeremy a column.

"You're three minutes late," Jeremy said to Vance.

"I know. Traffic." Vance winked at Sally. Not a lascivious wink, but in shared appreciation of Jeremy.

The trio walked down Van Nuys Boulevard, Jeremy working himself up about the upcoming NCAA tournament while Vance listened. Sally could understand why, when it was just Jeremy and her, he did all the talking about sports. The odd thing was, even when Jeremy was with someone who shared his interest in sports, he still did all the talking. And so loudly, at that. She wished he'd stop wearing earplugs.

They passed the usual line of people waiting to get into a hole-in-the-wall falafel place. "Hey, guys!" Sally called ahead. "I want to try this place for a change."

She entered the tiny restaurant, put her warm-up jacket on the only empty table, then went back outside to stand in line. Jeremy and Vance weren't there. To her astonishment, she spotted them across Ventura, heading into Hamburger Hamlet. Without her! Sally went to the corner and shouted across the boulevard. "Jeremy!"

He stopped and turned.

"Didn't you hear me? I want to eat here."

"I always go to Hamburger Hamlet," he shouted back. The signal invited him to WALK across the street, but he stayed on the curb.

"I know that!" she yelled over the crossing pedestrians. "But I want to try someplace new."

"Okay," he said. "We'll be at Hamburger Hamlet."

"Jeremy!" she screamed.

"Do you need money?" he asked.

"I have money! I thought we were going to have lunch *together.*"

"Me, too," he said. "But you want to go to lunch by yourself."

Jeremy turned and walked inside Hamburger Hamlet. Vance ran through the blinking DON'T WALK sign.

"Falafel is a great idea," he told her. "Let's go."

"I don't want to have lunch with you!"

Vance looked as if he was formulating something to say, then sucked in his lips. "Okay, then." He crossed the street and disappeared into Hamburger Hamlet.

Sally felt as if she might faint. What was happening? It didn't make sense. She and Jeremy had been going out three whole weeks, and he still hadn't said "I love you." And now this? Didn't Jeremy realize he'd never do better than Sally? She was thin—and sweet! She was a dancer! Why wasn't he terrified of letting her get away? She didn't understand. It literally left her dizzy. She braced herself against a lamppost.

The first time she had felt this way, she was three and David was reading her *Goodnight Moon*. They bid goodnight to the various things in the room. "Goodnight kittens / And goodnight mittens. Goodnight mush / And goodnight to the old lady whispering 'hush.'" Then, they turned the page and it was blank. The words read "Goodnight nobody." What did that mean? How did you say goodnight to *nobody*? Was *nobody* in the room with them now? After David put her to bed, would *nobody* still be there? That night, Sally couldn't sleep, imagining *nobody* settling in, breathing up all her air; not knowing if, at any moment, *nobody* would swallow her up.

Not knowing. It was the one thing Sally couldn't tolerate. Then something occurred to her: she had a way of finding out.

She let go of the post, retrieved her warm-up jacket from the restaurant, and headed back to Jeremy's apartment. She only had forty-five minutes until they returned. She decided to run.

VIOLET arrived at Kate Mantilini before one so she could score a booth. The busboy brought some of their fabulous sourdough bread. A week ago, Violet would have slathered it with butter and wolfed down the entire half loaf. But not today. Today she was flying. Today she was meeting Teddy. Her pulse raced. She felt utterly relaxed. This was where she belonged, right here, sitting in this booth, waiting for him.

The glass door opened. Through the sea of waiting people flashed pieces of Teddy. He made his way to the hostess and said something. She threw back her long, flat hair and laughed. Violet waved, but couldn't tell if Teddy saw her. He wore lopsided mirrored sunglasses that were too big for his face. Violet waved again. Teddy leaned in to the hostess and whispered. She whispered back. Teddy lifted his shirt. His stomach was a rich brown, with a treasure trail of dark hair running from his belly below the waist of his pants. The hostess slapped Teddy's hand and giggled. Violet sprang to her feet, but the edge of the thick table rammed her gut. She waved both hands. Finally, Teddy surveyed the room and spotted her. He stuffed his pockets with mints and toothpicks and pointed Violet out to the hostess, who shoved him on his way.

Violet got her first clean look at her lunch date. His hair was unbrushed. He wore a sleeveless cowboy shirt, long black sweat shorts, and…huaraches. His shirt had fresh threads hanging from the armholes, as if he'd ripped off the sleeves on the car ride over. Violet had picked this bustling showbiz watering hole because there might be people she knew here, as if to prove there was nothing sneaky about her rendezvous. But as Teddy neared, her terror grew. What if someone she knew *did* see her with this motley character? She needed an alibi: he could be a friend of a friend—who wanted to break into TV—who had just gotten out of rehab—and couldn't afford clothes—it was charity work for the Writers Guild Foundation—mentoring at-risk minorities—

"I figured out about you." Teddy slid into the booth across from her. "You're a Deadhead who took some really good acid, and your life is now one big magical hallucination."

Violet caught that Goodwill whiff again. "I'll think about that," she said, breathing through her mouth. A waitress passed carrying plates of food. Violet practically yelled, "Hi! We're in a hurry!"

"What can I get you to drink?" asked the waitress.

"Some codeine cough syrup," Teddy said.

"If we had any," the waitress replied, "it would be long gone by now."

"Don't I know it." Teddy held up his hand. The waitress transferred the plates to one arm and high-fived him.

"I'll have an iced tea," Violet said flatly.

"Make that two." Teddy watched the waitress leave, then stretched his arms across the back of the booth. "So, Baroness, what brings you here?"

"How's your car driving?"

"Fucking awesome. You have no idea what it's like for me to not have to worry about it breaking down."

"Your mother never taught you to write thank-you notes?"

"I had no way to get in touch with you."

"The mechanic knows my phone number and address. You could have asked him."

"Wow," Teddy said. "You really wanted to be thanked, didn't you?" His hair was ripe with grime and flecks that shimmered pink and blue under the hot halogen bulbs.

"I'm just saying it's kind of white trash of you."

"I'm the only thing worse than white trash," Teddy said. "Half-Mexican white trash."

Violet found herself smiling.

"You totally did miracle me," Teddy said. "I have no idea how I can ever repay you."

"One day you're going to have to step up."

"Shit," Teddy said with a twitch. "What does that mean?"

"I'm not sure," she answered. "It doesn't necessarily have to be with money. At some point, you'll just step up and do the right thing. When the time comes, you'll know."

"You mean like one day I'll have to drive you to the airport?"

"Oh, it's going to be a lot more than a ride to the airport."

The hostess led several black people to a table. Teddy waited for them to pass, then leaned in. "You know what I ask myself when I see niggers eating in a place like this?"

Violet quickly looked around to make sure nobody had heard. "I hope you ask yourself, Why do I keep using that word?"

"I know," he said. "It's bad. But when I was a junkie, that's who I'd hang around with. Everything was, nigger this, nigger that. I was living on the streets, so I was lower than a nigger. I forget I'm not there anymore."

"On behalf of Emily Post? Try keeping it to a minimum."

"Yes, ma'am."

"Thank you. Now, you were saying...."

"You want to know what I think when I see niggers eating in a place like this?"

Violet buried her smile in her hands and peered up. "You seemed determined to tell me."

"I think, How did they get this kind of money?"

"Money? This place is just for assistants and development girls."

"Gee, thanks a lot for the invite!" He laughed.

Violet studied him. "Do you have a girlfriend?"

"Yeah. I have this crazy girlfriend who I'm about to break up with. She's a performance artist. Her name's Coco." Teddy raised his eyebrows and added, "Coco *Kennedy*."

"Of the Hyannisport Kennedys?"

"Of the John-John Kennedys. He was her cousin."

It all clicked for Violet: her attraction to Teddy *wasn't* an aberration. He was objectively charming and desirable: to the hostess, to the waitress, even to American royalty. Coco Kennedy most likely had a plethora of glamorous suitors, yet she chose Teddy. "Really? A Kennedy?"

"Don't tell me you're obsessed with John-John, too?" he said.

"I met him a few times in New York, like everybody did. But I'd hardly consider myself obsessed."

"Good. Because I would barf if someone classy like you fell for those Kennedy poseurs."

"I'm not sure the first word that comes to mind to describe the Kennedys is *poseurs*."

Teddy rolled his eyes. "Why does God keep bringing people into my life who don't see bullshit for what it is?"

"JFK was responsible for the space program and oversaw the civil rights movement. That's more than posing."

"What are you, a fucking historian?"

"My father was." The colorful and dissipated Churchill Grace. He had moved to Hollywood in the sixties and kept company with his fellow countrymen Aldous Huxley and Christopher Isherwood. *Jam Today,* his slim but prescient jeremiad against all that Americans held dear, caused a minor stir when it was published in 1965. He was able to string together writing assignments, guest professorships, and Esalen weekends until his death thirty years later. His wife, Violet's mother, left and moved to Hawaii when Violet was just a baby. Churchill's devotion to his little daughter allowed him second and third chances with friends and benefactors. But finally, booze, regret, and anger were greater than his love of Violet. She had learned of his death from one of her father's devotees. The memorial service was at Churchie's favorite watering hole, Chez Jay in Santa Monica. Violet could have imagined nobody showing up, or five hundred. Twenty people did. That was the saddest part of all.

"How's she related to the Kennedys?" Violet asked. "Through Teddy or Bobby? Aren't they the only brothers?"

"Who the fuck knows? I try not to listen." Teddy ran his hands through his hair and checked his reflection in the window, then turned to Violet. "Anyway. Miss Kennedy aborted my baby this morning in Palm Springs."

"God…"

"Yeah, well. What are you going to do?"

"Why Palm Springs?"

"That's where she grew up," he said.

"How did a Kennedy grow up in Palm Springs?"

"Jesus. What does it fucking matter? She aborted my baby!"

"I'm sorry."

"I'm waiting a couple of hours until her sister drives her home from the baby-killing center, then I'm going to call her and break up with her. It's like the fourth kid of mine a chick has aborted."

"*Like* the fourth?" asked Violet. "You've lost count?"

"Four that I know of. I'm sure there are a dozen more." Teddy poured some salt on the table. He grabbed a sugar packet and started cutting the salt into lines. "Make me a promise." He looked up. "No matter what, never let me get back together with her. Okay?"

"I promise."

The booths, that's why Violet must have picked this restaurant. She knew they would be cocooned in one of these dark booths with the high backs that shut out the rest of the world.

"You seem to do okay for yourself," she said. "Sounds like you'll be onto the next in no time."

"No nice girl will ever go out with me."

"What makes you say that?"

"I'm broke, I'm an addict who will probably use again, and I have hepatitis C."

Violet blurted, "What's hepatitis C?"

"It's the consolation prize God gives the junkies he spares from AIDS."

"Did you share needles?"

"Ha! That's the *best* thing I did when I was a junkie. I'd cook heroin on a Christmas tree ornament and shove that up my vein if it meant getting high."

"Gee," Violet said lamely.

"I guess God gives you what you can handle."

"Then God must have a low opinion of me," she said. "He's given me money, health, the easiest baby in the world, and I *still* can't deal."

"Fuck off, you can't believe that. You're a saint. You know that, right? You're like this Johnny Appleseed of joy and light. Anyone who gets to feel your love is lucky. And I don't just mean lucky. I mean *one of the lucky*. The cosmically lucky."

"Are you dying?" she asked.

"Not really." He brushed the sugar onto the floor. "Hep C fucks up your liver and eventually you die of cancer. But if I eat right I'll be okay. I just get really fucking tired sometimes."

"You know what I'd do if I found out I was dying?" Violet asked. "I'd spend my last hours smoking cigarettes and listening to Stephen Sondheim."

"What, no Percocet?"

"Percocet would ruin the Sondheim. You've got to be all there for Sondheim."

"The Grateful Dead and 'Send in the Clowns'? That's a fucked-up combo."

Violet felt a ripple of relief that Teddy knew who Stephen Sondheim was. Not so much for Teddy as for Sondheim. It always made Violet sad when people didn't know who he was. It happened surprisingly—outrageously—often.

"Are there dating groups for people with hepatitis C?" she asked.

"It's called AA," he said with a laugh.

"How are you impregnating all these girls? Don't you use condoms?"

"I hate condoms."

"Oh man. I am sorry, but that is not cool."

"The doctors say you can't catch hep C from hetero sex."

"Are you sure about that?"

"You're totally disgusted by me, aren't you? See, this is AA at work. Three years ago, I never would have said that to anyone. Now I'm all like, Hi, I'm Teddy, I'm a junkie, I have hep C, and I don't use condoms. What's your name?"

"You're certainly honest," she said. "I have to give you that."

"*Certainly.* Listen to you with your five-dollar words."

"Wait until you hear me use the word *insouciant.*"

"Break me off a piece of that."

She assumed airs and said, "Your prejudice against condoms whilst infected with hepatitis C would indicate an insouciant disregard for safe sex."

The waitress had walked up. "I'll come back," she said, and pivoted away.

"Whoops," said Violet.

Teddy let loose a big, appreciative laugh, then stared into her eyes. She sunk deeper into his. Was he jaundiced? She couldn't tell. His bloodshot green eyes with the angry dark circles couldn't be considered beautiful. But they were arresting. And she couldn't look away.

"You're the one who's honest, Violet. You have this natural honesty that erupts from your heart then straight out of your mouth. I'm a manipulative junkie. Any kind of honesty I have has to be drummed into me by going to meetings every day. With you, it's pure."

Violet lolled in this gorgeous moment. Then she said, "You bring it out in me. I'm like this naturally, I suppose. But with you it's extreme."

"Jesus. I don't even know you and you're already using the word *extreme.* See what I do to people?"

"No, no, no," Violet said. "Extreme is good. We like extreme."

"No, we don't. Extreme is bad. I'm over extreme. I just want to play my music and write poetry."

"You're a poet?" Violet's heart swelled.

"Yeah, I'm always writing poetry," he said. "Poetry keeps me sane. And golf keeps me present."

"Golf?"

"I always start the day with golf. It pimp-slaps me into the here and now. There's no such thing as the past or the future when it's just you and the next shot."

Violet frowned. "I can't picture you on the links."

The waitress returned. "Have you decided?"

"Whatever she orders, I'll have the same," Teddy said. "And make it quick, because we've got somewhere to be."

SALLY already felt better. Concrete action was the only thing that worked in times like these, and here she was, taking it. The teakettle whistled. Sally held Jeremy's Visa envelope an inch over the steam. If she got one edge loose and peeled the flap from there, she'd stand a chance of not mangling this one the way she had Kurt's.

She realized this was not her finest hour, but she wouldn't have been reduced to standing here if what had happened back on the street were an isolated incident. No, a troubling pattern had formed. Jeremy always put his routine above her. He had difficulty looking her in the eye. He never shared his innermost feelings. What was he hiding? Another girlfriend? Could he be one of those men who had another secret family? Could he be opening up emotionally with his *wife?* Of course not! That's what was so maddening. Jeremy was faithful and predictable. Sally had never caught him in a lie or whispering into the phone, and his e-mails were all spam or work related. With Jeremy, what you saw was what you got.

Sally had once broached the subject with Maryam. "Compared to my other boyfriends," Sally had said, "I feel like there's something with Jeremy that's…missing." Maryam shot back, "The asshole part? If you're having problems with a guy who has a job and isn't running around on you, maybe *you're* the problem. Some girls can't be happy unless a man is treating them like garbage." Sally couldn't dismiss Maryam's analysis, as coarse as it was. Still, she didn't quite know what to make of Jeremy.

She tested the flap of the envelope. It lifted right off. She scanned the first page of the bill:

> Hamburger Hamlet
> El Torito
> Hamburger Hamlet
> El Torito
> Hamburger Hamlet
> El Torito
> Hamburger Hamlet

In case anyone didn't believe the man loved his routine! She turned to the second page.

> El Torito
> Hamburger Hamlet
> El Torito
> Hamburger Hamlet
> El Torito
> Cabot & Sons
> Hamburger Hamlet
> El Torito
> Hamburger Hamlet
> El Torito

She would have missed it if the dollar amount in the right column hadn't popped out: *$8,800.* Cabot and Sons was the jeweler just around the corner on Ventura! Sally neatly folded the bill and surrendered it to its envelope. The adhesive stuck, leaving no trace of her minor trespass.

"FOLLOW me" was all Teddy said when Violet asked where they were going. She found herself zooming along Wilshire Boulevard, lacing amid traffic, gunning through yellow lights, swerving into bus lanes—anything to keep up. The battered Mazda teased her late-model Mercedes through the Beverly Hills corridor, turned left at what was once CAA, then left again through Century City. Teddy's speed and recklessness were a throw-down, a sexual tease. Pure adrenaline, Violet was right there with him, proving herself worthy of the challenge. Approaching a red light, Teddy sharked into the left lane, as if to turn east on Pico. Violet, two cars behind, put on her blinker. But when the light turned green, Teddy lurched right. A car screeched to a stop and its engine died. Violet rammed into reverse, then drive, and stepped on the gas. She glimpsed Teddy's tail a long block ahead, sailing west, making no concessions to her. The light was green, but the walk signal a solid red. Violet was four cars back. She swerved into the right-turn-only lane and made it through the intersection. Violet neared Twentieth Century Fox. Right now, writers in smelly rooms were slogging through rewrites, eating take-out, unbuttoning the top button of their pants, putting in their order for the afternoon's coffee run, and debating where they'd order dinner. None of them had a clue that right now, Violet was airborne. She looked up. The light at Motor was red—it was too late to stop.

Fifteen years old: Violet's father drove her from the Zurich airport, up a verdant Alps road, for her first year of boarding school at Le Rosey. They entered a particularly long mountain tunnel. As they emerged from it, her father's eyes were closed. Violet screamed. "My dear," he said, in that blasé way of his, "when in the dark, it's easier to see with your eyes closed."

Now Violet closed her eyes and flew through the red light. She opened them. She had cleared the intersection unharmed. Teddy turned left into a parking lot outside Rancho Park. Just as she had thought…he was taking her golfing. Her phone rang.

"Have you arrived at the undisclosed location?" he asked.

"I'm here." Violet looked for a parking spot.

"May I draw your attention to the office building across the street."

Violet passed his car. It looked like he was taking off his shirt. "What are you doing in there?"

"Hey!" he said. "Don't look."

She found a space. "Okay, what?" she said.

"My ex-wife, Vanessa, used to work there while I stayed home smoking crack. And I wanted to fuck her, so I'd call her at work every five minutes saying, When-are-you-coming-home-when-are-you-coming-home-when-are-you-coming-home? She was busy, so I just sat on the couch all day, smoking crack and watching *Sanford and Son*."

"Come on. *Sanford and Son*?"

"You didn't love *Sanford and Son*?"

"I never saw it," she said. "I was at Le Rosey."

"What you say?"

"Forget it. Okay, I'm parked. Where do I go now?"

"Stay right where you are," said Teddy. "So there I was, out of my mind on crack, wanting to fuck my wife for sixty-five hours straight, but she was in a meeting all afternoon. And see that Jewish synagogue next door? Well, they were all worried about terrorist threats because it was right after September eleventh." There was considerable grunting coming from the other end of the phone.

"What are you doing?" Violet got out and walked toward his car, looking down.

"Stop. Hang on a second." After a long pause, Teddy resumed.

"Okay. Anyway, I wanted Vanesa to come home, so I called up the lobby of the building and said there's a bomb. And they evacuated like a mile of Pico. Everyone who worked up and down here was out on the sidewalk."

"Jesus! I remember that. I was working at Fox. It was after lunch, right? I was off the lot and couldn't get back on."

"Yeah! They evacuated the movie studio, too."

"That was you? You could have been arrested for calling in a bomb threat. That's a federal offense."

"See how far I'll go for the love of a woman?"

"I should be mortified to be having a conversation with you."

"But you're not," he said. "You think it's rad."

"It's pretty rad."

"Ha-ha. I just got you to use the word *rad*."

"It was my first time," Violet admitted.

"Okay, you can look." Teddy had changed into long black pants, a short-sleeved black knit shirt, and the black-and-white golf shoes. Topping it off was a straw porkpie hat. He leaned against a golf bag and had one of the toothpicks from the restaurant sticking out the side of his mouth. It was hard not to love him, standing there, jaunty and confident.

"Dress more like that," she said.

"Oh man. You don't get it."

Violet walked toward him, still talking on their cell phones. "Frayed clothes?" she said. "Who doesn't get it?"

"Maybe I get it on a whole other level that you don't."

"We can stipulate that. All I'm saying is this is one natty look."

"Who you calling natty?" Teddy barked, as Red Foxx. "And whatchyou doing wasting my minutes, woman?"

Violet snapped her phone shut. "Hey, look." A BMW had pulled into the space next to hers, about five cars down. A plump man had squeezed out and was writing something in the dirt on her window.

"What's he doing?" asked Teddy.

L-E-A-R-N T-O, the hothead spelled in the dirt. "*Learn to park,* prob-ably," Violet said. "The car next to me was parked over the line, so I had to park over the line, too." Indeed, the next word was P-A-R-K.

"There's more," said Teddy. They watched, side by side, Teddy leaning into Violet's arm. It was all she could do to concentrate on the man finishing his sentence: Y-O-U D-U-M-B A-S-S-H-O-L-E.

"That's amazing," Violet said. "Not only did he know I'm an *ass-hole,* but a *dumb* asshole, too!"

The guy got his golf clubs out of his trunk and stomped off. Teddy stormed over to Violet's car and wiped the words off the window. "That's not right," he said, blackening. "Hacker with his brand-new Pings." Teddy returned to his car, Violet at his heels.

"Once," she said, "I worked on a show on the Radford lot, and my parking spot was outside the *Seinfeld* writers' offices. They got so traumatized by my dirty car, which they had to stare at all day, that they wrote all over it 'Eat more meat, I love chicken.' Because I'm a vegetarian and they knew it was the only way to get me to wash my car."

"What a fucking hard-on," Teddy muttered. "I'll meet him on the dance floor." He pulled a ratty putter from his golf bag, then opened his trunk and threw the rest of the clubs back in. He choked the putter and headed toward the clubhouse, a wild look in his eye.

WHERE would it be? Sally had already scoured Jeremy's dresser, medicine cabinet, and jacket pockets. She pulled open his bedside drawer, which was filled with loose earplugs and scraps of paper scrawled with variations of "H-H-H-T-T-T-H." Jeremy had a habit of flipping a coin, then marking down if it was heads or tails. To what purpose, she had no idea. Why he kept them, still no idea.

Sally sifted through the fluff and shuddered: it was like running her fingers through the bottom of a hamster cage. She returned to the living room and opened his desk drawer.

There it sat, a pink velvet cube. She cracked it. Inside was a diamond ring. She opened it all the way. Her spirits flattened. She had always imagined nothing smaller than a four carat, and this was barely a two. Sally bucked herself up. The ring was gorgeous. Classic. Tasteful. And if anyone gave her attitude about the size, she could say it had belonged to his mother—

"Sally?"

She spun around. It was Vance. She dropped the ring box on the desk. "Vance! Hi! I thought you were at lunch!"

"I wanted to see how you were." He stepped closer.

"I'm dandy." Sally hopped up onto the desk to block his view of the ring, and closed the drawer with a calf as she twisted her legs.

"I know sometimes Jeremy can be tough. Today—the thing with lunch. Well, that's going to happen. But it's nothing personal."

"Couples disagree. It's healthy." She reached behind her, closed the ring box, and tented it with her hand.

"I know," he said. "And I'm glad you do, too. I always knew he'd find someone who appreciates him as much as I do."

"I'm an appreciator!" she said with a laugh.

Thump. Thump. Thump. Jeremy's big shoes pounded the stairs. His shadow rippled across the venetian blinds.

"Oh look, Jeremy's home!" Sally pointed. Vance turned. Sally opened the desk drawer, dropped in the ring, and slammed it shut just as the door opened. "Welcome home, my love!" she cried.

VIOLET followed Teddy through the cheesy wood-paneled clubhouse and out to the putting green. The darkness that had befallen Teddy in the parking lot was still in effect. His jaw worked the toothpick; his lion eyes scoped out the scene. Then Violet understood: the man from the parking lot was practicing his putts on the far side of the green.

"That guy thinks he can buy game," Teddy grumbled. "He doesn't have game." Teddy's animal spirits were on the rise, and Violet rose with them. He reached into his pocket and removed a ball. In one sinuous movement, he let it roll down his fingers and onto the tight grass. He gripped the putter with one hand, then the other, then snuggled both hands to form a grip on his old familiar friend. Violet caught herself staring and had to remember to breathe. She looked up. Teddy had seen her hunger. Violet waited—forever, it seemed—for him to call her on her carnal desire, to sentence her, humiliate her. Instead, he winked.

"So?" He putted the ball. He was loose, confident, unbelievably sexy. "What about you?" he said, his eyes never leaving the ball.

"What about me?" She looked around, hoping all could see that he was hers, and she, his.

"What's a rich husband doing letting you spend the afternoon with a guy like me?"

"*Letting* me?"

"No woman of mine would ever be allowed to eat at a restaurant like that with another man."

"Is that so?"

"It's my pimp nature," he said. "If you were my woman, there's no way I'd let you run around the way you do."

"It's lucky I'm not your woman," she said. "Because I don't like being told what to do."

"You would with me, though."

"I would not," she said.

"Oh, you would like it."

"I would not."

"Okay, then, you wouldn't." Teddy pointed to a hole about thirty feet away. "You think I can make it?" He hit the ball. It stopped just short.

Violet followed him to the cup. "Wait a second. You *do* realize that no guy will ever break me of my independence."

Teddy tapped the ball in and retrieved it. "I'll give you that one." He let the ball roll down his forearm, then snapped it high in the air. He spun around and caught it behind his back.

"Deal with it," said Violet. "You could never break me."

Teddy flashed a smile. "I already have." He hit his ball and called to someone, "Whoa! Look out!" His crusty ball knocked into a gleaming one, causing it to ricochet off course.

"What the fuck!" It was the BMW guy. He dropped his putter and glared at Teddy.

"Sorry about that, bro." Teddy made the putt.

"Are you done?" said the guy, yet to pick up his fallen club.

"I don't know." Teddy picked up the sparkling putter and returned it to its owner. "This hole is lucky for me. How about we putt for it?"

The guy picked up both balls and threw them fifteen feet away. "Happy to," he said.

"Jesus, here we go." Teddy shook his head. He putted his ball, and it swerved to the right. His rival made the shot. "Lucky shot!" cried Teddy. "Bet you a buck you can't do it again."

The guy reached into his pocket and rummaged through some bills. "All I got is a ten."

"If we're talking real money, I'll have to use your putter."

"Since when is ten bucks real money?"

"I'm not the only one playing at a public course. What, were there no tee times at Riviera?"

The guy took some phantom strokes, then lined up his shot and missed. "Fuck!"

He handed Teddy the overengineered putter.

Teddy marveled at its feel. "Sharp!"

Violet quickly looked away. The eroticism of Teddy handling another golf club was more than she could take.

Teddy putted; his ball rolled swiftly and directly into the hole.

Violet folded her hands behind her back so she wouldn't spontaneously embrace him.

Teddy plucked the ten from the guy's shirt pocket. "Thank you, ma'am." He led Violet off. "I'm going to buy you something pretty with this."

"Double or nothing," called the man.

Teddy stopped. He smiled at Violet, waited a beat, then turned on his heels. "You *do* know this time we're going to be shooting for that badass putter."

"It's an eighty-dollar Callaway."

"I'm good for the money." Teddy turned to Violet. "You got eighty bucks?"

"I got eighty bucks."

"One putt," said the man. "Eighty bucks or the putter." He went through the usual tortured deliberations and stood over his ball. Just as he was about to hit it, Teddy said, "You ever watch *The Partridge Family*?"

"What?" asked the man.

"I used to love that show when I was a kid. Especially the end, where Keith would sing the song. Then, one night, I'm sitting there watching the one where they all go to SeaWorld. And at the end, the mom starts walking around Shamu's tank, singing a love song about *whales*. The song ends, and I'm waiting for Keith to start singing, you know, the *real song* with his brothers and sisters. Then you know what happens?"

"What?"

"The show ends," Teddy said. "That was the song! The mother singing to a goddamned whale!"

"What's your point?" asked the man.

"It's just fucked up, is all."

The man took his shot.

As the ball swerved right, Teddy said, "Yippee kay yay!" The man hurled his club to the ground.

It was Teddy's turn. He picked up the putter, then stood over the ball. He turned his head to either side to loosen up his neck. He took an exaggerated backstroke, froze, then looked up at Violet. "This one's for you, baby." He hit the ball. Violet locked eyes with Teddy. Her father, her education, her husband, her career, motherhood, it all molted away. For this, Violet had driven through red lights, eyes closed. She looked. Teddy didn't have to. His ball was rattling in the cup.

"Jesus fuck me!" cried the man. He wheeled his bag away. "Fucking hustler."

Teddy turned to Violet. "Jesus fuck me? I'll have to remember that one." He handed Violet the club. "My gift to you, Baroness."

"In other words, you *do* know how to play golf."

"I shoot low seventies. When I was a kid, I spent all day on the links. My uncle was a greenskeeper at a public course and got me on the Junior Circuit. I placed top ten in enough tournaments to earn a golf scholarship to USC."

"I didn't know you went to SC." Violet sat down on a bench. "What did you major in?"

"I only lasted a semester. Not even. Couldn't deal with all those rich assholes. By Thanksgiving I was shooting up every day and stopped showing up for classes."

"But you could play professionally now, right? I mean, what was that?" She pointed to the putting green.

"That, my friend, was hustling." Teddy stood with one foot on the bench beside her. "That guy, I watched him. He's probably not a bad player. But when I asked him to putt me for the hole, everything about him changed. Sure, he made the shot, but I could tell he was feeling the heat. You want me to drop some science on you?"

"Go ahead, drop some science."

"When there's something on the line, when there's real heat, I play better than my abilities. Good players, even world-class sticks, can't do that."

"Can I just say, that was one of the coolest things I've ever experienced. And this from someone who saw the Clash at Bonds in '81."

Teddy took a seat beside her. Their legs touched, and stayed touched. "Do you have any idea what you've done to me?" he asked.

Violet braced herself. What he said next would lock them into a marvelous adventure, their future together, with Teddy calling the shots. "What?" she asked.

"Do you know what I'm going to spend all night doing?"

"Tell me."

"A tenth-step inventory."

"A…what?"

"An inventory. The tenth step: 'continued to take personal inventory and when we were wrong promptly admitted it.'"

"But—you didn't drink."

"You don't have much experience with alcoholics, do you?"

"My father was a drunk and died from it, if that's what you mean." Teddy threw his head back and laughed. Violet couldn't help but be charmed by such a wildly inappropriate reaction. "Thanks for the sympathy."

"I'm sorry. People like me and people like you…" Teddy trailed off.

"What?"

"We don't mix. Or, should I say, we mix way too well."

"Well, which is it?" she asked.

There was a long silence. "Hey, wanna see my track marks?" He held out his arm. There were some candle drips of scar tissue on the inside of his elbow. "First thing, when I meet people?" he said. "I check to see if they have track marks."

"That seems a bit self-defeating, doesn't it?"

"Meh?"

"You're clean now," she said. "You're living an honorable life. That kind of thinking just perpetuates the junkie mentality, which you've clearly outgrown."

"You may not believe it, but there are a few things I may be smarter about than you, Miss Violet."

She ran her finger along his track marks. Teddy lifted her dark glasses and looked into her eyes. She smiled. "What?" he asked. "What are you thinking?"

"I'd like to kiss you," she said.

"That probably wouldn't be cool, though." Teddy shuddered and scooched away.

"Oh—" Violet's hand was stranded in the air. She tucked it under her leg.

"Don't worry about it." He was plastered to the far side of the bench.

Violet had to get away before the skin on her face peeled off from her scorching humiliation. "I've got to get home." She stood up.

"Where do you live?" Teddy asked idly.

"Excuse me?"

"Where's home?" It was true! He hadn't a clue that he had just driven their budding affair into the ground. And with it, any hope of friendship.

"Up on Mulholland, with my husband and child."

"Who's your husband?"

"His name is David Parry." Violet waited for the inevitable.

"Holy shit! David Parry, the Ultra Records guy?" There it was, the inevitable. The intellectuals had this reaction when they found out who her father was. Most others had it for her husband.

"So you've heard of him."

"No fucking way! Ultra has the sickest jazz catalog. Ray Charles, Stan Getz, John Coltrane."

"Yep," Violet said. "Back in 2001, David saw into the future that the kids and every generation thereafter wouldn't pay for music. So he set about buying publishing catalogues and jazz labels. Old people's music. He's done quite well." It felt good, sticking it to Teddy with David's accomplishments.

"But he's also a big rock-and-roll manager."

"Yes, David is the star."

"Fuck. I can't believe David Parry's wife just tried to kiss me!"

"I've got to go to the market. David said he wanted pasta for dinner." Violet fished the keys from her pocket.

"I'm fucking depressed," Teddy said.

Her heart leapt: had he already regretted letting the moment pass? Would he try to win her back? "I'd give anything for a home-cooked meal," he said.

"Here's your putter. Sell it for gas money." Violet checked her watch. It was four o'clock. She could easily make it to the market and get dinner on the table by the time David returned home. She walked off, with a lightness to her step, immensely relieved that her abasement, though grotesque, was so short-lived.

FIRST people said "I love you," *then* they get engaged. It was this sequence of events Sally pondered as she sat in the teetering forest of shoe boxes stacked from floor to ceiling. She had already picked out some cross-trainers for herself. (That was ninety-five dollars she'd never see again!) Now it was time for the true purpose of the foray....

"Hey," she said to Jeremy. "While we're here, maybe *you'd* like some new shoes!"

"I already have these."

"I think you need some new ones," volunteered the marathon-running hippie who had been helping Sally. He had long hair, leathery skin, and an emaciated body. He looked like someone who'd been stranded on a desert island. "See how you're over-pronating your right foot?" The castaway pointed to the sole of Jeremy's gigantic docksider, which had, in fact, worn out at the inner heel.

Jeremy studied it. Sally liked where this was going. Her best strategy was to hang back and let the castaway fight this battle for her. "But these shoes are perfectly comfortable," Jeremy said.

"*Now*, maybe," said the castaway. "But if you don't get some stability in that right heel, you're looking down the barrel of a lifetime of heel spurs, plantar fasciitis, and shin splints. If you're lucky."

"Really?" Jeremy said.

"Absolutely. What size are you?"

"Ten," Sally said. The castaway disappeared into the back. She called after him, "Make sure they're dark! With dark soles!"

I love you. How would Sally get Jeremy to say the words? He was a man of habit. Saying "I love you" wasn't part of his habit.

He took a quarter out of his pocket and started flipping it. "Do you have a pen?" he asked.

"I love you!" Sally said, mortified at what had just squirted out of her mouth. "I mean—"

Jeremy looked at her. "Me, too."

"What—you do?"

"Of course I do."

"Well, when were you going to tell me?"

"I thought it was obvious."

This was all too odd and fabulous. But Sally couldn't rest. Jeremy still hadn't said the words. "You thought *what* was obvious?"

"I love you."

She gave him a shove. "You are *such a guy!* Do you realize how much of a guy you are?"

"Yes."

"Jeremy?"

"Sally?"

"Does it scare you?" She took his hand. "Our love?"

"No."

"I'm not scared, either."

"You shouldn't be," he said. "Real love, like the kind we have, is hard to find. We should be happy."

Sally's heart swelled with tenderness. It filled this cluttered little store, bursting through the wall, spilling out into Encino, and expanding up into the heavens. Everything that just moments earlier had annoyed her—the sun blisters on the castaway's cheekbones, the turned-over shopping cart blocking the good parking space, the drizzle that had started out of nowhere and would cause her hair to frizz—all of it was dissolving fabulously skyward.

Jeremy got a pen from the counter and fished out a piece of paper from the trash. He flipped his quarter several times and wrote out the results. T-H-T-T-T-H-H-T.

An image came to Sally, something she remembered from childhood. It was from the Carl Sagan series *Cosmos,* something called Flatland. Flatland was this two-dimensional world where everything was flat, even the Flatlanders who lived there. They could only perceive left and right, front and back, but no above or below. One day, a potato flew over from another dimension— really, Carl Sagan had said it was a potato—and this potato looked down and said, "Hello." The Flatlanders couldn't see it because it was hovering over them and they had no up or down. And when the potato entered their two-dimensional world, all the Flatlanders were able to see was this weird changing potato slice appearing from nowhere. It totally blew their minds because they had no concept this other dimension even existed. Then, when the potato went home and the Flatlanders who witnessed it tried to explain it to their friends, they couldn't. Because they literally didn't have words for it. Jeremy's "I love you" was like the potato materializing out of nowhere. Sally realized she had been living in a world where love equaled scheming, second-guessing, and game playing. Now she understood that there was a whole other dimension where love simply...*was*.

The castaway returned with a pair of dark brown hiking boot-sneakers with black soles.

Jeremy put them on and stood up. He smiled and turned to Sally. "These are more comfortable than any shoes I've ever worn," he said. "Thanks for making me come here."

Sally caught a glimpse of the two of them in a mirror. Jeremy and Sally. Sally and Jeremy. How she loved Jeremy, the kind genius. And how she loved that she loved a kind genius. And how she loved that the kind genius would no longer be galumphing around in those awful shoes.

VIOLET crawled up traffic-clogged Benedict Canyon, the words "I can't believe David Parry's wife just tried to kiss me" strangling her brain. Back at Whole Foods, she had to ask someone three times where the capers were, when she had been staring straight at them. She had to pull it together before she got home. What was she thinking asking Teddy to lunch? She'd never had an affair. If she did, it would certainly be with some genius rock star like Thom Yorke, not *Teddy Reyes*. She sat in traffic, her embarrassment so visceral she felt as if she were about to suffocate. She rolled down the windows. Her cell phone rang.

"It got pretty intense back there, didn't it?" It was him.

"It really didn't."

"Do you have Sprint?" Teddy asked.

"I don't know."

"You don't know? What do you mean, you don't know?"

"I don't concern myself with such things. We have people for that," she said, pleased with how haughty she just sounded. "What's it to you?"

"You're so fucking rich," he said. "I can talk for free to people who have Sprint. That's why."

"Do you work for them?" she asked.

"Do I work for them? It's my phone plan! What does your phone say?"

It said Sprint.

"Good," Teddy said. Without missing a beat, he started in. "How scary was that? Every time we see each other we almost fuck."

"Hardly." There was roadwork ahead. Hopefully, traffic would loosen once Violet passed it.

"I'm telling you, I'm totally hardwired for sex. Remember how you held my hand in the museum?"

"Yes." She sighed.

"After I left you, I went to the men's room in the park and jerked off."

"You did?" This was difficult for Violet to imagine. Twenty years ago, maybe. But after sixteen years of marriage,? And that stomach! A few weeks after giving birth, Violet had been taking a shower and accidentally ran her hand over it and nearly shrieked at how squishy it had become. Sometimes she found herself actually tucking her stomach into her pants! What had once been an admittedly curvy body was now the shape of a troll doll, with fat showing up in the most dispiriting places, like her upper back! The thought of a stranger—a young stranger with a Kennedy for a girlfriend, no less—jerking off to that? Okay, she liked it.

"You like that, don't you?" he asked.

"Are you a sex addict?"

"I don't concern myself with such things. I have people for that." Repeating what she said, that's what made her twinkle. "What positions do you like?" he asked.

"Have we already graduated to ribaldry—if there's such a word?" A horn blared. There wasn't a car ahead of her. Violet stepped on the accelerator, rounded the bend, and caught up with traffic.

"You love this, coming down off your mountain and giving the junkie a hard-on. Tell me. What positions do you like?"

"I don't know."

"Do you like doggy style?"

"I guess."

"Say certainly."

"I certainly like doggy...you know."

"You know what you like even more?" he asked.

"What?"

"Getting fucked in the ass."

"I should say not! I've never had the dubious honor."

"That's such a lie," he said.

"It's true."

"Then you've got a real treat coming to you. Chicks like you who think they're in charge are the ones who love taking it up the ass the most. What's your pussy like?"

"I don't know." She rolled up the windows and checked her mirror to make sure nobody she knew was in the car behind her.

"Do you shave it?" he asked. "Is it big and hairy?"

"Big? You mean like men have big dicks?"

"Is it hairy?"

"I wax it a bit. Not too much."

"David Parry likes hairy pussies! Ha! I knew we were brothers. Ask me some questions."

"Where are you?" Violet turned a sharp corner. A cheery patchwork ball that belonged to Dot jingled under her feet. She picked it up and tossed it over her shoulder.

"What do you mean?" he asked.

"You have conversations like this while you're driving, or are you behind a tree on the back nine?"

"I'm driving," he said impatiently. "Ask me a question."

"Will you recite a poem you wrote?"

"Not that kind of question!"

"Please?"

"Hey!" he said. "I have an idea. You put me on the payroll, and I'll write poems for you."

"I can be your Maria de' Medici," she said.

"Huh?"

"You know, the Medicis of Florence. During the Italian Renaissance they were patrons of Michelangelo and everyone. Rubens did those paintings of her that are hanging in the Louvre."

"Four out of five dentists surveyed said"—Teddy went into a Red Foxx impression—"*What you just say?*"

"Never mind," said Violet.

"Don't you worry. I'll be writing plenty of poems for you, Violet." She gripped the wheel with both hands so the flood of joy wouldn't knock her car off the road. He continued, "Ask me something."

"Why are you so broke all the time when you have an obvious talent for golf? Why don't you become a golf pro?"

"Are you trying to make me lose my erection?"

"You're driving with an erection? I didn't know such a thing was possible."

"Of course it is. Oh, my fucking God, will you just ask me about my cock?"

"I don't know. What's it like?" A fuzzy lamb stared at Violet from the passenger seat. She scowled and chucked it over her shoulder. When it landed, it emitted an ugly "Ba-ah! Ba-ah!"

"What the fuck was that?" asked Teddy.

"Nothing."

"Well, what about my cock? Ask me some questions."

"Is it…big?"

"Jesus, you have a lot to learn. Ask me if it's hard. Ask me if I'm stroking it. Ask me what I want to do with it."

"Can't you at least become a caddy? They do well with tips, from what I gather."

"I've been a caddy, and it doesn't do it for me, okay? Tips! Thanks a fucking lot."

"Aren't we in high dudgeon over a perfectly reasonable suggestion? Couldn't you—you know—do what you did today with that guy for money?"

"Hustle? That's not exactly what we at Alcoholics Anonymous call 'a manner of living which demands rigorous honesty.' What we're trying to do is live the life we're meant to live, which requires a restoration of ethics and morals. My cock is waiting."

"By the way, thanks for telling me that I'm responsible for you having to do an inventory."

"Oh man!" Teddy laughed. "You should have seen your face! You looked totally…" He kept laughing.

"The word is *chagrined*."

"You totally wanted me to say I was going to jerk off to you."

"I can just hang up. You are aware that cell phone technology makes such a thing possible."

"I'm sorry. You're right. You didn't make me do anything. I'm responsible for my own actions."

"He said, as if trying to convince himself." Violet neared her house and slowed down.

"Hey, I want to apologize for not thanking you for fixing my car. You're right, that was ghetto. So, thank you."

"You're welcome."

"I just didn't know how. You don't realize how much sixteen hundred bucks is to me. I mean, the most I've ever had at one time was eight hundred dollars. I had a real job, selling sunglasses on the Venice boardwalk. And one day a bus of Japanese tourists gets out and buys my entire inventory. When I got home, I spread all the money out on the floor and just stared at it."

"*Then* you spent it on drugs."

"No! I was clean then. I bought a sleigh bed."

"For the first time in your life you have money, and you go out and buy a sleigh bed?" Violet howled. "That has got to be the most low-rent thing I've ever heard!"

"Do you even know what a sleigh bed *is*?" he asked. "Those rad wooden beds with the iron metalwork."

"Of course!" Violet couldn't stop laughing.

"What's so funny?"

"It's just so nineties!"

"It was the fucking nineties. What do you want?"

"Where's the sleigh bed now?"

"I sold it for drugs two months later."

"How much did you get for it?"

"Fuck you." He sounded hurt.

"Two hundred bucks?"

"Can we change the subject?"

"One hundred?" Violet found a shoulder and pulled over behind a guy selling fruit from a truck.

"Is your husband always going out of town?"

"We're supposed to go to a spring equinox yoga retreat in Ojai. But I don't feel like going."

"So *that's* when we're going to fuck."

"You're pretty sure of that, aren't you?"

The fruit guy shuffled over, holding a three-pack of strawberries in one hand and a bag of oranges in the other. Violet waved him off.

"Just stepping up and doing the right thing like you asked," Teddy said.

"God! You totally don't get what I meant by that."

David's Bentley whizzed by. He seemed to be on the phone himself and didn't slow down. He probably hadn't seen Violet. She fumbled for the gearshift and jerked the car into drive. "I've got to go," she said.

"Why? What happened?"

"Don't you have a Kennedy to dump?" Violet waited for the Flying Spur to disappear up their driveway, then merged onto Mulholland.

"I get it," Teddy said. "Bye, Violet Parry."

"Bye, Teddy Reyes." Violet pushed the warm phone to her cheek. Her whole face ached from smiling so much. She drove through the Aleppo pines, making figure eights with her jaw to counter the cramps forming in her cheeks. If David asked—and she knew he wouldn't!—she'd say she had pulled over to finish up a phone conversation before she got home. That wasn't lying.

CHAPTER FOUR

Control It or It Controls You   ❀   And the Sultans Played Creole

"YOU'RE DOING GREAT," SALLY TOLD NORA ROSS, THE THICK-WAISTED WIFE OF Jordan Ross, head of one of the big talent agencies. Nora was doing some of the most pathetic *grande pliés* Sally had ever witnessed. "*Plié, relevé, plié, relevé.* Now with arms over the head."

"Ugh!" Nora's pudgy arms fell to her sides and she flopped breathlessly against the wall. "I am so stressed out. The guest list for tonight's party keeps *ballooning.*"

An army of Mexicans carrying heat lamps passed by the bay window.

"Next to the pool!" Nora shouted. "*Junto la piscina!*" She turned to Sally. "Is that how you say it?"

"I think so. How about we switch to *demi pliés?*"

"I hate you," said the wealthy butterball. "Can't I just do those kicky things?"

"Fine. *Dégagé,* with foot flexed. Third position." Sally set her feet and floated her arms into *grande pose.* "Right foot to the front. *Tendu* and *dégagé.* Heel leads the toe."

Nora flung her leg forward with all the grace of kicking a cat. "Please tell me these will get rid of my fat ass."

"You know what I say, Control it or it controls you." That was Sally's motto, from a bumper sticker she had on her three-ring binder in high school. "And one way to control your tush is *dégagé.* To the back. Toe leads heel. *Dégagé.*"

The phone rang. Happy to bail, Nora unlatched a cabinet door and answered it.

Since the Rosses' only child, J.J., had been diagnosed with autism, any object that could conceivably be picked up and hurled by a tantruming child—framed photos, telephone, ceramic bowls—had been secured behind custom-built glass-fronted cabinets. Last year, Sally had shown up to find the glass shattered and all the treasured memories in a million pieces in a heap on the floor. (Nora sent Sally home that day but still paid for the whole hour, which was really classy.) The following week, the glass had been removed and in its place, chicken wire. Behind which were imprisoned the images of Nora and Jordan smiling on the Great Wall, arms around Bill Clinton, huddled with Jack Nicholson at the *Vanity Fair* Oscar party, Nora, happy and pregnant on a yacht off Croatia. Before the diagnosis, before they stopped taking pictures.

Nora hung up and locked the phone back in the cabinet. "Can we just do abs and call it a day?" She kicked open the mat Sally had brought and sprawled out on it. "Jordan put the arm on all his big stars to show up. And word got out, so everybody, I mean *everybody,* wants to come." She rolled on her side and curled up. "That's what happens when you're only charging five hundred bucks a plate. Live and learn, am I right?"

"Let's try for twenty leg darts," said Sally.

"I hate those." Nora yelled out, "Zdenka!"

Sally braced herself for the entrance of the young Czech nanny, who clearly outranked her in the Ross household.

"Yes?" asked Zdenka in her hard accent. She nursed a bottle of exotic water. Anytime Nora outgrew a piece of clothing, it ended up on Zdenka. Today she sported a Dolce & Gabbana silk shirt, True Religion jeans, and Hogan shoes. Sally would have looked totally hot in that shirt, belted over leggings with her new Hermès belt. But did Sally ever get a crack at any of Nora's discards? No.

"The gals are coming to put together the goody bags in the dining room," Nora said. "Don't let J.J. anywhere near that, please."

"Of course," answered the nanny, and left.

Nora raised a leg in the air, an indication that she wished to be stretched out. Sally complied. Her student groaned with pleasure, then asked, "So. What's the latest on your beau?"

Sally had hoped Nora wouldn't ask. It had been two weeks since Sally had seen the ring. Still, Jeremy hadn't proposed. Sally was completely flummoxed. "We're doing fine," she said.

"I don't see a ring on your finger."

"If he proposes, he proposes. If he doesn't, I'm fine with that, too." This was what Sally had started to tell those who asked.

Nora yanked her leg free. "What do you mean? Two weeks ago you raved about what a good fit you two were."

"I know. But I think I'm looking for someone more…emotionally available."

"Please!" Nora crossed one leg over the other. Sally pushed the stuffed sausages into Nora's chest. "Men don't care about how you feel. That's what girlfriends are for. If you're waiting around for a guy who will share his feelings, you'd better pack Proust, because you're going to be waiting a mighty long time."

"I like that," Sally said.

"You don't have to like it or dislike it. You just have to accept it.

Jordan and I have a great marriage. But does he ever have a clue what I'm *feeling?* Never! That doesn't mean he's a bad husband."

"And you're a great wife."

"Well, thank you. I try to be. Sure, in the early days, we were screwing three times a day and making spectacles of ourselves in public and it was all very dramatic. But time passes. He has his career. I have my causes. We have a special-needs kid. We're partners who love each other."

Partners who love each other. Sally's thoughts quickened. It was as if she and Jeremy had fast-forwarded past the fireworks phase straight to the partner phase. And if she wanted to talk about feelings, she had friends for that. *Feelings.* They suddenly seemed so trivial in the context of a whole *life* together. "Can you finish off with ten basic crunches?" She really wanted to help Nora with that waist.

"Fine," moaned Nora. "But only ten."

Sally lay on the hardwood floor and led Nora in some crunches. "One, two, three—" The overhead lights flashed. Sally squeezed her eyes shut, then squinted. J.J. stood in the doorway, flipping the switch and staring expressionless into the bulbs. On the outside, J.J. was a beautiful eight year old with long blond curls. There was no way of knowing how damaged and creepy he was on the inside. Sally closed her eyes. The hot rays burned through her eyelids and into her retina, on-off-on-off-on-off. She shielded her eyes and shot a look at J.J., but he was transfixed by the repetition.

"Could someone get him to stop that?!" Sally cried. "My God! Stop it! Where's his nanny—"

Zdenka stared down at her. "I'm right here."

Sally quickly turned to Nora. "I'm sorry…." For all of Nora's complaining, she *did* pay cash and worked out in the middle of the day when the dance studio was closed. And Nora never once put up a fight about paying for canceled sessions. Sally couldn't afford to lose Nora, one of her bread-and-butter clients. "I apologize." Sally's voice trembled. "My eyes are just really sensitive."

"Zdenka, take him to the park or something, will you?" Nora said, unfazed by Sally's freak-out.

Sally flopped into a forward bend, fully aware she had just dodged a bullet. The Jeremy situation was beginning to affect her work. *Control it or it controls you.* It was time to apply her motto to Jeremy.

How do you look when you're interested? Violet tried to remember, as she and David drove up Beverly Glèn, Dot a bubbly passenger in her car seat.

"…Capitol is trying to get us to rerecord two of the tracks," David was saying. "So contractually, I can shop the record. I've got Columbia frothing at the mouth."

"Sultans of Swing" came on the radio. Violet loved this song. She was about to turn onto Mulholland, and music sounded better on Mulholland. She started to reach for the volume, but David was still talking; such an act on Violet's part ran the risk of igniting a conflagration.

"The question is," he said, "do we stay with Capitol and force them to release the tracks? Or would that make them lose enthusiasm for the single?"

A question. He had just asked her a question. Thank God it was still buffered in her short-term memory. Violet rewound it in her head and replied, "Is one of the tracks in question the first single?" Violet felt good about her reply; it was quick and informed, the reply of someone who cared.

"Yes. They gave me a list of producers. George Drakoulias was at the top."

"We love George," Violet said.

"Maybe I'll give him a call."

"Want dat. Want dat." Dot had spotted Violet's cell phone in the cup holder. Violet slipped it back to Dot, her gaze never deserting her husband.

"But all this—Hanging with Yoko, the record label, the catalogues—it's all starting to look like a fucking hobby compared to what the gold stocks are doing. You know what I say. Gold, it's the king of money. When it starts to run, it's going to be scary."

"I'm so happy for you," Violet said.

"Be happy for us. It's ours." David kicked at something on the floor. "What's this?"

"Oh," she said, "when I subscribed to *Cook's Illustrated,* without realizing it, I signed up for some cookbook-of-the-month thing. And most of the recipes involve meat, so I can't use them."

"Have you gotten off the list, at least?"

"I tried, but it's such a pain. So I thought I'd just give them to LadyGo."

David picked up a cookbook and leafed through it. "She can't understand this."

"I know, but there was a monster line at the post office when I went to return them. I'm sure LadyGo knows somebody who wants them."

David stared at her, jaw hanging. "That's your solution? For every month for the rest of my life, I'm going to pay, what"—he looked for a price on the book—"thirty-nine bucks for a cookbook that you're giving to someone who doesn't speak English, in hopes that she'll find someone who wants it? Come on, Violet."

"I'm sorry." She should have known this would happen. She should never have left these books in her car.

"It's not about the money," he said. "It's just—how are we living, here?"

"You're right. I'll get off the list and return the books on Monday."

David wasn't happy, but at least he had stopped talking. Just in time for Violet's favorite part of the song.

And a crowd of young boys, they're fooling around in the corner
Drunk and dressed in their best brown baggies and their platform soles
They don't give a damn about any trumpet playing band
It ain't what they call rock and roll....

Violet held her breath to better hear her favorite line, the one that never failed to slay her:

And the Sultans played Creole.

Violet's eyes welled up.

"Get that cell phone out of Dot's hand!" It was David, talking again. "She could get brain cancer."

"It's not on." Violet turned and held out her hand for Dot. "Mommy needs that back, sweetie."

"That's not the point. I don't want her in the habit— Shit— Violet, are you crying? What's going on?"

"I just really love this song."

"'The Sultans of Swing'?" David frowned and his head jerked back slightly, as if he was jolted by that fact. "Really?"

"Have you ever listened to the words?"

"No."

"It's about these working stiffs who play in a band every Friday night. And when they're onstage, nobody appreciates them. But they don't care. Because for those few hours, they're...free."

David looked alarmed. "Maybe you can go see Dire Straits next time they're in town. Or, you know what, Mutt Lange is friends with Mark Knopfler. We can all go to dinner next time we're in London."

Teddy hadn't called for two weeks! Two weeks tomorrow. Who jerks off to you five minutes after they meet you and asks what your pussy is like and doesn't call you for two weeks? Violet had called him. Twice. Left messages both times, but nothing. Who winds someone up like that just to go AWOL? Where was he? Did he know how much pain she was in? How she jumped any time she heard her cell phone ring? How his absence made time crawl? Was he dying of hepatitis C somewhere? Had he not broken up with the Kennedy girl after all? Were *they* somewhere fucking, him repeating everything *she* said, him laughing at *her* jokes? Did being in his aura make *her* drunk with submission? He had told Violet she was the most pure thing he had ever experienced. Didn't that merit a return phone call? She had gotten the mechanic's bill. Sixteen hundred dollars to fix his shitty car, and no phone call? He was going to write poems for her! He wanted to fuck her in the ass! Call her back! She wanted to twinkle! But ever since the putting green, ever since that thrilling phone call on Benedict Canyon, ever since all she had to do was close her eyes and he was there, she couldn't twinkle on her own.

David typed into his BlackBerry and flashed Violet a triumphant smile. "Mark Knopfler's number. I e-mailed it to you. You can call him when we get home. Done and done."

David had no idea. The last person Violet wanted to talk to was Mark Knopfler.

CHAPTER FIVE

The Ferrari

"TODAY WE'RE PROUD TO INTRODUCE OUR NEW COLLEAGUE, JEREMY White." A hot guy Sally recognized from TV—Jim Something-or-Other—spoke directly into the camera. "Many of you know the name from his 'Just the Stats' column, which appears in over a dozen newspapers nationwide. Beginning today, the big man himself will be joining the *Match-Ups* team every Sunday morning. Welcome, Jeremy."

Jeremy's face appeared on the dozen monitors throughout the dark soundstage. Sally's fingers were crossed in her pocket. She closed her eyes: her entire future hinged on the next three minutes.

"Hi, I'm Jeremy White. Let's take a look at one of sports' most exciting events, the NCAA Sweet Sixteen. First off, the matchup between heavily favored Georgetown and the little team that could, Canisius College...." The voice filling the air was soothing, almost musical. Sally opened her eyes. Yes, it was Jeremy, aglow on the enormous screen overhead, his face relaxed, his eyes gazing directly and calmly into hers. Finally, he wasn't wearing those dirty earplugs. His jacket and tie added a sexy look of authority. Sally blinked. It was as if she was beholding the man she *imagined* Jeremy to be when they were apart, only to have her heart sink when she saw how awkward he was in person. She turned around. In the booth, Maryam and the executives muttered excitedly, equally transfixed by this suddenly charismatic apparition.

"And who do you belong to?" Hot, wet breath tickled Sally's ear. It was Jim, the anchorman who had introduced Jeremy. Without waiting for an answer, he ambled over to the food table.

Sally scurried to keep up. "I'm a friend of Maryam and Jeremy's."

"Shush!" said a voice.

"First time on a set?" Jim whispered, shaking sugar to the bottom of five packets.

"No!"

"Shhh!" Maryam stepped out of the booth and shot Sally a nasty look.

"We're all heading to Marie Callender's after this." Jim poured the sugar directly into his mouth and took a hard swallow. "Maybe you'd like to join."

"I'm more Jeremy's friend than Maryam's. If you know what I mean."

"Say it isn't so." Jim's eyes slid down Sally, coming to rest on her ass. "Jeremy White picks seventy percent and gets to bang the likes of you? This dude is my idol."

Sally threw back her head and laughed. "He should be." Her long hair felt so soft against her bare back.

Jim reached forward and cupped the ballet slippers dangling from Sally's necklace. "Don't even tell me you're a dancer."

"Three years with the Colorado Ballet. I would have made principal, but I got injured."

He quickly dropped the necklace. "Here comes the queen bitch."

"You guys!" Maryam got in their faces and whispered, "Keep it *down*."

"She's *your* friend," said Jim. "It's not my fault she's never been on a set before."

"You!" Sally knuckled Jim in the shoulder.

"Easy," he said. "We're not in bed yet."

"That's the head of the network in there," Maryam hissed. "Are you trying to ruin Jeremy's screen test?"

"Of course not," Sally shot back.

"Then *shut up!*" Maryam headed to the booth, walking on the back edges of her heels so her footsteps didn't echo.

Sally returned her eyes to Jeremy and tried really hard not to giggle at Jim, who she felt watching her, maybe even making faces at her.

"…That's why I like Arizona's chances to upset Villanova," Jeremy was saying. "Until next week, I'm Jeremy White."

"Cut!" Applause erupted throughout the studio. Maryam received hearty congratulations from her beloved bigwigs as they all poured onto the set.

"You sure backed the winning horse, didn't you?" Jim said. Sally flashed him a saucy smile.

She was *so glad* she had called in sick to the ballerina birthday party this morning to drive Jeremy to this screen test. For the past week, she had withheld sex, not spent the night, and waited twelve hours to return his calls. It hadn't resulted in getting the ring on her finger, but she needed to give it time. She was, after all, a Flatlander going up against a mysterious potato.

"Jeremy?" the director asked over the PA system. "Next week, when we're live, I want you and Jim to do some happy talk. Jim, where did you go?"

"I'm right here!" Jim boomed from Sally's side.

Jeremy jumped out of his chair and headed straight for Sally, not even stopping to shake the hands of a dozen well-wishers. Sally got goose bumps; it was like the end of *Rocky,* when Sylvester Stallone called out, "Adrian!"

"Congratulations, sweetie!" Sally gave him a peck on the cheek.

Jeremy reared his head and turned to Jim. "What's happy talk?" he asked, rolling an earplug between his fingers, then sticking it into his ear.

"I'm sure this little lady knows a thing or two about happy talk."

Sally punched Jim in the arm.

"I don't understand what that means," Jeremy said to Jim.

"You know, banter," Jim said.

"Can you write it out for me?"

"Then it wouldn't be banter, would it?" Jim patted Jeremy on the butt. "Relax, big guy." He gave Sally a wink and walked away.

"Uh, hello?" Sally stepped into Jeremy's line of vision. "Sweetie?"

"I don't know what they mean by banter." Jeremy reached into his pocket, took out a quarter, and started flipping it.

"You just say stuff to each other," she said. "You know, chitchat. You see it all the time on TV."

"My contract says nothing about chitchat. Do you have a pen and some paper?"

"Jeremy!" She grabbed the quarter out of the air. "I congratulated you."

"Thanks. Everyone seemed happy."

Maryam rushed over. "We're all going to Marie Callender's. Do you want to come?"

Sally had resigned herself to the fact that spontaneity such as this wasn't possible with Jeremy. "Thanks," she said, "but no."

"Sure!" said Jeremy.

"Wha—" Sally said.

"Great!" said Maryam. "It's the one on Wilshire, west of La Brea." She ran off.

A woman with overprocessed hair plopped down a canvas gardening bag with pockets full of makeup brushes. "Hi, I'm Faye." She sidled up to Jeremy and started wiping foundation off his face. "Looks like we'll be spending lots of time together."

"Honey," Sally said, "they don't have anything you like at Marie Callender's."

"It's for my work," Jeremy said. "You don't have to come if you don't want to."

Faye brushed her fingers through Jeremy's hair. "There you are." Out of the side of her mouth, she added, "I've been doing this a lot of years. When the president of the network delays his flight back to New York to eat buffalo wings with a new guy—well, you better show up." Faye gave Sally the stink eye and walked away.

A fuming Sally led Jeremy through the studio and outside to the sunny parking lot in the gross part of Hollywood. The gigantic double-hatch doors sealed shut behind them. She spun around. "Jim asked me out just now."

"Are you going?" Jeremy asked.

"On a date. He asked me out *on a date*."

"But you're my girlfriend." He walked to Sally's car and waited at the passenger door.

"*Am* I your girlfriend, Jeremy?"

"Of course you are."

"Because I just don't know anymore. We haven't spent the night together in one whole week."

"You're the one who wanted it that way."

"Why would I want that?" She stood an inch from his face.

"You said you're on your menstrual cycle."

Everything with Jeremy was so frigging *literal*. It was impossible to give him a hint. Yes, Sally had told him she was having her period. But the last time she had her period, during the "honeymoon phase," she had given him blow jobs every night and slept over. Shouldn't the numbers guy be able to put two and two together?!

"What do *you* want, Jeremy?" Sally felt herself entering that zone that scared off all the other boyfriends, the one that gave her the reputation for being "crazy."

"I want you to stop getting mad."

"Then stop making me mad!"

"I want to. But I never know how."

"You're so freaking selfish, Jeremy."

"I don't understand. When I met you, everything made you so happy."

"I *was* happy. But you just manipulate me and walk all over me like I'm a doormat!"

"Do you need something to eat?" he asked.

"I'm sorry I'm not a *number,* Jeremy. Because you'd probably pay more attention to me. I'm sorry I'm not a hamburger at Hamburger Hamlet! I'm sorry I'm not a cheese quesadilla! I'm a human being who has feelings, who just wants to connect. But trying to connect with you is like trying to connect to a robot!" Sally shrieked and sobbed all at the same time.

Technically, she could rein herself in. But once she started losing control, she enjoyed the release and didn't want to pull back. It's what she imagined car buffs meant when they said high-performance cars "liked" to be taken out and opened up on an empty highway. Like the finest Ferrari, Sally enjoyed pushing the envelope of her emotional pain to see how far she could take it.

The horror on people's faces as she did—and it was always boyfriends who were on the receiving end of these spectacles—only reinforced her humiliation, which made her want to go further.

"I'm sorry I'm not a makeup whore or a television camera or a *quarter,* you bastard! I'm sorry I'm in love with you and turn down dates for you. I'm sorry I crushed the dreams of a dozen little ballerinas this morning so I could drive you here! *I'm sorry I exist!* I'm sorry I ever met you! Oh God, look what you've done to me! What have I become? I'm sorry I was ever born!"

Jeremy looked utterly bewildered. "I'm glad you were born."

"Don't lie to me!"

"If you weren't born, I wouldn't know you. And then what would I do?"

"Huh?"

"You're my life, Sally. I'll do anything for you. If you don't want to go to Marie Callender's, we don't have to."

"Really?" Sally looked up, her eyes moist. "But what about your career?"

"Television is just television. I can live without television. You, Sally, you're a person. A person I love."

"I love you, Jeremy." She hugged him. It was four o'clock. She *did* need some food in her. "Let's go to Marie Callender's."

CHAPTER SIX

Spring Equinox ❧ Thank God It's Just Diabetes ❧ Super-Rica

This Is It? ❧ Just the Check ❧ Standing There ❧ Ho!

TODAY HE WOULD CALL. SPRING EQUINOX. VIOLET HAD TOLD TEDDY THAT WAS when David would be out of town. It seemed so obvious when she had figured it out. Once she did, her torment gave way to the calm of having the upper hand in a delicious game of cat and mouse.

So Violet had spent the past two weeks preparing. Embracing the hunger pains she carried to the hairdresser, the waxing place, the facialist, the nail salon. Actually looking at herself in a full-length mirror while David was at work to see which outfits made her ass look the least gigantic. The expedition to a mall deep in the valley to buy size-large lingerie, then stashing it in the back of her T-shirt drawer. The body scrubs and cellulite massages using serum made of sheep colostrum.

While Violet attended to her body, she'd slip off into her life with Teddy—the one she'd lovingly write and rewrite. They'd live near the ocean in Santa Monica. On Georgina or Alta (west of Lincoln, of course!), where they could walk down the steps and across PCH to the Jonathan Club. Violet would fix up an old Craftsman. They'd buy the house next door and tear it down so they'd have a bigger yard and room for Teddy's studio. She'd fix him up as well—his teeth, his hair, his wardrobe. Because of her age, they'd have to have a baby soon. Maybe they'd get married. Maybe not. Paperwork might befoul the purity of their love. People would talk; Violet accepted that. But once they got to know Teddy, and watched her blossom, they'd wildly approve.

Violet had asked around about golf. It turned out that anyone, for a smallish fee, could sign up for amateur tournaments. If Teddy won enough—which he surely would—he would graduate onto increasingly larger circuits and ultimately the PGA. Even though he was no spring chicken—how old was he, anyway, thirty-something probably, she'd have to remember to ask—the main indicator for success in golf was that you started young, which Teddy had. How she'd burst with pride, standing by his side as he vanquished all nonbelievers. Their charity golf event would be the talk of the town. Lots of rock stars and movie stars, raising money for hepatitis C. That's right; Violet would not be ashamed of his disease. She had researched it online and was relieved to see that Teddy was correct: the virus was transmitted only by the exchange of blood, such as sharing needles, not from kissing or vaginal sex. There was even a cure for it, interferon, which was a long and expensive regimen, but one Violet would valiantly nurse Teddy through.

And of course, there was Teddy's poetry. He'd write epic, scrappy poems about Violet and their baby, Lotus. Lotus and Violet, his two flowers. (And Dot, of course, never forgetting Dot!) He could turn his poems into songs, which would lead to a robust music career. Ideally, Teddy wouldn't go on the road. He probably was a sex addict, and Violet didn't need to add that to her list of worries. So preferably he'd become a local sensation.

She sought solitude so she could filigree this future with Teddy. When David came home, she'd invent an excursion to the market. While there, she'd imagine the guest list for Teddy's listening party. Something low-key, a clambake perhaps? And David, happily remarried, would come with his new wife and give blessing.

Soon, Violet's high-flying life with Teddy was so vivid that the drudgery of her life with David and Dot felt like the distraction. A simple act such as David's popping his head into the steam shower—her beloved isolation chamber—asking, "Honey, have you seen my car keys?" felt like an act of violence. When conversation with David was unavoidable, she would still think about Teddy. That morning at breakfast, as David bitched about something, Violet had to check the urge to half-close her eyes, as she felt the softness of Teddy's tongue in her mouth, kissing her for the first time.

But there was a catch.

It was three in the afternoon on March the twenty-first, and Teddy hadn't called. Violet had carried her cell phone all day so as not to miss their assignation. Equally problematic, David refused to accept that his wife was not accompanying him to the yoga retreat. He was now standing at the car, ready to go.

"Where's your stuff?" he asked as he threw his duffel bag and yoga mat into the Prius—he knew enough not to drive his Bentley to a yoga retreat.

"I'm not going," Violet said for the tenth time.

"You planned it."

"I want to spend the weekend alone. Dot's with LadyGo, and I just want to relax."

"Thus, the yoga retreat."

"It will be more relaxing for me to be home alone," she said.

"You're always alone." He opened the front door of Violet's

Mercedes and popped the trunk. The obstinate bastard then grabbed her yoga mat, some sweats and tossed them in the Prius. "There. You're packed. Let's go before we hit weekend traffic."

Violet dug her fingers into her face. Teddy hadn't called yet. Should she just go with her husband?

David exploded, "What kind of face is that? I'm asking you to go away for the weekend like we planned, and you look like I just punched you in the stomach!"

Violet's cell phone rang. Her body knew it was Teddy before she saw the incoming phone number: 310-555-0199. Violet could have collapsed with relief. But she couldn't answer it in front of David. He grabbed the phone out of her hand. "Will you talk to me?!" It rang again. What if Teddy didn't leave a message?—oh God—"Say something, Violet!"

"I never said I was going with you!" she screamed. "I want a break!"

"From what? What do you need a break from? Spending my money? Spacing out? Driving off by yourself to God knows where? What do you even fucking do? I make the money. LadyGo raises your child. You do nothing! You're not necessary!"

"From that! You treat me like I'm a gigantic fuckup!"

"Does it occur to you that maybe it's because you're *fucking up?!* You're constantly out of the house but never doing anything. You're spending less and less time with Dot. We are your family. Live your fucking life. You haven't been UV-A for three years. You're not even UV-B. You're more like UV-Z."

"Don't call me that!" The phone! It had rung twice, now three times.

"What the fuck happened to you? You used to be a writer. Why don't you write anymore?"

"You know why," she said. "I don't want to be stuck on a show for sixty hours a week with Dot at home."

"Who said you have to write for TV? Write in your fucking

diary! But write. Why am I even having to tell you this? You used to know these things. You used to be a dynamo."

"Those days are over."

"As your husband, don't I get a fucking vote on that?"

"No!"

"That's your solution? For me to just go about my business while you slip away?"

Violet knew it was her turn to say something. But the phone had stopped ringing. Would Teddy leave a message? She was stranded on the silence, staring at the phone in David's hand without shame, like a dog fixated on the slimy tennis ball he wants you to throw.

"Your silence speaks volumes," David said.

The tinny trumpets of Pachelbel's Canon in D heralded. A voice mail! Violet panted, her eyes locked on the little blinking mailbox.

David opened his hand. "Your phone." She snatched it. "I hope you realize how much you stand to lose, Violet." He slammed the trunk, got into the car, and peeled out.

Violet's fingers trembled as she hit the voice mail button. *One new message.* "Hi, it's your spring equinox call." Teddy's voice was higher and more nasal than she'd remembered. "I need a favor from you. And ask me what I did last night."

Violet hit the reply button.

"That didn't take long," Teddy said. "Aren't you impressed that I know when the spring equinox is?"

"What did you do last night?" Violet said, feral with impatience.

"I downloaded pictures of chicks who looked like you and jerked off to them."

Violet swirled with delight. "Really?"

"I thought you'd like that."

"What favor do you want?"

"I'd like Geddy Lee's 4001 Rickenbacker bass."

"When's your birthday?"

"Listen to you," he said. "Like you're going to get it for me."

"We know Geddy Lee."

"*We* know Geddy Lee! Ha!"

"We used to spend every Christmas with him in Anguilla."

"Do you have any idea how much I love Rush?"

"And you're giving *me* shit about being a Deadhead? When's your birthday?"

"May first is my AA birthday. I'll have three years."

"May Day," Violet said.

"What's that supposed to mean?"

"May Day. It's a pagan celebration where children with ribbons dance around a maypole."

"Are you tripping on that hippie acid again?"

"All I meant is, congratulations on being sober for three years." There was a puddle of oil on the floor. Violet grabbed a rag from the tool bench and started to mop it with her foot.

"If I make it."

"Of course you'll make it."

"We have to stay humble in the program," Teddy said.

"Let's have a birthday party for you."

"We can't do that."

"Why?"

"Because it's my sponsor's birthday, too. And he always wants to have our birthdays together."

"That's cool." Violet picked up the dirty rag with her fingertips. "I can throw a party for both of you."

"He doesn't exactly know about you."

"Why not?" Violet headed toward the trash cans.

"He's this very by-the-book AA dude and he'd be really down on our relationship."

"Why?" She froze.

"You're a rich married lady I jerk off to who gives me money. That's not exactly part of the program."

"Oh." Violet dropped the rag.

"Don't worry. I've got it figured out, though. What's your address?"

"Why?"

"So I can come over tonight. Don't you love it how little old junkie me knows when David Parry's going to—" A roar from his end overpowered his voice.

"Where are you?" Violet asked.

"I just dropped off Her Majesty Coco Kennedy at the airport. Her sister is going on tour with the *Cats* of Japan and she got Coco a free plane ticket. Don't ask, because it doesn't make sense to me, either. You should hear her voice mail. It's filled with all these producers who want to make her a celebutard reality star. What a crazy bitch." Violet was speechless. "What's wrong?" he asked.

"I thought you broke up with her. Is she still your girlfriend?"

There was a pause. *No; that's all he had to say, no. Come on, say it: no.*

"Yes." There must have been another pause, because Teddy was now saying, "Violet? Does this upset you? Hello?"

Violet's throat throbbed. "No."

"Great. You're upset," he said.

"You made me promise I wouldn't let you get back together with her, that's all."

"Oh that. I forgot. Well, relationships are complicated. Am I right, Mrs. David Parry?"

"So you still have a girlfriend."

"I'm only eighty-five percent faithful to her."

If Violet could just hit "pause," she might be able to separate out the vagaries tangling up her brain.

"Hit me with the deets," he said. "What's your address? All I've been eating are blueberry bagels. I need some healthy food or my liver's going to balloon. You have no idea what it's like. I have the body of an eighty year old. You're a vegetarian. You can make me some healthy grub, right? Come on, where do you live?" Violet was too addled to do anything other than recite her address. He'd be there at eight. "And Violet?"

"Yeah?"

"We're just going to hang out. No funny stuff." Teddy hung up.

Violet felt repellent, like a duped sex predator slavering over the phone in a grimy carport. Her Mercedes was right there. She could jump in and catch up with David. She called Teddy back to tell him not to come. But his phone rang and rang and rang, then went to voice mail. She was certain he had seen it was her and not picked up, figuring she was trying to cancel. She closed her phone. The only thing to do was to have him over, whip up some spinach from the garden, and never see him again. Tomorrow morning, she would drive up to Matilija and make things right with David.

SALLY, Jeremy, and his two lesbian neighbors were gathered around his kitchen counter. "To Jeremy!" Jennifer raised a plastic cup of two-buck chardonnay she and Wendy had brought over in celebration.

"Good luck on Sunday," Wendy said, digging into the supermarket veggie-and-dip platter. She was the guy in this relationship, judging from her bulging khakis and rugby shirt. "We'll always be able to say we knew you when!"

Sally bristled at the sense of ownership these girls felt over Jeremy. Sure, they used to drive him places, but Sally did the driving now.

"Come on, Sally!" said one of the gals. "Have some wine."

"I'll stick to Diet Coke," she said. Wendy and Jennifer launched into reminiscences about the old days. Sally excused herself. "I have to use the little-girls' room."

"Don't forget your purse," Jennifer said. Wendy stifled a giggle.

"Thanks for reminding me." Sally smiled and grabbed her purse. Apparently dykes thought it was the height of uptightness to bring one's purse to the bathroom. They had commented on it before. But Sally wasn't offended. Jeremy had asked her to pick a romantic restaurant where they could have dinner later tonight. Deviating from his routine could only mean that he was finally going to pop the question. Sally had picked the Ivy, a place she had always imagined herself getting engaged. Soon enough, she and Jeremy would be kissing off Jennifer, Wendy, and this whole crappy apartment complex for a new life over the hill.

Sally shut the bathroom door, unzipped her Liberty of London cosmetic bag, and got out her lancet and glucometer. She washed her hands with soap and hot water. In honor of the occasion, Sally pricked the ring finger on her left hand. She stuck a test strip into the glucometer, squeezed her finger, and touched the blood to the plastic. The meter beeped. She sucked her finger and waited seven seconds for the reading. She had to smile: diabetes didn't know happy days from sad ones. It didn't care if she was getting engaged to Jeremy or dumped by Kurt, rejected by Juilliard or dancing the part of Giselle: ten times a day she'd still have to prick her finger and inject herself in the stomach.

The glucometer read 230. Sally had counted on her blood sugar being lower, considering her three o'clock injection and forty-five minutes of cardio. She would definitely want at least half a tarte tatin, the Ivy's signature dessert. Plus, the maître d' would probably send over champagne when he heard the joyous hullabaloo. That would give Sally another ten grams of carbs. Should she take some Humalog now and not have to worry about it until tonight's dose of Lantus? But her sugar levels might spike from the champagne and excitement. Then, if she ate even a couple bites of tarte tatin, she might feel too crashed to make love later. And tonight was a night she and Jeremy had to make love.

Sally decided to be safe and take a shot now, then test herself at the restaurant. She removed the tiny cushioned bottle of Humalog and the syringe dedicated to it, then drew out four units. She lifted her dress, felt her stomach for a spot that wasn't tender, and injected herself.

One of the things Sally loved most about Jeremy was the way he had reacted when she told him she was type one diabetic. And that she had lost half of her little toe to it. He frowned and said he was sorry, then never brought it up again. Everyone else got so maudlin when they found out. (Especially about the toe!) Sally knew from that point on, she'd be "poor diabetic Sally." So she never brought it up. And always wore closed-toe shoes.

As much as she would have liked to say to Jennifer and Wendy, Hey ladies, I bring my purse to the bathroom because I'm *diabetic,* Sally never once used the diabetic card for sympathy. Not even with her boyfriends, who might have forgiven her some of her histrionics had she blamed low blood sugar. Diabetes was simply something she was born with. Her eyes were blue, her teeth were straight, and her pancreas didn't produce insulin. If Sally didn't deviate from her four-hour plan, she was no different from anybody else. Control it or it controls you.

When Sally was three, she fainted while Mom videotaped her practicing her mouse dance for *The Nutcracker.* David and Mom rushed her to the hospital. When she was diagnosed with juvenile diabetes, her mother said, "Thank God it's just diabetes." The one and only time Sally went to a shrink, she recounted this story. He was astonished at Sally's unwillingness to allow that diabetes was something she should feel anger or sadness over. She left before the hour was up.

If anything, diabetes taught her the self-discipline necessary to excel at ballet. She attended the Academy of Colorado Ballet, then joined the company. Years passed as Sally watched her fellow graduates make coryphée, soloist, and principal, while she remained stuck in the corps. But then she got lucky. A guest choreographer from Russia was so inspired by her that he created a ballet around her in celebration of the hundredth anniversary of women's suffrage in Colorado. A month before Sally's premiere (the governor was scheduled to attend, and Don Johnson!), a blister on her little toe split open. She practiced through the pain, then the tingling, then the numbness. She ignored the black spots. The swelling and stiffness spread to her foot. She wrapped it tight, which bought her a couple of rehearsal days. Then her ankle started to swell. By the time Sally made it to the hospital, the toe was mottled white and scarlet, and even light blue. It looked like an exotic coral. The infection had spread to the bone. They had no choice but to amputate. A dancer four years Sally's junior ended up dancing the part and was now a principal with the San Francisco Ballet.

Sally prided herself on her ability to bounce back—indeed, what else was there to pride herself on?—and she considered it a badge of honor when someone close to her didn't know she was diabetic. None of her students had a clue. Her manager at the dance studio had no idea. When Violet sent over those crates of chocolate, it made Sally think *she* didn't know, either. Sally had certainly never brought it up with her sister-in-law. But she found it hard to believe that after seventeen years, David had never mentioned it to his wife. It had been such an enormous part of his life, too. He still paid Sally's insurance and doctors' bills. That would be one of the sweetest aspects of marrying Jeremy: getting on his insurance, so David could finally stop paying her bills.

Sally withdrew the needle from her stomach and returned the syringe to the section of her cosmetic bag where she kept the Humalog syringes to reuse. Even though they said you shouldn't reuse syringes, all diabetics did, because of the cost. Insurance didn't cover five needles per day, which Sally averaged, so it made sense to use one until the tip became so blunt it made her bruise. She did it as a courtesy to David.

"Let's see." It was Jennifer's muffled voice from the other room. Jeremy clomped across the floor. Even with his new shoes, his walk was loud and clumsy! Sally held her breath and leaned against the door. The desk drawer slid open and shut. Jeremy clomped back to the kitchen. Sally cracked the door. Jennifer and Wendy leered at the ring. Jeremy closed the velvet cube and dropped it in his jacket pocket. Sally flushed the toilet to make it seem as if she had been peeing, then rejoined the party.

SUPER-RICA, a funky taco stand on the outskirts of Santa Barbara, was a favorite of David and Violet's. It wasn't on the way to the yoga retreat, but it was worth the half hour detour. David stood, puzzling over the hand-painted menu board above the window. Violet always ordered for them, and none of this looked familiar. The line behind David was long and impatient: UCSB students and NPR-listening foodies who had made the pilgrimage to Super-Rica and knew precisely what they would order when they finally arrived at the window.

"There's some melted-cheese thing?" David asked.

"*Queso de cazuela,*" the Mexican said.

"Fine. And a horchata." The man gave David a number and a cup of the rice drink he'd been craving on the drive up. David handed the guy a twenty. "Keep it." He sat down under the tented dining area and, in its blue glow, thought about Violet.

She had sought refuge and stability after being raised by an unreliable father. Done. She wanted to move to LA. Done. She wanted to quit her job. Done. She wanted a fabulous house. Done. She wanted a baby. Done. She wanted a full-time nanny. Done and done.

And I'm the fucking asshole?

Did she have any idea how it stung when David said something and she met him with silence? At best, she'd fake it with a zombie smile or a vacant "Really?" He knew what it was like to have Violet head over heels for you. There was nothing like it. When he met her, she was a bubbly, brilliant chatterbox, always with a million questions. Now she was remote, weepy, mute.

What was her fucking excuse? That the pregnancy was *hard?* That she had a baby over a year ago and the adjustment was *hard?* That the house she had found was *harder* to remodel than she thought? That she stuffed her face during her pregnancy and it was so *hard* to lose the weight? That having a husband support her lavish lifestyle was just so *hard* on her self-esteem? That making two breakfasts in the morning, one for David and one for Dot, and not having time to make one for herself was so darned *hard?*

How about spending high school waking up at four AM to deliver newspapers in a shitty blizzarding Denver neighborhood, then doing the afternoon *and* evening shifts at Baskin-Robbins to work a forty-hour week to qualify for benefits? That was pretty *hard.* How about a teenager filing for legal guardianship of his diabetic sister so she could be covered by his health insurance? Or never going to college, getting an accounting degree through the mail, and now sitting on $32.8 million, liquid. With compounding interest, probably $32.85 after the car ride up here. Last time David checked, that was a *hard* thing to do. How about being a goddamned visionary and seeing the music business about to fall off a cliff, then leveraging everything to buy publishing catalogues that had since grown into cash cows? He had done it, and would consider it *hard.* How about booking a band whose debut album hadn't even been released to open for Green Day this summer? David had finalized that just this morning. These days, that was a mighty hard thing to pull off. How about the forty e-mails that came in on the drive up? From bands and record executives and road managers and art directors and the friend of a friend of a friend who didn't want much, just help becoming a *gigantic rock star!* Handling all that with grace only to come home to a crazy cunt of a wife was *pretty fucking hard!*

Were any of these people e-mailing or calling just to check on how David was doing? Or to thank him for always being there? No. They wanted jobs or favors or rescuing from some fuckup. Since David was a teenager, he'd been the daddy. To his mother, to Sally. Now to Violet, to Dot, to his bands, and to the hundred or so people he employed at any given time. David would consider that *harder* than making a pot of coffee in the morning and handing a baby off to LadyGo.

Earlier, in the carport, his wife couldn't take her eyes off her cell phone as it rang in his hand. Just six months ago, he had to persuade her to carry one. Now she was Susie-fucking-cell-phone. Her peculiar fixation on it had made him look down at the incoming number. Bad news for Violet, David was good at memorizing numbers.

310-555-0199.

It wasn't one he recognized. Who could have reduced Violet to such possum-eyed stupidity? A lover? That would explain a lot. But Violet fucking somebody? It wasn't the Violet he knew. If he called the number from his cell phone, whoever it was could trace it back to him, so David went to the pay phone and dialed it.

"Please deposit two dollars, fifty cents."

David smashed the receiver against the phone and let it dangle. A bunch of jocks, finishing up their lunch, snickered at him. On their table, among the empty red plastic baskets, was a cell phone. David pulled a fifty from his money clip and slapped it down. "I have to make a call. Keep the change."

"Wow, sure." A kid wearing a Def Leppard *Hysteria* T-shirt handed over his phone. David had managed that tour. He dialed the number. It went straight to voice mail.

"Dude, it's Teddy. Leave a message."

David tossed the phone back onto the table. The kids looked up, hushed. "Here, you want to use mine?" said one. The others exploded in dumb laughter.

David returned to his chair. Teddy. The name sounded familiar.

He navigated his BlackBerry to e-mail, then searched for "Teddy." One message came up, last month from his assistant.

> To: David@ultra.com
> From: Kara@ultra.com
> Re: mechanic bill
> Hi David,
> The accountant just called about a bill for $1588.04 for
> repair work on a 1989 Mazda 323 belonging to a Teddy
> Reyes. We don't show you owning a Mazda 323 and
> there's no one by that name on the payroll, so we wanted
> to make sure this bill wasn't sent in error.
> Kara ☺

David scrolled through Kara's other e-mails. He found one from later that day:

> To: David@ultra.com
> From: Kara@ultra.com
> Re: Re: mechanic bill
> Hi David,
> I just spoke to Violet and she cleared up the charge. She
> said you were super busy and I shouldn't bother you with
> this kind of stuff. Sorry about that. ☹
> Kara ☺

So. Violet had fixed a car belonging to some guy named Teddy Reyes. David vaguely remembered being in the bathroom a while back and Violet saying she had helped someone whose car had broken down. She had failed to mention the part about paying for it. Then she tried to hide it from David. And now Teddy Reyes was calling.

"Fifteen!" shouted the man from the window. "Fifteen! You number fifteen, mister?"

David checked his ticket and got his tray of food. It wasn't the thing he liked, the thing that Violet ordered for them.

THE tofu was grilled; the rice had about ten more minutes; the fresh ginger was grated into the soy and rice-vinegar mixture; the garlic cloves were fried and awaiting the spinach Violet had picked. She popped a jar of peanut butter into the microwave. Fifteen seconds should soften it sufficiently to whisk into the sauce.

Her cell phone rang. "I have to tell you something before I see you." It was Teddy. Violet had been so absorbed in her preparations, she'd almost forgotten for whom she was cooking.

"Okay." The microwave beeped. Violet tested the peanut butter. It needed thirty more seconds. She put it back in.

"My mother's in jail," he said.

"Oh." Violet frowned, not quite sure how this concerned her.

"She tried to kill one of her boyfriends," he said haltingly. "You know what I mean."

Violet didn't, nor did she want to imagine.

"There was this main one who'd beat the shit out of her. And I was around for a lot of it. For all of it."

"Oh," she said.

"You think I'm totally disgusting and beneath you, don't you?"

"No!" she said, too brightly.

"I get really weird after I fuck a chick. My relationship with Coco is totally abusive. I'd never want to do that to you. It's such a gift from God to have you in my life."

Finally, a judo moment, where Violet could use his words against him. "Thank you for telling me," she said. "Because it's abundantly clear we should just be friends."

"Why? Because I'm so gross?"

"Because, if I'm inferring correctly, you have mother issues and I'm an older woman who has recently stopped breast-feeding."

"Hot. Do you still have milk in your tits?"

"No!" Violet said as she fluffed the rice. "I've cared for you in a way a mother would and you sexualized it. It's classic repetition compulsion."

"The doctor is *in!* I've never met anyone like you before. Dig?"

"Yes," Violet said, almost wistful for the time when these words would have thrilled her. "I dig."

"You can't say, Yes, I dig. You have to just say, Dig."

"Dig." For Violet, his attempt at badinage had all the lightness of a protein bar.

"Nobody's ever been nice to me like you have," he said. "I've never felt this loved by somebody." The creature now sounded needy. Violet was sick at herself for what she had allowed to develop between her and this . . . person. She needed therapy. She'd get it, starting Monday. She owed it to David.

"Now, open up these gigantic gates." He was outside! There was no point in panicking. Violet simply had to make it through dinner, bid him adieu, and change her cell phone number. She pushed the button to open the gate and waited at the front door. "Jesus Christ," he said from the darkness as he tripped on something.

"Sorry. I should have turned on the lights."

Teddy emerged wearing jeans, a T-shirt, and a dark wool coat. His face was much more prepossessing than she had remembered. It filled her with calm, knowing she'd cast him back out into the world so handsome. He'd find another girl in no time.

"Don't kiss me," he said. "I have a sore on my mouth."

"Is it herpes?" Violet retracted the mixing bowl into her body.

"No, I don't have herpes yet. Ha! Listen to me. I don't have herpes *yet*. Aren't you glad you know me?"

He beat her to her own thoughts; Violet had to give him that. Standing there tentatively in his secondhand clothes, Teddy reminded Violet of that line in *Sweeney Todd* where Mrs. Lovett says to Toby, the street urchin who has developed a fondness for her,

What a lovely child it is. A rush of warmth filled Violet. For Stephen Sondheim, for putting it all down in words. And for her father, for telling her he would.

"Welcome," she said.

Teddy stood in the foyer and scoped out the place. "This is it?"

"It's not the biggest house. But it's by a good architect and we like the spot."

"You're seriously apologizing for this house? Jesus Christ. The view out this window is like a fucking airplane." Teddy followed Violet into the kitchen and sat at the counter. He checked out the valley lights to his right and the city lights to his left. "Okay, I just got a contact high from that magical acid you and David took." He opened a *New York Post.*

"David gets the New York edition Fed-Exed to him." Violet turned on the burner for the spinach. "He likes it better than the national edition."

"When I get to be a rich rock star, I'll have to start doing that with the *Desert Sun.*" Teddy twirled around on the kitchen stool. "What's for dinner, Lucy?"

"I might have conjured up some brown rice, sautéed spinach, and tofu. Oh! I forgot the peanut butter." Violet opened the microwave and removed the jar. She dug in a spoon and plunked some into the ginger-soy mixture.

"Wait," he said. "You're putting peanut butter in spinach?"

"It's a ginger-soy-peanut sauce." She pulled a small whisk from a Tuscan ceramic.

"Peanut butter? I don't think so."

"It's a common ingredient in Asian cuisine."

"I can't eat sugar," he said. "It's bad for my liver."

"Who's talking about sugar?"

"There's a ton of sugar in peanut butter."

"Peanuts are nuts. Nuts are fat and protein. Not sugar."

"You're so fucking out of touch up here in your glass castle that you don't even know what's in peanut butter!" Teddy gave her a lusty laugh and did another 360.

"*Peanuts* are in peanut butter." Violet wondered what the Kennedy girl must think of her boyfriend's intelligence, or lack of it.

"Say what you want," Teddy said. "All I know is spinach and peanut butter don't go together."

"They do, though." Violet stabbed the glob of peanut butter with a fork and raised it in the air. "But it's up to you. In or out, just tell me."

"Out."

Violet pitched the fork into the sink.

"Ha!" Teddy said. "Did I tell you I have a pimp nature?"

Violet threw the spinach in the pan. The flash of steam caused her glasses to fog. She didn't bother wiping them.

"WE'D like the tarte tatin, please," Sally said. "To share."

"Right away." The waiter withdrew the menu and retreated.

"Are you nervous about Sunday, my love?" she asked.

"Not really." He patted his jacket. "I was wondering. Do you—"

"Yes, Jeremy?"

"Have a pen? I wish I knew the breakdown of viewers in terms of sharps and squares. I want to remember to ask the producers tomorrow."

Sally knew herself well enough to know she was on the verge of one of her "Crazy Sally" episodes. The dinner wasn't over, she reminded herself. Perhaps Jeremy needed some space to gather his thoughts before he proposed. It was time to check her blood sugar anyway.

"Excuse me," she said.

To get to the bathroom, Sally had to walk through two rooms and a patio. She wasn't sure, but she thought that meant they had a bad table. In the front room, Sally came upon the entire band

Aerosmith, dining with some music business types. She could introduce herself as David's sister.

When David was just eighteen, he had joined a corporate accounting firm in Denver. Soon after, Aerosmith had come to play Red Rocks, where the band's manager had discovered someone was embezzling money from the tour. The manager called David's firm to send over their "most straitlaced" auditor. David ran the numbers and found a rat's nest of improprieties. The manager was so impressed he hired David to join the tour the next day. A year later, in a hotel lobby in Sydney, some local kids saw David emerge from a limo with Aerosmith and gave him a demo tape of their band. Not knowing what else to do with it, David passed the demo to a guy from the record label. That's how David had "discovered" Commonhouse. His reputation as a no-nonsense manager with an ear for music was on its way. Her geeky brother, David! The only record he'd ever bought was a Beach Boys greatest-hits album.

The guys in Aerosmith would certainly remember David if Sally dropped his name. But any time she had tried it in the past, a pall settled over the conversation. People still had to be civil to her—David's stature required it—but it was obvious what they were really thinking: David was an asshole. Sally opted to let Aerosmith dine in peace, and continued to the patio.

Adam Sandler was eating with his posse. He locked eyes with Sally, then returned his attention to his friends. Sally felt a jolt of humiliation that he had seen her emerge from Social Siberia. But, then again, for all he knew, she could have been eating with Aerosmith. Sally knew he'd glance back up at her, so on her way to the bathroom, she made sure to sway her hips.

Sally sat down on a toilet seat and took out her diabetes kit. She pricked her finger, dabbed the drop of blood on the test strip, and stuck it in the glucometer. Her seven o'clock reading had been a low 79, but with the swordfish and rice she'd just eaten, she had figured on something between 90 and 110. The glucometer read 260. *Dang.* It might be a false reading, considering she'd just eaten. Under normal circumstances, she'd hold off until her nighttime shot of Lantus. But not tonight. If Sally was going to indulge in a couple of bites of tarte tatin and a real sip of champagne, not a fake one, she'd have to counteract it with three units of Humalog. She washed her hands, dug out her syringe and insulin bottle, and lifted her dress. Her stomach had begun to bruise, which wasn't the most romantic sight in the world. She'd better take this shot in the leg. She drew out the insulin and stabbed herself in the quad. It hurt. The needle was dull. Time to throw it away. She applied pressure to the injection site. If she stood still for about a minute, it would help with the bruising.

Sally had to be especially vigilant about keeping her blood sugar near 100 because she'd gone off her birth control pills without telling Jeremy. This morning she had peed on the ovulation wand and it had come up pink, which meant she was in the all-important forty-eight-hour window. If the egg traveling down her fallopian tube was to get fertilized tonight, her sugar levels had to be absolutely consistent.

She recapped the syringe and returned it to the cosmetic bag, where she put the needles to throw away when she got home. She checked her smile in the mirror from the right, the side Adam Sandler would see as she returned to her table.

The maître d' stood at the star's table, blocking her line of vision. Sally considered it inappropriate for a maître d' to bother a celebrity like that. She paused.

"Excuse me." The hostess gently touched Sally's arm. "Can I help you with something?"

Sally jerked from the woman's touch and returned to her table. Jeremy was flipping a quarter and scribbling the outcome on a scrap of paper. The tarte tatin had been split onto two plates, and Jeremy had already wiped his clean. She waited for him to acknowledge her, but he didn't. She sat down, cut into her dessert, and took a bite. *There goes thirty carbs for nothing,* she thought.

"Try it with the whipped cream," Jeremy said eagerly. *The whipped cream!* That was it! He had hidden the ring in the whipped cream.

Sally gave him a beguiling smile. "I think I just might." The joy she'd kept bridled for the past month broke free. She had to steady her hand as she sliced across the dollop. The edge of her fork clinked against the hand-painted plate. Sally's eyes, her face, her past and future, fell on the fork positioned over the only remaining portion of whipped cream big enough to contain a ring. She slowly lowered her fork. It hit ceramic. She mashed the whipped cream. Once, twice—

"Just get a little bit." Jeremy helpfully stuck his fork on her plate. She attacked his fork with hers and smashed flat the whipped cream and the apple tart. Growls came out of her mouth. "Sally?" Jeremy asked. "Are you okay?"

"Sorry to interrupt," said a familiar voice behind Sally.

Jeremy looked up. "Hi," he said.

Sally spun around. Adam Sandler had come to their table! Had their chemistry in that one glance been so powerful that he'd brazenly ask her out right in front of her boyfriend?

"Look who's here!" she gargled.

"Sorry to interrupt." Adam Sandler shifted his weight and looked down bashfully. *What a sweetie!*

"Not at all," she said.

His eyes still on the floor, Adam Sandler said, "You're—"

"Sally!"

"Jeremy White," said Adam Sandler.

"Huh?"

"The maître d' tipped me off. You've got to believe there's like nobody I'd come up and bother while they're eating. Basically, you and any Pittsburgh Steeler. And Al Gore. But that's because I heard he was talking trash about my mother."

"What did he say about your mother?" Jeremy asked.

"He's joking!" howled Sally, rolling up her eyes.

"I've got to thank you for your Rose Bowl pick last year," the movie star said.

"Number one versus number two is a terrific angle," Jeremy said. "Works nine percent better in bowl games than regular season."

"I bet the money line," said Adam Sandler.

"You got plus one fifty, then. One sixty at kickoff."

"You're a fucking genius." Adam Sandler turned to Sally and said, "May I?"

"Sure." She had no idea what she had just permitted.

Adam Sandler grabbed Jeremy's cheeks and shook his face. "I love this guy," he said. "If you didn't have a girlfriend, I'd kiss you." He let go of Jeremy's face. "Good luck Sunday, by the way. They've been promo'ing the shit out of you."

"Thanks," said Jeremy.

"I'll let you go," Adam Sandler said, and walked off.

"Don't!" cried Sally after him.

The waiter swung by. "Would you be needing anything more this evening?"

"Just the check," Jeremy said.

DINNER was delicious and the conversation, covering topics from Teddy's favorite movie (*Vanilla Sky*) to his theory on the origin of hepatitis C (invented by drug companies), airless. Violet had let Teddy's misnomers, conspiracy theories, and harebrained schemes go undisputed, and even feigned interest in his idea for a TV show he proposed they team up to write.

"I can't believe it's almost ten o'clock," Violet finally said.

"What is that, a hint?"

"Not at all." She stood up and cleared their plates. He had eaten around the cloves of garlic. She didn't trust people who didn't like garlic, especially big fried pieces.

"It is a hint!" he said with a laugh. "Look at you. You're throwing me out."

"If that's what you want to call it."

"Well, thanks for dinner." He reluctantly got up. "I haven't had a home-cooked meal in years. I hope David realizes what a cool chick you are."

"Who knows anymore." Violet walked to the front door, but Teddy lingered at a painting.

"Is that you?" he asked.

"It's a portrait David had commissioned for our anniversary. That's me at the pool. You'll recognize the view."

"Coco's family is totally into art, too," he said. "They just sold a Picasso for like seventeen grand."

"Seventeen grand? It must have been a print."

"No, it was a painting. It was just really small."

Violet let that one go, and opened the door.

"So, we'll hang out again?" he said. "Maybe with your husband?"

Teddy and David friends? David would last about two seconds in conversation with this jejune nitwit.

"Teddy?" Violet said.

Teddy twitched.

"What's wrong?" she asked.

"That's like the second time I've heard you actually say my name. I still kind of can't believe I know you."

"I was about to say something intimate."

"Shit," said Teddy. "What?"

"I want you to know that the intensity I felt for you wasn't something that had ever happened to me before." Hopefully, Teddy would find comfort in these words when she stopped returning his calls.

"Hey," he said. "What are you doing tomorrow? You want to see me play in this gooney Rolling Stones cover band in Long Beach? We totally rock, even though the lead singer is a fucked-up junkie. I'm going to fire him after the show." He couldn't have known that David had once managed the Rolling Stones, and Violet had spent her honeymoon jetting through South America on the *Steel Wheels* tour.

"Really?" she said. "Bill Wyman kicking Mick Jagger out of the Stones? That can happen?"

"Shut up. Just come check us out."

"I wish," said Violet. "But I'm driving up to meet David at the yoga retreat in the morning."

"I thought he was going alone."

"I decided to join him."

"While we were having dinner? Jesus. Am I really that dull? I told you I'm tired, right?"

"Like you said, relationships are complicated." She kissed him on the cheek and closed the door. She returned to the kitchen and started the dishes.

Then her cell phone rang.

Without even looking at the number, she went to the front door and opened it. Standing there, phone in hand, was Teddy.

To be on the road with a rock band was to become intimately familiar with *Scarface*. The movie was on a constant loop in tour buses, dressing rooms, and hotel suites. Roadies had *Scarface* tattoos. Production offices were indicated by life-size cutouts of Al Pacino in that white suit. The video game was a recent annex to the riders of David's bands. Snippets of the movie's dialogue were played between songs on the precurtain mix tape. David knew them all: "First you make the money, then you get the power, *then* you get the women." "You think you can take me? You need a fucking army if you gonna take me!" "You're all a bunch of fucking assholes. You know why? You don't have the guts to be who you wanna be.... You need people like me so you can point your fucking fingers and say, 'That's the bad guy.' ... Well, say good night to the bad guy." "I never fucked anybody over in my life didn't have it coming to them." Before their encore, Commonhouse would blast, "You wanna fuck with me? Okay. You wanna play rough? Okay. Say hello to my little friend!" Then they'd rip into "Light Sweet Crude."

David's personal favorite moment was when a business associate suggested doing something that displeased Tony Montana. Tony considered it, then said, "So that's how you wanna play it?" One of the most sinister lines in the history of cinema.

So that's how you wanna play it?

Violet had sent David off to a yoga retreat so she could fuck some guy named Teddy Reyes in David's ten-million-dollar house while their daughter slept at LadyGo's in Pasadena. Did Violet take him for a fucking chump? Had lust damaged her brain? Didn't she realize that David had spent the past fifteen years beating off groupies? What did she think happened on the road, anyway? But had he ever cheated on his wife? Never once.

When David had first met Violet, he was seeing a girl in Sacramento whom, to this day, he had never told her about. Sacramento Sukey, she was known to any band that rolled through town. She was famous for the blow jobs she generously bestowed, not only on the band members but roadies, too. No doubt, she was a skank. Still, David found her kindhearted and a good listener. She had a kid and cut hair or something. David found himself spending hours on the phone with her every night. He even flew her to Japan and Australia on one of the tours. He kept her quarantined in his hotel room, of course, for fear of getting ruthlessly teased if anyone discovered he'd developed bona fide feelings for the blow job queen of central California. In the early days of Violet, David had rendezvoused with Sukey a few times. But the moment he got engaged, he cut Sukey off. And now, sixteen years into a marriage, fresh from weaning their baby daughter, Violet was cheating on *him*?

So that's how you wanna play it?

David zoned out into the wet tea bag stuck to the side of his handmade cup. Dinner was over and everyone had trickled outside for the sweat lodge ceremony. He was alone in the mess hall, frozen, a state he had found himself in more than once since his arrival at the Matilija Retreat Center. During the afternoon yoga class, Shiva had asked David if he was okay. Only then had he realized he'd been standing, lost in a knot in the wood floor, while the other students were arched in backbends at his feet.

David looked up from his tea. A hand-painted sign on the wall read ONLY TAKE WHAT IS FREELY GIVEN.

Did Violet think David had earned eight million dollars last year in a music industry that had turned to shit because he didn't enjoy a *street fight*? For starters, he'd throw her out of the house. Change the locks. Cancel the credit cards. Shut off her cell phone. Impound her Mercedes. Send LadyGo and the rest of the minions packing. Then he'd kick the party into high gear and go about winning sole custody of Dot.

You wanna fuck with me? Okay. You wanna play rough?

All it would require was money. Any judge would sympathize with hardworking David, whose stay-at-home wife spent more time with her south-of-the-border lover than with the baby she could barely conceive.

Her womb is so polluted she can't even make a fucking baby.

David couldn't wait for the scabrous trial so he could enumerate Violet's maternal transgressions. The time she was changing the battery on a smoke alarm and Dot swallowed a bunch of pennies and David had to perform the Heimlich in order to save her life. When Violet had left Dot unattended in the rocking chair while she went outside to show the phone guy some junction box. Or when Violet was in another room and Dot had sucked on an indelible-ink marker, which left her with a sickening black mouth and tongue for a week. The jury would gobble that shit up. David wasn't the one who had been desperate for a baby, but at least he understood that once she was born he had an obligation to keep her alive!

The table David sat at was made of wood. Burned into its surface in wavy lettering were the words THIS PLACE OF FOOD, SO FRAGRANT AND APPETIZING, ALSO CONTAINS MUCH SUFFERING. David pondered its meaning, then caught himself softening and looked away: anger reloaded.

So that's how you wanna play it?

Did Violet actually think she could get by without David? The most she'd ever earned in a year was a million. And that was before she took five years off. The television business, like the music business before it, was fucked. If she was even able to get a job, she'd be lucky to make two hundred grand, one hundred after taxes. He'd love to see her try to scrape by on that! Private trainers, nannies, assistants, maids, first-class travel, limos, restaurants, shopping sprees whenever she got bored. That cost *real* money. Their nut was a million a year. Did Violet even know that? Had she ever thought to ask? Did she fucking care? She'd start caring come Monday, when she'd return home from some goddamned manicure and her gate clicker wouldn't work. When she finally tracked down a pay phone—she'd have to, as he'd have canceled her cell phone—David would be unreachable because he'd be out to lunch with one of the long list of women who would die to be seen with him. And how old would they be? Twenty-five. What would they look like? A perfect ten.

I never fucked anybody over in my life didn't have it coming to them. You got that?

She thought things were rough now? She didn't know the half of it. Her life would be spent *never knowing*. Would Dot get dropped off for her supervised visit? Would the alimony be there this month? Sometimes yes, sometimes no. David would fuck with her payments as much as possible without getting hauled into court. There were pettifoggers who specialized in shit like that. Violet would become one of those divorcées deformed by plastic surgery who descended into madness and isolation because all they could talk about was how evil their ex was. Violet would be forced back into the workplace. She liked houses; she could always become a realtor. He pictured her face on the bus bench, VIOLET PARRY, THE CONDO QUEEN OF ENCINO!

You think you can take me? You need a fucking army if you gonna take me!

What did Violet think was so great out there for a fat, divorced, forty-two-year-old woman with a kid? Oh, that's right, some guy who didn't have the wherewithal to fix his own car! For that Violet had sabotaged sixteen years of marriage and a family? For that she was willing to abdicate all claims to David's riches?

Say good night to the bad guy.

David hoped Teddy the King would still be there for Violet when the money dried up and the friends mysteriously scattered. LA wasn't kind that way. All their friends would fall in line behind legendary impresario David Parry, not his aging, unemployable wife. How long would it take Violet to realize that all she was to Teddy Reyes was a rich lady who paid to have his car fixed? If *Señor Reyes* could stomach fucking *Señora Gorda,* there might be more bills paid. Perhaps a new cell phone. He'd gladly eat some stretched-out gabacho pussy for one of those stylin' Apple phones! Was Violet deluded enough to think Teddy Reyes was in it for her sparkling personality?

"David?" It was Shiva. She stood in the open door. "Are you going to join us for the sweat lodge?"

"I'll be right there."

And David *would* be there. He honored his commitments. Violet had been the one to sign up for the yoga retreat, but she apparently preferred staying home and getting fucked by a beggar!

David brought his cup to the kitchen. Above the sink hung a colorful sign, WASHING THE DISHES IS LIKE BATHING A BABY BUDDHA. THE PROFANE IS SACRED. He smashed his cup in the sink and went outside.

The night sky was not an LA night sky, where streetlights hit the haze and ricocheted back a constant glow. It was a night sky that meant business: black, the stars-you-could-touch each had their own twinkle. David walked under the canopy of ancient California oaks and startled as the stars popped out from between the web of branches. The roar of the water sliced into his ears. He had noticed a river before, but only now really heard it. David hung at the perimeter of affluent yogis and yoginis who, like him, had driven up from the city. They stood around a roaring fire, attention rapt on Ruth, an abdominous woman with tough skin and scarecrow hair.

"The ceremony will last for roughly an hour and a half," she said. "Hot stones will be brought in between each prayer round...."

"Can I see your wrist?" whispered a young guy with a scraggly beard who wore pajama bottoms. "This sweet grass will form a band of protection around your heart."

"If it's supposed to protect my heart, why are you putting it around my wrist?" asked David.

"It's to protect *your heart*," the kid said. He was either stoned or stupid. David offered his arm. The hippie, tongue hooked over his lip in concentration, braided some grass around David's wrist and gave it a tug. "Make sure you let this fall off naturally. If you cut it off, everything you receive tonight from the Great Spirit will disappear."

"Thanks for the tip."

"There are about thirty of us," Ruth was explaining. "That means we'll need to have an inner and an outer circle. It's going to be a tight fit." She nodded to a chest-high dome constructed from branches; it measured about twelve feet in diameter and was covered in animal hides.

Tight fit? When Shiva had said there'd be a sweat lodge, David pictured a *lodge* lodge, like an Ahwahnee or an El Tovar. Not as grand, obviously, but something wood paneled, with a place to sit, like a big sauna. *That puny twig thing was* the *fucking sweat lodge?* During the evening yoga class, David had contemplated some hippies pulling pelts out of a plastic storage bin, the kind Violet kept stacked in the carport to store Christmas decorations and the like. The hippies had laid the pelts across this wood structure. David had assumed there'd be one structure per person. *Jesus,* they were all expected to fit into this *one?* And hot stones, too?

"The temperature will reach a hundred and fifty degrees," said Ruth, oblivious to the growing terror in the Westsiders' eyes. "I will pour water onto the stones throughout the ceremony, which will make it about two hundred degrees with humidity."

There was no way Violet would have been able to take this. David remembered when she was pregnant and she tried to cajole him into letting her have a home birth. He pointed out that she had once complained for three days after swallowing a piece of gum. "I have a high tolerance for pain but a low tolerance for discomfort," she had explained. It was very Violet, and David was charmed, as ever.

"Earth Mother," Ruth intoned to the night sky, "we ask you to accept us into your womb and return us to our innocence. Please cleanse us of our ignorance and spiritual *dis-ease....*"

Dis-ease. This, too, would have sent Violet fleeing to the nearest Four Seasons. Nothing vexed her like hippies mangling the English language. Once, during a yoga class at home, Shiva had said,

"We're all members of the *one song*." She repeated it several times, *one song* this, *one song* that. Finally, Violet couldn't take it anymore. She stood up out of her Warrior II pose and demanded, "Why do you keep saying that? What is that? *One song*?" Shiva answered, "Uni-verse. *Uni* means one and *verse* means song. One song. Uni-verse." Violet rolled her eyes. "Oh, for God's sake," she said, always her father's daughter!

Ruth started banging on a drum. "We call upon the spirit guides of the Four Directions. We beseech you to grant us your wisdom so we may be re-birthed into the world with a healed heart."

A pleasing array of yoga asses swayed to Ruth's *a capriccio* drumbeat. David used to fetishize yoga chicks for their hot bodies and free-loving spirits. But enough yoga classes had made him realize these hotties were no less crazy or manipulative than strippers. Both were willfully ignorant and directed their limited intelligence into their bodies. There was a yin-yang to it. Yoga chick on the one side, crazy stripper on the other.

"Now that we've blessed the stones," Ruth said, "it's time for us to take off our clothes and enter the lodge." She ripped off her T-shirt and sarong. David wasn't the only one to quickly look away.

If Violet were here, she'd have been having a complete breakdown. He'd have to go through the whole rigmarole about how she wasn't fat. A lie! But what else could he say? David had never pressured his wife to lose the baby weight. He was painfully aware of the looks on people's faces any time Violet stopped by the office, their eyes aglimmer because the almighty David Parry's wife had gone fat on him. He had been heartened this past month to see Violet exercising and losing weight—for Teddy! *It was for her new lover, Teddy.*

"Aaagggh!" He punched a nearby tree. The skin across his knuckles split open. He felt the sting but didn't bother to look.

Apparently, nobody wanted to be the first to strip. All just stood there, eyes downcast. At least nut job strippers had no problem getting naked! David pulled off his T-shirt, stepped out of his shorts, and walked over to Ruth.

"What is it you want us to do?" he said.

"Enter the lodge on your hands and knees, prostrating yourself to Earth Mother. Crawl counterclockwise until you're nearest to the door on the other side."

David spiked his clothes, dropped to his hands and knees, and hightailed it into the so-called lodge. Inside, he hesitated. It was darker than dark, the dark of nothingness, and impossible to determine where his body ended and the blackness began. He proceeded gingerly, the twig wall brushing his right side. Suddenly, a pain pierced his knee. A sharp rock was sticking out of Earth Mother. David's hand was already raw and throbbing from the tree. He didn't want to fuck up his knee, too. He stood up, and the whole lodge popped off the ground with him. He fumbled for a branch to balance the sweat lodge before the whole goddamn hunk of junk capsized.

"Jesus Christ!" He dropped to his knees, and the structure crashed down on his back. "Fuck me!"

"Hey, what happened?" called Ruth. "Stay prostrated close to Earth Mother."

David continued crawling, then felt something soft on his face. Before he realized it, he was inhaling a musty animal pelt. "Gaaah!" He slapped the germs off his face, then a head rammed his legs.

"Did someone up there stop?" asked a voice.

David decided to bail on this perimeter bullshit. He clambered across to where he sensed the door would be. But then his arm buckled and his face was planted in some loose dirt: he had fallen into a pit. "Cock-sucking fucking shit cock motherfucker." David spit out a mouthful of dirt and licked the rest onto his forearm.

"I think someone's hurt," called a frightened woman.

"I'm fine!" David lifted himself back on all fours. He had lost any sense of direction. He decided to crawl until he reached the wall, then hang a left. He put one hand in front of the other until the crown of his head tapped a branch. He turned to the left. He felt something soft and fuzzy against his arm. Only when it pressed harder against him did he realize he had brushed up against a dick and some hairy balls. "Aah!" David jerked his arm away.

"Just breathe in, buddy."

"Yeah, I'm trying."

"One hand, then one knee," offered another voice.

"Then the other hand and then the other knee," someone else pitched in. "Break it down."

How had this fucking happened? Just this morning, David had booked Hanging with Yoko to open fifty dates on the Green Day tour. And now a mob of new age dipshits was instructing him on the finer points of *crawling?* These privileged half-wits who drove up for the weekend in their Mercedes Kompressors, did they actually think they had money? David would put his portfolio up against theirs any day. *Bring it, motherfuckers!*

"Why are we stopped?" squeaked a woman.

"I thought we were supposed to go counterclockwise," said a deep voice.

"Is something wrong?" It was Ruth. She must have stuck her head in. "You've got to keep moving in there. Is someone confused?"

"It's the guy who punched the tree," volunteered a woman.

Anger ripped through David. Violet would pay for this. He would put a dollar amount on his rage and humiliation and deduct it from her settlement. He took a deep breath, then knocked heads with somebody.

"Ouch!" cried a woman.

At least it meant he'd reached the door. David felt for the edge, then planted himself beside it and pulled his legs into his chest. The dick-and-balls guy plastered himself next to David. Why didn't he just lean in for a kiss while he was at it? David attempted to get comfortable, but a knot from a branch poked into his upper back. He reached around and broke it off. It didn't do any good. He shifted his weight and nestled between some bigger branches. He licked his injured knee and sucked the dirt from the raw wound. Big salty flaps of skin came off in his mouth. If Violet were here, she'd give him a peck on the cheek. She understood how hard his days were....

A fleshy ass dropped onto David's feet. He quickly widened his stance to avoid his toe up someone's butt. A slender back leaned into his shins. He scrunched his legs closer, but the person just pushed deeper into them.

Something heavy landed in his lap. Jesus Christ, it was a *braid*. One of the yoga-chick-slash-strippers had a big one. He had marveled at its lack of hygiene in the dinner line. David lifted the braid with his thumb and index finger and dropped it off to the side. In an instant, it was back in his lap. Once again, David picked up the braid.

"Excuse me," whispered a woman. "It throws off my alignment if my braid falls to the side."

"How's that my problem, Rapunzel?" David tossed the braid off to the side.

"I need it to fall straight back," she said. The braid-that-wouldn't-die landed in David's lap.

"Cut your hair, why don't you?" David chucked the braid to the side, making sure to yank the woman's head in the process.

"Ouch!"

"Fuck you!"

"Hey—" admonished someone. "Language."

"That energy is totally inappropriate," said another.

The fetid thing once again appeared in David's lap. He wiped his bloody hand and knee on it.

"What are you doing?" said the woman.

"Nothing." David spit into his palm and smeared that on the braid, too.

Violet would have found this hilarious. If she were here, this incident would be added to their rich annals of happiness: how the sweat lodge kept getting worse and worse and then…the hippie braid fight. Knowing it was being shared with the woman he loved would have made David's increasing misery almost thrilling. But no, it was just David, alone in the dark with a bunch of strangers.

Fat-lady grunts announced the arrival of Ruth. "O Great Spirit of Life," she adjured, "we are gathered below in our pitiful little lodge on Earth Mother." Ruth needed to read that book of Dot's about using your "inside voice." If David had whispered that to Violet, she would have cracked up. He smiled. Violet had a zesty, unapologetic laugh. After all these years, it still took him by surprise.

"We shall invite the helpers of the Great Spirit to enter our lodge," said Ruth, who continued on with some mumbo jumbo. The drum sounded three times, then there was silence. Not even the river could be heard. Did their bodies absorb its roar? The hides deflect it? David couldn't comprehend the physics of it. A glowing orange orb floated past him. Smooth wood touched his shoulder. The fire guy must have been using a pitchfork to lay down the hot stones. Three more were brought in and lowered into the pit. Sweat dripped down David's face. A hiss filled the darkness. Wet heat blasted him.

"O Wakan Tanka," Ruth said, "we thank you for providing us with life-giving rains, which this water symbolizes." Her voice had become low and spooky, like Sally and her little friends when they'd put on séances.

David closed his eyes. It seemed no darker than before. He opened his eyes to make sure. Indeed, there was no difference. His eyelids fell and, in turn, his body levitated slightly. He knew it wasn't levitating. Obviously, his body wasn't levitating. Still, he kept his eyes closed to enjoy the strange sensation.

"We will now begin our four rounds of prayer," said Ruth. "I will begin, then we will go around one by one, starting with the first gentleman who entered." That would be David. He smiled as he imagined Ruth's words entering through his legs and traveling up to his brain that way. "When you are finished praying, you are to say, Ho! Then, as a way of acknowledging your prayer, the group answers, Ho! That will indicate that it's time for the next person to speak." David didn't really understand what he was supposed to do and didn't really care. "Great Father Sky," entreated Ruth, "you are the protector of Mother Earth. We call upon your power to heal our hearts. May we be free from danger. May we be free from *dis-ease*. Until we feel happiness and peace ourselves, we will be unable to walk down your great Red Path. Kindly listen as we go around the circle and pray for ourselves." Ruth shook her rattle. "Great Father Sky, I ask you, please free me from depression," she said. "Ho!"

"Ho!" answered the chorus of yogis.

Shit, that was quicker than David had expected. It was now his turn to pray for himself. What did he want? The man who had everything. David liked to tell people that the only thing money couldn't buy was poverty. Maybe he could lay that line on these new age bozos. Or, better, he could say, "My wife's back home fucking a Mexican. What does that make her? A..." And then they'd answer, "Ho!"

Instead, David found himself saying, "To be understood. Please, let me be understood. Ho!"

Violet thought he was an asshole. Everyone at this retreat thought he was an asshole. LadyGo walked around on eggshells because she thought he was a big asshole. Hanging with Yoko had signed with him because, after meeting with all the top managers, they said, We wanted an asshole on our team. None of them understood: David was no asshole. He was responsible.

"Free me from attachment," said the man to his left. "Ho!"

"Please," said a woman, "let me live in a world…" She paused to gather her thoughts, then continued, "…not *without* men, but with men who are more in touch with their inner woman."

David had taken care of Sally since she was two. Their dentist father had died suddenly of a heart attack, leaving the family shockingly in debt. Their mother's response was a rapid descent into frailty: physical, mental, emotional. Twelve-year-old David had no choice but to quit sports and devote his afternoons and weekends to working. A year later, Sally was diagnosed with juvenile diabetes.

"Money problems," someone was saying. "I promise I will get everything under control if you remove my debt. Ho!"

It was up to David to take Sally to her doctors, check her heartbreakingly tiny feet for cuts, monitor her blood sugar, ride his bike to the pharmacy to get her insulin, cut the Chemstrips in thirds to save money, fill out reams of insurance forms. And always, the shots. Any kiddie birthday party, David would take the bus to the only bakery in Denver that carried sugar-free desserts. It was down on Colfax and Franklin, the one that stuck day-old doughnuts on tree branches for the birds. He'd buy something for Sally so she wouldn't feel any more ripped off by life. On Halloween, he would tie ribbons around baggies of celery and deliver them on his paper route with a note that read "When the drum majorette trick-or-treats tonight, please give her this. She's diabetic." He'd stay with her at ballet class, long past the age when the other girls got dropped off, making sure she ate, and ate properly. But he never saw Sally as a burden. It filled him with lofty purpose, doing the work of Sally's pancreas so she could remain a child.

"Free me from fantasy," a voice cried in the dark. "Ho!"

But everything changed when Sally turned eleven. David had driven her to Dr. Turner to discuss recent advancements in diabetes treatment. The doctor asked Sally about her regimen and David jumped in with the answers. The doctor instructed David to step into his office, where he called the Denver Children's Hospital and requested a bed for the next week. "It's time Sally learned for herself how to be a diabetic." David said, "But I'm her big brother; I want to help her." The doctor replied, "Help her, you'll kill her." David didn't visit Sally once that week, as she learned for herself to count carbs, prick her finger, read a glucometer, and give herself multiple shots. A month later, Aerosmith offered him the job. David's first call was to Dr. Turner. He said leaving Sally would be the best thing for her. So David left. She didn't tell him about the amputation until after it happened, after she moved to LA. He could see the terror in her eyes as she pshawed it as a silly inconvenience. His heart broke for her, so he went along with the charade. A charade he'd kept up for the past ten years.

The drum sounded again. More rocks were brought in. David leaned into their unbelievable heat. It was soothing in the same way that biting down on a sore tooth made it feel better.

"Now that Great Father Sky has healed our hearts," said Ruth, "we ask Earth Mother to do the same for a beloved friend. May this beloved friend be happy. May they be physically well. May they feel safe. May they know peace." The rattle sounded. "To the man out there who hasn't found me yet," she said. "You, beloved life partner, may you feel joy. I love you so. Ho!"

It was David's turn. He had only one beloved friend. "My wife," he said. "Please help her. She is suffering. Ho!"

Why else wouldn't she be here? The Violet he knew and loved showed up. The first time he had laid eyes on her, she was sitting in that ticket holders' line ahead of time. She was a stand-up chick. She didn't bail. She didn't lie. She certainly didn't *cheat*.

"My children," another voice said. "Ho!"

Violet must have been suffering. What else could explain her behavior? She had wanted a baby more than anything. But she seemed to be running away from little Dot. That must have been so confusing to Violet. Violet, who was so intelligent and empathetic.

Violet, who had said just the right thing innumerable times to all different types of people. This time, Violet was unable to help herself.

"I pray my boyfriend finds the clarity to accept my love," said someone. "Ho!"

Violet was radiant and honest and impeccable with her word and serious and vulnerable and remembered things you said ten years later and played the piano and could quote Shakespeare and wrote thank-you notes and once even a letter to the boss of the guy at the airline counter who had been especially helpful on their way to Aspen and she kept secrets and listened to what you were saying not just with her ears but with her eyes and also her smile and she left five dollars in the hotel for the maids and knew a hit song the first time she heard one and baked teething biscuits for Dot and grew the most lovely smelling roses and knew how to crochet and spoke four languages and when someone complimented her on her perfume she'd send them a bottle the next day and anytime David looked across a crowded party and saw her talking to somebody he had no doubt they'd adore her just like he did and she never wore makeup and people remembered her for her dinner parties and big crazy words and without her he was just an asshole rock-and-roll manager that's why the guys from Hanging with Yoko said he was an asshole because they hadn't met Violet yet and when people met Violet they realized there must be something more to David because why would such a successful and worldly and gorgeous, he couldn't forget gorgeous, woman be married to David if that was all he was, an asshole? To the uninitiated, David seemed like the star of the marriage. This was the truth, though: people came for David, but they stayed for Violet. And now she was gone.

David wept. Others did, too. More stones had been brought in. Water had been splashed on them. More steam arose. These things must have happened, for Ruth was praying again.

"O Great Spirit," Ruth said, "we give thanks for the rich bounty that results from the water of springtime. You have heard our prayers for ourselves. You have heard the prayers for our dear friends. Now let us summon the Buffalo Calf Woman to send similar healing to a teacher. A difficult person who has been placed on our path to teach us compassion. The rains of the Great Spirit are not selective. They fall equally on one and all, and so should our love. We now ask the Buffalo Calf Woman to birth this equanimous love and let it rain on this difficult person who has caused us so much suffering."

David's head flopped down and landed squarely on the wet braid across his knees. He smiled and up bobbed his head.

"To my father, who beat me," Ruth said. "I hope he feels safe. I hope he feels free. Ho!"

"Teddy Reyes." David spoke the forbidden name. "Ho!"

David knew what it felt like to have Violet's eyes fall on you and you alone. It was as if you'd been singled out for life's greatest honor. Just minutes into their first date, in line for popcorn, David had felt it, and it made him believe he could accomplish anything. And he had! To meet Violet for the first time was to be seduced by her strange brew of curiosity and high-mindedness. Now Teddy, whoever he was, had gotten a hit of it, too. Of course he was calling. He needed another fix! Maybe he thought he was rescuing the rare, exotic Violet. From her asshole husband.

Because David was an asshole. He was mean to her. The shameful part was, he had only started being mean when she began to show signs of weakness. When she had trouble conceiving, then the remodel, and finally the pregnancy. With no money and no job of her own, David only bullied her more.

In the delivery room: Violet had been in labor for twelve hours, refusing the epidural. (She had been right; her tolerance for pain *was* high!) Violet, writhing and grimacing. David, horrified at his helplessness. In front of Dr. Naeby and the nurses, Violet said to her husband, "Please, don't be mean to me anymore. Look at me. See how hard I'm trying? Please don't be so mean, especially now, with the baby." Having watched his wife endure such pain, David had already resolved to do the same. But to be called out by a woman in labor, in front of a roomful of strangers, was unendurably humiliating. David rolled his eyes to Dr. Naeby and the nurses. The good doctor smiled, oh-the-things-I've-seen, and shrugged. Despite Violet's plea—indeed, perhaps because of it—David had, if anything, been crueler to her since she became a mother.

What had happened to them? When he met her she was Ultraviolet. That's why he loved her. Not for the fantasia of good food and laughter and sex that had become their life together. But for her supreme confidence. Her boundless energy. He had found a teammate who, like himself, could take care of business. For their one-year anniversary, right after they had moved to LA, he had bought her a gold necklace from the Elvis Presley estate with Elvis's "TCB quick as a flash" logo encrusted in diamonds. Sure, even in those early days, Violet would break down when it all got to be too much. She'd cry some mornings. But before noon there would invariably be a call. "I'm okay!" she would declare, and the sparkle was back. The mojo intact.

But this time Violet wasn't bouncing back. She had escaped into the arms of Teddy Reyes. Poor bastard. He probably thought he had a chance with her! He may have even convinced himself that he understood her. But before Violet was David's wife, she was her father's daughter. David knew the stories well. Had Teddy heard them, too? Of the often drunk and always grandiose Englishman driving his erudite little girl around Los Angeles in a convertible Jag, quizzing her on Greek versus Roman gods, or the legacy of Sputnik, or devouring the latest Broadway cast album? Did Teddy know Churchill Grace once sent his daughter to bed without pudding because she didn't know the exact round in which Muhammad Ali knocked out George Foreman in Zaire? David understood only too well that Violet was an inveterate snob. She would protest wildly when accused of such a thing. This blind spot was her most charmingest of charms. Soon, David knew, the snob in Violet would stir from its slumber and forbid her from spurning her Croesus husband and heiress daughter for a man incapable of scraping together sixteen hundred dollars to fix a car!

The drum sounded. Ruth spoke, "Now we will begin our final round of prayer. Let us commit ourselves to the transformative love we have generated and which connects us to the Great Spirit."

Right now, at this moment, David loved Violet.

And now he loved Violet.

And now he loved her, too.

The marriage had turned to shit. At least Violet was doing something about it. She was taking a leap. So David would take one, too: no matter what Violet said or did, from this moment on, he would love her as he loved her now.

Ruth shook the rattle. "I promise to slow down and appreciate life's precious gifts," she said. "Ho!"

It was David's turn. "I will love her. Ho!"

CHAPTER SEVEN

Present/Wonderful Moment ❧ I'm Hearing Something ❧ The Message

The *Pietà* ❧ Ritz-Carlton ❧ Elephant Slaying ❧ *Mas*

The Dress Hollow ❧ God Is for Poor People

VIOLET CARRIED DOT INTO THEIR SUNDAY MORNING RIE CLASS. RESOURCES for Infant Educarers, or RIE, was a parenting approach that Violet had flipped over. It was founded in the sixties by a Hungarian, Magda Gerber, and based on the research of Dr. Emmi Pikler, a Budapest pediatrician. RIE held that all babies were born competent, inner directed, and confident. Only by well-intended but misguided parenting in which babies were wheedled, praised, and entertained did they become insecure, overly dependent, and quick to bore. Unlike in other mommy-and-me-type classes, in RIE class, parents were asked not to initiate conversation with their babies, so the teachers could model how and when to respectfully communicate. Thus RIE classes were rather solemn affairs.

"Good morning, Dot," said Sharon, the serious but gentle teacher. Violet found it demoralizing that a woman in her sixties had a better body than she did.

Violet put Dot down and joined the wall of trendy moms. One man was there, a young tattooed father who took every opportunity to mention that he had directed an episode of *Entourage*.

Dot stood at the door, watching the group of infants play with wooden toys, plastic kitchen items, and such. She took a deep breath and looked at Violet. Violet nodded. Dot took a deeper, quivering breath.

"Ball," she said. Violet acknowledged this with a smile. Dot bustled over and picked up the ball.

"What we just saw was wonderful parenting on the part of Violet," said Sharon. "Dot was able to choose *on her own terms* when to initiate play. Violet did not order Dot to go play. How wonderful life would be if, as adults, we could take a couple of deep breaths to assess *our* comfort level before *we* jumped into a strange new situation."

Violet nodded. She hadn't heard a word of what Sharon had just said.

TEDDY *stood in the door, his hands nestled in the pockets of his pill-covered peacoat. His downcast eyes said he well understood that what they were about to embark on was grave and dishonorable. He entered the house and hesitated. Violet removed her glasses and placed them on a table alongside her car keys, some dry-cleaning tickets, and Dot's spare EpiPen. She locked the door, then walked to the couch and sat on its edge. Teddy followed and sat beside her, his head down, his hands still in his pockets. His profile betrayed his inferior breeding: weak chin, narrow nose, no cheekbones to speak of. Ashy skin, sparse eyelashes.*

He turned to Violet. "So?" he asked. Through a crack in his jacket, Violet saw his beating T-shirt. She moved closer and touched both palms to his cheeks, then ran her fingers through his thick, unclean hair.

"Oh Jesus." Unloosed, Teddy kissed Violet. She released into the pillows. They searched each other's mouths. Tenderly, roughly, trading off leads, as if to say, This is who you are? Well, this is who I am. *All with the aching thrill that is impossible with a husband of sixteen years.*

A blond-haired boy wearing a Hanging with Yoko T-shirt and kabbalah bracelet struggled to fit a hair curler into the wide mouth of a water jug. When he finally succeeded, the *Entourage* director glanced up from his text-messaging and said, "Good job, Django!"

Sharon smiled. Violet braced herself. She knew this guy was going to get it.

"In RIE," Sharon told him, "we think of praise as sugarcoated control. Django was peacefully enjoying the challenge of putting the roller in the jug. By telling him, Good job, you sent the message that something arbitrary to him is of great import to you. Not only does this confuse a child, but it also erodes his inner peace. Pretty soon, you will have a praise junkie on your hands whose only motivation in life will be to perform for other people because it's the only way he knows how to feel good about himself." Violet had never much cared for the *Entourage* director, and even secretly hoped he'd get on Sharon's bad side. But now that it had happened, it made her kind of sad.

VIOLET luxuriated in the teenage playfulness of making out with Teddy. With her tongue, she explored the gap in his teeth. On one side was the sharp edge of his front tooth. On the other side, the flat, smooth molar.

"I know," Teddy said. "When I first lost that tooth, I always did that myself."

"How did you lose it? Did a dealer beat you up?"

"I'm such a fucking cliché. You know me too well."

Violet kissed him again. He answered back. "Oh God," she said. "Can we kiss forever?"

"No!" Teddy laughed and pushed his hand down her pants, beneath her underwear, and slid his fingers up inside her. "God, your pussy's wet." For years, Violet couldn't get like that for David. It was unspoken, that they needed to use spit to fuck. It had been awkward and embarrassing at first; now it was just fact. "Take off your clothes," Teddy said, and pulled his T-shirt over his head.

Violet undid one button on her shirt, then the other. Luckily, she was wearing one of her new bras, a lacy confection that smooshed her breasts together to yield a fulsome, almost cartoonish cleavage. "Take that fucking thing off," he said. "Hurry it up."

"I have a question," said a young mother. "Tess fusses when I'm at my computer doing e-mail."

"What's your question?" Sharon said.

"I feel bad. I mean, I need to check my e-mail—and I never do it for more than fifteen minutes—but Tess hates it. And I want her to be happy."

"Wanting your child to be happy is a misguided goal," said Sharon. "The goal shouldn't be to raise a constantly *happy* child. The goal should be to raise a child who is capable of dealing with reality. Reality is boring. Reality is frustrating. Reality isn't about getting everything you want the second you want it. Even a one year old is capable of handling these things."

Violet was back in the living room with Teddy.

HE undressed with frenetic purpose, as if stripping in the snow before jumping into a hot tub. It allowed Violet to match his lack of shame with her own. Naked, supine on the velvety couch, she felt giddy nonchalance. She was Manet's Olympia, sumptuous, alert, being attended to by a dark figure. More shocking than the tableau was the trust she felt in the supplicant standing before her with the big erection.

"I can't believe how hard I am right now," he said, stroking himself. "Jesus, you have great tits." He reached down and cupped one of her breasts, her soft

white skin super-sensitive to his every hangnail and cracked cuticle. Teddy sidestepped between the couch and the coffee table until he stood squarely before her, then dropped to his knees. Violet pushed the table away with her heels.

"Thanks," he said. "I didn't know if it was a million-dollar antique or something."

It was a Donald Judd and it cost fifteen grand, but Teddy didn't need to know that. He sucked her breast. His hands moved to her legs. He pushed them apart, wide. Violet smiled-winced at the pleasure-pain of her ligaments stretching. Teddy sat back on his heels and examined her. "Your pussy is more gorgeous than anything on the internet. You just ruined jerking off to porn forever."

"I think that makes me happy."

"You little minx," he said. He gave her inner thigh a sweet kiss.

"That's me all right. A little minx."

He rammed his face between her legs and worked his fingers, his tongue, even his teeth, it seemed, only coming up for air, face shiny, to exclaim, Fuck, or, Jesus.

For fun, Violet said, "Jesus, fuck me," but Teddy didn't get the reference.

OLIVER, a darling two year old, shook the water bottle full of hair rollers. Dot ran to look and tripped over a plastic bucket.

"Dot, I saw that," said Sharon. She walked over and sat near Dot, who was about to cry, or maybe not. "You fell and hit your head." Sharon picked up the bucket and showed it to Dot. "This bucket. You tripped on it."

Dot took in Sharon's words, then sprang up and ran to join Oliver.

"All Dot needed," Sharon said to the parents, "was acknowledgment that someone saw what had happened to her. Parents think they need to fix every little painful thing that happens to a child. Children are born with an incredible capacity to get over things.

They just need to know that someone saw it. It is evident to me that Violet is adhering to the RIE principles at home."

"Thank you," Violet said.

KNOWING that Teddy preferred going without, Violet was relieved when he dug through his pants and pulled out a condom. "Just happened to have one handy?" she teased.

"I never know who I'm going to run into. One time, I was coming out of the men's room in Beverly Hills, and there was this hot lady just sitting there."

"Oh yeah?"

"I totally could have fucked her."

"You think?" Violet watched Teddy put on the condom. She had been married and faithful for so long that sex with a condom was a racy novelty.

She lay back and hung one leg over the back of the couch. Deep in a trance, Teddy positioned himself and thrust inside her. Once, twice. He brushed his hair out of his face and pushed himself up on his hands and looked down. He was transfixed by the rhythmic penetration. Like a stupid animal, his mouth hanging open, watching.

"Fuck," he kept saying. "You're so fucking hot."

Now Violet knew: this was all she'd ever needed. Not the money, not the career, not the landmark aerie. The moment she recognized it, a panic filled her: it wasn't enough. Teddy was on top of her, fucking her hard, grunting with each thrust. They were sticky with sweat. She breathed him in. It still wasn't enough. Violet pulled his body close into hers and stuck her tongue in his mouth. It still wasn't enough. She clawed her nails deep into his back. He reached for her hand, singled out her index finger, and pushed it toward his asshole.

"Do that," he said. She stuck her finger in deep. "Like that," Teddy whispered. "I like that." She grabbed his hair with her free hand. "You fucking whore," he whispered. Teddy's cock was in her, his tongue in her mouth, her finger up his ass. There was nothing more she could do. This had to be enough. She closed her eyes.

Present Moment, Wonderful Moment.

That was a mantra the Vietnamese monk Thich Nhat Hanh had given at a teaching in France. Each time Teddy pulled out, Violet thought, *Present Moment*. Every thrust in, *Wonderful Moment*.

Present Moment, Wonderful Moment. She finally understood what the simple Buddhist had meant.

There was one problem: the future.

Violet opened her eyes. What would she do with all the moments that weren't this present moment, this wonderful moment? There would be so many, too many to endure. She was forty-two. If she lived to eighty, there would be almost forty years of moments that wouldn't be this wonderful. Violet closed her eyes. She had to stop thinking that way. Be present, she scolded herself. In. Out. In. Out. *Present Moment, Wonderful Moment.*

"Get on your hands and knees," Teddy said. She did, and he pushed deep inside her. The force of it sent her face into the arm of the couch. Violet grabbed onto it for support. He reached under her and lifted her so they both stood on their knees. Their reflection in the sliding glass door was beautiful, haunting. Violet naked, hair cascading down. Behind her, Teddy, his dark arms entwined around her luminous skin, playing her like his upright bass, attuning himself to her subtleties. The overlay of dappled moonlight reflecting off the pool reminded Violet of that Gustav Klimt painting The Kiss. Once, in Vienna, it was on some rock tour, she couldn't remember which, she had gone to see it three days in a row. There it was, in the reflection.

Suddenly, Teddy stopped. "Is that a tat?"

"A what?"

Teddy lifted her hair off her ear. "It is. Ha! It's a fucking tattoo."

"Oh yeah. Violets."

"When did you get all tatted up?"

"In Amsterdam, one spring break."

"You hung out in Amsterdam? With the hash and hookers?" He pulled out and turned her around.

"With the Anne Frank house."

"The what?"

"Anne Frank House."

"Who's that?"

"The Jewish girl who hid from the Nazis in the attic and then died in the Bergen-Belsen concentration camp."

"Hey, nice thing to bring up while you're getting fucked."

"You're the one who brought it up."

"I just asked about your tattoo." He kissed her neck.

"It seemed like the punk thing to do at the time."

"Do you think I should get a tattoo?" He sat down on the couch to give it serious consideration.

"No." She flopped on her back, her legs straddling him. "I think they're pretty reductive."

"Heh?"

"I can either fuck you or give you a vocabulary lesson. What's it going to be?"

"Jesus, look at you."

"Are you kidding?" she asked. "Look at you."

"I need to come on you." He ripped off his condom.

"Be my guest." In his animal trance, that Violet felt so privileged to be part of, Teddy jerked off on her stomach.

RIE class was over. Violet was collecting her things when the *Entourage* director approached. "Hey, I saw on the class roster, you're Violet Parry."

"Yeah," she said. Here it comes, Violet thought.

"I directed an *Entourage* once."

"Really?"

"Yeah. So I'm sure we know lots of the same people. Are you working on anything now?"

"Nope," Violet said. "I'm out of TV. You know, raising the kid."

"Your husband's David Parry?"

"Yeah." No matter how successful she was, it always came around to David.

"Did you see Django's T-shirt?"

"It's cute."

"Maybe we can have a playdate sometime," he said. "Django is always talking about Dot."

"Maybe." Violet pulled out her cell phone to make busy, then saw it: a red message light. She practically yelped. "I'll get your number next week. Dot! Hurry!"

"WE'RE one minute away!" alerted the assistant director.

Jeremy sat at the anchor desk, all alone under the bright lights. He was full-fledged handsome in his Zegna suit and tie. Faye finished powdering his nose, then checked his hair. Jim sat at the next desk and gabbed on his cell phone.

And like a big dummy with nothing to do, Sally stood at the snack table, free falling. She had exhausted her arsenal of threats and emotional stunts. Never before had her wiles failed her like this. No matter how bad things had gotten in the past, she always had one more trick up her sleeve. Not this time. It had left her in such a state of panic that last night she needed something to help her sleep. But when she searched her medicine cabinet for a sleeping pill, anti-anxiety drug, or antidepressant—things she'd been prescribed over the years by doctors but had never actually taken—Sally remembered all the bottles were empty. Years back, she had dumped the contents of every one into her cupped hands and threatened to swallow them in front of Kurt. His reaction? He barely looked up from the TV. "Go ahead, take them. You don't have nearly enough there to kill yourself. They might make you more tolerable." In a frustrated rage, Sally had flushed them down the toilet.

So today, she came armed with her old standby, the single business card in her jacket pocket. She ran the edge of it between the flesh of her thumb and fingernail as she tried to catch Jim's eye. Coming to her boyfriend's first day of work with the purpose of hitting on his coworker: it wasn't Sally's proudest moment. But Jeremy had given her no choice.

"Twenty seconds!"

Maryam and her bosses settled onto their thrones in the control booth.

"Ten seconds!"

Jim, who hadn't even seen Sally yet, clicked his cell phone shut. Like a quarterback, he held the phone behind his head with one hand, pointed forward with the other hand, then...spiraled it right at Sally! She snatched it out of the air like a bride's bouquet and hugged it into her chest, suppressing a squeal of delight.

"Five, and four, and three," the director announced.

One second before the light went on, Jim winked at Sally, then turned to the camera. "This week," he said, "we have the pleasure of introducing our new feature, 'Just the Stats.' It's brought to you courtesy of Jeremy White. And if you've never heard of Jeremy White, lucky you. You don't have a gambling problem. Welcome, Jeremy."

The red light on Jeremy's camera came on. "Thank you, Jim," he said.

Maryam flew onto the set. Since gambling was illegal, it was a humongous no-no to use words such as *betting, point spread,* or *money* on *Match-Ups*. Jim must have ad-libbed that part. Sally, who loved the bad boys, found it an auspicious start to their future together.

"With their rebound-to-turnover ratio," Jeremy said, "I'd give Duke a big edge."

Maryam stared daggers at Jim, who mocked her with a schoolmarm face, then winked at Sally. Maryam spun around and caught Sally mid-giggle. Sally quickly turned to watch Jeremy.

"My picks are Duke and Villanova," he was saying. "Until next week, I'm Jeremy White and those are Just the Stats."

Jim's camera light came on and he turned to Jeremy. "I'm with you, Professor. The Duke D was impressive against the Wildcats."

Jeremy responded by silently staring into his own camera.

"Yoo-hoo!" Jim gave Jeremy a wave. "Over here, Professor."

An eternity passed as the studio hung on Jeremy's silence.

"Hey." Jim's voice was tense. "You okay over there?"

"Jim, you know what they say," Jeremy finally said. "Don't get on the bus with Cinderella."

"There you have it, boys and girls," Jim said. "Jeremy White has spoken. Call your bookies before the line moves."

"Cut!" boomed the director's voice.

"Jim!" shrieked Maryam. "You can't mention bookies!"

"Whoopsie daisy!" Jim cracked up.

"It's not funny," Maryam said.

"She thought it was hilarious." Jim pointed at Sally. All eyes turned to her.

"I did not!" Sally shook Jim's cell phone at him. She marched over to whack him, but tripped over Jeremy, who hadn't budged from his chair. His face was twisted, his eyes fixed to the floor. "Jeremy," Sally said, "the segment is over." He was unresponsive. She jiggled his chair. "Get up."

"I'm hearing something," yelled a sound guy. "It started at the end of the last segment. I need everyone to be quiet." The studio went silent and everybody stood still. "There it is," said the sound guy.

First, Sally smelled it: a pungent odor.

Then she heard it: a strange gurgling sound...

Sally looked down. It was coming from Jeremy. A brown stain spread down the inside of his pant leg. He looked up at her, helpless.

In an interview about his secret to success, David said that you only needed to get lucky once; after that, you had to get really smart, really fast. Sally had gotten lucky by capturing the imagination of that visiting Russian choreographer. But she hadn't followed David's advice. It was a mistake she was still paying for.

Standing in the studio, Sally recognized that luck had once

again presented itself. This time, she was going to get really smart, really fast.

"My bad!" she said to the crew as she touched her stomach. "I forgot to eat this morning." With a big smile, she tossed her purse into Jeremy's lap. "Let's go get some breakfast, sweetheart." She swiveled his chair and gave it a playful push toward his dressing room.

THE SUV that had been lurking for Violet's parking space honked, and honked again. Violet didn't care how long the bitch had been waiting, nor that Dot was crying because her shoe had fallen off, nor that it was boiling hot in the car with the windows rolled up. Teddy had finally called after thirty-six long hours. Violet replayed the message, to pillage it for meaning.

"Violet, Violet, Violet," her lover said. "Poor little rich Violet. Where y'at, woman? I just set up for my nonpaying big-band gig at a totally lame AA Sober Picnic in the valley. We're going on at eleven and playing for half an hour. There are like a thousand people here, and that rocks, but I had to haul my upright and amp across an entire soccer field to set up. These morons found the place farthest from the parking lot and decided, Hey, let's put the stage here. That's alcoholics for you. Maybe if David Parry managed me he could get some roadies written into my contract. But what am I saying? La la la la la la. I'm saying that I'm going to marry you. And you're going to cook for me and I'll golf in Pebble Beach and I'll never have to suffer through these ridiculous gigs again. Holler back, baby."

Violet shifted into drive and headed up the hill.

SALLY stood at the teeny sink in Jeremy's dressing room and scrubbed his underwear with warm water and a bar of soap.

Jeremy sat on the loveseat, a throw pillow covering his manhood. "I was fine when I was looking at the camera," he said to the floor.

"This is nothing to be ashamed of, my love." Sally rinsed and wrung out his underwear, then rifled through the drawers for a hair dryer. "Bingo!"

"I like looking at the camera," Jeremy said. "It was when I had to look over at Jim—"

Sally turned on the hair dryer and aimed it at the undies. Jeremy sat frozen, as if in a shock-induced trance. She held the underwear to her cheek. They were dry enough. "Here you go," she said. She glanced up and caught her reflection in the mirror.

Her face, tilted slightly downward and her arms outstretched, reminded her of the replica of Michelangelo's *Pietà* in St. Martin's church in Denver. As a child, Sally would stare at it during mass. She'd grow enraptured by the Virgin's look of sorrow, cradling her dying son. After receiving communion, Sally would pass by the statue and try to stop in Mary's direct line of vision. But the Virgin's flat marble eyes made it impossible. Sally spent her whole life secretly cuddling the feeling that love such as Mary's was her destiny.

Sally turned to Jeremy. He still wasn't getting dressed. "Get up," she clucked. "Turn around. I want to make sure all the poop is off." Jeremy shuddered, then complied. There was a trace of brown on the inside of his right knee. She wetted a paper towel and scrubbed it. "As good as new," she said. "I think it's best if we bring the suit to the dry cleaners ourselves. She stuffed the offending Zegna into a plastic shopping bag." Jeremy stepped into his khakis. Sally removed his blazer from the hook and helped him into it. She felt the pocket. The ring box was still there.

She led Jeremy to the parking lot. Words weren't necessary. From this point on, no matter how rich or famous Jeremy became, Sally would be the only one who knew that he had diarrhea on camera and she had saved him from career-ending public humiliation. He knew that she knew. It never had to be spoken of again.

Sally drove them straight to the Ivy. The maître d' had seen Jeremy on TV this morning. With great fanfare, he led them to a table, on the patio this time, where they dined on crab legs and mimosas. Over dessert of flourless chocolate cake—the tarte tatin wasn't as great as everyone had made it out to be—Jeremy proposed.

VIOLET stepped out of the shower and did the unthinkable: stood squarely in the mirror and examined her naked body. Over the years, she had perfected the art of getting out of the shower without catching even a fleeting glimpse of herself in the mirror. But it was imperative to know what Teddy would be seeing tonight so she could offer him only the most flattering angles. She had lost fifteen pounds in the past month and a half, but God she was fat! She might *feel* thinner, but that didn't mean she was objectively *thin*. And the skin on her cheeks hung off her high cheekbones. Sometimes her face looked plump and youthful; sometimes it looked like an arid hide. This is what happened when you were forty-two: sometimes it all came together and you looked okay; sometimes you looked fifty.

It was noon. On his message, Teddy had said he was going onstage at eleven to play for half an hour. It would take another half hour to load his gear back into his car. He was in the valley, but where exactly? Violet figured it would take him half an hour to drive home. Assuming that he *didn't* loiter at the gig—and why would he, he had called it lame in his message—that would put his estimated time of arrival back home anywhere between twelve thirty and one. Violet had to leave pronto if she wanted to catch him.

She picked up the phone on the wall to call him. The message light was flashing. Violet's whole body seized up.

"Hi, girls." It was David! "I'm leaving early so I can come home and see my two favorite people. I miss you both and can't wait for a group hug." *Beep.* "Received Tuesday, 4:35 AM." *Shit.* Violet hadn't reset the date and time since the power went out last month. If David had left this message an hour and a half ago, she was in good shape. But if he had called just after she left for RIE class, he might burst through the door any minute.

"LadyGo!" Violet screamed. "LadyGo!" She had told the nanny to pack the car for a trip, but there was no way to tell how much LadyGo actually understood. LadyGo's English seemed to have somehow gotten worse over the past fifteen years. All Violet could do was instruct her and hope. Violet called LadyGo's cell phone. The one reliable law of the universe: nothing got between LadyGo and her cell phone.

"*Allo?*" LadyGo said.

"Could you please come into my bathroom?" Violet hung up. She grabbed a duffel bag and pell-mell crammed it with handfuls of underwear, pants, and shirts.

LadyGo plodded in. "Yes, *meesuz?*" Violet had relinquished command of the household to the El Salvadorian, who hadn't missed a day of cleaning in fifteen years and who now reigned supreme as the nanny. Violet had never enjoyed a relationship as simple as this, where the more she paid someone, the happier they were. Most people turned on her and got resentful for the vulgar wealth on display, but never LadyGo. She lived in an apartment in Pasadena with a rotating cast of sisters and cousins fresh from, as she'd wistfully say, "my country."

"When did Mister David call?" Violet asked. "Did you hear the message?"

"I don't know, *meesuz.*" LadyGo smiled. Violet never knew what LadyGo was always smiling about. It had even occurred to her that LadyGo wasn't smiling at all. Rather, it was just the deepening contours of her Indian face. There was no use trying to wring information out of the inscrutable nanny.

"Did you pack Dot's things like I asked?"

"Yes, *meesuz*."

"Please have her in the car and ready to go in five minutes."

"Yes, *meesuz*."

"We're going away in the car. For a trip. In five minutes. You understand?"

"Yes, *meesuz*." LadyGo wasn't moving.

"We're going to the Ritz-Carlton." Perhaps the lure of purloined shoe mitts and sewing kits would light a fire under LadyGo's ass.

"Ritz-Carlton, *meesuz*?" Indeed, the name enlivened LadyGo. "Ritz-Carlton is *spencie*."

"Yes, very expensive."

"Club floor?" asked LadyGo. The club floor with its twenty-four-hour buffet of shrimp, Coca-Cola, and miniature pastries was a veritable pleasure dome to the El Salvadorian.

"Yes. And we need to be out the door in five minutes." Violet held up five fingers.

"No *Meester* David?"

"No Mister David." Violet then noticed LadyGo's T-shirt. It read HOLD MY PURSE WHILE I KISS YOUR BOYFRIEND. It was a mystery to Violet where LadyGo got these things. (They seemed to have a connection to her prodigal nephew, Marco, who LadyGo was constantly bailing out of jail.) It mortified Violet to be seen at the Brentwood Country Mart or the Wednesday farmers' market alongside LadyGo pushing the stroller, wearing one of her bizarre T-shirts. The best/worst was last summer at an engagement party for someone from David's office. LadyGo had worn one that read ASS IS THE NEW MOUTH. Violet thought it was hilarious and dragged David over to see. David exploded; Violet had been apologizing for it ever since.

Violet grabbed a fleece and tossed it to LadyGo. "Here. Put this on."

"For me?" LadyGo smiled big.

"For you. Now go!"

"We go now?" asked LadyGo.

"We go now."

"Why you call me for?"

"Just be ready to go in five minutes."

LadyGo left and Violet took a breath. She had her phone, cash, clothes. She raced down the hall and found Dot in the middle of the kitchen, completely naked and eating a bag of Flamin' Hot Cheetos.

"LadyGo!" called Violet. LadyGo *knew* Dot shouldn't eat processed food; it made her eczema flare up. More important, Violet needed Dot hungry for the hour-plus drive down to Laguna. That way, she could ward off Dot's fussing with grapes and juice. The last thing Violet wanted was to scare off Teddy with a crying kid in the backseat. Violet squatted down and held out her hand. "Dot, sweetie? I don't want you eating Cheetos. Please give me the bag."

"*Want* Cheetos," replied Dot.

"I know you do. You can have some grapes later, when we're in the car."

The back door creaked open. Violet jumped. It was just LadyGo, speaking animatedly into her cell phone in Spanish, something about the Ritz-Carlton.

"Please, would you put a diaper on Dot," Violet said. "I want to leave in five minutes."

"Yes, *meesuz*." LadyGo took Dot's hand. "Come, *Mama*."

Violet grabbed hold of the counter and pulled herself up. She dialed Teddy on her cell phone. It went straight to voice mail. *Shit.* Violet dialed his number again. Voice mail. Again. Violet closed her phone.

The orchid on the counter. It was abloom in scowling, pinched faces! Slanted black eyes and yellow puckering mouths teetered under gigantic velvety white headdresses.

"Gaah!" Violet chucked the plant into the sink. She called Teddy again. Voice mail. She knew it was risky to show up without notice to whisk him off. But what qualm could he possibly have about an ocean-view suite at a five-star hotel? Violet dialed his number again. Voice mail. She hung up.

Dot emerged from the bathroom, dressed but still clutching the bag of Cheetos.

"Honey, give those to me," demanded Violet.

"*Want* dem," said Dot.

"You can't have them!" Violet tore the bag from Dot's hands. Angry red Cheetos flew all over the floor. "LadyGo!"

"Cheetos!" wailed Dot.

The back door opened. "LadyGo!" Violet scooped up the Cheetos. "Dot can't have these. It's what causes that rash on her feet—"

"*Meesuz,* you want LadyGo put Miss Dot in car seat now?" LadyGo appeared from the bathroom.

Violet froze. Who, then, had just entered through the back door?

"Knock-knock," a woman's voice chirped. "Anybody home?"

Violet spun around. Walking toward her were Sally and some guy she'd never seen before.

"HELLO!" Sally called. "David? Dotty Dot? Anyone here?" She breezed down the hall, Jeremy right behind.

Finally, it was Sally's chance to prove *there was nothing wrong with her.* Not that her brother or sister-in-law had ever come out and said as much, but it was what that shrink one time called "the elephant in the room." The elephant in Sally's room was that something must be wrong with her if she was so pretty and thin and still single. It was also why Sally had stopped telling people she was David's sister. At first, they'd be impressed. But then, the elephant in the room: that there must be something wrong with Sally if David Parry was her big brother and she was still driving around with a trunk full of tutus. This engagement ring would slay both those elephants, and even a third: that Violet was somehow better than Sally. Now Sally would also be the wife of a rich guy. Plus, hers was on TV.

Sally stopped. Violet was in a dogfight with her wailing baby over a bag of chips. Dot's face and hands were covered in red dye, and that awful nanny just lurked and smiled.

"Hi, sis," Sally said.

"Sally. How did you get in?"

"I know the code to the gate." Sally prayed she was wearing enough foundation to hide that her face was most likely as red as Dot's. "From when I house-sat for you. I just wanted to stop by so you could meet my fiancé."

"David's not with you?" Violet asked.

"No." Sally hooked her arm in Jeremy's. "Violet, this is my fiancé, Jeremy White."

"Oh." Violet stuck out her hand. "Nice to—" She looked down. Her hand was covered in red dye. She wiped it on her pants. "Shit," she said.

There was a long pause. "Where are you going?" Sally asked.

"What?"

"Your car is packed."

"Ritz-Carlton, m*eesuz*," chimed the nanny. "They give you steak and shrimp all day. I bring my wallet, but lady go, If you have special key, you no pay. No charge extra, nothing."

Violet told the nanny, "Put Dot in her car seat, please," then turned to Sally. "I'm sorry," Violet said, "but this isn't a good time to chat."

This wasn't a flipping *chat!* Sally had just announced she was getting *married*. Wasn't the big whoop about Violet that she was so classy with her fancy-pants upbringing? Sure, Violet was *rich*. The kitchen alone screamed money. The French sea salt in the silver dish. The Montblanc pens, some without their caps, stuffed into a Rolling Stones mug. The Cartier watch tossed into a bowl of miniature red bananas. The slim basket of boysenberries they wanted ten bucks for at Whole Foods. The shoes with the red soles that Nora Ross sometimes wore, so they had to cost a fortune, just kicked into the corner. But *class?*

Violet was a wreck! Her home was a pigsty. There was a two-hundred-dollar orchid — that their "orchid guy" came once a week to "switch out" — crashed in the sink. Her brat was screaming. The word *congratulations* had yet to be uttered! She was probably a size twelve. What was the use of having money and health if you weren't grateful? If you didn't look good? If you were going to act so weird and rude?

"We didn't want to stay long, anyway." Sally tightened the grip on her purse. "We just wanted to share the good news."

"I'm glad you did. But we're in a rush. I'll make it up to you."

"That won't be necessary," Sally said with a swallow. She took Jeremy's hand and turned to leave. "Oh, and Violet?" Sally added. "You look *amazing.* When I get pregnant, I want all your secrets so I can be tiny like you a year after giving birth."

"Oh, yeah…" Violet said. Then her face dropped.

Sally turned. David had entered, an uncharacteristic spring in his step. "David," she said. "Hi!"

"Dada!" Dot raced into his arms.

"Hey, beautiful!" David scooped up his daughter. "The whole gang's here! All my Parry girls! What's the occasion? Where's everyone going?"

"Ritz—" the nanny started in.

"David!" Violet jumped in. "Sally got engaged."

"Wow! You what?"

"I'd like you to meet my fiancé, Jeremy White."

"Wait," David said. "Jeremy White from the *LA Times?*"

"And now TV." Sally demurely held out her left hand.

"How about that sparkler! Jeremy White part of the family; who would have thunk such a thing? Welcome."

David grabbed Jeremy's hand, then winced in pain. David's hand was bandaged and he wore some hippie-looking braid around his wrist. "I forgot," he said. "I messed up my hand." Both knees were cut and swollen, too. "Honey," he said to Violet, "you know who Jeremy is. He's the one who picks the NFL games. He had an amazing run last year."

"A zillion percent or something," Sally mooned.

"Seventy-one against the spread," Jeremy said.

"Yeah, right." Violet's words looked like torture to get out.

"Hi, gorgeous." David walked over and hugged Violet. But she just stood with dead arms, car keys in one hand, cell phone in the other. David then announced, "There's something outside I want everyone to see."

Violet grabbed Dot and said, "We'll be right there."

Sally and Jeremy followed David outside. David stood at the edge of the lawn and pointed toward the horizon. "See them? Painted lady butterflies." Indeed, butterflies, in groups of a dozen, were flying in a straight line. "They're migrating from Mexico," he said. "They'll end up in the Pacific Northwest. It only happens once a decade. See them, Sally?"

This was the David she knew. The David who loved nature. The David who had been an Eagle Scout. The David who had taken her overnight camping in the Rockies and hung their food from a tree so bears couldn't eat it. The David who had brought her to a pond to study the movement of frogs for her solo in *The Frog Prince*. But *that* David left home the first chance he got, never to return. Now theirs was strictly a business relationship. David paid Sally's medical insurance and she kept away. Another elephant in the room.

"Yeah," Sally answered. "There are hundreds of them."

"Back in '98, Violet and I drove to this spot in Topanga that the entomologists projected would be on the migration path. It was like a Dead show. There were a hundred cars on the side of the road, and people were hanging out, listening to music. But the butterflies ended up migrating about five miles east. By the time everyone packed up and caravanned down Topanga, across PCH and up some other canyon, it was too late. The butterflies had gone. Just now, when I pulled up, I saw them. Of all places, of all times, they chose Stone Canyon, right now. What are the odds?"

"I've been trying to calculate them," said Jeremy.

"I bet you have!" David let out a big laugh, then turned to Sally. "Maybe these butterflies are a sign that you two should get married here."

In all of Sally's fantasies about her wedding, she had never allowed herself to imagine getting married at David's house. It was so obvious and within reach that for it *not* to happen would have been too cruel to endure. She looked up at Jeremy. "What do you say, sweetie?"

"Anything you want."

"Isn't this wild?" David said. A butterfly had just landed on his hand. "It's a chemical that builds up in their brains. Every ten years, the switch is flipped and nothing can stop them. Who ever thinks of a butterfly on a mission?"

Sally saw it before David did. She didn't know what it was exactly, but she wanted to protect him from it: Violet was in the car with Dot and the nanny, screeching onto Mulholland.

VIOLET felt LadyGo staring daggers at her from the backseat. "This Ritz-Carlton?" Violet said. She adjusted her mirror, but LadyGo averted her eyes. "It's supposed to be the best. Beautiful beach. Big pool…" Unimpressed, LadyGo shook an elephant rattle in front of Dot.

The scene back at the house was certainly inelegant. Sally barging in trailed by that sportswriter with the earplugs. And David. Bounding in, wearing a grass thing around his wrist, acting like Mr. Natural? His last words before he had driven off for the weekend were, You're not necessary. That's what Violet was fleeing, a dead marriage with a cruel husband who raged at her. His bruised knuckles told the real story. The peace-and-love David would soon revert to the volatile wall-punching David. Violet ached for Teddy—to be entwined in his dark, scarred arms, treated rough, exalted, laughing, kept guessing but always knowing. She crossed the double yellow line to enter the car pool lane.

"Truck with cars!" Dot pointed to a transporter loaded with Mini Coopers.

"That's right," Violet said. "A truck with cars."

"*Mas!*" Dot said. It had been her first word, *mas*. "More" in Spanish.

"It's right there," said Violet.

"*Mas!*" said Dot. "*Mas!*" She started to cry.

Violet slowed down so Dot was abreast of the transporter. "See it? It's right there. You don't need *mas*." But Dot was implacable. "Baby, what's wrong?"

"Right turn ahead," said the computer lady on the GPS.

"*Mas!*" wailed the little girl.

"Give her some juice or something," Violet told LadyGo, and exited onto Sepulveda, then turned left on Venice.

"Your destination is ahead on your left."

Violet cruised past a ninety-*eight*-cent store. A place to refill your water jugs. Piñatas hung from a bodega's tattered awning.

"SpongeBob!" said Dot.

"*Sí, Mamacita*, SpongeBob!" LadyGo said, full of pride. "Miss Violet, the baby is too much intelligent." How would Dot know about SpongeBob? Violet and David didn't let her watch TV. LadyGo must be plopping Dot in front of it while Violet was away.

"You have arrived at your destination," announced the voice with an almost grotesque calm. Next to a Mexican dentist's office with bars on the windows, set back from a patch of dead grass, was a small two-story building.

Violet pulled an illegal U and parked the car. "I'm going to run in and pick up my friend," she told LadyGo. "*Then* we'll go to the Ritz-Carlton."

"Miss Dot stay in Mercedes car," said the nanny. Violet had seen where LadyGo lived and it was no step up from this. But get LadyGo in a Mercedes with a blue-eyed child and she became the queen of England.

"I'll be right back," said Violet.

There were two units in the stucco building, one above and one below. 11838 was upstairs. Violet passed some rusted rosebushes and climbed the steps. She opened the screen door and knocked. No footsteps, nothing. She knocked again. She scanned the street for Teddy's car. LadyGo pointed up to Violet. Dot waved. Violet waved back. She walked to the rear of the landing to see if there was parking behind the building.

"*Allo.*" A black man with braids, wearing just athletic shorts, appeared behind the screen. Violet remembered Teddy once saying he had a roommate named Pascal, someone from AA, who worked in catering.

"Hi," she said. "Is Teddy here?"

"*Zey* went out this morning."

Violet wondered, Did he say *they* or was it just his accent? "You must be Pascal?"

"*Oui.*"

"My name is Violet Parry." She held out her hand.

"The lady who paid to have his car fixed."

That wasn't exactly how she would have put it. "Yes," she said.

Pascal opened the door but wasn't happy about it. "Does Teddy know you're coming?"

"Not exactly." As Violet passed Pascal, she got the strong sense he was checking her out. She was overcome with guilt for letting Teddy down with her fat ass.

The apartment was bright and uncluttered. The beige wall-to-wall carpet—while beige wall-to-wall carpet—was surprisingly unworn. Violet was emboldened by the restraint of the decor. It struck her as adult and lent her confidence in having chosen Teddy.

"I'll call him to see where he is," Pascal said.

"I already tried. His phone is turned off."

"Let me try." Pascal disappeared to his bedroom and closed the door. Violet devoured her surroundings. An unobjectionable sectional sofa they had probably found on the curb. Some bookshelves made of cinder blocks and two-by-fours. French gangster movie posters on the wall. Teddy's golf bag. A boom box with lots of cheesy flashing lights. Jazz CDs. Rush CDs. Free weights in the corner. An unopened Homer Simpson Chia Pet.

"Teddy will be here in five minutes," Pascal returned to announce.

"Great, thanks."

"So, your husband is David Parry?"

"Yep." Violet went to the window.

"Must be nice, eh?"

"It's okay." LadyGo and Dot kicked a ball on the lawn. Violet had to give that to LadyGo: she never went anywhere without a ball. "My daughter and nanny," Violet explained.

Pascal looked out the window. "That's your S600?"

"My what?"

"S600."

"Oh, right. My Mercedes."

"Must be *very* nice."

Violet's cell phone rang. She checked the number. It was David. "I'm not going to get it."

The screen door creaked open and slammed shut. "Wazzup, bro?" There he was, Teddy, in the room with her.

Violet's intention had been to act cool, but a gigantic smile hijacked her face. "Nice to see you," she said.

"Look who found her way into Beaner Central. I hope you left some bread crumbs so you can find your way back."

"I have to change for work," Pascal said.

"Thanks, man." Teddy gave him a jive handshake and seemed to whisper something, then turned to Violet. "To what do I owe this honor?"

"I have a surprise for you."

"I'll say! Is that your kid and nanny outside?"

"Yes."

"Your daughter's beautiful. What's her name again?"

"Dot."

"That's right, Dot. Anyway." Teddy put his hands on Violet's hips. This was what it felt like to belong to Teddy. She didn't want to talk, just sink deeper and deeper until she no longer existed. "I'm waiting," he said.

"Oh—" she said. "Pack your bags. I got us two rooms at the Ritz-Carlton in Laguna Niguel, where we can eat healthy food and you can play golf at Torrey Pines."

"Wow!" Teddy's hands flew apart.

"Like you said, I make shit happen."

"Yeah…but I can't go."

"Why not?"

Teddy looked perplexed. "I have a job."

"You do?" Violet felt the blood rising in her cheeks.

"I'm not just a pickup cat. I work at a music store."

"Oh—I—"

"That's why my fingernails are black. It's ebony dust. I repair guitars. What? Did you think I was just *dirty*?"

"No—I—" Violet sputtered. "Can't you call in sick?"

"Not if I want to keep my job!" Teddy laughed. "Plus I have a commitment at an AA meeting tonight."

"Oh."

"My sponsor has me on a ninety-in-ninety. I have to do ninety meetings in ninety days. And I don't know any meetings down there."

"The concierge can help us find them," she said.

"The concierge can help us find them! Jesus Christ, I've arrived."

Violet felt like she was finally establishing a beachhead and carefully moved forward. "The concierge can also tell us where to buy you a new bass," she said. "Rickenbacker 4001, if my memory serves me."

"You get some serious points for remembering that." Teddy crept closer. "It can't be a new one, though. You've got to get me a vintage."

"Done."

"*Pura vida*, baby." He stepped in and gave her a rough kiss. There it was. She kissed back, matching his aggressiveness. "Shit, you're a good kisser," he said.

"How about we leave tomorrow?"

He pulled her head close and stood on his toes to kiss her again. David was six foot two and Violet had to stand on *her* tiptoes to kiss him. It seemed unnatural to lean down to kiss a man. Teddy suddenly jumped back.

Dot was climbing the stairs, LadyGo's head bobbing behind her. Neither had seen Violet and Teddy.

"Thanks," whispered Violet. She opened the door for her daughter and nanny. "Dot and LadyGo, this is Teddy. Teddy, this is Dot and LadyGo." Teddy and LadyGo exchanged pleasantries in Spanish. Violet was encouraged by how swimmingly it was all going, until Pascal emerged from the bedroom. LadyGo stiffened. She had made it clear on numerous occasions that she didn't care for the company of *los negros*.

"Hey, Pascal, where are you working today?" Teddy said, for everyone's benefit.

"Brian Grazer's house in Malibu." Pascal buttoned his white shirt and tucked it into his pressed black pants.

"Pascal's father was a slave," said Teddy. "A real bona fide slave from Africa. He escaped and moved to France. Am I right, brother?"

Pascal grunted in affirmation. He walked to the door and lit a Gauloise.

"Kunta Kinte, I wish you wouldn't smoke those things," Teddy said. "There's a fucking baby here."

Pascal waved him off and exhaled through the screen door. "I feel like shit."

"Then stop smoking cigarettes." Teddy turned to Violet. "When he was a kid he sold incense in the Paris flea market."

"*J'aime bien le marché aux puces à Paris,*" Violet said to Pascal.

"*Vous été allée à Paris, eh?*" he asked with a bright smile.

"*Parfaitement,*" answered Violet. "*Et même plusieurs fois. Je suis allé à l'internat en Suisse. A Le Rosey.*"

"I love it." Teddy beamed with pride. He punched Pascal's shoulder. "Listen to her. I told you she was the real deal."

"So," Violet asked Teddy, "are you coming with us?"

"I don't know...." Teddy bit his nails.

Violet slapped his hand down. "Don't do that. I'm going to spray you with skunk oil so you don't chew your fingernails."

"How did I all of a sudden go from a five-thousand-dollar bass to skunk spray?"

"Come here," Pascal said to Dot. "I want to show you something outside."

"Go with them, please," Violet ordered LadyGo.

LadyGo, who had probably pictured herself being offered a complimentary fruit drink at the Ritz-Carlton right about now, did not take kindly to being ordered outside a run-down apartment to play with a black man. "Yes, *meesuz.*" She heroically followed them outside.

The door slammed and Violet turned to Teddy. "We can stay here tonight and go down tomorrow, if that would be easier."

"I can't have you and your posse crash here. It's not fair to Pascal. He paid my rent this month. I'm lucky he didn't kick me out."

"I'll send Dot and the nanny down in my car now, then you and I can take a limo down tomorrow," she said.

"Where's your fucking husband during all of this?"

"He's still out of town," she said quickly.

Teddy gnawed at his fingernails. It was impossible to tell what he was thinking. "Fine," he said. "But I have to leave for a little while to take care of some stuff."

"Now?"

"I have a commitment."

"At the music store?"

"No, not at the music store. I'll meet you back here in two hours. Let's walk out together." Violet wanted to interrogate him about where he was going, but thought better of it. Tomorrow they would be in a suite on the Ritz-Carlton club floor. That was all that mattered.

Outside, Dot and Pascal were running around, trying to catch something in the air. "Bugs!" cried Dot. Violet took a closer look. They weren't bugs. They were painted lady butterflies.

SALLY floated up the escalator to the bridal salon. It had felt wrong to be cooped up in Jeremy's apartment watching basketball on the first day of her engagement, so she left him there and raced over the hill to Saks.

She opened the door and discovered a plush forest of glimmering mannequin brides. In the corner was an antique desk where an okay-looking brunette and her mother quietly flipped through a gilded leather portfolio.

An impeccably groomed salesman stepped toward Sally. "Hello," he said.

"Hi! I'm here to buy a wedding dress."

His eyes darted to her ring finger, then back to her face. "I'm with a customer," he said with finality.

Sally shot a glance at the other bride's ring. It was gigantic. Sally lifted her eyes. The woman had also spotted Sally's measly ring. Sally's hand twitched. "That's okay," she told the salesman. "I'll wait." How Sally would have loved to show them all who they were dealing with and buy the most expensive dress on the spot! But long ago, she had stopped carrying credit cards.

The money she had taken out to start Kurt's leather jacket business had mushroomed from the original six thousand to forty-nine thousand, spread across eight credit cards. Sally would never forgive Kurt for sticking her with the debt, then changing his phone number and telling everyone *she* was the psycho.

She had called the credit card companies in an attempt to negotiate the runaway debt. They'd offer the option of making a small down payment, which would lock her into a fixed interest rate that was only one-tenth of a percentage higher than the current one. She would make the payment only to discover that the new "fixed interest rate" was just fixed for fifteen days. And then *it* shot up eight whole points. Once, she had Fed-Exed a payment to arrive on the due date, March 12, so the "penalty rate" wouldn't kick in. But she hadn't seen the fine print that stated it had to be received by *seven AM* on the twelfth. So it triggered something called "universal default," where all the credit card companies talked to one another, and once you defaulted on one payment, they *all* went into penalty rate. Before Sally knew it, she had eight credit cards, each at 29.9 percent interest. She felt so stupid and alone; the shame compounding inside her like the interest itself.

Last year, she had screwed up the courage to ask Maryam if she knew of any credit consolidation places. "Why?" snapped Maryam. "You're not in credit card debt, are you?" "Of course not,"

Sally replied. "It's for a student." Maryam said, "Good. Because only morons get into credit card debt." Sally never mentioned it again to Maryam or anyone else. She'd lie in bed at night, with open eyes, the weight bearing down on her chest from above. When it got too great, she'd roll onto her stomach. But the debt would push up through the mattress. She'd turn onto her side, but it squeezed her like a vise grip.

She wandered through the glittery dresses and stopped at a gorgeous lace-upon-lace creation. She then realized it was an A-line cut. A-lines were for fatties. She wanted a super-fitted, strapless, low-back mermaid cut.

The really annoying thing about Sally's financial straits was that she made good money! After taxes, forty-five grand a year. Her rent was two thousand a month. Her living expenses another fifteen hundred, which left her a three-thousand-dollar cushion. But she always managed to spend that, too. A friend would get married in Seattle, and she had to fly there and buy a bridesmaid's dress. Or her laptop would get a virus and crash. Or, to keep up with the trends, she needed to replace all her birthday party tutus with princess dresses.

For the past couple of years, Sally's whole focus had been on trying to find a rich husband. Now that it was a reality, Sally saw that what may have been sound in concept was vague in execution. Did she have to have an actual conversation in which she'd tell Jeremy she was fifty grand in debt because of an ex-boyfriend and please pay it off? The thought of it made Sally sick. Literally. She closed her eyes.

David had generously offered to "take care of the wedding." Could Sally ask him for cash, then siphon off fifty grand to pay off her credit cards? Perhaps, but it would mean skimping on her big day. She deserved to have the wedding of her dreams, nothing less. Maybe she could tell guests that instead of presents, she wanted cash. That might be considered tacky, though, getting married at David's fabulous house and asking the guests for envelopes of money....

Or. Or. Or. There was personal bankruptcy. People on the radio were constantly singing its praises. Sally had looked into it once but decided against it because it would show up on her credit report for ten years. That meant she couldn't get a new car or move into a better apartment. But...after she married Jeremy, she could use *his* credit cards. Married couples did that all the time. And he would pay for their new house. She could get him to buy her a new car. So, really, there was nothing to prevent her from filing for bankruptcy. And Jeremy would never know....

"Are you okay, miss?" the brown-haired bride asked Sally with sweet concern.

"I'm fine." Sally opened her eyes and straightened. She must have been leaning against the wall for some time, because the bride was touching her back. The mother and salesperson were looking over. "I'm fine!" Sally said with a wave. "Nothing to look at!"

The other bride returned to the desk.

Sally made a show of spotting a dress in the center of the salon and walked toward it. Just the couple of steps were enough to make Sally feel like fainting. What was wrong? Hypoglycemia or hyperglycemia never made her feel sick in this way. And her blood sugar was 120 when she left the apartment half an hour ago.

The trio were whispering and glancing over.

Did that mean Sally looked as sick as she felt? She smiled, but the effort almost made her barf. She touched the first gown she saw. "Aaah." She stepped behind the mannequin, as if to inspect the back of the dress. She was now in a secret hollow of outward-facing headless brides.

Oh God. Tulle, bows, rhinestones, flowers, crystals, glass slippers, necks, corsages—they all spun fantastically around her. Sally had trouble fighting her way out of the kaleidoscope of dreams. One mannequin teetered. Sally was about to be sick. But not all over the beautiful dresses! She fumbled her purse open, buried her head in it, and hoped she wouldn't vomit.

It had been two and a half hours since Teddy's car disappeared down Venice Boulevard. Violet had dispatched LadyGo and Dot to the Ritz-Carlton with a credit card, then trekked to the Whole Foods on National. She now sat on Teddy's steps, teeming grocery bags against her shins, and brooded over whether Pascal had said *they* went out this morning or *he* went out this morning.

Zey, he. Zey, he. Zey, he.

The words did sound similar. For argument's sake, if Pascal had said *they*, who would *they* be? Teddy and who? Surely not Coco. As of Friday night, she was on a plane to Japan. And it didn't make sense for her to be back in Los Angeles two days later.

"Sick!" Teddy leapt up the stairs and stood over the groceries. "You have no idea how hungry I am. Whole Paycheck is like Oz for an evil junkie like me."

"Hello." Violet closed her eyes and surrendered herself to the possibilities. They had the apartment to themselves. What would it be? Would Teddy drag her by the arm into his bedroom, pimp-style? Would he take her right here on the steps? Would it start with a tender kiss? . . . She opened her eyes.

Teddy was hoisting himself up by the handrail, clearing Violet and three steps' worth of groceries. He let himself into the apartment.

"Oh," Violet heard herself say.

She gathered the bags and deposited them in the kitchen. Teddy was splayed on the couch, chimplike with one arm stretched overhead, listening to his cell phone messages. Terror shot through Violet: something had happened, something terrible.

"I can't wait to crash after I eat." Teddy kicked off one motorcycle boot, then the other, and scowled at their smell. He shut his phone. "That was my white-trash aunt from Palm Springs." *Palm Springs*. The words scalded Violet, a cruel reminder of the history Teddy shared with Coco. "My aunt has this son who wants to learn to play bass, and she asked me if I could find him a used one. I said I had an extra I'd sell to her for forty-five bucks. So, I box it up and stand in this long fucking line at the post office, and then they tell me it's gonna cost *twenty-five* bucks to ship. So I call my aunt and ask if she'll pay that, and she says no. She wants me to *drive* it out. Sure, I say, if she pays for gas—"

"Where did you go?" Violet said.

"Huh?"

"I'll pay to mail the bass, if that's what you're getting at."

"Fuck you." He looked genuinely hurt. "That's not why I was telling you. I was sharing something that was going on in my life. Or isn't that something the hoi polloi like you and David Parry concern yourselves with?"

He had confused *hoi polloi* with *hoity-toity,* but this was no time to scrap it out over a malapropism. "I'm sorry," Violet said. "What did your aunt say?"

"It doesn't fucking matter."

"That was rude of me," she said. "I duly apologize. Let's have some dinner and start over."

"Do-over granted."

"Good." Violet retreated to the kitchen and emptied a still-warm container of brown rice and vegetables into a clean-enough bowl and placed it on the counter. "So," she asked, "how are you?"

"I had a really rough time last night." Teddy pinched some rice in his fingers and ate it standing up.

"Why?" Violet handed him a fork. "What happened?"

"I came this close to using. It was like three in the morning, and Pascal had some Almond Roca and I ate the whole fucking can." Teddy pulled out a julienned green pepper and flung it on the counter. "Next time, don't buy me anything with peppers.

Peppers make me fart. Anyway, I started going through the trash to see if there were any nuts left in the foil. That's what you do with crack. You go through the packets of foil to see if you missed any. I felt like I was on the verge of slipping."

"Why?" Fearing a body blow, Violet crouched down and made busy with the groceries. "What happened?"

"I cheated on my girlfriend, that's what happened." Teddy stood agape. A square of tofu rested on his tongue. "God, am I that bad in bed? Did you forget?"

"But you said you were only eighty-five percent faithful to her."

"Ha! Did I say that?"

"Yes."

"I'm such an alcoholic! No wonder I'm on a ninety-in-ninety." He chuckled and took a giant bite of food.

"So what happened?" Violet asked. "Did you drink last night?"

"Jesus! Of course not."

"So stop calling yourself an alcoholic."

"We don't say, 'Hi, I'm Teddy, I *used* to be an alcoholic.' We say, 'Hi, I'm Teddy, I'm an alcoholic.' It's a progressive disease."

"Whatever."

"Whoa, whoa." Teddy pointed at the bag. "What's that I see?"

"Rice cakes?" She had debated buying them, on account of their being so cheap and ordinary.

"I fucking love rice cakes. You have no idea how many of those babies I can scarf down." Teddy's vim was appreciably on the rise.

Violet decided to ride its momentum. "But Friday night," she said, "didn't you have fun…you know…?"

"Fucking you? Of course." He let out a loud belch. "I'm a sex fiend. I guess I'm just not mature enough to fuck a married woman and not feel like shit afterwards."

"I don't think it's a matter of maturity." Violet pulled out a spray of ranunculus and stuck them in a pitcher.

"You and me can fuck," he said. "And it's instant gratification and all, but eventually I end up back in my shitty apartment with the chain-smoking Nigerian and I have to go for days eating the free shit they put out at AA meetings just to pay my cell phone bill."

Violet dithered. This might be the perfect time to announce she had left David. Or might that spook Teddy? She needed to work on him a little more. She held up a pastry bag. "Sugar-free vegan ginger cookies."

"You have no idea what you've done for me," he said. "You've opened the door to everything I've been praying for my whole life. To be a famous musician, to eat good food, to have a friend I can count on." *Friend:* the word was an arrow slung into Violet's chest. She opened the refrigerator door and stood behind it for cover. "Our friendship is a gift from God," he said. "I don't want it to get all muddy from fucking. I think I told you, I'm a much better friend than boyfriend."

Violet was in that *Far Side* cartoon where the man scolded his dog, Ginger, but all the dog heard was: *Blah, blah, blah, Ginger, blah, blah, blah, Ginger.* All Violet could hear was *friend.* She felt like screaming for Teddy to stop, but the words caught in her throat.

"God has blessed me with your friendship and generosity," he continued. "He's blessed me with Coco, who's so beautiful. It's ridiculous to think I have to choose. So I want to offer you my friendship. I usually charge a million bucks. But I'll give it to you for the low price of five hundred grand."

"Wait," Violet said. "She aborted your baby."

"I don't really know if that happened."

"You mean she's still pregnant?"

"Fuck no," Teddy scoffed.

"What are you saying? She *lost* the baby?"

"You never know with Coco Kennedy."

"What does that mean?" A torrent was rising within Violet and she was powerless to quell it. "You're either pregnant or you're not. You have an abortion or you don't. Those things are immutable."

"You sure like to concern yourself with stuff that's none of your beeswax, don't you, Baroness? That's what I should start calling you, Baroness von Beeswax."

"It *is* my fucking business!" Violet slammed the refrigerator door. "Two hours ago you were shoving your tongue in my mouth and now I'm a *treasured friend!*" Violet picked up the box of milk thistle tea bags that the lady who worked in the nutrition aisle had said helped balance the liver. Not the three-dollar box of tea bags, or the eight-dollar box, or even the twelve-dollar box, but the *sixteen-dollar box of milk thistle tea bags because only the best for the king of 90066!* She threw it full force at Teddy's head. He swerved just in time.

"Gee, Violet," he said, "have you communed with God yet today?"

"I don't believe in God." She looked around Teddy's apartment, with its thrift shop decor and Holy Bible on the table, and thought, God is for poor people.

"Godless Violet. It's all starting to make sense." Teddy picked up the tea bags and walked over. Violet took them. His hand and hers, not even touching, just touching the same dented box, it was enough to make her melt. Teddy brushed his hand across her cheek and pushed her hair behind her ear. "Let me see that ink again," he said. Violet lowered her head and leaned into his hand. "That is so fucking rad."

Violet was mute, a beggar. This was Teddy's chance to erase the past ten minutes. She'd forgive him everything if he'd just kiss her....

"Do you think I should get a tattoo?" he said. "They say you should get one on the best part of your body." He turned to a wall of mirrored tiles and lifted his shirt. "I'm so fucking obese."

Violet blinked. She breathed in through her nose. She touched the counter. Yes, it was true: she was standing in squalor, and the bootless pauper who had just rejected *her* preened in a mirror. She opened her phone and dialed LadyGo.

"I need you to come back," she told the long-suffering nanny. "Pick me up at the empanada place on Venice. The one we went to that time after the beach." Violet hung up.

"You let a fucking beaner drive your car?" Teddy still hadn't peeled his eyes off his reflection. He held his hair in a topknot, which he admired. "That car costs a hundred and fifty grand."

"Probably."

"What do you pay her, like a million a year? Oh Violet. Why did we fuck? Now I can never be your nanny. It wouldn't be clean." He dropped the clump of hair.

Violet folded the grocery bags, stacked them on the counter, and headed for the door.

"Wait, you're going?" He dove into the grubby sectional. "Come on. Just because we fucked once doesn't have to change anything. I'll always love you."

"At last," Violet said. "My poem. I thought you had forgotten." Her phone rang. She didn't look to see who it was. Anybody would be better than this vainglorious dirtbag.

Of all people, it was Sally. "Don't you go to that fabulous hard-to-get-into gyno, Dr. Naeby?" she asked breathlessly. "The one who's really good with delivering babies? Well, could you get me an appointment? I've tried in the past and the nurse said he wasn't taking any new patients." Violet said she would and hung up.

Teddy examined something he'd mined from between his toes. "Does this mean we won't be spending Christmas with Geddy Lee?"

"Affirmative." Violet opened the door.

"Are you okay?"

"I'm more than okay. In fact, this moment marks the end of my self-immolation and the rehabilitation of my *amour propre*. If you don't know what those words mean—and why would you, they have nothing to do with seventies television—I invite you to look them up in a dictionary."

The screen door slammed behind Violet. She didn't bother looking back to see if Teddy would come after her. She knew he wouldn't.

CHAPTER EIGHT

Fantastic Voyage

It was a sunny day, but Sally kept the windows of her truck rolled up to seal herself into her hothouse of happiness. Was it possible? Was she really out of debt? *Out of debt!* If she'd known that declaring personal bankruptcy would be this easy, she'd have done it years ago. After the debacle in the bridal salon, she'd spent all week downloading forms and gathering her financial records. She made an appointment at an out-of-the-way law office and had just dropped off the paperwork with a check for three hundred dollars. It took all of ten minutes. The only thing left to do was attend a hearing — which, she'd been assured, was a mere formality — and the whole nightmare would be in the past. She could now indulge herself in her delicious future.

"Woo!" Sally screamed as she reached Santa Monica Boulevard. "Woo-hoo!" But she was too happy to go home. She wanted to keep going. At the top of La Cienega, she got in the left lane and headed west down the curvy part of the Strip. Mulholland, PCH, Sunset: driving these streets made Sally feel as if she *was* Los Angeles. Like in that movie *Fantastic Voyage*—where shrunken scientists were injected into a dying man's bloodstream—Sally zoomed along Sunset with the flow of traffic. She caught the light at Sunset Plaza, then surged ahead with the pack. She felt integral to the city she loved, as if her driving were keeping it alive.

In that interview David had given, another thing he said was "Go with the green lights. Don't try to make people do things they don't want to do." Sally finally understood what he meant. She was literally going with the green lights, and her courtship with Jeremy had been just the same. Their setup, their humble life at his apartment, his audition, the proposal, there was such a beautiful inevitability to it all. And now she was going to be a mother!

Dr. Naeby had accepted Sally as a patient and confirmed that the episode in the bridal salon was morning sickness. So Sally was carrying the ultimate accessory, a Naeby baby. Sally loved, loved, *loved* Dr. Naeby. He was so handsome and relaxed. During her appointment, he'd accidentally left the image of Sofia Coppola's uterus up on the ultrasound monitor. So that was cool. Sally hadn't yet shared the news of her pregnancy with Jeremy. The books said not to tell people until the second trimester, in case something happened.

She adjusted her hand on the steering wheel so the diamond looked bigger than two carats. "Woo-hoo!"

Could it be that not having to worry about money was really this transformative? Back in the days, Kurt began every morning by chanting. It was part of the Buddhism he was into where you'd chant for money. Sally didn't think it was all that Buddhist to have your one wish in life be to get rich. But Kurt had explained he was only chanting for money so, once he had it, he could devote himself to world peace. Money first, world peace second. Sally was suspicious. Still, as a show of support for his spiritual journey, she went to Pottery Barn and bought big golden letters that spelled out the words WISH and DREAM and hung them from fishing line over his altar.

Traffic slowed as Sally passed what used to be Le Dôme. Once, when she had her convertible Rabbit, some men had pulled up alongside her and asked if she'd like to have a drink at Le Dôme. They were Seiko reps in town for a jewelry show. Over drinks, they opened a display box and offered Sally her pick of glittery watches. She chose a gold with mother-of-pearl inlay. She hadn't had to "do anything" for it, because she told the guys she had to run home and change before meeting them back at their hotel. She slipped them a wrong phone number and never saw them again. Later that night, she told Kurt the watch had been a gift from David.

Kurt...Kurt... Now that Sally was free of his debt, she felt a pang of guilt about how psycho she'd gone when he dumped her. Was it really necessary for her to have retaliated by hacking into his e-mail program and sending a group message to his entire address book, as him, saying he liked to have sex with dogs? Now that she had some perspective, it did seem immature. Sally rounded the bend where Tower Records used to be and found herself stopped at the first red light. Right outside Mauricio's Boot Shop. Where Kurt worked. There was a parking spot smack in front. With time left on the meter. This had to be some kind of sign. Sally glided into the space.

She entered the tiny atelier wedged between Duke's Diner and the Whiskey. Mauricio was a quiet man who made custom cowboy boots for rock stars, socialites, and Japanese tourists. The walls of the shop were plastered with framed magazine covers, auto-graphed pictures, even gold records given to Mauricio as thanks for his master craftsmanship. All boots were handmade to order and started at eight hundred dollars. For the truly hip, it was never a question of *if* you owned a pair of Mauricio's but *how many*. Get some margaritas in Kurt and he'd be hi-larious about the "shit that went on." Sally thought he should partner with Violet on a sitcom about Mauricio's. Kurt had considered it but decided he didn't want someone to rip off his stories and steal all the credit.

The store was empty. Part of Mauricio's mystique was that there were no boots on display, just a wood bench that ran the length of the narrow store. Kurt would chat up the customers and determine whether they were worthy of Mauricio's. If Kurt deemed them unhip, he'd say Mauricio was backed up for three years. Japanese tourists were preapproved because they'd pay three grand for a pair of eight-hundred-dollar boots.

Kurt emerged from the workroom carrying a box. He wore one of his vintage Hawaiian shirts and the Peter Criss cat boots Mauricio had made for the 2004 KISS reunion tour, which Kurt got to keep when Peter Criss quit the band. Kurt's shoulder-length ringlets were as perfect as ever, just blacker. He looked up and saw Sally, but nothing registered on his face. He was always so cool, so Zen. He stepped behind the counter and shelved some bottles of leather conditioner. Sally wished she could just turn around. But she was stranded in the middle of the empty store.

"If it isn't Sally Parry," Kurt finally said, barely opening his mouth. "Or maybe it's not Parry anymore?"

"Not for long." She swatted the air with her left hand.

"Who's the lucky guy?"

"Just a TV personality." Sally narrowed her eyes. "How are *you?*"

"Could be better, could be worse," he said, always the Buddhist. "How's your brother?"

"He's great. We were just up at his house."

"Was he out of town?" The corners of his mouth curled.

"He was there," snapped Sally.

"I checked out Hanging with Yoko at the Troubadour. I was going to go up and say hi to David, but the band was so derivative. I mean, give me' the Velvet Underground any day." Kurt stepped out from behind the counter to check the display. His shirt was tight around his gut. Sally, on the other hand, had maintained her figure.

"You look great," she said.

"Flea was in here the other day. I delivered his boots because the Chili Peppers are like family. Has David ever taken you over to Flea's house?"

"No," Sally said.

"You should ask him to, because it's really cool." He used both palms to line up the bottles.

"Are you still living over on Curson?" she asked.

"Nah, I moved."

"Are you still a Buddhist?" she asked.

"Oh yeah. I chanted this morning for forty-five minutes. You should try it. It can really transform your life."

"I'm doing fine," she said.

"Still, never hurts to make the world a better place."

"I am making the world a better place," Sally said. "I'm getting married."

"Well, good luck." Kurt picked up the empty box and headed to the back. "Tell David I said hey."

"Kurt!" she said. He turned around. "I—I wanted to invite you to my wedding." His eyebrows lifted, but just barely. She added, "It's going to be at David and Violet's house."

Kurt rested the corner of the box on the counter. "Do they still live in that place near Coldwater?"

"Oh no!" Sally said with a guffaw. "They bought an important architectural house and spent two years restoring it. It's been in all the magazines. Anonymously, of course. You'd have no way of knowing it was theirs."

"Let me give you my new address."

"I'll mail the invitation here. If there's one thing I know, it's that you'll always be working here." She spun around to leave. Kurt was an ass man, and Sally wanted to make sure he saw that hers was better than ever.

CHAPTER NINE

Gilbert Osmond ❧ **Better and Better, Faster and Faster** ❧ **Mayday**

ALL THAT MATTERED WAS THAT VIOLET GET THROUGH TODAY WITHOUT CALL-ing him. The past five weeks had left her sleep deprived and shaky. But she hadn't gone and done anything crazy. Sure, she had called Teddy a hundred times, but she had never left a message or uttered a peep when she heard his voice, Hello…hello…hello?

There were, however, other lapses. Every few days, Violet had found herself buying a present to give him today, May 1, his three-year AA birthday. There was the cell phone, the golf clubs, the 1980 Rickenbacker bass she'd had Geddy Lee sign and send her. The moment she'd purchase one of these lagniappes, hope and self-loathing would ricochet within, leaving her jumpy and demor-alized. But the important thing was: she hadn't made contact. If she could just survive today, she'd be over a significant hurdle. To ensure success, Violet had composed an itinerary, one to which she would adhere no matter what.

7–9 AM:	Wake up, make breakfast.
9 AM:	LadyGo arrives. Say good-bye to David.
9:20 AM:	Go down to garden. Dig cell phone out of hole. DON'T TURN ON PHONE TO CHECK TO SEE IF TEDDY HAS CALLED. HE HASN'T. Give phone to Dot.
9:30 AM:	Leave for LA Mission.
10 AM–6 PM:	LA Mission: Feed homeless. Disperse Teddy's presents to homeless.
7 PM:	Pick up David at office. Take one car to Paul McCartney at Hollywood Bowl.
8–11 PM:	Paul McCartney concert.
11 PM:	Get David's car back at office. Drive home.
12 AM:	Sex with David. Sleep.

So far, Violet hadn't deviated from the plan. It was 9:30 and she'd made it out of the house and into the car ahead of schedule, sans cell phone. The phone had been her most formidable adversary in her attempt to banish Teddy from her thoughts.

A week into her travail, Violet had announced to David that she wanted to change her phone number. "Why?" he asked, glancing up from his breakfast. Violet blanked. She couldn't remember what she had just said. That's how bad it had gotten. She'd often start a sentence and, midway through, realize she had no idea what she had just set out to say. That's where Teddy lived, in the interstices. Between sentences, between words, between thoughts. "Never mind," she told her husband. "I don't care one way or another," David said with uncharacteristic alacrity, which only served to rattle Violet further. He continued, "I'm just asking because if there's a problem with Sprint, I'll have Kara get on it."

"No, I was just thinking about it." Violet knew it wasn't an answer. But now she was trapped into keeping her phone number, a cruel reminder that Teddy had forsaken her. All she could do was change her ringer, so it wouldn't turn her into a Pavlov dog and unleash a stampede of hope every time it rang. Last night, she had woken up at four in the morning and gone to the kitchen, where her cell phone was charging, and checked for messages. She called voice mail over and over in a sickening loop, in case Teddy had called while she was dialing. Then she'd heard a voice. "No!" it said, "No! No! No!" It was Dot, from the baby monitor. She was scolding her dolls, something she was into these days. Violet then realized it was daylight. She'd been standing there for two hours! Disgusted with herself, she walked to the garden, dug a hole, and buried her phone.

She turned south onto Beverly Glen and passed a cluster of real estate signs. She remembered: it was Tuesday. The morning rush clogged the canyon road, but Violet eschewed the quicker Benedict Canyon because that's where she was driving when Teddy had called her after their idyll at the putting green. It was in front of the shoddy alcazar, with the flesh-colored VW bus abandoned halfway up the curb, that Teddy had made it known he'd jerked off to her the day they met. It was while she was driving by the once-proud family of deep green palms, now stiff and cappuccino colored since the cold shock a month ago, that Teddy had asked her to say, I *certainly* like doggy style. It was as she was passing the Craftsman with the sycamore trees, strange ones that grew more horizontal than vertical, that Teddy had said he would write plenty of poems for her. Because of Teddy, Benedict Canyon was now ruined. So were Wilshire, Beverly Drive, RIE class, the 405. And Sondheim. The know-nothing had even managed to ruin Sondheim!

A few weeks back, Violet had made an appointment with a shrink she'd seen on and off. But his earliest availability was two weeks away. "I can come in early one morning if it's an emergency," the therapist had offered. "No!" Violet answered. She hung up and decided to cut through the yackety-yak and get on some fucking meds. She called her agent—who had frequently spoken of the rainbow of pills he popped—to get the name of his psychopharmacologist. Violet was tickled to be put right through, even though she hadn't worked in several years. "Oh God, don't tell me it's you, too?" the agent had said on speaker. "I've got a thousand former show runners who will work for nothing just to keep their houses. Don't tell me I have to find work for the wife of a billionaire." His laughter and that of others filled his office. Violet said she was calling to secure an item for the RIE auction, and quickly hung up. Two weeks later, she drove to the therapist's office but never got out of her car. What would she tell him anyway? He'd never understand Teddy. There was no way to convey his laugh, what a great kisser he turned out to be, so playful, so obliging…

Violet snapped the rubber band on her wrist and said, "Gilbert Osmond Gilbert Osmond Gilbert Osmond."

This morning, she had written GO on a rubber band and put it around her wrist. Any time she thought about Teddy, she was to snap it and repeat her mantra: Gilbert Osmond Gilbert Osmond Gilbert Osmond. Were their affair to proceed, that's what Teddy would have been, Gilbert Osmond to her Isabel Archer. Invoking *The Portrait of a Lady,* one of Violet's favorite novels, gave her strength and clarity. Everyone but Violet would see that Teddy was utterly beneath her and only interested in her money. At least Gilbert Osmond was a suave aesthete. Teddy didn't know who the Medicis were!

Crawling to the intersection where the Four Oaks restaurant used to be, Violet saw an open-house sign. Taped to it was a handwritten piece of paper: LAND!!! She checked her watch. She had time, and it was always fun to look.…

She followed the signs up a mile of increasingly narrow streets, through the land that curb appeal forgot, and arrived at a dirt cul-de-sac. Among a forest of blue-and-white GWEN GOLD flags was a white Lexus SUV with the driver's door open. Inside was a woman in her sixties who wore a dowdy Ann Taylor suit. She seemed utterly surprised to see Violet.

"Pull up behind me," Gwen shouted. "Make sure you turn your wheel to the right." Gwen pantomimed turning the wheel. A former actress, Violet thought. Violet introduced herself as a neighbor in an attempt to quell any hope of a sale on the part of the eye-lifted realtor.

"It has fabulous estate potential," Gwen said. "Ten acres, which is unheard of in 90210." Two huge gates, held together by a rusty chain, lay in the dirt at the bottom of the hill. "As you can see," Gwen said, "the driveway needs some work."

"What was once here?" asked Violet. "Was there a house?"

"Over the hill. It's the old George Harrison estate. He lived here in the seventies. The next owner tore the house down and never rebuilt."

George Harrison. The name sent a bolt through Violet.

Five years ago, in a book of Linda McCartney photographs, Violet had seen a photo of George Harrison sitting in a Los Angeles house that overlooked a lake. She and David couldn't figure out where in LA it was. Violet had even asked Barbara Bach about it at a dinner party; she said the house was in Beverly Hills. Violet knew there wasn't a lake in Beverly Hills, but felt it would be insolent to challenge the wife of a Beatle.

"The house—or what's left of it—is it up there?" asked Violet.

"You can hike up if you'd like." Gwen handed Violet a spec sheet. "I wore the wrong shoes. I have a meeting with a mediator at noon. I thought it was next week, but my ex's lawyer informs us this morning that it's *today*."

Violet headed up the rocky path. At the first switchback, she stopped to catch her breath. Below were tightly packed hippie shacks. It was quite charming, this incognito hamlet. She continued her ascent. The driveway, if widened and stabilized, could be stunning blanketed with acacia groundcover and Aleppo pines. She reached the top of the rise. Stone Canyon Reservoir shimmered below. She made her way down the cushiony gopher hole–riddled hillside to the foundation of the former house. There wasn't a building in sight. The reservoir was so close, it bounced sunlight onto her face. The water lapped against the shore. It felt like Lake Tahoe. David loved Lake Tahoe. She could build a Lake Tahoe retreat in the middle of the city.

Violet owed it to David. When she had arrived home with LadyGo and Dot after her humiliating trip to Teddy's, Violet explained her sudden disappearance with a convoluted story involving a birthday party at Chuck E. Cheese, a freeway closure, and a note she thought she'd left on the counter. She had expected a merciless interrogation, which she was only semi-prepared for. Instead, David gave her a big hug, then took Dot and did her night-night all by himself.

Could it really be? Had David become more loving and patient than ever since the night of her betrayal? Or was it a cruel illusion, another facet to her madness? She didn't know anymore. A week ago she'd left her credit card at a restaurant on purpose just to provoke some of David's good old-fashioned rage. But he had patted her on the head and driven back to get it himself. Had there never been any basis for escaping into Teddy's arms? If there was a God, Violet was convinced it was a cruel one, for turning her husband nice on her.

Building a house. It was a huge project, but she needed a huge distraction. The other house was cursed. Violet's unemployment, miserable pregnancy, empty bank account: these could all be traced back to the Neutra house. She had to get away from the front door she had opened to Teddy. The living room ceiling she had stared at, trying to coax Father Time into making the sex last forever. The bed of roses where Teddy had taken her, his brown body with its huge cock, ramming into her from behind, her pussy throbbed now just thinking about it, God, if she could only feel it again, just one more time, she'd tried to replicate it, lying in bed while David slept, touching herself with one hand, pulling her hair with the other, but she couldn't, she needed Teddy, oh, to be on her knees, sucking that cock, that's all she needed, to feel her mouth around that glorious—

Violet snapped her rubber band. *Gilbert Osmond Gilbert Osmond Gilbert Osmond*. She forced a breath through her pounding chest.

The spec sheet said there were ten acres of land. For $1.9 million, it was a steal. David, a huge Beatles fan, would heartily endorse buying a part of Beatles history. And how fortuitous that tonight was the Paul McCartney concert? Violet needed to get to David's office ASAP. She clambered up the hill, her feet sinking into the rodent-softened soil a good six inches with each step.

IF the past five weeks were any indication of what the rest of her life would be like, Sally hoped to live a long, long time. Between planning the wedding, Jeremy's growing fame, and her pregnancy, things were getting better and better, faster and faster. Life was a thrill ride, and Sally's hands were up in the air.

"Will all debtors please stand up?" It took Sally a second to realize this meant her. The two hundred others who had appeared for their 341 bankruptcy hearing in this ballroom-turned-courtroom stood up. Sally sprang to her feet.

"Do you solemnly swear," said the bailiff, "to tell the truth, the whole truth, and nothing but the truth, so help you God?"

"Yes," answered the cacophony.

A small Japanese woman had taken "the bench." The bailiff said, "Bankruptcy court under the Honorable Aiko Yashima on this first day of May, is now in session."

"You may all be seated," said the tiny judge.

The notice had said to plan on being here all day. Sally had come prepared with wedding-related paperwork. Even her bankruptcy hearing, which she had imagined as a bunch of towering figures with distorted faces hissing indignities at her, turned out to be altogether civil. Most of her fellow "debtors" were white, middle-aged, and looked pleasantly bored. Sally untied the ribbon on her wedding organizer and spread out her flowchart, bridal magazines, and RSVPs on the empty chairs beside her.

Who knew that planning a wedding could be this deeply satisfying? David had told her to spare no expense, so Sally had hired the wedding planner to the stars. Under Pam's guidance, Sally had discovered she possessed a unique talent for picking the rarest lily, the most sought-after calligrapher, the tip-top-of-the-line tent. Any time Pam presented Sally with makeup artists or photographers from which to choose, she would pick the most expensive. "Why do I bother?" Pam would ask, shaking her head. It became one of their many hilarious inside jokes.

Sally dove into the RSVPs that had arrived yesterday. The first one she opened—wouldn't you know—was an acceptance from Kurt. Sally's heart sank. How would she ever explain his presence to her friends? Sally had attempted to work Kurt into conversation. "I thought it would be fun to wear white cowboy boots with my wedding dress," she had said to the gang at their girls night out at the Laugh Factory. Maryam barked, "Don't tell me you're even *considering* talking to that creep Kurt again." Sally blushed. "Of course not!" When she returned home, she called Kurt to disinvite him, but got the machine. The outgoing message was normal enough, "Hi, it's Kurt. I'll catch you later." Then a woman giggled in the background. With laughter in his voice, Kurt seemed to turn to her and say, "Wha—?" *Beep.* Sally was so flustered that she hung up. The best option at this point was to act indignant that Kurt was there and blame his presence on Violet.

"That's me, Your Honor." A man in the row behind Sally stood up using the back of her envelope chair, which caused them to spill all over the worn carpet. Sally shot him a dirty look and gathered her RSVPs.

"Is this a complete list of your assets?" asked the judge. "A 2006 Formula Sun Sport boat, a 2005 Porsche Cayman S, adjoining properties at 2860 and 2862 North Beverly Drive in Beverly Hills."

"That's right, Your Honor," answered the man.

Sally looked around for someone to exchange an eye roll with. But most were too absorbed with text-messaging to even be listening.

"The court will appoint a trustee to sell your nonexempt assets. Once you complete the required course in personal-finance management, you will receive a notice informing you that your debts are hereby discharged."

And that was it! The guy with the speedboat, Porsche, and not one but *two* houses in Beverly Hills made his way down the row of chairs and out the door!

Dum-dum da-dum-dum-dum-dum. The wedding march trilled from Sally's cell phone. It was her new BFF, Pam. NO CELL PHONES signs hung everywhere. Sally crouched down and whispered, "Hi, Pam."

"What's this message about you inviting the entire Lakers franchise to the wedding?"

Jeremy's star was rapidly rising, and with it, the number of guests. Jeremy would never think of inviting his new business associates, but as his better half, Sally considered it her duty. What had started out as a once-a-week spot on *Match-Ups* had turned into a nightly appearance on *SportsCenter*. Jeremy had just been assigned to broadcast from the floor of the NBA semifinals. So on their first day as man and wife, they'd be crisscrossing the country, first-class.

"Don't kill me." Sally giggled to Pam. "But we just found out that Jeremy is doing some print ads for the Gap!"

"Get out!" squealed Pam.

"I know. They're doing a new campaign called 'You Will Be Famous,' starring people who just got famous. Jeremy's going to be on billboards!"

"Girlfriend, you have landed yourself such a hottie."

"I know. But it means I have to invite the Gap people *and* his commercial agents."

"Oh God. How many?"

"Ten," Sally said in an itty-bitty voice.

"Can I renegotiate my deal so I'm paid by the guest?"

"Shut up!"

"You'd better not stop by any Starbucks between now and then," Pam said, "because you'll invite all of *them* to this thing, too." Sally loved Pam. She was so salty.

"Sally Parry," the bailiff called. "Sally Parry!"

"Gotta run," Sally whispered, then sprang up. "I'm right here!"

"I see you have no assets," said the judge without looking up. "Your debts total forty-nine thousand dollars to eight credit card companies. Is that accurate?"

"Yes." Sally straightened herself. Compared to that last guy, she felt a flush of pride over her fiscal responsibility.

"You want to reaffirm the debt on your 2006 Toyota RAV4. Is that car insured?"

"Yes, Your Honor."

"Have you cut up all your credit cards?"

"Yes."

"The court has received certification that you completed the personal-finance-management course," said the judge with an impressed pout, "ahead of schedule. Your debts are hereby discharged. You will receive a written notice within thirty days."

"Randall Kline," said the bailiff. Just like that, it was over. Sally collected her wedding stuff and skipped out. What did she care if Kurt came to the wedding?

VIOLET stood outside David's glass-fronted office. His newish assistant, Kara, sat at her desk. "So, what's it like out there?" she asked Violet. "Did it ever start raining?"

"What—oh, no," Violet answered.

"I'm from Arizona, and every morning I think it's going to rain, but it never does."

"Yeah...." Violet would normally make small talk with an assistant, especially one this mousy and sweet, but she had the rare opportunity to observe David at work. He was on his headset, elbows on his knees, looking out the floor-to-ceiling window behind his desk. No checking e-mail or leafing through *Billboard* while on the phone. Completely tuned in. A rare quality in this day of multitasking, it had impressed Violet seventeen years ago.

She'd never forgotten that conversation outside the Murray Hill Cinema. "*You're* Violet Grace?" David had said, as if in disbelief. "Yes." Violet scrambled to her feet, peeled off her Walkman, and tucked the newspaper under her arm. "You already bought the tickets?" he asked, with a bluntness that belied his sad eyes. The incorrigibly self-possessed Violet found herself stammering, "I—I thought it might sell out. I got here early. I hope that's okay." He looked deep into her face and said, "I'm surprised." "Good surprised or bad surprised?" Violet was born with an instinct for people. Sure, she had the education and worldliness that was out of reach of an accountant-turned-rock-manager from Denver. But she somehow knew that David was a better person than she. "Good surprised." The glint in his eye said he was wild with approval. She craved more. She'd been chasing it ever since.

David finished his call and removed his headset. This was his element, making big decisions. All of them the right decisions, for his clients, for his record label, for his family. He never once let them down.

"Hey, look who's here!" He jumped up.

Violet pushed open the heavy door. "Hi, sweetie. Sorry to bother you."

"Of course not!" David gave her a hug and held the door open with his foot. "Kara, you've never met the beautiful Ultraviolet herself."

"I have just now, Mr. Parry," said Kara. "I mean, we've talked on the phone. And I *feel* like we've met—"

"Hold my calls," David said, and let the door close. He took Violet's hand. "I'm glad to see you. What's the good word?"

The office had been the same for ten years. Shelves crammed with books, stacks of CDs everywhere. Good, not great stereo. Violet had resisted the wifely urge to storm in, decorator in tow, and put her stamp on his domain. Like her husband, the office was what it was: no airs, all business.

"I came upon something that might intrigue you," she said.

"I'm listening."

"You know behind the Four Oaks, where that preschool is? Well, there's a lot for sale that overlooks Stone Canyon Reservoir."

"Okay…" David said.

"Not high above it like we are now. Just thirty feet above the water. There's not another house in sight."

"Are we in the market for a new house?" he asked.

"I was driving by and I saw the sign. Ten acres for one point nine."

"How much is buildable?"

"About an acre. It's the old George Harrison estate."

"Really." David blinked, big.

"You have that book here, don't you?" Violet went to the bookshelf. "Remember, we were looking at that picture, wondering where it was, and I asked Barbara Bach about it?" David pulled out the Linda McCartney book. "That's it!" Violet found the photograph of George Harrison sitting in a bay window. He had scruffy clothes and long hair, so youthful and at peace. Behind him were pine trees and a body of water.

David studied the photograph. "That is Stone Canyon," he said. "We can see that curve from the bathroom. Son of a gun."

"Isn't that wild? There's no house there now. Just the foundation. The city would probably make us build within the footprint."

"So we're buying the land?"

"It seems to happen any time I stop by," Violet said. "Maybe next time you won't be so pleased to see me."

On his desk was a framed picture of Violet and David holding Dot. They had been on vacation in Lake Tahoe. Violet was smiling so hard her face looked like a fun-house distortion of happiness. Was there really a time when standing in the snow with David and Dot could have made her so happy? That was the last weekend in January. She had met Teddy on February 1, a Tuesday. Little did she know when this picture was taken that just three days later, she would desecrate a good life. Of all that Teddy had absconded with, that was the cruelest. Worse than her self-worth—he could have that!—he had robbed her of any proclivity to find joy in life's simple pleasures.

"You keep saying fixing up the Neutra house almost killed you," David said.

"I know."

"One question. Why isn't this that definition of insanity, doing the same thing over and over and expecting different results?" David studied her. He was direct. He was even. But he was saying something Violet didn't want to hear, and this is what made him seem like an asshole. It wasn't fair, but Violet understood the reputation.

"I know what you mean," she conceded.

"I'm amenable to it," said David. "We have the dough. If every five years you fix up a house, there are worse vices in the world. I just need to know *you've* thought it through." The phone rang. One of David's rules was to never go home without returning every call, which often meant staying in the office until late in the evening. Knowing the exigencies were piling up in the outer office made Violet anxious. "Don't worry about the phones," David said. He ran his finger along the grass bracelet around his wrist. "Do *you* understand why you want to do this?"

Violet's heart skipped. For the first time, it occurred to her that David knew about Teddy. He sees it all, thought Violet. My ecstasy, my shame, my madness. It was so obvious that she feared she might explode in laughter. What else would explain the queer expansiveness that had befallen David since the yoga retreat? Was it part of a twisted game? Was he waiting to pounce? Would the dreaded confrontation happen here, now? Violet had rehearsed for this moment. "I fell in love," she would say, "or thought I did." "With whom?" he'd want to know. "A musician, no one you've heard of. It's over now." Violet wouldn't attempt to gainsay any of her husband's accusations. How could she possibly defend her swath of destruction? *Nostalgie de la boue* run amok? Sure, David had lost his temper every now and then, but that surely didn't justify Violet's going off and fucking someone with hep C and trying—unsuccessfully!—to buy his affections with David's money. "It's not your fault," she would tell her husband. "It's all on me. I went crazy or something. I developed a frantic attachment to the first person who showed some interest. I know how feeble that sounds, but I don't know how else to put it. I love you, and I want our family to work. If you don't, I understand. But please know I will spend the rest of my life making it up to you, if you'll let me."

The glass door opened. Kara entered. "I'm sorry—"

"I'm talking to my wife," David said.

"It's just—I finally tracked down Yuri. He's on his cell phone for the next ten minutes and then he's getting on a plane—"

"Take it, take it, take it," Violet said.

"I'm talking to my wife," David repeated to Kara. She slunk away and shut the door, trapping Violet in the phantasmagoria that David's office had become.

"So?" he asked. "Do you know *why* you want to buy this land? Yes or no."

"Yes, yeah," Violet stammered. "I do."

"Okay, then." David had chosen to spare her. She could breathe again. "Do you want me to call the broker and get into it?" he asked.

"I know what to do."

"Truer words were never spoken," he said.

Violet laughed. David was her salvation. Love would come. "You keep saving me, David."

"Thanks for noticing."

"I'll see you tonight," said Violet.

"Yeah," he said. "Paul McCartney. Oh! I got us the fresh hookup." It was something that had always endeared David to her. He was an accountant by nature, yet used phrases like "fresh hookup" with perfect ease. "If we go back before the show, Paul will take a picture with Dot."

"You're kidding!"

"LadyGo can bring her over for the photo op, then take her home. She'll be going to bed late, but it's worth it for a picture with a Beatle, am I right?"

"I love you, David."

"I know that. And I love you."

"I don't know why sometimes. But thank you."

"I knew you were complicated from the start," he said. "You announced as much when you wanted that song sung at the wedding."

Violet cringed. He was referring to Stephen Sondheim's "Sorry-Grateful," from *Company*. It was what she had been listening to on her Walkman outside the movie theater that day, so she always considered it "their song." Violet had asked Def Leppard to play it at the wedding. When the band saw the lyrics, they checked with David. He confronted Violet and she quickly withdrew the request.

"That's the best thing Def Leppard ever did," she said now. "*Not* sing that song. I don't know what I was thinking."

Violet was shaky as she walked out of David's office and down the hallway. She took Gwen Gold's card out of her pocket, then remembered she didn't have her cell phone. She opened the door to the conference room.

A couple of interns unpacked the day's lunch. MR. CHOW, the thick glossy bags read.

"I need to use the phone," Violet said. "I'm David's wife." Neither reacted. They wouldn't get far in the business. She reached for the phone. Her fingers dialed a number.

310-555-0199.

"Hello?" It was Teddy.

"Happy birthday." Violet panted like a sick animal. With dead eyes, she gazed at the rubber band on her wrist. GO, it said.

"I knew you'd remember," he said. "You looking for that ride to the airport?"

CHAPTER TEN

KURT SLITHERED UP ROSCOMARE IN HIS CHARTREUSE DODGE SATURN. HE had closed Mauricio's early to get a chant on before the wedding. Kneeling at his altar, Kurt had chanted *Nam myōhō renge kyō* for an hour, then shampooed his hair. While his curls air dried, he chanted the Lotus Sutra ten times before heading out.

The song "Tiny Dancer" came on the radio.

> *Blue jean baby, LA lady,*
> *Seamstress for the band*
> *Pretty eyed, pirate smile,*
> *You'll marry a music man.*

Last year, before Kurt kicked his chanting up a notch, this song would have made him go postal. *What the fuck was "Tiny Dancer" doing on KLOS? Since when did some fruit's B-side take over for "Stairway to Heaven" as the quintessential classic rock anthem?* The dudes next door at Duke's Diner would blast "Tiny Dancer" just so Kurt would come over and honor them with his genius rant.

But now "Tiny Dancer" played and Kurt had equanimous mind. *Nam myōhō renge kyō* once again delivering the goods. In a videotaped speech, President Ikeda had said the universe's offerings were abundant. Most people walked around in delusional states and couldn't see what was theirs for the taking. Only by chanting *nam myōhō renge kyō* could they transform their karma.

If someone had told Kurt a year ago that he'd one day drive to David Parry's house and *not* seethe with revenge fantasies, he would have told them to take another hit of crack. When the custom leather jacket business didn't take off, Kurt had a brainstorm. He'd introduce a cheaper line of ready-to-wear and sell them at rock concerts. He had dragged his sample case to David's office for a meeting. The deal was simple: Kurt would set up a booth at David's gigs and kick him twenty percent of his profit. But before Kurt even got a chance to unlatch the trunk, David shook his head. "Kurt, it doesn't fly. I have an exclusive agreement with my merchandiser. I'd have to pay you and him. That's just not gonna happen." Kurt said, "You don't understand—" But David cut him off. "As a favor to Sally, I'll give you an internship if you're interested in learning how the music business works." Kurt *knew* how the business *worked*. For the past ten years, he'd seen it firsthand from the boot shop. He wanted to be David's *partner,* not the guy who brought him coffee!

But, like President Ikeda said, painful experiences were necessary to motivate us. Once you devoted yourself to the Mystical Law, the hidden connections of the universe started working for you. And he was right. Kurt had chanted for months to live in an apartment without roommates. One day, he saw a giant balloon that read CONDOS FOR SALE, ZERO DOWN. It was a brand-new building with a pool on the roof. Kurt took out an interest-only mortgage for three hundred dollars a month more than his rent. Within a week, he had moved in, set up his Gohonzon, and hung the letters WISH and DREAM.

Turned out, three hundred bucks was more of a dent than he'd imagined. After a couple of months, things were getting dire. In order to make the April mortgage, Kurt had been forced to sell all his CDs, disconnect his Internet, and never set foot in a Jamba Juice. He kept chanting, but with a fierceness he'd never before applied to anything in his life. He'd show up for work barely able to speak, his voice was so hoarse. And then what happened? Crazy Sally Parry walked through the door. At first, Kurt was terrified. He knew he'd stuck her with massive credit card bills. He had been haunted by the prospect of the cops coming after him, or worse: her brother. Every time the sleigh bells on the shop door jingled, Kurt jumped, fearing it was David Parry coming to kick his ass. Kurt's paranoia had consumed him to the point where he had to take codeine cough syrup to get the edge off. But what did Sally do? Invited him to her wedding. *Nam myōhō renge fucking kyō*.

Kurt stopped at the light at Mulholland and checked his hair. His curls always looked sharpest two weeks after a perm. And the goatee was a nice addition. The single gold hoop earring was pure inspiration, which came to him while chanting. This Captain Morgan look was a keeper.

> *Hold me closer, tiny dancer*
> *Count the headlights on the highway*
> *Lay me down in sheets of linen*
> *You had a busy day today.*

The light turned green. Kurt trusted that the universe was leading him to David Parry's for a reason. He just needed to stay openhearted when the opportunity presented itself. He turned off the radio and chanted the rest of the way there.

"Nam myōhō renge kyō, nam myōhō renge kyō, nam myōhō renge kyō...."

WHEN Violet had offered Sally and her entourage the "spare bedroom" to use as her bridal suite, Sally couldn't picture it. That's because there was nothing to picture! The room was the size of a postage stamp, barely big enough for the measly twin bed shoved in the corner. Here Sally sat, having her hair ironed by Clay, a ghoulishly Botoxed, brow-lifted, and spray-tanned hairdresser.

"Ouch! That burned my scalp!" Sally swatted his hand away.

The door opened, knocking into a tiny Vietnamese manicurist who carried a pan of swaying soapy water. A caterer, balancing plastic-wrapped cookie sheets, entered and zeroed in on a small dresser piled with purses. "Whose are those?"

"Mine," offered the old-lady makeup artist from the bed, where she lounged on her side, recovering from "the altitude." Her name was Fern and she smelled musty. Who knew where Pam had dug her and the rest of these clowns up?

"I'm going to need to move them," announced the caterer.

"Wait a second!" Sally jumped up and accidentally flipped over the pan of water.

"Oh no!" squawked the manicurist.

"This is the *bridal suite!*" Sally blocked the caterer from the flat surface. "You can't put those here."

"Is that sushi?" asked Fern, coming to life.

"Soft-shell crab rolls," said the caterer. "Have one."

"No!" Sally said. "Stop that! They're all about to touch me. Put those somewhere else! Where's Pam? Could someone get Pam!"

"Honey, I need you to sit down," said the hairdresser.

"Is my scalp burned?" Sally patted her forehead.

"Your scalp is not burned."

"It's still stinging." Sally went to the teensy bathroom and examined her hairline in the mirror. She could make out a faint red mark. "There it is," she told Clay, not a little triumphantly. "A burn."

"So Fern will fix it with powder," he said.

"Hunh?" Fern looked up from her deteriorating sushi roll and touched Sally's face with roe-speckled fingers.

Sally yelped. "Wash your hands! They're covered in fish!" She felt her face. Tiny orange fish eggs stuck to her fingers. "Oh, my God! Where's Pam? Or Maryam or anyone? I need help! Did someone call Pam?"

"Everyone looks so beautiful," hummed Fern, perched at the window.

"My guests are arriving?" Sally jumped out of her chair.

"I *will* burn you next time you do that." Clay slung the curling iron over his shoulder.

Sally peeked through the blinds. A familiar Escalade pulled up to the valets.

"Nora and Jordan Ross are here!" Sally cried.

Nora emerged, draped in yards and yards of chiffon. Sally prayed that Nora would identify herself as Sally's friend, not a Core-de-Ballet student. Sally wanted no accountability for *that* body. Nora had some kind of Band-Aid on her cheek. Why was it that you reached a certain age and you suddenly had no qualms about leaving the house with Band-Aids on your face? The passenger door opened, and out climbed Nora's son, J.J.

"I didn't invite *him!*" Sally's eyes widened. "Where's Jordan? Don't tell me *that boy* is Nora's plus one!" The valet got in the car and zoomed away.

"Relax!" laughed the hairdresser.

"You have no idea!" spit Sally. "That boy is autistic."

"He looks very sweet," said Fern.

"Yes, but he could throw a fit and ruin everything!"

The manicurist, ready with a pair of cuticle scissors, tapped one of Sally's feet. Sally would be wearing closed-toe pumps, of course. Still, she wanted her feet to be beautiful underneath.

"No cut cuticles," Sally said. "Only polish."

The hairdresser opened the door and shouted into the hallway, "Can someone please tranquilize the bride? And me, too, while you're at it!"

"That is *not* funny!" Sally fought back tears. She had made a special trip to the foot doctor yesterday to get her nails cut. "I just want nail polish."

"Polish?" asked the Vietnamese woman. Her accent made it sound as if she were talking around a big ice cube in her mouth.

"Polish only. No cutting."

Finally, Pam traipsed in, swinging a glass of champagne. "The peach Bellinis are to die for," she said. "I'm taking orders."

"Get us all doubles!" said the hairdresser. "With a Valium chaser."

"Pam!" Sally grabbed the wedding planner. "We've got to move Nora Ross. She brought her son instead of her husband."

"No Jordan Ross?" Pam pouted. "Boo-hoo. I hear he messes around."

"Put them at table sixteen," Sally said, "with Maryam and the people from the gym."

"I'll figure something out."

"There's nothing to *figure out*. I told you, table sixteen."

A sweaty man carrying a video camera poked his head in. "I'm looking for Pam. I'm here to videotape."

"*C'est moi*," said Pam.

"You haven't started yet?" Sally shrieked to the man.

"I kept going up and down Mulholland, trying to find the house. It isn't very well marked."

"Everyone else has managed to find it," Sally said. "I want you out there shooting the arrivals!"

"The *arrivals!*" hooted the hairdresser.

Pam swallowed a guffaw and lunged for the door. "I'll show you where to set up," she told the videographer.

"Don't go!" Sally seized Pam's arm and whispered, "Don't leave me alone with him."

"Who?" Pam blurted, "Clay?"

"Everybody's treating me like I'm a *C-U Next Tuesday.*"

"A what?"

"A *C-U Next Tuesday,*" Sally whispered. "Spell it out."

"A cunt? Darling, just say it. A cunt."

"Now I'm a *cunt*, am I?" The hairdresser scratched the air. "Mee-oww!"

Sally turned to Pam. "Have you found out what band is playing?"

Although David had given Sally carte blanche to throw the wedding she wanted, she put him in charge of the band. She'd taken every opportunity to hint at how much she loved Coldplay. Def Leppard had played at Violet and David's wedding. Why not Coldplay at hers?

"I'll go check," said Pam.

The videographer hadn't moved from the doorway. Sally asked, "What are you doing standing there?"

"You're right. I should get some balloons."

"What?"

"To put out. So people can find the wedding."

"People are finding the wedding," Sally said. "People have found the wedding. We need that fact videotaped. The ceremony is going to start in forty-five minutes and you're not shooting videos!"

"What's important," Pam said, "is that you relax, Miss Beautiful Sally Parry-soon-to-be-White. Now, you kids play nice." She left.

The hairdresser turned to Sally. "Honey, you need to let me

finish your hair so I can grab a cupcake and go to the gym to work it off."

"Those cupcakes are the wedding cake. You can't eat them now!"

"Everyone else is."

"What do you mean? Who's eating them?"

"They have cupcakes?" Fern rose from the bed.

They were interrupted by an echoing screech. Sally ran to the bathroom window. A banged-up van had pulled into the adjoining carport.

"The band!" Sally eagerly watched as some middle-aged men tumbled out. None looked like Chris Martin, but he'd probably arrive separately, in his own limo. Sally turned and opened the door to the hallway.

David happened to be passing by. He wore a blue suit and a floral tie. It was the first time in forever she'd seen her brother in a suit, and she was struck by how handsome he was. "David!"

"Hey, don't you look beautiful?"

"I can't stand the suspense." She pulled him into the room. "You have to tell me."

"What?"

"Who's the band?" Sally prepared to explode in excitement.

"I have no idea." David looked confused. "I told Violet to take care of it. I don't know any wedding bands."

"Oh." Sally's mouth trembled. "Of course."

"Let's clear the area!" Pam was in the hallway herding out David, the video guy, and several caterers who had somehow packed themselves in. Sally found herself marooned with the original gang of idiots.

"Was that really David Parry?" asked Fern. "He's just a baby."

Sally returned to the bathroom window. The band was mostly in their thirties or forties. Long hair, tight jeans, all pretty skeevy to be playing at a wedding. The van door slid open to reveal a drum. On it was the famous lip logo of the Rolling Stones! Sally's heart jumped. On another drum was printed THE ROLLING STONERS. THE WORLD'S GREATEST ROLLING STONES TRIBUTE BAND.

VIOLET zipped up her dress. She had told Sally she'd be a bridesmaid only if she could give Sally's fabric to her own dress designer. The result was a chic A-line gown. Violet grabbed one boob and hiked it so it sat high in her bra, then the other boob. Everything is okay, she reminded herself, and slipped on her shoes. Hiring Teddy's band to play the wedding was *not* a desperate attempt to win back her ungovernable lover. It was a tender beneficence for a dear friend who had sounded despondent when she called him on his birthday.

May Day, when Violet phoned Teddy in the conference room, she had asked, "How are you?" Teddy's voice was scratchy and slow. "My bones ache and I want to sleep all the time. My boss sent me home last week because he said I was depressing the customers." Violet smiled for the benefit of the interns setting out the Chinese food. She asked, "Is he paying you?" "Is he paying me?" Teddy laughed. She'd forgotten about the laugh. She asked, "What are you doing about money?" "Pascal paid the rent for May. I'm eating at AA meetings. Plus, there's this store in Malibu that gives away oranges. Sometimes I drive up there, but with gas, it's cheaper to eat at the Ninety-Nine-Cent Store even though the food there fucks up my liver." If this was legerdemain on Teddy's part—working in the rent, AA, gas money, and the condition of his liver in one breath—Violet would have to give him a ten. "Why didn't you call me?" she asked. "Because you made it more than clear that unless I fucked you, you didn't want to know me." Violet felt as if she'd been punched in the throat. It all flooded back, the scorching humiliation. She had somehow blocked out how dour and recalcitrant he could be. Put the phone down, she said to herself. But now that Teddy had injured her so grievously, Violet couldn't stop until she'd reclaimed some dignity. What came out of her mouth was "Oh." She dug her fingers into the back of a conference chair. "My hep C is fucking *on*," he said. "Have you seen a doctor?" One of the interns was looking at her. Violet met the kid's gaze, and he quickly resumed stuffing chopsticks into an NPR mug. "I'm not going to LA Country," Teddy said. "Which is the only place that will take me. It's fucking gross." "You're such a prince." "Make fun of me," he said, "but people die there." "Are you collecting unemployment?" "I was thinking about applying for SSI." "What's that?" "You're so fucking rich," he said. "I can't talk to you." She asked, "You mean, like welfare?" "Yes, I mean like welfare. Thanks a fucking lot for making me say it." "What about golf? Can't you get some money that way?" He scoffed, "I told you, that's not part of the program. I have to live my life with rigorous honesty." "I don't mean *hustle*. Can't you get a job as a caddy?" "What's up with you?" he said. "You suddenly have a thing for niggers?" "What?" He shot back, "Then stop trying to turn me into one." That's when Violet had devised the plan to hire Teddy's band to play at the wedding. The Rolling Stoners charged a thousand dollars. She'd give Teddy three thousand in cash. "You can disperse the moneys at your discretion," she told him. "Now, those are two words that have never been spoken to me in one sentence: *money* and *discretion*." "What do you say?" Violet asked with a laugh. He answered, "I can eat your pussy a couple of times for three grand." Violet thought she would vomit. The interns had just opened a container of that crispy orange tofu Mr. Chow made especially for her and David. She knew she'd never be ordering it again. "I hope you're joking," she said with faux gaiety. "Of course I'm joking," he said. "You're just doing what friends do, watch each other's backs."

The din of the wedding guests grew louder. Violet ran her fingers through her wet hair and headed into the bedroom, then stopped.

A man in a tuxedo sat perfectly upright on an Eames bench in the sitting area.

"Jeremy?" she asked.

He lifted his eyes, then gazed down. His hands were clutched tightly together. Fluorescent earplugs stuck out of both ears.

"I can't do it," he said to the floor. "It's a big mistake. I know I'm lucky to marry anybody. Especially Sally. But she doesn't care about me. It's like I don't exist."

"Okay...." Violet sat down beside him.

"She doesn't love me. She tolerates me. There's nothing worse."

"It's intolerable being tolerated."

"What?" Jeremy flashed her a look.

"Stephen Sondheim. From *A Little Night Music*. 'As I've often stated, it's intolerable being tolerated.'"

Jeremy doubled over and hugged himself. "I only bought her the ring because Vance made me. I tried not to give it to her. But she's too strong. She scares me. I don't know why I have to get married. I don't know why anyone has to get married."

"Jeremy?" Violet wanted to take his hand, but he still hadn't looked up. "What do you want to do?"

"I tried not giving her the ring, but she's too strong. I can't stop the wedding."

"You *can* stop the wedding, though." Violet knew the customary course of action would be to deliver a buck-up speech about pre-wedding jitters. But she could attest to Jeremy's fears. Sally always stood a little too close when she talked to you. Her eyes sparkled a little too brightly. Her makeup was too dewy perfect. She would frequently touch Violet's shoulder in sympathy when there was nothing to be sympathetic about. Violet was always at ease around aberrant personalities. As a girl, her father's coterie had made it a necessity. But with Sally, Violet felt as if she were being manipulated, to what purpose was never clear. It terrified Violet.

"I can't stop the wedding," said Jeremy.

"Jeremy. You have no idea how hard-core I am. If you want me to go out there right now and announce that the wedding is canceled, I will do it."

"Really?" He finally held her gaze. His eyes flickered hazel with hope.

"Absolutely." Violet took his hand. "I just need to make sure it's what you want to do."

"What about Sally?"

"You will have to go talk to her."

Jeremy quaked. "I can't. She'll start screaming. Or ignore me. She won't let me cancel the wedding."

"It's not up to her," said Violet. "It's up to you. Sally has lots of friends who can help her through this."

"I'm scared," said Jeremy.

"I'm scared for you. This is a big move. But it's imperative you do what's right for *you*. Ultimately, it will be what's right for Sally. She deserves better than to marry someone who feels this way about her."

"That's true," said Jeremy.

"Do you want some time alone while you think about it?" Violet stood up.

"No!" Jeremy pulled her arm. "Stay here."

Violet placed her other hand over his and sat down. She turned her head to give him some privacy.

Out on the lawn, fifty people sipped Bellinis and plucked appetizers off silver trays. Some admired the view, others the house, all giddy at finding themselves surrounded by such impeccable taste. But then, a piece of seared tuna flew off a woman's cocktail napkin. A man grabbed an old lady who had suddenly tipped over. A plume of champagne shot through the air.

Then: a young woman, wild with anger, ripped through the crowd. And in the girl's chaotic wake: Teddy. He seized the girl with the short black hair and porcelain skin.

Violet watched the ruckus, unable to hear any of it behind glass.

Teddy—ludicrously attired in lopsided mirrored aviators, red-white-and-blue terry-cloth headband, and shiny shirt unbuttoned to his waist—lunged at the lithe girl. The crowd widened around them. She pushed Teddy. He yanked her. She fell sloppily to the ground. She leapt up. Teddy grabbed her face with one hand. He snared his arms around her waist and grimaced. The black from his missing tooth screamed, *This is who you chose to fuck, a wino from the gutter!* Violet squeezed Jeremy's hand, lest she fly apart. Teddy dragged the girl away. One of her Ugg boots dropped to the ground.

And they were gone. With a collective shrug, the guests resumed their enjoyment of the party.

Dot, festooned with colorful pipe cleaners, skipped through the crowd, followed by LadyGo, who nibbled on a bouquet of satay. Violet had averted disaster earlier today by giving LadyGo a blouse to wear over her JOHN TRAVOLTA IS A HUGE FAG T-shirt.

Violet shook loose Jeremy's hand. "Excuse me," she said. "I have to ask my nanny a question." Violet opened the door and waved. "LadyGo! LadyGo! Come here!"

"Mommy!" Dot charged over and mightily hugged Violet's legs.

"Hi, sweetie." LadyGo walked over at funereal pace. Violet grabbed her arm. "Who was that girl who just ran through?"

LadyGo needed a few seconds to gulp down the chicken. "I don't know, *meesuz*," she said. "Somebody ask and lady go, I'm a friend of the band. Lady who plan the party? Lady go mad."

Jesus Christ, Violet thought, could it be Coco?

"I want you to go find that girl and ask her what her name is." Violet dug her nails into LadyGo's jiggly upper arm. LadyGo looked down. Violet released her grip. "You must find out that girl's name. Do you understand?"

"Yes, *meesuz*." LadyGo brushed the phantom wrinkles from her sleeve and made a big show of regaining her composure. She trudged out the door.

"Faster!" Violet said. "Run!"

"Who dat, Mommy?" Dot pointed at Jeremy.

He was stuck in some kind of sickening loop. "She screams and I keep talking until I say the right thing, then she's fine, then she screams and I keep talking and then it stops when I say the right thing, she screams—"

"That's Jeremy!" Violet half-squealed. "He's a friend of Aunt Sally's!"

"And I keep talking until I say the right thing, then she's fine, then—"

"Jeremy?" asked Violet.

He looked up, his eyes flashed a plea for Violet to help him stop. Then he looked down. "It's nice for a while and we have fun and I say the wrong thing and then it starts over—"

"Jeremy!" Violet dropped to her knees and grabbed his cheeks. "Stop it!"

"And then she keeps talking and I talk and then she says something and then I say the right thing—"

"Stop it!" parroted a delighted Dot.

"Dot, it's not funny. Mommy needs to talk to Jeremy. Go look at the books." Violet nudged Dot in the direction of the coffee table, then turned back to Jeremy. "You are going to call off this wedding."

"I want that," he said.

"I want dat!" chuckled Dot, pushing the art books onto the floor. The Robert Williams book thumped down; so did the first edition of *Uncommon Places* by Stephen Shore.

"You need to find Sally and tell her," Violet told Jeremy.

Dot found the book she wanted, the Andreas Gursky with that marvelous photograph of the Ninety-Nine-Cent Store. "Dot has those chairs." She pointed to the chair that she did indeed have.

Violet dipped her head so she was in Jeremy's line of vision. "You have to do it now. The wedding is in ten minutes." She stood up, hoping he would follow her lead, but he didn't.

"Candy." Dot pointed to some licorice in the photograph. "Dat candy has no nuts."

Violet pulled Jeremy up by a dead arm. "Do you know where Sally is?" she asked.

"No."

"Off the garage, in the guesthouse. It's where the wedding party is gathering."

"*Meesuz?*" LadyGo rushed in, her eyes dancing with excitement.

Violet held up a finger to LadyGo while she dispensed with Jeremy. "Go talk to Sally. Don't make it more complicated than it has to be. Just say the words, I want to call off the wedding."

"I want to call off the wedding," he repeated.

"That's right. That's all."

"You'll be here?" asked Jeremy.

"I'll be here. Everything is okay."

"*Meesuz,*" said Violet's agent provocateur, unable to contain her reconnaissance. "Lady go name is *Coco Kennedy*." The Spanish accent made the name even more grotesque.

"Lollipops!" said Dot.

LadyGo noticed the wreckage of expensive books. "Miss Dot! Very bad girl." LadyGo dropped to her knees and matched the books to their jackets.

Jeremy just stood there. "You'll be here?" he asked Violet.

"I'll be here," Violet said flatly.

"Everything is okay?"

"Everything is okay."

SALLY, an opaline vision of silk and lace, navigated the carport, careful not to brush against the dirty Bentley and Mercedes. Maryam dutifully followed, holding the bride's five-foot train.

"Careful of the bikes," Sally warned, then stopped suddenly

before she stepped in a puddle of oil. Maryam smacked into her. "Watch out!" said Sally.

"What are you doing?"

"Uh, trying not to ruin my dress?"

"Tell me next time if you're going to stop," said Maryam. "I can't see anything."

"You know this wouldn't be happening if I was getting married at the Bel-Air Hotel," Sally said to Maryam's tulle head. "Where is Violet, anyway? *She* should be the one helping me."

"I don't know," Maryam said, with a tinge of sullenness.

"You're not still steamed about me making Violet the maid of honor, are you?" Sally asked. "It's her house. I had no choice." The tulle mushroom cloud was silent. Sally lifted her dress with one hand and reached for the Mercedes mirror with the other, careful to keep arm's length from the dusty car. She hurdled the oil spill. One foot landed. Just before the other one did, her body jerked back. "Aaah!" Sally's leg swung in the air, but she miraculously regained her balance.

"Oh God!" cried Maryam.

Sally turned. Her follower was splayed on the concrete, Sally's train triumphantly overhead. Sally grabbed the wad of lace.

"Did I get dirty?" Maryam scrambled to her feet. Black goo covered one side of her dress, arm, and leg.

"Not too," Sally chirped. But she couldn't keep a straight face as Maryam registered the extent of the disaster. A laugh escaped Sally's pursed lips.

"It's not funny!" Maryam said.

"I'm sorry—it's just—how did you possibly get that—it's in your *hair!*"

Maryam started crying. "How can you laugh? In five minutes I have to get up in front of everyone."

"You don't have to get up in front of everyone if you don't want." Sally prayed Maryam would take the hint.

"If I don't want?!" Tears streamed down Maryam's face. "I'm a bridesmaid! I spent a hundred dollars on my hair and three hundred dollars on this ugly dress I'll never wear again. You're such a fucking bitch!"

Sally gasped. "I can't believe you just said that."

"I swear, I hate you sometimes." Maryam stood on one leg like a flamingo, using her clean leg to wipe her dirty one. "You wouldn't even know Jeremy if it weren't for me."

"What does that have to do with anything?" Sally said. "Are you jealous?"

"Of you?" Maryam cried. "Give me a break."

"You *are* jealous! Because now you're the only one who's not married."

"Can you stop being a selfish bitch for one minute of your life? I'm covered in black engine oil!"

Sally took a deep breath. "Maybe Violet has a robe you can wear over your dress."

"I'm not walking around all night in a robe!"

"Or you could turn the dress inside out?" Sally offered.

"Fuck you." Maryam stormed into the guesthouse.

Sally called after her, "How dare you! After I paid to have your makeup done with my own money! And you *know* how much trouble I went to picking out bridesmaid dresses that you *can* wear again!" The door slammed. Sally stood there, red faced, holding her own train. She stomped into the guesthouse.

Jennifer, Jim, David, Vance, Clay, Fern, and Pam were in a tizzy over Maryam. Not a word about how magnificent Sally looked. And still no trace of Violet, her maid of honor!

Sally went into the bathroom, shut the door, and screamed in frustration. She pulled her diabetes kit from her garter belt and checked her blood sugar. She wanted to inject herself at the last possible minute so she could enjoy a four-hour stretch of unadulterated bliss. Her glucose was 210, on the high side. With the champagne and wedding cake and pure joy, it was certain to climb. Sally drew four units of Humalog into her syringe. Suddenly the door swung open.

It was Jeremy.

"Oh!" Sally fumbled to hide her diabetes kit, but it fell from the edge of the sink. Syringes, glucose strips, and insulin bottles showered the floor. Sally swept them into a pile with her foot and stood over it. "Jeremy!" she said. "What a lovely surprise!"

Sally saw the look on Jeremy's face and she knew: *he wants to call off the wedding.* She was so sure of it that a strange calm befell her. She gingerly closed the door behind him. "You know it's bad luck to see the bride before the wedding," she tut-tutted.

"I have something to tell you." He met her eyes with a coldness she'd never before seen.

"Well, I have something to tell *you*," she said.

"No. I have something to tell you."

"I want to tell you mine first." She scrunched her nose.

"I have something to—".

"Jeremy—" she said.

"I don't want to get—"

"I'm pregnant!"

"What?"

Sally closed the toilet lid. She tapped Jeremy's chest and he dropped onto it. "Dr. Naeby confirmed it yesterday," she lied. "I wanted to surprise you tonight."

"I didn't know," Jeremy sputtered.

"We're going to have a baby!" She took his hand. It was heavy and cold. Her heart began to race. *He still wants to call off the wedding.*

"I don't want to—" he attempted again.

Sally kissed him, stuffing the words back in his mouth. "Darling," she said, her lips still pressed against his, "I've been so emotional this past month, wanting our wedding to be perfect. And now that all our friends are here, some of them flying in from all over the country, I'm so glad that I *did* make it perfect. And all your colleagues are here and they're going to be so impressed. I know I've been a little crazy. But now we know it was the pregnancy hormones that made me act a teensy bit cuckoo."

Sally withdrew her face just enough to see that Jeremy had the wild, defiant look of a caged animal. He was calm now, but sometimes caged animals looked defeated when they still had one flurry of fight left in them.

"I don't want to worry you," Sally said, hating herself for the lie she was about to tell, "but my diabetes has been out of control this past month. My doctor wanted to hospitalize me. There's an ambulance waiting on Mulholland, just in case."

"There is?" Jeremy said. "What's wrong?"

"I'm stabilized now, so there's nothing to worry about."

Jeremy stared at the floor.

Sally felt a rush of relief. "It's six o'clock!" she said. "You'd better go and take your position."

"Okay." Jeremy got up, shoulders still slumped.

"You look gorgeous, my love," she said. "Or should I say, Dad!" She plucked the earplugs out of his ears. "Not today."

Jeremy zombie-walked back into the main room. Just then, Violet breezed in with wet hair. She stopped and gave Jeremy an urgent, quizzical look. Sally withdrew into the bathroom to watch. Jeremy said something to Violet. Violet grabbed him by the shoulders. Sally could read Violet's lips. *What happened?* So that's where her maid of honor had been this whole time! Jeremy walked off without responding to Violet, who looked up and spotted Sally.

"There you are!" Sally said, arms swept outward, like a soap opera *grande dame*.

"Sally!" Violet said. "Is there something I can help you with?"

"Thank you," Sally said. "But you've already done so much."

THE ceremony, in all its banal splendor, had come and gone. Dinner, too. After the meal, Violet had found herself maundering drunkenly to some Gap executive, so she plopped herself down at a deserted table, content to be the requisite drunk whom all others avoided.

The guests were spilled across the lawn, basking in the balmy night and jetliner views. Some had been drawn to the edge by the sound of coyotes attacking an animal. The terrifying screeches and even more terrifying high-pitched clicking sounds were nothing new to Violet, who had grown up in the hills. Tonight, there seemed to be some meows thrown into the clamor. Perhaps the wild things had scored a neighbor's cat.

Teddy's band wasn't scheduled to begin until after the cake ceremony. Just before, Violet would blame a migraine and slip off to the Beverly Hills Hotel, where she and David had booked a room to avoid the racket of the cleanup. Violet hadn't seen Teddy since he had dragged off Coco, caveman-style. At first, Violet was appalled that her beneficiary hadn't come looking for her. But after six Bellinis, she no longer gave a shit.

She fished the booze-soaked peaches out of her glass and closed her eyes, willing the fruit to deaden her emotions even further. She grabbed an abandoned glass from across the table and scooped the peach mash from it, too.

In lieu of a wedding cake, Sally had opted for the *de rigueur* tower of cupcakes. Several caterers had just carried it out and nervously lowered it onto a rose-petal-covered table. The tower, topped by a groom and ballerina, reigned over the crowd, its frosted finery beckoning all to come hither and have a taste. But a caterer-sentinel was positioned nearby to prevent any such thing.

Guest after guest was politely but firmly rebuffed. Violet lived for shit like this. She couldn't stop grinning.

But the cake ceremony was nearing, time for Violet to make her escape. First, she needed one of those cupcakes. She pushed herself up, then grabbed the table to steady herself. She wobbled to the cupcake tower and reached for a chocolate with coconut frosting.

"I'm going to have to ask you to wait," the caterer said, "until the cake ceremony."

"I won't be here for the cake ceremony." Violet snatched a cupcake.

The caterer grabbed her arm.

"It's my house," she said.

The caterer instantly released his grip. Violet smiled. Aah, how cozy it was, being David Parry's wife with all its attendant perks. She ripped the top off the cupcake and crammed it in her mouth. All she needed now was a blast of caffeine to sober her up for the drive. She stepped unevenly to the bar and ordered a Diet Coke.

A partygoer approached, eyes on Violet's cupcake. "Oh! Are they letting us eat those now?"

"Knock yourself out." Violet stuffed the bottom half of the cupcake into her mouth, but had forgotten to peel off the paper. She pulled it out, saliva and cake spilling onto her chest. She needed a trash can.

On the bar sat an empty jar. Taped to it, a grainy color Xerox of a British flag. Written in big letters, the word TIPS. Beside it, a fan of business cards that read "The Rolling Stoners."

"Wait—what are these?" Violet said to the bartender.

"Some guy started putting them around. He said David Parry, whose house this is, said it was cool."

Violet scanned the soirée. Tip jars had sprung up on every conceivable flat surface! She stuffed the business cards into the tip jar and thrust it at the bartender. "Throw this away!"

"But David Parry said—"

"I'm his wife. Go. Get rid of all of them. Now!"

"Aaaaah!" A shriek erupted from inside the house. A woman's voice? Coco's voice? Violet staggered toward it.

"Aaaaah!" There it was again, coming from the master bedroom. Violet flung open the door. The bedroom was quiet, tranquil. But someone was in the bathroom—a woman—and sobs, too.

"It's okay, don't worry," said a soothing voice.

Violet hurtled through the door.

A whimpering boy stood in the corner. A woman with kind eyes stroked his hair. "Hi," she said to Violet. "I apologize. J.J. was using the bathroom and saw a spider."

"Oh!" Violet laughed with relief. "A spider!"

"It's there! It's there!" J.J. pointed to the bathtub.

"That's a big scary one, all right," Violet said. "Do you know what we do with spiders here?" The boy was silent. "We help them." Violet picked up a newspaper and brushed the spider onto it. "If you open the window, I can put him outside." The boy did. Violet shook the newspaper and the spider fell off. "Now he's back with his friends."

His mother stuck out her hand. "I'm Nora Ross. Thanks for your patience. He's on the autism spectrum and can get a little fixated."

"He's a sweetheart," Violet said.

"He's my teacher, that's for sure!" Nora tousled the beautiful boy's hair.

Violet wanted to hug this shell-shocked woman who still somehow managed to radiate such tenderness. The boy sprinted through the bedroom and out into the thick of the party.

"I'd better go," Nora said, and followed.

Violet stepped into the yard. People were being herded in the direction of the cupcake tower. Violet needed to split. She didn't need to say good-bye to David. And Sally, well, who cared about Sally?

"Violet!" It was David. He was holding Dot, who devoured a cupcake the size of her face.

"Hi. I was about to come find you. You know what? I'm not feeling well…." Violet trailed off. Under Dot's arm was a dirty pink Ugg boot.

"Violet, what's going on?" David asked.

"What—what do you mean?" Her stomach tightened.

"Did you book this band?"

"A friend of mine plays in it." Shit. She'd forgotten to lie. "Why?"

"Apparently there's a girl with them who's in the house causing some kind of commotion. The wedding planner tried to kick her out, but she claimed she was a friend of yours."

"Shit. I'll take care of it."

"Shit," said Dot in her small voice.

"Since when do you have a friend who plays in a Stones cover band?" David asked, incredulous.

"He's the nice guy I met on the street that day. He's a nice guy, a friend, who needs the money. His name is Teddy."

David practically dropped Dot. "Teddy Reyes?"

"Yeah," Violet said as casually as possible. She furiously tried to remember if she'd ever mentioned Teddy's last name. Oh God, David's face was reddening. His jaw was working. His neck was tensing.

"That's it," he said. "I'm done." He shook his head and walked away.

Violet caught up and grabbed his arm. "David! David!" A nearby group of Sally's girlfriends glanced over. Violet lowered her voice. "What do you mean?"

"You're smart about some things," David said, heedless of the girls who had paused their conversation to listen. "But you're not smart about others. You grew up around intellectuals and loveable eccentrics. I grew up around poor people. What do I always say?"

There was no way Violet could answer that. David was always inculcating her on so many different topics.

"Troubled people are trouble," he said.

It was one of their common themes: that Violet didn't understand people. Sure, she floated with ease among the most rarefied strata of society. But her idea of a scary lowlife was someone walking around with JUICY COUTURE emblazoned across their ass.

David continued, "Some people think the worst thing in life is to wear white after Labor Day. Others think nothing of throwing their babies into dumpsters."

"What babies, Dada?" Dot asked.

"Down-and-out people are down-and-out for a reason." David's voice spewed venom. "They're drunks. They're liars. They're lazy. They're insane. If you want to pay to have their car fixed or whatever the fuck you're doing with them, do it on your own time." And now he started screaming, "But don't let them into my house! Don't let them near my fucking daughter! Do you hear me?! What is wrong with you?!"

Dot began wailing. The guests, who had only moments ago taken pleasure in watching the rich people fight, scurried away.

"You're right," Violet said. "I'm sorry. I'll change."

"You'll change." He spit out a laugh. "I really tried, Violet."

Dot tried to worm out of David's grasp. "Mama!"

"Come to me, sweetie," Violet held out her hands, but David jerked Dot away.

"I want Mama," Dot cried. "I want Mama!"

"It's okay, Dot," Violet said. "Mommy and Daddy are happy."

"Don't lie to her!" David raged. "Will you stop lying for once in your fucking life?! Lie to yourself. Lie to me. But don't lie to Dot!"

"What should I do?" Violet pleaded. "Tell me what you want me to do."

"What you always seem to do: whatever the fuck you want." He stormed off with Dot. Violet swayed like sea grass in the ocean of the lawn.

The bartender came over with a glass. "Your Diet Coke."

"Whoooooaaaa!" A collective moan rose from the crowd. The cupcakes had tumbled to the ground. Nearby, J.J. was crying in shame. Nora was on her hands and knees, frantically picking up cupcakes.

EVERYONE'S attention diverted by the cupcake avalanche, Kurt skulked into the house. David Parry was the kind of macher who was probably swimming in codeine cough syrup or better. Rich people, they got a hangnail and some Beverly Hills doctor was writing them a scrip.

He cased the living room. Nice shit they had here. Smaller than their other place, but right out of *Dwell*. In the corner was a door. Kurt scuttled toward it.

Shit, his head ached. His hands felt arthritic. A swig of codeine should lube the joints just right. It was a sweet party. Except for Maryam, who kept shooting him dirty looks, or at least tried to through her crazy makeup. He got a ton of compliments on his Peter Criss boots, but that was to be expected. He was seated at a table with a bunch of people from the Lakers. Maybe he could do a search-and-replace on that leather jacket proposal he wrote up for David and give it to them. Selling leather jackets at Lakers games…Kurt was warming to the idea.

He closed the door and flipped on the light. It was a fucking kid's room. Crib, quilts on the wall, a stuffed rocking hippo in the corner. Kids got coughs, too, right? Maybe they gave the brat codeine cough syrup. Kurt entered the bathroom and shut the door. In the medicine cabinet sat a promising-looking bottle. Zyrtec. Kurt had never heard of it. He chugged the whole thing and stuck the empty bottle in the pocket of his Hawaiian shirt. If he caught a buzz, he could call into the pharmacy and get the refills.

Something slammed. At the other end of the bathroom was

an open door Kurt had missed. His instinct was to beat it, but he paused. A familiar voice drifted in from the other room.

"How could you show up here with her?" It was Violet; he'd know her voice anywhere. Even though she was a heifer, he wouldn't mind hitting some of that million-dollar snatch. She always smelled so nice.

Kurt crept closer to the door.

"Did I tell you she was crazy?" A man was talking now.

Kurt couldn't resist taking a peek. The guy was short, had dark skin and good hair. Kurt drew back.

"She doesn't belong here!" Violet screamed. "I don't care if she is a fucking Kennedy."

"Well, good. Because she probably isn't."

"What did you just say?"

"Her driver's license says Carolyne Portis. She just goes around posing like a Kennedy because people are lame enough to be impressed with it. Personally, I always had my doubts. I mean, think about it. What's a Kennedy doing growing up in Palm Springs?"

"You asshole!" There was a struggle. Violet was trashing the poor fucker with both arms. In Kurt's humble opinion, she needed to start altering her life state big-time. Violet screamed, "How could you invite her up here?"

"I didn't *invite* her. She hacked into my e-mail and found out where the gig was. She walked here from the Greyhound station."

"And that's meant to mollify me? Jesus Christ!"

"She's gone now. She bit one of your caterers, so I had a friend pick her up and bring her back to my apartment."

"She's biting people now?! What the fuck is going on? Do you realize my life is over? And for what?" Violet started really crying. "What happened that day? Was *she* there? Is that where you disappeared for those two hours? To find your girlfriend and tell her to give you a minute, the rich lady just showed up and you needed to string her along? Do you have any idea how infected my brain has become because of that night? Right now, the trunk of my car is full of presents for you. Golf clubs, a cell phone, even a bass I had Geddy Lee sign, waiting to give you when you finally called me to tell me that *you felt it, too!*"

Kurt shivered. The connections were flying, just like President Ikeda said they would.

Violet continued, through tears, "Do you realize what you've done to me? I grind out my days with my husband and child, but by night, I'm yours. I'm yours, but you don't want me. Thanks to you, I'm a ghost, drifting through life, craving something I'll never taste again."

"Violet, I didn't know."

"David is going to leave me."

"I'm sorry. I really am."

"Why didn't you at least fight for me?" she asked. "Aren't I worth a fight? Or a poem? You never wrote me a poem. Do you think about me? Every day, every waking hour? Tell me the truth."

"No."

Violet laughed and shrieked at the same time. It was more fucked-up sounding than those coyotes.

"I think about my rent and my car and getting laid and staying sober and how shitty I feel and my roommate who's always coming home after work and calling France while I'm trying to sleep."

"So in the end it all comes down to your shitty little existence? Is that who I was to you, then? A cash cow? Well, cash cows have feelings, too."

"Tell me," he said. "What can I do? I want to make amends."

"You can think about me every day until you die."

"Of course I think about you."

"And you can suffer!"

"Ha! That can be arranged."

"You smelly creep. You shiftless fucker. This is not a joke. I am not a joke. You watch out for me. You fear me. I'm so vast you'll never know. I'm the weather."

The door slammed. It was like the universe had dumped a fucking fruit basket in Kurt's lap. He had to hightail it to Violet's car before the other dude did. That shit could pay his mortgage for the entire year.

SALLY had imagined dancing and being serenaded by Coldplay until the wee hours. Instead, it was 9:45, most of the guests were gone, and a no-name band played "Street Fighting Man" to a deserted dance floor. Sally stood at the front door, Nora holding both her hands. "I am so, so sorry about the cupcakes."

"Don't worry about it," said Sally. "It wasn't J.J.'s fault." It was *Violet's* fault. She was the one who had grabbed the first cupcake before it was time. From that point on, the wedding was doomed. With no cake ceremony, the release of the doves and the center-piece raffle stood no chance of being magical.

"Where are you two newlyweds off to?" Nora asked.

"We're back and forth, traveling with the NBA for the month...." Sally trailed off. She couldn't remember what month it was....

"Oh!" Nora grabbed an envelope from her purse. "I wanted to give you this. It's a save-the-date card for a thing I'm having on June first, if you're in town."

"Ooh." Sally took the envelope, with the faint realization that she had in her hand something she'd wanted ever since she started working with Nora—an invitation to one of her parties. But Sally's mouth was so dry. She wandered away from Nora and bumped into a man.

"Hey, nice party, babe," he said. Sally couldn't remember his name. He worked with Jeremy.

"Right..." said Sally. She needed some water. And someplace to lie down.

"I've never heard a whole Stones set without a bass player."

Who was this guy? Jim. That's right, Jim. When did she last eat? Some fruit, a bite of cupcake. She'd raised a champagne flute to her lips during the toasts, but hadn't swallowed any. Was she low or high? When did she take her last shot...?

"I asked Jeremy how it felt to be married," Jim said, "but he was neither zero nor one about it." He cracked up. "Come on, that's hilarious. Jeremy has two emotions, zero and one."

Sally hiked the hem of her dress, felt for her garter, and pulled out the diabetes kit she'd had made in matching satin just for the occasion. She stabbed her finger with the lancet and squeezed some blood out.

"Oh—what are you—I'll just give you some privacy." Jim slunk off.

Sally pressed the blood onto a test strip and stuck it in the glucometer.

Beep.

404.

That couldn't be right. Sally blinked. 404. She pulled out a fresh test strip and tested her blood again. 412.

Oh God! She'd never taken that shot before the wedding. Jeremy had come in and she'd totally forgotten! At over 400, she risked slipping into ketoacidosis. She could go into a coma. What if she passed out here? *Please, no. Not at my wedding, not in front of the guests.* She needed some insulin now! Her medicine was in the guesthouse. Sally staggered down the hall, her heart rampaging throughout her body.

Her baby! What if she had ketones in her urine? If any passed into her placenta, it might damage the baby's developing organs. Sally picked up her pace. Oh God, how could she have let this happen?!

Sally flew into the carport and beheld a sight that under any other circumstance would have bowled her over.

Kurt stood at the open trunk of Violet's Mercedes. When he

saw Sally, his jaw dropped and eyes flew open. In the whole five years they were together, Sally had never seen so much…*expression* on Kurt's face.

"Sally!" he yelped.

But Sally kept running, her dress dragging across the oily floor. She tumbled into the guesthouse and lunged for the bathroom door.

It was locked.

"Hello!" She knocked on the door. "Please hurry! I have to get in." She pounded it with both fists. "It's the bride; I need to get in!" She rattled the knob. "Hello! This is an emergency! Please!"

The door opened. A man stood there, nobody she recognized. A red-white-and-blue terry-cloth headband tamed his unruly hair. He looked sleepy, as if he'd just woken up. His green eyes, sickly and bloodshot, stared into hers. Sally froze, as if this man were a portent of evil.

"Who are you?" she asked. But he just walked away.

Sally shut herself in the bathroom. Her Liberty of London bag was on the floor behind the toilet, where she had kicked it when Jeremy burst in. She'd forgotten to put it away! Bottles of insulin, test strips, caps, lancets, alcohol wipes, were scattered everywhere. She grabbed the Humalog. Now she needed a syringe. She couldn't find one. She shook her bag and turned it inside out, then dropped to her knees and checked behind the toilet. She picked up the rug, turned over the trash can—there it was: a syringe! Among the tissues—in the trash can! Sally laughed. It must have landed there when Jeremy surprised her!

Sally jammed the needle into the little jar. Her hand shaking, she drew out ten units. She didn't bother lifting her wedding dress. She stabbed the syringe through the satin and injected herself in the stomach. She could finally breathe. Her baby was going to be fine.

CHAPTER ELEVEN

Double Secret Probation ❀ **The Game Show** ❀ **Coachella**

Now Do You Believe Me? ❀ **I Never Really Liked You**

"TEN FIVE PER EPISODE?" VIOLET SAID TO HER AGENT AS SHE BACKED OUT OF the carport. Violet's friend Richard had just gotten a pilot picked up. There was a bit of money left in the budget, and he had asked if she'd consult a couple days a week. "We can close the deal," she told her agent. "Let me know my start date." She hung up, tickled to be once again employed.

The night of the wedding, Violet had stayed up for David in their hotel room, bracing herself for his excoriation, but he never appeared. Instead, he had checked into his own bungalow. It was where he'd been living for the past month, coming and going from the house only to see Dot, get the mail, and drop off laundry. He was always perfectly agreeable, exchanging pleasantries with

Violet, who trepidatiously followed his lead. It was as if she were on some type of double secret probation.

All Violet could do as she awaited her sentence was live her life, their life. She kept the house in order and tended to Dot. Every night, she'd snuggle in bed with her little girl and, after the books, tell her, "Mommy loves you. And Daddy loves you. And Mommy loves Daddy. And Daddy loves Mommy."

Teddy rarely appeared in her thoughts. When he did, it was so benign—she'd read a reference to JFK and think, Oh—that Violet would smile at the utter lack of emotional charge.

However, there were some loose ends. First, she had to wiggle out of the George Harrison estate. The geology report was a disaster, which gave her an excuse to cancel the purchase. The paperwork had to be signed and delivered by five o'clock tomorrow.

The second issue was a bit more unsettling. The myriad of gifts stashed in her trunk had disappeared the night of the wedding. Violet resisted calling Teddy, not only because she didn't want any contact with him, but because her gut said he didn't do it. His code of honor was rife with nuance, to be sure. But burglary was something that just didn't fit. There was the additional matter of hepatitis C. She and Teddy had used a condom. Still, she would get a blood test, just to be sure.

Violet reached the bottom of the driveway and stopped at the mailbox. Despite all of David's success, his face would fill with childlike anticipation at the sight of the mail. She'd bring him the mail, the lunch she had made him, the escrow cancelation papers, and word of her new job. David had wanted her to start writing again. Perhaps he'd be so happy he'd sleep at home tonight. Perhaps he'd already made up his mind to throw her out. There was no way to tell. Yesterday at the market, she had reached for a dozen eggs, and realized they had a good chance of lasting longer at her house than she did.

She dialed David's office.

"Violet!" burst the startled voice of David's assistant.

"David's wife."

"I know. He was out of the office all morning, I have no idea where, and I've got a million people trying to get a hold of him."

"Oh," Violet said. "He's not around?"

"He just got on a helicopter to Coachella. Even though the concert's not until Saturday, he went today to make sure the sound from the main stage won't drown out the second stage—" The assistant gasped.

"What?" asked Violet.

"Nothing," said the girl. "I don't know why I'm telling you all this."

Violet had been thinking the same thing. "Well, just tell David I called." She hung up, disappointed she would miss him.

SALLY ascended the steps of her Crescent Heights apartment. Strewn on the landing was a month of mail laced with shriveled wisteria blossoms. The state seal of California jumped out at her. She opened the envelope. "Sally Miller Parry, this letter informs you that your debts have been discharged, blah, blah, blah...." Could she have really gotten away with the whole thing? She was out of debt, married, and pregnant, all in four months. She gathered the mail and opened the door.

Before her was a wonderland of wedding presents, all shapes and sizes. They were just gigantic chunks of cardboard, of course, but Sally's X-ray eyes saw the light blue Tiffany boxes, gold Geary's ones, and more! It was as if she had opened door number two and won the grand prize. She half-expected Bob Barker to step in and hand her the keys to a brand-new convertible. The audience would lustily applaud, knowing Sally deserved it all.

She could have ripped open every box on the spot, but she had to organize her medicine before the car arrived. Game One of the NBA Conference Finals was tonight in Houston, and the plane left in two hours. Sally picked her way to the kitchen, where she loaded medicine into her extra diabetes kit for the plane. Hopefully, Houston would be more fun than Sacramento. It ended up that there was only so much you could do, or charge, at the Sheraton Grand Sacramento. She and Jeremy had ventured out once, to the California State Railroad Museum. At the ticket booth, Jeremy got recognized by a bunch of scary black people wearing Kings jerseys. They kept shouting, Hey, Professor! and taking pictures with their cell phones. The newlyweds left before the guide showed up for their VIP tour.

Sally zipped the kit shut, then couldn't help it. She had to open just one present.

She raced into the living room and chose a giant box from Tiffany. She yanked off the red ribbon. Inside was a peacock cachepot. Sally's spirits sank. She *had* registered for it, but what would she do with a five-hundred-dollar cachepot? Maybe start a charity where people gave away their wedding presents to those less fortunate. Sally had once read in *Town & Country* that Jessica Seinfeld, Jerry's wife, founded a charity that distributed baby stuff that her friends didn't want. Now that she was Sally White, she needed to start taking herself seriously like that, too.

Sally looked at the mail. Maybe there was something good *there*. She recognized a return address as belonging to Nora Ross. The envelope was heavy, the paper thick and expensive. Sally opened it and removed a little book bound with red silk cord. On the cover were the words:

Brilliant

Absentminded

Mathematically Inclined

Structured

That was a perfect description of Jeremy! This must be some kind of personalized thank-you note for the wedding. She turned the page.

Repetitive
Clumsy
Literal Minded
Socially Inept
Obsessive

Sally frowned. Sure, all those things applied to Jeremy, but they were hardly appropriate for a thank-you note. And where was the part about *her*? She turned the page.

ASPERGER'S SYNDROME

A Pervasive Developmental Disorder
that has reached
epidemic proportions.

Please join
Nora and Jordan Ross
as they Shine a Spotlight
on the Autism Spectrum.

There was a Web address on the bottom of the invitation. Sally went to her laptop and typed it in. A blare of words and phrases appeared on the screen.

Asperger's syndrome is considered to be a lesser form of AUTISM…

Wait, Sally thought, J. J. has autism. Jeremy is nothing like J.J.

Asperger's syndrome is often marked by high intelligence and a tendency to become abnormally fixated on one subject. This often results in a successful career in that field.…

That did describe Jeremy, but lots of people were successful.

> They have trouble empathizing and reciprocating emo-
> tion.... Their speech often lacks inflection....

Sally? She could hear Jeremy's flat voice as if he were right there in the room.

> Many people with Asperger's syndrome have difficulty
> making eye contact....

Sally.

> They have an unusually low tolerance of loud noises.

Sally.

> They rigidly adhere to specific arbitrary rituals, any devia-
> tion from which can cause significant anxiety.... Despite
> their intelligence, everyday activities such as driving a car
> can seem impossibly complicated....

Sally!

> Asperger's is highly hereditary. One in three girls born to a
> parent with Asperger's will inherit it. Double that with boys.

Sally grabbed her stomach and closed her eyes. Jeremy's horrible voice echoed in her brain. *Sally. Sally. Sally.*

"Stop it!" She covered her ears.

"Sally. The car is waiting." She turned. Instead of Bob Barker standing among the boxes, it was Jeremy. "Sally," he said, "it's time to go."

"Jeremy. Is something wrong with you?"

"No."

"Why do you always wear earplugs?" Sally had never even asked him this, always having attributed it to the delightful eccentricity of a genius.

"Do you want some?" He reached into his pocket and offered her a pair. She hit them to the floor.

"Look at me," she said. He flashed her a glance, then looked down. "Look me in the eyes." She stepped toward him. He didn't look up. "What is wrong with you?"

"Our plane leaves at twelve fifty and it's eleven now. The driver said there's lots of traffic."

"Why don't you drive?"

"I don't have a license," he said.

"Have you ever tried to get one?"

"Six times."

"What happened?" Her voice trembled.

"It didn't work out."

"*What* didn't work out?"

"I scored a hundred on the written, but I didn't like the driving portion."

"Don't you think it's weird," she said, "that you got your PhD in a week, but you can't drive a car?"

"I got my PhD in five semesters."

Then it occurred to her. "That's why you pooped that day. You can look into a *camera* just fine. But when it came time to look into Jim's *eyes,* you got so nervous, you shit your pants!"

Sally had played everything right. The dating, the proposal, the pregnancy, the wedding. The one thing she had overlooked was that Jeremy was retarded. And chances were, the baby in her belly was, too.

"Go," she said. "Go to Houston by yourself."

"You have a plane ticket."

"Get out!" Sally said. Jeremy turned and walked out of the apartment.

THE helicopter began its descent. David stared out the window. The Coachella Valley looked as if someone had begun to methodically stick postage stamps in different shades of green to the desert floor, only to abandon the task halfway through. He could make out the festival site up ahead, its monster main stage and dozen white tents scattered on the hyper-green polo field. David's Black-Berry vibrated. There it was.

> To: David@ultra.com
> From: BartonC@TMBB.com
> Re: divorce papers
> Just been filed. Let me know when you want them served.

David contemplated the grass bracelet that still clung to his wrist.

At the fire pit, the stoned kid had cautioned that the sweet grass must fall off naturally, otherwise the transformative power of the sweat lodge would be lost. Over the past months, David had grown increasingly preoccupied with the bracelet, never tugging on it, careful not to get it wet, even wearing his watch on his right hand so it wouldn't rub against it. He hated himself for his superstition. What had happened there anyway, other than David and a bunch of strangers getting really, really hot together? Still, he hung on to the hope that something life-changing had actually taken place.

Indeed, compassion had flowed in the weeks after the yoga retreat. How couldn't it have? David had returned home to find Violet a lying, distracted wretch. Pity was a cinch. Until Sally's wedding.

David had been prepared to storm into the hotel room that night and announce he was leaving her. Heading down the palm-plastered corridor, Dot in his arms, thoughts ablaze with the invective he'd been rehearsing for the past five hours, he held the door open for a couple of women. "Awwww," they both cooed, in such a maudlin way that David almost turned to see what it could be. But of course it was Dot. Bundled up in her quilt, clutching her froggie, her fancy dress stained with berries and chocolate, God, what could compare to the peacefulness of that sleeping face? And David thought: *Violet had turned him into a chump and a cuckold, but there was no way she was going to turn him into a man who walked out on his child.* He turned right around and checked into a bungalow.

And amazingly, this past month, Violet had seemed to find her way back. But with every wifely duty she performed, David's rage grew. He could get his own lunch. He had an assistant for that. How about a fucking apology with his tofu and brown rice? Violet was perfectly plucky to go about her business as if nothing had ever happened! Which meant that *David* would be the one stuck suffering a lifetime of suspicion and betrayal.

The helicopter touched down on the empty polo field. All but one strand of the bracelet had frayed. He would serve the divorce papers when it finally fell off.

The pilot opened the door. David was met by a woman who worked for the promoter.

"David! Hi!" she said. Thirties, skinny, in jeans and tank top showing off great arms. "We've got the whole Ultra village set up. Five Airstreams, all with wireless and *Scarface*."

"How about Guitar Hero?"

"Guitar Hero on big screens. I had to lock up the mini guitars because the crew won't stop messing around with them." She laughed and touched his shoulder and kept it there a second too long. He knew that word had leaked out that he was living apart from his wife. The promoter chick wore too much makeup but had full lips, the kind that never quite closed. "Are you staying through Saturday," she asked, "or going back to LA tonight?"

"I don't know," he said. "It depends how it goes."

SALLY sat across from Dr. Naeby at his cluttered desk.

"What's up?" he asked.

"I'd like to get an abortion," she said. "Now."

Dr. Naeby's eyebrows jumped. The walls of his office were covered with framed pictures of his own children. The lyrics of "Teach Your Children Well" were handwritten and signed by David Crosby, with a personalized thanks to the OB/GYN.

"You're not going to tell me why," he said.

"No," said Sally.

Dr. Naeby flipped through her chart and looked up. "You never called us back about the blood test."

Sally now remembered receiving a message from him last week about needing to draw more blood for some routine tests. "I was out of town," she said.

The doctor pushed a button on the intercom. "Diana? Could you get room four ready? And tell Marcella we're going to need some blood." Dr. Naeby paused at a flimsy ultrasound of Sally's fetus that was stapled to her chart. He appeared lost in thought for a moment, then shook his head wistfully and looked up. "Okay." He hit his hands on the desk. "See Marcella first and I'll meet you in room four."

Compared to her other two, this abortion was pure class. Dr. Naeby, Diana, Marcella, they all struck the perfect tone, not too solemn, not too cheery. Basketball was discussed as Sally got the IV of Valium, and the whole thing was over before she knew it had started.

"Stay as long as you like," Diana said, removing the IV. "We don't need the room. You have someone to drive you home?"

"Yes." It was easier to lie.

"Here are some pads and some pills," Diana said. Sally didn't bother looking. "These are to help your uterus contract. And some painkillers for cramping. Give us a call if the bleeding doesn't stop by tomorrow."

"Thanks." The door opened and shut. Sally lay there, comfy-cozy, drifting in and out. She thought it was funny when people talked about abortions as though they were so tragic. If only she could have one every day. Nothing could compare to the satisfaction of knowing a potentially ruinous situation had been averted.

On the wall was a photograph of a cheetah or a leopard, peering out over some green hills. It must have been a cheetah. Cheetahs were the ones that looked as if they were crying black tears. The picture was signed in the corner, Charles Naeby. Dr. Naeby probably took it when he was on safari with his family. Sally loved Dr. Naeby.

She would tell Jeremy that she had lost the baby due to diabetic complications. She could fly to Houston in time for tonight's game. Wait—what was she thinking?—the secret was out—there was something wrong with Jeremy. She had no choice but to divorce him. A good lawyer could prove that Sally was the only reason he had gotten the ESPN job, which would entitle her to half of his contract. But that might get canceled once everybody found out he had…whatever that thing was he had. All she'd need was enough for her apartment—no—she had given up the apartment, and somebody else was set to move in on the first. And now she couldn't get a new one because she'd declared bankruptcy. Plus, she'd given up all her classes and privates, so her career was dead. And she'd canceled her health insurance through David. The wedding presents! The presents must be worth thirty grand. She could return them for cash—no, probably not; most were engraved. God, did that mean she had to stay with Jeremy? How could she not have seen what was wrong with him? All the signs had been there on the very first night! Jeremy was so literal minded. He didn't drive. He didn't look her in the eye. He wore earplugs. She always knew there was something a little *off* about him, but she was happy to live with it. Now that it had a name, now that it was all over the internet, now that Nora Ross was having parties celebrating it—Sally sat up.

Weird hospital-issued maxi pads the size of bricks were stacked on the counter. She looked down. They had put one of those abortion garter belt things on her. Sally's thighs were smeared with blood. Dr. Naeby and the nurses had just left her there, bottomless. The paper sheath she wore from the waist up had shadows of blood on it, too. She ripped it off. Here she was again. It didn't matter what movie star was in the next room, an abortion was an abortion. A jumbo maxi pad was a jumbo maxi pad.

The first abortion Sally had, she was fifteen years old. Def Leppard had just played the first of four sold-out shows at McNichols arena. After flirting with Joe Elliott, the lead singer, at the Brown Palace bar, Sally went upstairs with him to his room. He was practically passed out on the bed, wearing the same ripped jeans and Mott the Hoople T-shirt from the show. She was a virgin and didn't have a clue how to proceed when he unzipped his tight pants and peeled them down to his knees. He never took his eyes off the *Top 10 Video Countdown* on MTV. Sally locked her mouth around his uncircumcised thingy—it was the first and last time she'd seen one of those!—and blew, while he yelled instructions in a stupid Eliza Doolittle accent. "Suck! Slower. Softer. Watch your teeth. Suck. Deeper." *Deeper?* Sally was already worried she might gag. Still, he kept barking at her, "Deeper, deeper." Sally knew there were a dozen girls at the bar who would take her place in a second. So she slowed down, sucked, shielded her teeth with her lips, and pushed her mouth down as far as she could without gagging. "I'll do it myself." He pushed her out of the way and grabbed his pecker. The VJ had just announced the most requested video of the day, "Pour Some Sugar on Me" by Def Leppard. "It's okay!" Sally said. "I'll do it!" She stuck his dick as far down her throat as she could, and something came up. She couldn't stop herself. She vomited on his stomach. Not too much, though. "What was all that?" He rose to his elbows. "Nothing!" Sally pushed him back and frantically licked up her vomit. He shoved her aside and passed out. The next day, the roadies made a big deal out of giving her a special laminated pass with her picture on it. She proudly flashed it to all the yellow jackets at that night's show. At the after party, David marched over and ripped off her lanyard. "Give me that thing," he said. The whole party went silent. "You fucking assholes," David shouted to the crew members. "She's just a child!" He spiked the pass onto the concrete floor and stormed out. Sally picked it up. Above her picture, it didn't say DEF LEPPARD. In the same triangular letters as their logo, it said BAR FEEDER. Sally didn't see anything wrong with being called that. "Bar feeder," she said to herself. Then, the kick in the stomach: it *read* "Bar Feeder." But spoken, it *sounded like* "Barf Eater." The roadies burst into laughter. The only one who took pity on her was the one-armed drummer. An hour later, she lost her virginity to him and got pregnant. That's how pathetic her one attempt as a groupie had been; she couldn't even fuck somebody with two arms.

Her second abortion had been paid for by the travel agent who didn't leave his wife for her. He drove Sally to and from some clinic by the airport and never spoke to her again.

Tears flowed down Sally's cheeks and tickled the back of her neck. *Drip, drop.* They landed on the paper covering the exam table.

Throughout her childhood, all the other kids were frightened of her. She was the weirdo who couldn't eat sweets and had to go to the nurse's office to test her blood sugar. The isolation she felt only made her try harder, which only further repelled her class-mates. The one person who understood her isolation was David, but he left home. So Sally marshaled her fear into ballet. The better she got, the more the teachers yelled at her, the bigger her smile. But then "3 mm X 3 mm" of her toe was taken. All she had to show for her years of grueling practice was the lying smile on her face. When she just wanted to tell someone, "I'm scared."

Nobody could understand how much she hurt, how hard she tried, for how little she was asking. She'd have been happy to stay in the *corps de ballet* at a regional company. It would have been fine to marry a guy who worked in a boot shop. She knew her place.

Now, fresh from abortion number three, she had nowhere to go. "I'm scared," she whimpered.

She had always ached for a baby, just so she could hold it and say, "I know you're scared. I'm scared, too." And now that baby was dead in the wastebasket. Why had she run out and had another abortion? From now on, she'd be a girl who had gotten three abortions. Prostitutes and sluts had three abortions, not nice girls. Maybe this was her last chance to have a baby and she'd just murdered it. Maybe it wasn't even a boy, and chances were there was nothing wrong with it. What if she'd murdered her daughter for no reason? God, she had to check to make sure it wasn't a little ballerina—Sally jumped off the table and her legs gave out. She crawled to the trash can and smashed the pedal with her hand. It was full of white shiny paper. She reached in and touched something small, hard, and slimy—it stuck to her hand.

"Aaaah!" Sally shook her hand wildly. It was just a piece of gum, which went flying. "I'm scared," she sobbed. "Now do you believe me?"

"She's right in here." The nurse's voice grew louder from the hallway.

"Who?" said another voice.

The door swung open.

"Violet?" Sally said.

"Sally?" said Violet.

"Oh shit." Diana, the nurse, turned white and ran to help Sally to her feet. "Are you okay?"

"I'm fine, I'm fine."

"I'm sorry," said Diana. "I assumed she was here to take you home."

"No," said Violet, who had a cotton ball and white tape on the inside of her elbow.

"I'm so sorry," said Diana. "This has never happened. I mean, I just assumed, since you're family—"

"It's okay," Violet told her. "It's okay." Diana left. Violet stepped into the room and closed the door. "Are you okay?" she asked Sally.

"I'm fine. I'm great, really. I had no choice but to get a little abortion." Sally grabbed her jeans and stepped into them. "Because of my diabetes."

"I'm sorry—I—" Violet stammered. "I didn't know. Here, let me help you."

"I can manage." Sally slipped her shirt over her head.

"Gestational diabetes?" Violet asked. "I thought they tested for that later."

"Regular diabetes. *My* diabetes."

"You're diabetic? Since when?"

"Since I was three. Type one."

"Jesus Christ," said Violet. "I had no idea. David never told me."

"He didn't?"

"I'm sorry. I don't want to make it about me. But I'm just kind of reeling here." Violet gulped. "Let me drive you home."

"I'm fine." Sally grabbed the handful of pads.

"Where's Jeremy?" asked Violet.

"He's in Houston. He knows, and all. I'm just going home. I'll be fine." The stupid pads wouldn't fit in her purse. No matter how hard she crammed them, they fell to the floor.

"Here." Violet took Sally's purse. "I'm going to drive you to our house. You can spend the night there."

"I don't want David to know," Sally said.

"He won't."

They walked down the hall to Diana's desk. "I am so sorry, you guys," she said. "Nothing like that has ever happened before."

"Don't worry about it," said Violet. "How are we paying for this?"

"I'll send a bill to the Crescent Heights address," said Diana, off Sally's chart.

Before Sally could protest, Violet handed Diana a black American Express card. "How about we put it on this?"

VIOLET drove up the canyon, Sally curled in the passenger seat, her back to Violet. Violet reached for the Tupperware container containing David's lunch, pulled off the top, and offered it to Sally. "If you're hungry, I made them."

Sally took it.

"And for the tenth time, I can't believe David never told me you were diabetic." Then it struck her. "Oh, my God. I sent you *chocolates* on your birthday!"

"I thought that was pretty insensitive." Sally bit into one of the fritters. "You made these?"

"Chard and quinoa. They're better when they're hot."

Sally rolled onto her back and wolfed down another one. Violet felt Sally studying her face. Sally finally said, "I didn't have an abortion because I was diabetic. I had an abortion because I found out there's something wrong with Jeremy. It's something called—I don't even know how to pronounce it—it's a syndrome or something."

"Asperger's?"

"You knew?" Sally looked stricken.

"Well, no. But now that you mention it, I'm not surprised."

"I'm the only one who didn't know he was retarded?"

"He's not retarded!" Violet couldn't help but laugh. "It's a spectrum disorder. Our accountant definitely has it. People speculate that Bill Gates has it, and Albert Einstein probably did, too. Seriously, it's no big deal." Sally stared out the window. Violet continued, "Every woman in America at some point must think her husband has it. You think I never wanted to throw myself off a cliff because David is so unemotional? I mean, not telling his own wife that his sister is diabetic. What is that?"

"Everyone knew but me!" Sally dropped the Tupperware.

"Nobody *knows*," Violet said. "And if they did, they wouldn't care. I think it was Oscar Wilde who said, You wouldn't care about what other people thought about you if you realized how seldom they actually did."

There was silence. Then Sally said, "Why did you tell Jeremy to call off our wedding?"

For a moment, Violet was speechless. "I just happened upon him. There was no treachery on my part. He said you scared him."

"That's the best you can do?" Sally said.

Sally had been painfully honest with Violet. Now it was Violet's turn. "I never really liked you," she said.

"I never really liked you, either," Sally shot back.

"Thank you!" Violet laughed. "That makes me feel so much better. From the first day I met you, I could tell something was off. And I thought I was crazy. I mean, this whole time, I thought it was me."

"It *was* you," said Sally. "I didn't like you. I thought you were a snob masquerading as a nice person."

Violet was impressed. "I've never heard it put that way before." She drove past a eucalyptus grove on Mulholland. "When I was a little girl," she said, "I remember driving by this exact spot with my father. He was shit-faced as usual, and he told me, If there's one thing I know how to do, it's drive these canyon roads drunk."

Sally forced a smile.

"From now on," Violet said, "it will always be the spot where you said, I never really liked you."

CHAPTER TWELVE

KARA DROPPED HER PURSE ON HER DESK WHEN THE PHONE RANG. SHE WOULD have let it go to voice mail, but it was five after ten, and it might be David calling in for messages. She grabbed the phone, making sure she didn't sound out of breath. "David Parry's office."

"Hi, is David there? It's Geddy Lee."

Geddy Lee. The name sounded familiar, but Kara couldn't place it. "He's not in yet. May I take a message?"

"I'm calling to razz him about my bass showing up on eBay. Tell him if he's really that cheap, I'll give his wife the money."

Kara didn't have a pen and her computer was asleep. There was no way she would remember what this guy had just said. "Do you want me to try him at home?" she asked, then gasped. David never wanted people put through to his house. "Or," she said, "maybe he's in his car, but I can't reach him because it's hard to get reception in the canyons." Kara cringed at how lame that just sounded.

"Just give him the message when he gets in."

"He's usually in by now," she said. "But he was at Coachella for a sound check yesterday and probably got back late to the—" Oh God! Kara had almost told this Geddy guy that David was living at the Beverly Hills Hotel! Even Kara wasn't supposed to know. "I'll give him the message," she said.

"He knows my numbers."

Now Kara was back at square one. Who was Geddy Lee? How did you spell Geddy Lee? And what was the message? Something about eBay and a bass. She *so* didn't want to get fired for this.

"KNOCK, knock."

Sally roused from an oozy semi-slumber and found herself back in the bridal suite.

"I'm sorry if I woke you." Violet entered with a breakfast tray. "Egg white omelet with low-fat Jarlsberg, sautéed mushrooms, and ten blueberries. Everything low in sugar for my diabetic sister-in-law."

"Yeah, thanks." Sally sat up. On the tray were a vase of flowers and some gossip magazines.

"Your medicine is in the bathroom. Your mail is in the kitchen, and your clothes are there." Two of Sally's velour sweat suits were folded on a chair, along with her washed and ironed clothes from yesterday. Sally vaguely remembered having changed into Violet's silk pajamas and giving her keys to her apartment.

"I really appreciate it," Sally said. "I'll be out of here this morning."

"Don't even think about it. You're staying the night."

Dot, the shiny-eyed force of nature, hurtled in. Nothing had ever gone wrong for this quizzical girl in the crooked pigtails.

"Hi, Dot." Sally tried not to smile too big.

Last month, when she was planning the wedding, Sally had made an extra effort to connect with her niece. Dot had hidden her face in her hands and told Violet, Mommy, tell the lady to stop smiling at me.

"You read me a book?" Dot handed Sally a stiff copy of *Goodnight Moon*.

"What," Violet said, off of Sally's look. "You don't like *Goodnight Moon*?"

"It was a little weird," Sally admitted.

"Goodnight nobody. Don't you love that? It's so random." Violet turned to Dot. "I'll read it to you later, sweetheart."

"Uppy, uppy." Dot raised her arms. Violet scooped her up.

"Well, we're off. I have errands and a playdate, then the realtor wants to meet me at that land we're not going to buy. Be here when I get back."

"I will." Sally watched Violet leave and couldn't resist. "Violet, those cargo pants…"

"I know, I know. They make my ass look gigantic, but I trekked to Everest Base Camp in them a million years ago and I have a sentimental attachment."

"Wear them around here if you have to," Sally said, "but get some low-rise jeans to wear in public."

"I'm starting a new job next week. We can go to Barney's and blow my paycheck before I get it. You can be my stylist." Violet left.

Sally picked up a magazine. It was brand-new and didn't have an address label on it. Neither did the other magazines. Violet must have picked them up especially for Sally. Maybe Sally had it backward: Violet was a nice person masquerading as a snob.

Sally ate her breakfast and took a shower. She carried her tray to the kitchen and tripped on something. An overstuffed laundry bag from the Beverly Hills Hotel had appeared in the hallway.

"Sally." David stood at the kitchen counter. Violet had said he was out of town. "Are you feeling better? Violet left a note."

"Hi! Yeah, I'm fine. I hope it's all right that I spent the night."

"I have to talk to you about something."

Sally opened the dishwasher. "Sure, what?"

"I was looking through the mail, and before I realized it was *your* mail, I saw this." Swinging between his thumb and index finger was her bankruptcy letter. "You declared bankruptcy?"

"Oh, my God—" Sally dropped a glass in the sink.

"The creditors listed are credit card companies," David said. "What do I need to do?"

"Nothing. It's over. The bankruptcy went through. Isn't that what the letter says?"

"How were you able to file for Chapter Seven? After the Bankruptcy Act a couple of years ago, didn't they make that more difficult?"

"I get paid in cash, so most of my income didn't show."

David considered this and nodded. "Remember that correspondence course I took to get my accounting degree?"

"Yeah."

"Here's what it taught me. Those who understand compound interest earn it; those who don't, pay it. Got that?"

"Yes."

"Next time, come to me, will you?"

"There won't be a next time," she said.

David handed her the discharge letter. "On another unpleasant topic: my wife called me last night, none too pleased that I never told her about your diabetes."

"Oh."

"You made me promise not to tell anyone, right?"

"Right." She had, but that was way back in high school.

"Could you clarify that fact for Violet next time you see her?"

"I'm sorry," said Sally. "I just assumed, because you were married, it would come up."

"A promise is a promise, unless I'm instructed otherwise."

"Well, what do you tell her when the bills come?" Sally asked.

"What bills?"

"My doctors' bills."

"I'm paying your doctors' bills?" David's head jerked back ever so slightly. She'd forgotten he did that.

"And my insurance."

"That's news to me."

"Wait," Sally said. "You didn't know?"

"I believe you," said David. "Anyone who screws in a lightbulb around here ends up on my insurance."

The phone rang. David answered it. Sally held herself up, both hands on the counter. Her insides stung as if she'd just been eviscerated.

David handed her the phone. "Dr. Naeby, for you."

"Oh," said Sally.

"Okay. I'm going to the office. See you later." David left. She waited for the door to shut, then took the call.

"Hi, Sally," said Dr. Naeby. "How are you this morning?"

"Fine."

"No cramping or excessive bleeding?"

"No, everything's fine."

"That's the good news." Dr. Naeby changed gears. "Now, about your blood test. Something of concern showed up in the first one, and that's why I wanted to run another...."

KARA stood proudly before David. Not only had she pieced together Geddy Lee's message, but she'd also found the eBay auction and e-mailed David the link. David seemed unusually interested in it and had asked her to get Geddy Lee on the phone. David had just hung up and called Kara in.

"The bass?" he said.

"Yes?" Kara had pen in hand, ready to take notes.

"Pay for it with cash. I want that bass, the seller's name, and where he lives on my desk before lunch."

It took Kara a second to realize she was committing the number one cardinal sin of an assistant: standing there with the deer-in-headlights look. She had to say something, but all that came out was "Muawh—"

"Get it done," David said.

"Of course." Kara calmly walked down the hall to the office of the guy who did the bookings. "Hi, would you mind covering David's phones?" she asked his secretary.

"Sure," said the older Hillary, who had no choice. As David's assistant, Kara outranked her.

Kara returned to her computer and found the auction. There was an option that let you "Buy It Now." Which was a whopping $10,000. The actual auction had only reached $1,200 and it closed at five. It seemed stupid to pay $10,000 now, when David could probably buy the bass in a few hours for much less. Kara rose from her chair to point this out, then sat back down. It wasn't her job to second-guess David. She bought the bass, contacted the seller, and got his address. He wanted to know more about her, but she said nothing. Any information was too much information.

The messenger from the bank arrived with the cash, and Kara walked him into David's office. David tore open the plastic envelope, counted the money, and signed for it.

"I have the address and I'll leave now to get the bass," Kara said.

"Where is it?" he asked.

"Really close: 8907 Sunset Boulevard."

David's head shot back. "That's on the strip, right?"

"A place called Mauricio's Boot Shop."

David blinked. And blinked again. "Mauricio's?"

"Yeah."

David stood up. "I'll get it myself." He started out. The brick of hundreds was still on his desk.

"Don't forget the money!" said Kara.

"Go to the bank and deposit it back into the account."

"Of course," said Kara.

Now she's fucking Kurt Pombo! David fishtailed onto Sunset Boulevard. All he could figure was that Violet had moved on to Kurt Pombo and was funneling him rock memorabilia to sell on eBay. Had the great Violet Grace Parry truly stooped this low? It was impossible to fathom. David double-parked outside Mauricio's and left the front door of his Bentley open. He flew into the boot shop. If he had a baseball bat he would have been wielding it.

The joint was empty. But not for long. Kurt entered from the back room. "Hey, David," he said with a yip. "What's up, bro?"

"So that's how you wanna play it?" It must have come out pretty fucking menacing, because Kurt fled into the back like the little bitch he was. "You want to fuck with me?" David charged him. Kurt had nowhere to run in the tiny workroom. He cowered in the corner. David grabbed him by the Hawaiian shirt and threw him against the wall.

"I'm sorry," Kurt yowled. He slid to the floor. "I'll give it back. It's right there—"

"I don't give a fuck about the bass." David kicked Kurt in the gut. After two lonely months of Saint David, kicking the shit out of a wannabe lowlife sure hit the spot. "I'm here because of my *wife,* you asshole. But I don't want her back, either. Whatever the fuck you two are doing together, she's all yours." He kicked him again.

"I swear—I didn't—I swear. I'm not the one fucking your wife."

David stopped.

"I just stole that shit from the car." Kurt stood up. "I took the shit she was about to give to that other dude—the guy in the Stones cover band."

David cocked his head and walked himself through the logic of this new information.

"I promise you, man," Kurt said, "I never touched your wife. Take the bass. And the phone and the golf clubs. It's all there. And your kid's cough syrup."

On the cobbler's bench, among cowboy boots in various stages of finish, sat Dot's eczema medicine. David had to smile. He extended his hand to Kurt, who recoiled. David grabbed his daughter's medicine and left.

VIOLET sat in her car at the bottom of George Harrison's former drive-way, flipping through the escrow papers. Gwen had insisted on meeting at the property before Violet made any "rash decisions." Violet had finally acquiesced. She felt a strange tenderness toward this older divorcée, her very own Ghost of Christmas Future. Violet then noticed that David had forgotten to sign the middle of page four.

"Shit," she said.

"Shit," said Dot.

"No, darling, we don't say shit."

"Mama? Out. Out."

"We can't get out." Violet turned on the stereo.

> *Bobby...Bobby...Bobby...Bobby...Bo-bo-bo-bo-bo-bo-bo-bo-*
> *Bobeeeee.*

Violet checked the rearview mirror. Dot was mesmerized, as always, by the opening number from *Company*.

> *Bobby, baby. Bobby, Bubby. Robby. Robert, darling. Robbo.*
> *Bobby, baby. Bobby, Bubby.*

Dot whispered along, keeping up as best she could. Violet smiled. It was never too early to indoctrinate Dot into the glories of Stephen Sondheim. Dot, named after the artist's muse from *Sunday in the Park with George*. David was dismissive of Sondheim, saying, He can't write songs. Violet fervently disagreed. She didn't care if other children grew up to the Wiggles or Dan Zanes. Hers would adore Sondheim. Violet had declared it that joyous day of the first ultrasound. David conceded her Sondheim if she'd give him the Mets. They shook on it in front of Dr. Naeby, who raised his brow and went about his business.

There was a knock on the window. "Ooh, you brought the munchkin!"

"Gwen, hi." Violet turned down the volume.

"I have my walking shoes on!" Gwen lifted a hiking boot to the window. Perhaps she'd been a dancer once.

"I really can't," started Violet. "I have the baby. You know how enthusiastic we were, but the geology report leaves us no choice but to cancel. You understand."

"Oh." Gwen's face came crashing down.

"Mommy?" said Dot.

"Yes, sweetie?"

"Shit."

"I'm ignoring that," Violet informed Gwen. "Thanks for everything, but our decision is made. Here are the papers. David didn't sign page four, but he signed everywhere else—"

Gwen swung her hands up, as if avoiding being served. "Nope. Can't accept those. No point in trying. Papers gotta be signed. No can do."

It was impossible to hate Gwen. Violet would send her a check, or a client, even see if there was a one-line part for her in the new TV show.

"I understand," Violet said. "I'll fax them to your office by five." Gwen pivoted, climbed into her car, and drove off.

"Out!" said Dot. "Mommy, want out!"

Dot had been a trouper all day, plus it would be good to burn off energy before the nap. "Just for five minutes."

A green car crunched up the dirt road and stopped. "Green car," said Dot.

"Yes," Violet said. "That's a green car."

"What dat man's name?" asked Dot.

"I don't know," Violet said. "Now run around and then we're going to go home and take a nap."

A door slammed. The green car's trunk was open. Behind it was that guy Sally used to date, with the hair and the Hawaiian shirts.

Violet's instinct was to protect Dot. "Honey, don't go far."

Then, this guy—Kurt, she thought—loaded his arms with Geddy Lee's bass, the set of Callaway golf clubs, and the bag from the Apple store. He walked over and dumped them at Violet's feet.

"Take them," he said. "Get them out of my life. I don't need the karma." He turned around.

"Where did you get these?"

"I took them out of your car."

"Oh." Violet said. "Wait—" She glanced at Dot, who was climbing the nearby hill. It was rocky and steep, but thanks to RIE, Dot had good balance. Violet turned to Kurt. "How did you know I was here?"

"I went to your house and Sally told me. I'm sorry. I'm a fucking moron. If suffering serves as a springboard to expand your life state, then I'm going to have the biggest life state in the universe." His Hawaiian shirt was torn, his hand bandaged, and one eye was starting to swell.

"What happened?" she asked.

"Ask your fucking husband."

"Oh God." Violet's stomach roiled.

Dot was squatting, completely absorbed in some discarded

strawberry baskets. "Bobby baby, Bobby bubby," she sang to herself as she filled a basket with rocks.

"He thought I was fucking you or something," said Kurt.

"Why would he think that?"

"Don't ask me. What goes on between you and your husband is your business. My only business is to chant until I transform my destructive tendencies from poison into medicine. I'm like Pigpen with a black cloud of bad karma following me everywhere."

"Hang on a second." Violet frantically tried to calculate the bits of information. "How did you even know this stuff was in my car?"

"I overheard you telling the guy you were fucking."

"Is that what you told David?!"

"I really don't remember. I was too busy trying not to get my face kicked in." He turned to leave.

"No—you can't go—tell me." She grabbed both of his arms. "What did you hear? What did you tell David—"

"I told him I'm not the guy you were fucking."

"What?!" Violet's whole body throbbed. "What did he say? What did you tell him—"

A shriek echoed across the canyon. It was Dot. No *Mommy,* no *Mama,* just one cry, then silence. It was what Violet had always feared the most, silence.

"Dot!" she screamed. Her daughter had vanished from the hill. Blades of grass and fragile California poppies swayed in the breeze. It was silent and idyllic, like the day-after scenes of Chernobyl.

"Shit," Kurt said. "She was right here. Where did she go?"

"Dot! Baby! Say something!" Violet fought her way up the hill. "Dot! Mommy's here. Dot! Where are you?!" Violet screamed to Kurt, who stood at the bottom of the hill, "Help me! Maybe she's down on the street. Or in a house. Knock on the doors. Oh God—"

Violet thought she might vomit: the reservoir. "No, no." She scrambled to the top of the rise.

Twenty feet below, splayed among the rocks, was the still body of little Dot, facedown, pigtails askew, wearing her beloved Spider-Man T-shirt and the frilly pants Violet had sewn for her just last week.

JEREMY entered his Sherman Oaks apartment. "Sally?" It had been twenty-nine hours since she had told him to get out. She never arrived in Houston, as he figured she would. She hadn't called once.

He removed the pad of graph paper he kept in his jacket. After the wedding, Jeremy had begun to graph Sally's moods. He entered the intensities and frequencies onto a basic Cartesian graph. He had intended, through Fourier analysis, to break the master waves into component waves and extend the graph out to predict Sally's mood swings. But he could only realistically predict sixty-three percent. Although that may have been an impressive number for sports handicapping, it didn't help when applied to the person you were married to. He then came up with the idea of inputting his own actions into the sine-cosine equation in an attempt to see if he was indeed responsible for his wife's terrifying moods. She always said they were *his* fault, for being so selfish. But what was he so selfish about? Wanting to go to a restaurant he liked? Wanting to walk instead of drive? Wanting to read the papers every morning in silence? Why wouldn't *she* be considered equally as selfish for wanting to go to the restaurants *she* liked? Or wanting to drive everywhere? Or blathering on about some television show while he was trying to read the paper? How did that make *him* selfish and not her?

Jeremy had tried to make this point many times, but how did you prove to someone that you felt as much as they did? All the feelings Sally was always accusing him of not feeling—love, anger, fear—he *felt* them. He just didn't feel the need to talk about them. That was a feeling, too, not feeling like talking about your feelings. If all feelings were so great, why didn't that one count? Besides, whenever he did try to talk about his feelings, she told him he was stupid to feel what he was feeling. In Jeremy's opinion, the things *Sally* felt were stupid. Therefore, they should just cancel each other out.

But Jeremy had taken Sally as his wife. All he could do now was try to figure her out. Coin flipping, formulas, first-order discrete differential equations, propositions: all had proven to be dead ends. But Jeremy had noticed that, like his favorite number, the imaginary number i, Sally's moods were cyclical. So he decided to graph them out.

Even though the graphs were ultimately of no use, entering data points and curve-fitting served to calm him. Over the last couple of days, he had recognized that Sally was nearing an instantaneous inflection point and he had braced himself for an outburst. But yesterday's tirade was a true anomaly. He tried to input it, but the curve had gone parabolic!

He looked through the mail. Among the rectangles was a square. A pamphlet. He flipped it open and read:

Repetitive

Clumsy

Literal Minded

Socially Inept

Obsessive

On the last page, it said, "To learn more about Asperger's syndrome, please call Nora Ross at…"

Jeremy picked up the phone and dialed the number.

VIOLET took a deep breath, then walked steadily toward the Ultra office, Dot on her hip. It was imperative that David sign the escrow papers in the next fifteen minutes, or they'd lose their $50,000 deposit. If pressed, Violet could attribute her shakiness to such a tight deadline. Before she opened the door, she ran through the story one last time.

I was meeting Gwen Gold at the George Harrison property when I discovered you forgot to sign page four. Dot wanted to chase butterflies. I let her, never being more than two steps away. All of a sudden, the ground gave way. She must have stepped into a gopher hole. The geology report talked about them, remember? Next thing I knew, Dot rolled down the hill. I was right there. There was a little blood, but she hardly cried. On my way over, I stopped by Dr. Naeby's, just in case. He thought Dot needed a couple of stitches and offered to do it there. I tried calling you, but Kara said you couldn't be disturbed.

It was a good story. The only collateral damage would be to Kara. David would demand to know why she hadn't put Violet through when his daughter was getting stitches. Kara would claim no such thing had happened. Ultimately, it would come down to Violet's word against the assistant's. Kara was young; she'd find another job.

Violet entered the office.

"Mommy, down," said a squirmy Dot. "Down, Mommy."

"In a second, sweetie."

Even though Dot's CAT scan and neurological had been normal, the ER doctor had said it was imperative for Violet to monitor her for drowsiness, headache, balance issues, or vomiting. Any of these symptoms could indicate a hematoma and would require immediate surgery.

David was behind glass at his desk, his back to them.

Kara was at hers, taping receipts to a sheet of paper. "Mrs. Parry, hi!" she said. "Finally, I get to meet Miss Dot. Hi there!" She gave Dot's hand a squeeze. "Aren't you beautiful? And isn't that the cutest hat ever?"

"Mommy, what's dat?" asked Dot with an impish smile. She pointed to a can of Coke on Kara's desk.

"What do you think it is?" Violet said.

"*Coca-Cola*," said Dot, in an unmistakable Spanish accent. "Want dat."

"Just this once." Violet put Dot down. Kara punched something into her computer and led Dot toward the kitchen. David switched to a wireless headset and walked over. Violet took a deep breath: this was it.

When Violet had reached the bottom of the hill, Dot was whimpering. Violet scooped her up. Dot's mouth was full of blood; it flowed down her chin and onto Violet. Dot looked at her mother, indignant, as if to say, How dare you allow such a thing to happen to me? Violet wept with relief and cradled Dot's head. Instantly, Violet's hand became soaked. Blood flowed from a gash behind Dot's ear. Violet pressed her fingers against the cut and ran to the Mercedes. On the drive down to UCLA, Violet had phoned their neighbor, the head of surgery there. By the time mother and daughter arrived at the emergency room, a team was mobilized and waiting on the curb. It reminded Violet of when she would arrive early for a party and there were too many valets.

David muted his headset and stuck his head out of the office. "What's up?" he asked.

"I need you to sign page four in the next fifteen minutes and fax it back." Violet handed him the papers.

"I'll be right there." He shut the door. Violet welcomed the chance to review her story one last time.

Dot tripped in a gopher hole. She didn't cry. Only upon Dr. Naeby's insistence did I let her get a couple of stitches. I tried to call, but Kara wouldn't put me through. It was over before Dot even knew what happened.

Dot and Kara returned, Dot holding a can of Coke with both hands. Her balance, vision, and mental acuity all appeared perfect.

"Dot," Kara said, "do you want to see pictures of my nephew? His name is Lucas. He was only four pounds when he was born, teeny tiny." The screen saver on the assistant's computer was of a curled newborn covered with monitoring devices. "I'm so excited," Kara told Violet. "I get to go to Coachella this weekend. David said he'd let me stand on the stage for Hanging with Yoko. I'm going to totally wave to all my friends."

"Come here, baby doll." Violet adjusted Dot's cashmere cap so it hid the inch-long tape protecting her stitches.

Kara said, "And next week is going to be crazy with drummer auditions."

Violet thought of something. Coachella was this weekend, so David would probably spend at least two nights there. And with Yoko drummer auditions all week, his nights would be tied up. There was a good chance he wouldn't be dropping by the house at all. Dot's stitches were coming out in five days. If Violet could keep David from Dot, he might never know about the stitches. Violet's new story was:

Dot fell into a gopher hole while we were walking around the George Harrison property and—

Actually, there was no reason to tell David any of it!

In the UCLA parking garage, Violet had changed into some yoga clothes she always kept in the trunk. She didn't have clean clothes for Dot, so she had called Daniel at Hermès. Fifteen minutes later, he was standing on the curb with a six-hundred-dollar (!) ensemble for Dot. And hats for Violet, of course. Other than the tiny stitches that were hidden by the Hermès knit cap, Dot betrayed no evidence of the fall. David always went out of his way to avoid talking to the neighbors, so he wouldn't find out about the accident from the surgeon. And if Violet brought cash to UCLA, she could pay the bill and there'd be no paper trail!

David was now off the phone.

One last time, Violet ran through the story—there was no story! And sweet Kara would be spared! If David confronted Violet about the stuff Kurt stole, she would say she'd gotten it for the RIE silent auction and figured a valet at the Beverly Hills Hotel had stolen it.

David opened his office door and handed Kara the papers. "Fax these immediately and get a time-stamped confirmation they were received. Thanks."

Dot galloped into David's office and jumped up and down upon seeing all the pictures of her. "Dot!" she exclaimed. Dot's favorite subject was Dot. She was like a miniature rapper, always referring to herself in the third person.

"I have lots of pictures of my girls here," David said.

"Daddy?" Dot held up a framed picture. "*Dat* man eating nuts?"

"No, that's Dada."

"*Dat* man eating nuts," Dot insisted.

David studied the picture, then laughed. "How about that?" It was the photograph of them at Lake Tahoe, the one where Violet looked so incomprehensibly happy.

They had flown up to ski and had watched the Super Bowl while playing Texas Hold 'Em at a casino. Violet was up two grand at one point, then gave it all back and more. David won a monster pot early and cashed out. Violet's style was to raise and bluff, even when she knew she'd been beat. At halftime, when her stack had started to dwindle, David had come by and whispered, "Learn the thrill of a smart lay-down."

"Do you see that?" David asked Violet. "In the corner. See that man eating a Mr. Goodbar?" He turned to Dot. "You're just a little smartie, aren't you?" David swept up his daughter and emitted a roar of love. "God, I love this little girl. I'm never going to let anything bad happen to you."

Back in the hospital examining room, Violet had held her bloody daughter. Their neighbor Dr. Driscoll entered. A highly decorated Vietnam vet, the surgeon commanded fear from the orderlies. "Thank you so much for coming, Dr. Driscoll," she said. "I really appreciate it." "What's going on?" he asked. "It's right above her ear. A cut." Dot's hair obscured the injury. Violet lifted it, but the blood had dried, sticking strands of hair to the wound. "Owww!" howled Dot. The surgeon shot a withering look at the nurse and growled, "Will someone get me a sponge with some warm water?" The nurse did, and Violet pressed it against Dot's head. "How did it happen?" asked Dr. Driscoll. "We were walking on a hill and she fell—I was right there." "With kids," the surgeon said, "the worst ones happen when you're right there. Jonah fell off the changing table when he was three months. I swear, I had my hand on him!" He smiled at the recollection, then looked at the cut and frowned. "I'm going to have to sew this shut." Violet trembled as the nurse prepped the forceps, needle, and syringe. "Relax, Mom," laughed the doctor. "I'll have her looking like she went to a Beverly Hills plastic surgeon." The nurse popped her head into the bustling hallway. "I'm going to need all hands," she called. "We've got a baby." It required four nurses, as well as Violet, to hold Dot down for the lidocaine shot and the stitches. Violet repeatedly telling her daughter, "It's okay, Dot. Mommy's here." Then whispering: "I'm sorry I didn't want to be with you. I'm sorry you weren't enough." It was the only time during the ordeal Violet had cried. Once the final suture was in, Dot's shrieks abruptly turned into strange high-pitched barks, "Oof! Oof!" Violet panicked that her daughter's brain had been damaged. "What, Dot?" Violet looked desperately into her daughter's eyes. Dot pointed to a wall where a calendar of West Highland terriers hung. "Doggies. Oof! Oof!"

Violet watched Dot now, sitting in her Dada's lap, playing with his headset.

"Mine," Dot said.

"Mine," David teased back.

Dot grabbed the grass bracelet around David's wrist. "Mine," she said.

"Mine," David parroted back.

Dot yanked the bracelet, and it came off in her hand. "Mine!" She squealed with delight.

David looked up at Violet. His eyes, always so sad and incongruous with his temper, finally looked like they belonged on his face.

And Violet knew it was over.

She walked to her husband and daughter, then even closer so that all three touched. God, she loved her little family. And Dot, what a scrapper! She had barely cried when she was born. She came out eyes open, as if not wanting to miss any opportunity to drink in life. David had said if there was a thought bubble over Dot's head those first moments, it would have been, What else ya got? He also said he would entirely trust Violet's instincts when it came to raising Dot. All he asked in return was that Violet keep her safe.

Violet fell to her knees. Dot cupped her mother's cheeks with her small hands. Violet closed her eyes. Dot's impossibly soft skin on her face, it felt like being held by little whispers.

"Ultra?" David was calling her name. "Ultra?"

The door opened. Someone entered.

"Kara?" he said. "Could you take Dot?"

"Of course."

The door closed.

"Violet? Ultra?"

Violet looked up. "David," she said. "I have something to tell you."

"I know you do." His eyes swelled with understanding.

"I'm scared."

"I know you are." He took her hands in his.

"I got really off track, baby."

"I know you did."

And she told David the story.

CHAPTER THIRTEEN

Surprise Me ❊ Thank You ❊ Surprise!

Reyes, T. ❊ Genotype Two

FOR THE PAST SIX MONTHS, SALLY HADN'T MUSTERED THE COURAGE TO RAISE her hand. But last week, out of nowhere, Flicka, the eighties runway model who ran the group, approached Sally and asked if she would "tell her story."

The eight double-spaced pages quivered so in Sally's hands that the words darted about in a game of catch-me-if-you-can. In an attempt to steady them, Sally dug her elbows into her sides. Don't look up, she reminded herself.

"I was born in Denver. And I had a happy childhood. I loved ballet and I had diabetes and I collected horses." Sally stopped, realizing how that sounded. "Not *real* horses. Those plastic Breyer ones. You know what ones I'm talking about." She looked up. The dozen or so people in the room, most of them familiar, appeared baffled and bored. Flicka winced. Sally quickly dropped her eyes, but had lost her spot on the page. She vamped as she tried to find it. "Horses…diabetes…ballet…Everything was great.…I was happy." She turned the paper over. "I'm sorry. I'm new at this."

None of the others had ever written out their speeches, but most of them were seasoned AA people and seemed perfectly at ease with offering up the most humiliating version of themselves to complete strangers.

Sally still couldn't find her place, and now all the pages were out of sequence—she'd have to do without. She quickly fixed her gaze on a smoke alarm above the sea of eyes.

"Like I was saying, I had a happy childhood and everything was great. Even the diabetes wasn't so bad. I don't remember a time when I didn't have it. And if you think like a pancreas, you'll be fine. And I was. I had friends, a job teaching ballet, a husband."

Sally's eyes drifted down. Flicka picked at a thread on her jeans. A man stood at the coffeemaker, and several people waved to him to get them some coffee, too. Most other eyes were on a baby a lady bounced on her lap.

In one breath, she looked at the audience and said the dreaded words, "I'm Sally and I have hep C."

Everyone swung their attention to her. Instantly, their faces were filled with that combination of curiosity and sympathy that had kept Sally coming back to this little church basement in the valley.

"I found out I had the virus six months ago," she said, "during a routine blood test when I was pregnant. I don't even know why they tested for EIA, but I guess they test for everything these days. And I tested positive. And then I retested positive. And then I reretested positive. Because, you see, if it wasn't for my denial, my life would have been crap."

Sally heard a guffaw that was unmistakably Simon's. She stole a peek at the Irish motorcycle mechanic who was covered in tattoos and got infected, like almost everyone here, from sharing needles. He was the only one to make small talk with Sally at that first meeting, the one Violet had dragged her to, the day of her diagnosis. Simon had asked Sally if she was new and given her his phone number, right in front of his hot girlfriend, Petra, who, like Simon, was also HIV positive. Sally hesitated before touching the piece of paper, which only seemed to endear her more to the couple.

"So, I went to a hepatologist and I tested positive for EIA, CIA, and RIBA. Luckily, my viral load was low. My ALT levels were normal." Sally scrunched her shoulders to her ears and spoke in a small voice. "And please don't hate me, you guys, but I'm genotype two."

The vast majority of those infected with hep C were genotype one, which responded poorly to interferon treatment. Only fourteen percent were genotype two, which had an eighty-one percent cure rate.

"Listen to me," Sally said. "I feel guilty because I have the *less* deadly form of hep C!" If there was one thing she had learned from the denizens of this room, it was gallows humor. "I started the twenty-four-week course of Pegasys and ribavirin. I went in last week and..." Sally paused. She hadn't included this part in her written speech, for fear of seeming cruel. "I tested clear."

Her friends applauded. Sally, an expert in detecting mixed emotion, knew their happiness was pure. "Oh, you're just clapping because you want to get rid of me."

"We do!" called a leather-faced granny.

"Not more than me!" said Sally. But really, she rued the thought of saying good-bye to these people, her unlikely tribe. Although she'd never be far. David had given her money to start the Sally Parry Foundation, which would raise money for hep C research by staging marathons. The first event would be a 10K run/walk whose finish line would be in David and Violet's yard.

"I still need to wait another six months before I'm declared virus free," she said. "And even then, it could reappear as another genotype. But I can't help it, I feel lucky." Sally laughed. "Not *too* lucky, mind you. The interferon just about killed me. I couldn't work, which was especially horrible, because I'd just declared bankruptcy—" Sally couldn't believe she'd actually admitted that. "That's right. I'm diabetic, hep C positive, bankrupt, *and* single! Men in the audience, I'm *available!*" Once again, the group laughed.

Sally was still waiting for the complete nervous breakdown to hit her because of the divorce. As Violet had put it, You can't secretly abort your husband's baby because you think he's retarded and expect to stay happily married. Tonight would be hard. Sally would be seeing Jeremy for the first time since they broke up.

Sally sighed. "I know as the speaker I'm supposed to share my difficulties. In my speech, I wrote about how horrible the interferon treatment was, with the vomiting and the fever and my sister-in-law having to hold me still while my brother gave me my insulin shots. And I became severely anemic, so I had to get blood transfusions, which terrified me. I think I ended up in the hospital four or five times. I lost count. But really, that was nothing." She looked up. She'd lost the crowd again. "Okay, don't believe me, but I'm diabetic. I had to have one of my toes amputated." She shook her left flip-flop at the crowd. Several people craned their necks to get a look at her half-toe, the one with the ring on it. "It cost me my career as a ballerina. Next to that, interferon was a breeze!" She paused. "I didn't plan on telling you about the hardest part for me, because it's going to sound so stupid." She looked at the faces. Nobody was going to make her say it. And so she said it. "The hardest part for me"—Sally's voice filled with tears—"is not knowing how I got it." She didn't try to stop the tears. She knew nobody minded. Mascara was a thing of the past, anyway. "Most of you are ex-junkies, so *you* know how you got your hep C. And I'm just telling you, be grateful, okay? I'm serious. I'm sure you're all thinking, Oh, she's diabetic; she probably got infected from a needle. But I promise you, I never shared a needle once. I've never had a blood transfusion. Diabetics never even *hear* about hep C. It's not something that happens."

Sally sensed a presence. Violet had appeared and was standing against the back wall. Today was one of Violet's workdays, an important one, as they were shooting an episode she had written. Sally had begged her not to drive all the way out to the valley just for this, but there she was, beside the sign that read BETWEEN BLACK AND WHITE ARE ALL THE COLORS OF THE RAINBOW. Violet winked.

Sally continued, "I would give anything to find out how this disease happened to me. I know it's stinking thinking to say all I need is this one thing and *then* I can be happy. But I swear, if I could just know how I got infected, then I'd be okay." Nobody in the room seemed to hold this against her. "Can I just say? When I first got here, I really hated you people." Everyone laughed, Violet the loudest. "See! That's why. You all laughed too much. Some of you looked so sick and scary, and I hated you for it. But I really, *really* hated those of you who *didn't* look sick. I thought, How dare you walk around in your nice clothes and try to pass yourselves off as *normal*. Don't you just love how I thought that?" Sally laughed. "I couldn't see what was so funny about a bunch of dying people. Worse, a bunch of dying people who talked about how hep C was some frigging *gift from God*."

Sally smiled at the housepainter who had spoken at that first meeting. "God is the ultimate physician," he had said. "He is open for business twenty-fours hours a day and he still makes house calls." At all the God talk, atheist Violet had twisted so much in her chair she practically tumbled to the floor.

"When I first came to this room," Sally said, "I knew better than everyone. I had all the answers. I woke up every morning with a plan. But now..." Sally started crying again. "I hate you guys—you've turned me into one of *you!* Because I *do* feel so blessed by this disease. And for the first time in my life, I wake up and I don't care what happens. I'm just so happy to be alive. Now I wake up and I say…" She raised her eyes, as if talking to God.

"Surprise me."

VIOLET had been to enough Emmy ceremonies to know her way around the Shrine Auditorium. She hurried along the deserted red carpet, brandishing her jumbo ticket to the security people, who, at this late hour, just talked among themselves.

The banquet room was hushed and dim. Violet looked for her table number atop the wilted centerpieces. These weren't the Primetime Emmys or the Technical Emmys, which had been held over the weekend. These were the Sports Emmys, held on the following Monday night. Regardless, it was a bunch of people in black-tie, unimpressed with the food. A familiar voice from the stage caught Violet's attention.

"Seventeen years ago, our son Michael was diagnosed with autism." It was Dan Marino.

Violet wove through the tables and slipped into the empty seat beside David. He'd saved her the best one, facing the stage. "Nice to see you, Ultra," he whispered. "How was work?"

"It went well, thanks." She kissed his cheek.

"Since 1992," Dan Marino was saying, "the Dan Marino Foundation has raised over twenty million dollars to fund spectrum disorder research."

Violet reached across David and squeezed Sally's hand. In support of Jeremy, David had bought a table. It was brave of Sally to come. She flashed a smile at Violet, then returned her attention to the stage.

"Tonight," said Dan Marino, "to present the First Annual Dan Marino Humanitarian Award, I'd like to introduce a tireless warrior in the fight for spectrum awareness."

A waiter set a plate in front of Violet. "Spinach, potatoes, grilled mushrooms, and Diet Coke," he said, then turned to David with trepidation. David nodded. Everyone else was eating dessert. David must have ordered it especially for Violet. She smiled. She was cared for.

"Please welcome Nora Ross," Dan Marino said, then stepped back.

Violet's heart still broke for Dan Marino's Super Bowl loss to the Forty-Niners, his second year as a pro. "Never made it back to the Super Bowl," Violet whispered to David. "Isn't that so sad?" David shook his head in mock exasperation and gave her a kiss.

Nora looked as disheveled and fabulous as ever. She stood at the podium and spoke extemporaneously. "My husband and I are proud parents of a son who has autism. As Dan alluded to, I spend every waking minute raising money, having meetings, going in front of Congress, and in general, haranguing anyone who crosses my path into helping us find a cure. So you can imagine how pleased I was, six months ago, when I received the most extraordinary phone call. It was Jeremy White, saying he wanted to know more about Asperger's." Nora dropped her jaw and affected an exaggerated look of amazement. "I had met Jeremy a few times. He wasn't one for chitchat, so of course I thought he was on the spectrum. But ask my husband; I think every neuro-typical is on the spectrum. I *did* know Jeremy was a television personality, so I asked him if we could use him as the face of our SOS campaign. He obliged, and we coordinated the media message with his Gap ad."

Jeremy's ad appeared on the screen. In it, he wore khakis and a button-down shirt, and flipped a coin. Across the top were the words YOU WILL BE FAMOUS. It was the same giant Jeremy that graced Sunset Boulevard, Times Square, and every other bus in America.

Nora continued, "I got Jeremy in touch with a fabulous cognitive therapist. A few months later, he started driving for the first time in his life!"

Violet knew how hard this must be hitting Sally. She looked over. Sally's smile was huge, her eyes fixed on Jeremy. She wore the same look as Dot did when she'd spot a woman breastfeeding in the park. Dot would walk over and stand an inch away, enthralled, delighted, not knowing it was socially unacceptable to look so nakedly interested in another person.

"The *New York Times* picked up the story," Nora said, "and it's been the most e-mailed article of the past month. That shows you just how hungry people are to learn about spectrum disorders. Jeremy White's brave 'coming out' has been the tipping point that made people realize a person can be brilliant, successful, *and* still be on the spectrum. Ladies and gentlemen, please welcome this year's recipient of the Dan Marino Humanitarian Award, Jeremy White."

Sally jumped to her feet and applauded. David and Violet did, too.

The day Violet had gone to Sally's apartment to pick up her medicine and clothes, she came across the Hermès belt she had given her for her birthday. To Violet, it was an afterthought, something she'd thrown in because she knew Daniel would deliver the chocolates if she bought a gift from Hermès. There was the belt, proudly displayed on a shelf in Sally's closet. It was coiled in the original orange box, the brown ribbon neatly tied around it. Seeing the tender care Sally had taken of a dumb belt somehow repelled Violet. She decided then to step up and love Sally well.

Everyone in the ballroom was on their feet. Although Jeremy had continued to write his column and appear as a commentator, he had never publicly addressed his Asperger's. Jeremy stepped to the podium. There was a palpable sense in the room that tonight they would all witness a small piece of history. He leaned in to the microphone.

"Thank you," he said, then turned and walked off the stage.

Dan Marino stepped up to the mike. "And people say there's no difference between typicals and spectrum disorders!"

Nora thwacked Dan Marino with a program.

"Hey!" Dan Marino said. "I can joke. The guy picked twelve-and-two against the spread yesterday."

Nora shoved Dan Marino, who sheepishly spoke in to the mike. "You're cool, Jeremy?" he asked. "Right? You can take a joke."

"Yes," Jeremy said, off stage. Everyone applauded. Sally covered her face with her hands, smiling and shaking her head. The next presenter took the stage.

"I have to pee," Violet told David. "Don't let them take my food." Violet passed the staging area where a regiment of caterers loaded coffee onto silver trays.

She stopped. Pascal was one of the waiters, his dreads tied back with a black ribbon. He saw Violet and smiled as if it were yesterday. She bounded over. "*Pascal, bonsoir. Ça va bien?*" She kissed him on both cheeks.

"*Oui, Violet,*" he said. "*Et vous?*"

"*Ça va bien, merci.*"

"*Avez vous entendu qui est arrivé à Teddy?*" he said.

"No!" Violet froze. "What happened?"

Sally appeared, grabbed Violet's arm, and hung from it. "I'm freaking out," Sally said. "Jeremy was so adorable. I want to go say hi. Will you come with me?"

"Sally—" Violet shook her arm loose.

"I'm sorry." Sally stepped back with a frown.

"Did something happen?" Violet studied Pascal. He hesitated and threw a glance toward Sally. Violet said, "She's okay."

"It happened a couple of days ago," Pascal said. "He was on the bus and started vomiting blood. An ambulance took him to the hospital."

"Why?" Violet said. "What was wrong?"

"He went out."

"Where did he go?"

"He got high, got drunk," Sally volunteered. "That's what they say. Who are you talking about?"

"My friend Teddy, the one with hep C." It had been of great comfort to Sally when Violet first mentioned she had a friend who was infected and living a full life. Violet had marveled at the coincidence that *two* people she knew could have the virus. It made her especially grateful that her own test was negative. Sally had questioned Violet on and off about this infected friend, but out of respect for David, Violet kept it vague.

"First he shot drugs," Pascal said. "Then he started drinking. And now he's in LA County."

"LA County?" Violet's chest froze. "He hates LA County. He says people die there."

"That's what happens if you drink with hep C," Sally said. "It's a real no-no."

"It was because of me." Violet gulped. "Because of what I said at the wedding. Oh God, I should have apologized. It's my fault."

"He started shooting drugs for one reason," Pascal said.

"Because of me," Violet said.

"Because he had the cash."

"What?" Violet asked.

"He had three thousand dollars cash in his junkie hands, and he went out and got high. It's as simple as that."

"I have to go," Violet said.

"Violet, don't," Pascal said.

"I need to do this." Violet took Sally's hand. "I have to get David and I have to go." She started off, then stopped. "Pascal?"

"Yes."

"Thank you."

SALLY watched Violet hustle off and stood there with the French waiter. . . .

Violet's mysterious friend with hep C.

He was shooting drugs.

He was at Sally's wedding.

The frightening man who emerged from the bathroom.

The syringe in the wastebasket.

It had no cap on it.

That's how Sally had contracted hep C.

He used my needle to get high at my wedding.

The waiter looked at Sally, as if waiting for her to speak. There was nothing to say. This guy—Teddy was his name—the one responsible for infecting Sally. He was now at LA County Hospital.

VIOLET ran-walked-ran down the hall of the ICU, reading the patients' names off the doors. The nurse had told her Teddy's room number less than a minute ago, but she'd already forgotten.

FLORES, L.

This is all my fault. Before you met me, you were playing jazz, golf, going to AA meetings. I shouldn't have given you the money. I meant well, but I didn't know. You were right; there's a lot I'm not very smart about.

IDELSON, E.

This was my fault. I won't stop until you're sober and healthy again. I promise.

TOLL, J.

David can help your career. You can audition for one of his bands. Or, if touring would be too hard on you, you could be a session musician. That pays great.

REYES, T.

Violet stopped.

She'd gone back to the table to tell David the news. "What do you want me to do?" he asked. He didn't press her for details. He didn't get angry. He didn't point out that in a marriage, you take care of the marriage, not the people outside the marriage. "I want to go," she said. David put down his napkin and stood up. "I'm going with you."

Teddy was on a respirator, a tube sloppily taped to his mouth with too much tape, in a too-big X. Both arms were tucked under a thin blanket. A bag of brown liquid hung from the bed rail. He was awake and staring at the ceiling. Several clear bags of drugs hung from an IV drip, their contents landing in his vein. Was one of them morphine? She hoped so; she knew how fond he was of the opiates. At Kate Mantilini, Violet had studied the whites of his eyes to see if she could detect jaundice. Now they were a solid yellow. Yellow and green, Green Bay Packer colors...

Teddy slowly turned his head in her direction, just like the first day they met, when she had run to his parked car. He had known it was her then; he had known that she would come. As he did now. And just like then, he nodded.

"Oh, fuck you," Violet said with a laugh. With that laugh, Teddy's laugh, warmth filled her body. She sprang closer to the bed. Pieces of his hair were braided with colorful beads. "*There's* your look," she said. "It took you a while, but you finally found it."

He rolled his eyes but didn't try to speak. He studied her face. On the TV, Jay Mohr told Conan an unremarkable story about being given the wrong hotel room in Vegas. Violet let Teddy's eyes wash over her, savoring what felt like his touch.

"You paged me?" A sandy-haired doctor breezed in.

"Hi," Violet said, startling. "Yeah. Could you tell me what happened?"

The doctor looked at Teddy, then back at Violet. "I can only discuss a patient's care with immediate family."

"I'm his aunt," Violet said.

The doctor frowned and turned to Teddy. "Do I have your consent to discuss your case with this woman?"

Teddy nodded.

"Is he going to be okay, Dr. —" Violet looked at the doctor's name tag. "Dr. Molester?"

The doctor quickly corrected, "*Moleester.*"

Violet didn't dare look at Teddy for fear they'd both erupt in laughter.

Dr. Molester unhooked Teddy's chart from the foot of the bed and gave it a cursory look. "He was brought in two days ago with acute esophageal variceal hemorrhage, caused by alcoholic hepatitis."

"I'm sorry, you're going to have to dumb it down."

"Mr. Reyes's liver was already compromised from hepatitis C. Excessive alcohol consumption caused the liver to enlarge and block certain veins from draining. Pressure built up in the esophagus to the point where his esophageal veins popped, causing a massive bleed. He's lucky he didn't bleed to death."

Teddy stared at the ceiling, a majestic beast, caged, yet not deigning to make eye contact with his captor.

"Why is he on a respirator?" Violet asked.

"We inserted a Blakemore tube in his esophagus to put pressure on the varices to stop the bleeding. It's coming out tomorrow."

"So it's not a permanent condition? He'll be off the respirator and able to talk?"

"That's correct."

She grabbed Teddy's foot and gave it a shake. "I guess it's premature to break out the cigarettes and 'Send in the Clowns.'"

The doctor scowled.

"What, no Sondheim fans?" asked Violet.

"There's not a lot to joke about," he said. "A biopsy indicated his liver is severely cirrhotic."

"Oh God." Cirrhotic livers, this was her father's bailiwick. "How bad is it?"

"The liver is a regenerative organ. Sometimes it can recover from the injury of alcohol. Unfortunately, the scarring is permanent, so it remains vulnerable to any alcohol and infections."

"But if he doesn't drink, he'll be fine," Violet said.

"If he doesn't drink, he might get better. We don't know yet. If he drinks again, he'll probably die."

"That's easy enough." She looked at Teddy. "Right? You can stop drinking."

Teddy raised his eyebrows skeptically.

"Oh, come on. That's the easy part. I can get you one of those minders David hires to go on tour with his bands." She turned to the doctor. "Can I sign him up for a liver transplant?"

"They don't put active alcoholics on the transplant list." He looked Violet up and down with disapproving eyes. "As you know, livers are hard to come by. You have to show that you want to live enough to not drink."

"But if he stays sober, he can get on the list."

"I'm not sure." The doctor clanked the chart back onto the rail. "There's a screening process that I'm not completely familiar with."

"So tomorrow I'll talk to someone and get you on the list," she told Teddy. "I know the best hepatologist in the city. Dr. Beyrer. We'll have her take over your case."

"If you really want to help?" said the doctor.

"Yes," said Violet eagerly.

"I suggest you donate blood. When Mr. Reyes came in, his liver was unable to manufacture the compounds required for clotting, so he required a massive blood transfusion. The hospital is always in need of blood."

"Oh," Violet said, deflated by the meagerness of the request.

"Unless, of course…" he said.

"What?" she asked, brightening.

"You're infected, too."

Violet felt a stab of humiliation. "No," she said. "Of course I'm not infected."

"Good. Then you can give blood on the fourth floor. They're open all night. Is that all?"

"When will he be released?" Violet asked.

"He's on a strong regimen of somatostatin to lower the pressure within the portal system. Also, his abdomen was showing preliminary signs of ascites, which caused an infection to develop. We've got him on diuretics and broad-spectrum antibiotics."

"Well, whatever. The important thing is he won't drink again and we'll get him a new liver."

The doctor raised his eyebrows. "Excuse me, but we're short staffed here."

"Of course. Thank you, Dr. Mol-*eester*."

The doctor departed. Teddy laughed, and coughed so hard he was thrust upright. The respirator tube snared him back like a fish on a hook.

"Jesus! I'm sorry!" Violet frantically pushed her fingertips into the milky tape to keep the breathing tube affixed. She placed one hand on Teddy's chest to push him back down, and left it there. He closed his eyes.

"Don't worry," she said. "The Baroness von Beeswax is in the house. I'm going to make sure you stay clean and get you a new liver." Violet quoted Shakespeare, "Come, let's away to prison; We two alone will sing like birds in the cage." Teddy opened his eyes. "You do know where that quote is from," she said. "It's what Shirley Jones sang to Shamu in your favorite *Partridge Family* episode."

Teddy laughed again and started coughing.

"Stop it, stop it," she said.

And then: in traipsed Coco.

On a chair and table were a mangy rabbit-fur coat, cans of Red Bull, and a *Vogue*. They'd been there the whole time; Violet just hadn't noticed.

Coco was dressed the part, in all black. Laced into her black bob were braids with colorful bangles. Also on the table was a Ziploc bag of beads. Coco must have woven them into his hair. Her doll.

"Who are you?" Coco's voice was breathy and her words choppy. Her eyes, evacuated. There wasn't even the slightest attempt at affability. Violet stared into the face of crazy. Not good-crazy. Mean, hard, mentally ill crazy. Violet looked to Teddy. His eyes were closed.

"I'm his aunt," Violet said, the words getting stuck in her throat.

"No, you're not." Coco sat down on the bed. She took a swig from a can of apricot juice, then tore open some Oreos. "That lady in the blood place was a real bitch," she told Teddy. "She wouldn't let me give blood because of the hep C. But I stole some cookies and juice." She seemed to have completely lost interest in Violet.

Teddy opened his eyes but stared at the ceiling. He wouldn't look at Violet. The fucking coward.

Coco was a crazy liar who didn't love Teddy, yet he kept coming back for more.

Teddy was a crazy liar who didn't love Violet, yet she kept coming back for more.

So who was Violet, other than a crazy liar…who kept David coming back for more?

But Violet could change that. She would make herself worthy of David. It might be the only thing of note she would do for the rest of her life.

It would have to be enough.

She hoped it would be enough.

"Turn it up," Coco said to no one in particular. "I love this commercial."

Violet looked at Teddy one last time, his eyes still closed. She turned and walked out of his room and down the corridor.

She thought about the zucchini in the garden. Winter weather hadn't yet arrived, so the summer vegetables were still thriving in December. Tomorrow, she'd pick some and make David that pasta he liked, the Marcella Hazan recipe with the mint and garlic and red wine vinegar. She picked up her pace; she couldn't wait to tell David about the dinner she was going to make. She'd fry green tomatoes, too, with herb aioli. Because of the heat, the dill and cilantro Violet had planted last month were beginning to bolt and needed to be picked. Dot could help Violet. She loved helping her mama in the garden.

Violet turned into the waiting room. David sat cross-legged on the floor, playing dominoes with a black family. She had no idea her husband knew how to play dominoes.

He looked up. "What?" he asked.

She decided against telling David about the pasta. It would be better to surprise him.

SALLY watched, undetected, from across the nurses' station, as Violet left. Once the coast was clear, Sally moved to a chair beside Teddy Reyes's room. She didn't know what she'd been waiting for, but when the girl in black left, Sally floated to her feet and entered.

The respirator was so loud it seemed to overpower the patient asleep in bed. Sally walked closer. Yes, this was the man from the wedding. Not that she had doubted it, but seeing him gave her the serenity of knowing she'd put the pieces together correctly.

Sally glanced at his chart. There it was, hepatitis C, genotype two. Fourteen percent of all hep C cases were genotype two. At least he'd given her the *good* hep C.

He was beautiful. Gorgeous fuzzy eyebrows, the kind you wanted to gently brush your lips across. A crooked nose. Sweet ears. One had been pierced several times but was now free of adornment. Short, sparse eyelashes. His forehead smooth, kiss-able. His arms rested above the blankets. So tanned, the jaundice only showed on the inside of his elbows. He must have loved the sun—a day laborer, a beach rat, a water baby?

A tattoo peeked above the blood pressure cuff and continued down his inner arm. Sally couldn't tell if it was a vine or some kind of snake.

His thumb bled at the fingernail. He must have chewed it just before he fell asleep. Poor guy. What had he been so worried about that he pushed the respirator tube away and risked his life just to chew his nails? Was it something Violet had said? On the blanket, near his right hand, was a bright red dot. Fresh, virus-infected blood. Before Teddy, Sally might have been afraid of it. Tonight, she touched it. She leaned over to behold his face. Her hair brushed his cheeks.

"It's okay," she whispered. She reached under his neck and felt the warmth of his skin, happy warmth. She slipped her fingers farther down his back and felt the ripple of his ribs. In his slumber, his head rocked, then lolled on her arm.

"You did the best you could," she said.

Sally's free hand was slightly cupped and turned upward. She closed her eyes. Teddy was alive in her. As was the person he had contracted the virus from. And the person who'd given it to them. And anyone else who had hep C. Or any other disease. Or who'd ever been delivered impossible news. Or whose life was not what they'd hoped it would be. They all rested in the palm of her hand.

"I know you're scared," she said. "I'm scared, too."

When Sally opened her eyes, his were open and gazing into hers. Their yellow glow only added to their beauty, such a gorgeous icy green.

"I forgive you," she said.

His eyes absorbed her with such courage. His lower lids rose slightly. He was smiling. And then he closed his eyes.

CHAPTER FOURTEEN

Those Violets

DAVID HADN'T TOLD HIS WIFE WHERE HE WOULD BE TODAY. IF VIOLET CALLED, Kara was under strict orders to tell her he was unreachable, not back at the hospital.

"What's the name of this ambulance service?" asked the woman in the billing office. She was fat and peppy, a combination David found endearing.

"It's called Private Ambulance Providers of Los Angeles," he said.

"And it's not one of ours?"

"It's a private ambulance service."

"You know insurance isn't going to cover that?"

"I know."

"Can't be cheap." The woman shook her head.

"It isn't." David had arranged for Teddy to be transferred to Cedars and to be cared for by Sally's hepatologist, Dr. Beyrer. David would pay the bill, no questions asked.

"Okey dokey," said the lady. "We're just about ready. Let me get one more authorization." She pushed herself up with a celebratory groan.

"Take your time," David said.

Last night, when Violet had found David in the waiting room—he was playing dominoes with the father of a guy who'd been shot—there was a peculiar look on her face. David knew what it looked like to be wildly loved by Violet, he could tell by the twinkle in her eyes, and for the first time in years, he saw it. He had no idea what had transpired in that hospital room. But David's final act of faith in Violet, and he knew it was the last one that would be required, was loving those she loved.

In the sweat lodge, David had chosen to believe in her. It had brought him the truth that day in his office. What she told him, the depths to which she had sunk, and in the name of what, he still couldn't comprehend; it nauseated him. What she described, not the details as much as the madness of the affair, was all too familiar.

Back when David and Violet were newly engaged, Sacramento Sukey had called David's office every day and every night. He never took her calls, naively willing her to just go away. His heart still raced, remembering that white-knuckle moment when he was heading out to meet Violet at Orso, before *Falsettos*. His secretary had buzzed him, "David, it's Sukey again." "Tell her I'm out of the office." "She's out *here*," whispered the secretary, "*in my office*." David slipped out the back door and raced down the thirty-eight flights of stairs, to Seventh Avenue. Somehow, there stood Sukey, jangly, puffy faced, *desperate*, outside a souvenir shop. She held the hand of her little boy. David wrote Sukey a check for five grand, right there on the sidewalk—for what, he didn't know, but he became unglued by the prospect that Violet would surprise him at his office, as she sometimes did, and discover he was a cheat. Sukey never called again. Still, David hadn't set foot in Sacramento for seventeen years. In fact, when Violet landed her first TV job and wanted to move to LA, the only hesitation on David's part was that it was too close to Sacramento. This was why he hadn't cheated since. Not because fidelity was sacrosanct, but because infidelity turned good people bad. David sometimes wished he could give himself points for his rectitude. But he had made up his mind, so it wasn't even a choice. Other people apparently had a harder time sticking to things. Not David.

On the hospital worker's desk was a clownish ceramic bowl with pinched edges. In it were fifty cards the size of shirt labels. David grabbed a bunch and fanned through them, reading the single word calligraphed on each.

> Gratitude
> Healing
> Compassion
> Play
> Tenderness

"I see you found my angel cards," sang the woman.

"Oh. Yeah."

"Every morning you're supposed to pick one and use it for inspiration."

"Ahh," said David.

"Pick one."

He tossed the cards back into the bowl, stirred them with his finger, and picked one. "*Courage,*" he read. Beside the word was a drawing of an angel in a bathing suit, jumping off a high dive.

"Do you like it?" asked the lady. "Because if you don't, you can take another one. I do it all the time."

"Courage is fine."

"You, young man," the lady said, handing him some papers, "have gorgeous credit."

"I get that a lot." David filled out a check for a whopping $23,545.99.

"Come with me," she said conspiratorially. David followed her down the corridor. "I sprained my ankle a couple of months ago." She winced with each step. "It keeps flaring up. I guess I should have taken better care of it."

"Rice," said David.

"What?"

"It's an acronym. Rest, Ice, Compression, Elevation. It's what you should do for an ankle sprain."

"You'd think working at a hospital, someone would have told me that!" She laughed. "Here you are, room 833."

David hadn't realized it, but she had escorted him to a door that read REYES, T. David balked. "Oh."

"Have a nice day, Mr. Parry," she said, and hobbled off.

"Yeah, you, too."

Last night, David and Violet had taken his car to and from the hospital. Back home, Violet slept, but David couldn't. He had called a taxi to take him to the Shrine to get Violet's car. That was LA for you—a voracious gobbler of time and energy over car logistics.

The best example had been ten years ago, at a Grammy party at the old Morton's. David couldn't leave until he had said hi to Mick Jagger, who was in serious conversation with some chick. David lingered a few minutes. Then, to give Mick a hint, he sat on the edge of the banquette. David overheard them fervently debating whose car to take home. They could take both cars, but if they did, Mick would have to park his Bentley on the street, which wasn't safe, but if they left his car at Morton's, the valet would be closed in the morning, so maybe they should park one car on the street now, but this neighborhood had overnight parking by permit only, so they would risk getting towed…Christ, it went on for an eternity! David realized that if Mick Jagger wasn't immune to LA car bullshit, nobody was. From then on, David had always found it amusing.

Driving Violet's car home on the 405 early this morning, David had the freeway to himself. The shoulder was dotted with tough orange garbage bags. Parolees in stenciled vests picked up trash in the dry hills. A deer had one of the bags in its teeth and shook it with a dumb violence not usually associated with Bambi. David smiled. He'd have to tell Dot about it. He turned on the stereo. A CD was playing, something Violet must have been listening to on the way to the Shrine last night.

> *You're always sorry,*
> *You're always grateful…*

It was that Sondheim song she had wanted sung at their wedding. David couldn't remember exactly what about the lyrics had made him so upset. It was some song where married men explain to a bachelor what it was like being married. David turned up the volume.

> *You're always sorry.*
> *You're always grateful.*
> *You hold her thinking,*
> *"I'm not alone."*
> *You're still alone.…*
>
> *You're sorry-grateful*
> *Regretful-happy.*
> *Why look for answers*
> *Where none occur?*

You'll always be
What you always were,
Which has nothing to do with,
All to do with her.

It had taken him long enough, but driving north on the 405, just past the Getty, David finally got Sondheim.

A man coughed. A dry cough that wouldn't stop. Teddy Reyes. David stood at the open door. Courage, the angel card had counseled.

Teddy Reyes sat on the bed, his back to David, naked it appeared, his hospital gown in one hand. His hair was shaggy, his back brown and slight. Seeing the skin his wife had touched, loved once, it made David's stomach tighten. Teddy Reyes pulled a T-shirt over his head. Before he stuck his hands through the armholes, he rested, depleted from the exertion. The small man who had sundered David's marriage barely had the strength to put on a T-shirt! Still, he had somehow managed to wrest Violet's sanity. David knew she wouldn't have relinquished it without a fight. Teddy got his arms through the shirt and sat there, slumped.

That's when David saw them: the violets tattooed on Teddy's arm. A garland, exactly like those behind Violet's ear. They snaked from the inside of his wrist, up his arm, around his elbow, then disappeared inside his shirtsleeve. The violets. *Those fucking violets.*

LATER that day, David was returning calls at his desk when Kara entered with a Post-it: "The driver from PAPLA." It took David a second to register, Private Ambulance Providers of Los Angeles.

"Get him on the phone," David said. As he waited, there was a terrific squawking through the double-paned window.

A flock of birds, big ones, swooped down Beverly Drive and, in a glorious watery movement, alighted on the cheesy Santa sleigh that spanned Wilshire Boulevard. David knew from their silhouettes that the birds were Amazon parrots, giant and Christmas colored. He had never seen them before, but there was much lore surrounding this flock of LA parrots. Some believed them to have escaped from the set of *Doctor Dolittle* in the sixties. Here they were now, shimmering red and green in the tinsel under the harsh December sun. Marvelous!

The phone rang. "This is David Parry."

It was the ambulance driver. Teddy Reyes was nowhere to be found. David got his friend with the sprained ankle on the phone. She was as surprised as anyone. When nobody was looking, Teddy Reyes had unhooked the IVs, gotten dressed, and walked out of the hospital. The only trace of him was a note on the bed. It read "Went to pick up a friend at the airport."

TEDDY

I GIVE YOU THIS GIFT. COME CLOSER. ALL I HAVE TO GIVE IS THIS, AND I GIVE it to you.

I'm a know-nothing, my ignorance is immense. (You would call me a philistine.)

I'm a jailed crazy, a sobbing drunk in the garden, a diseased pirate, the scorpion king of Venice. Still you come, basket in hand, to collect more of my booty.

Come closer....

I gave until you lit up the night sky. I took until you were a madwoman wandering the canyons.

Oh, how your basket trembles for my gifts.

Shall I fill it with my sick roses and counterfeit coins, my long nights, my sweet heart, and the birdsong of my brilliant parrots circling overhead cawing your name?

Look at your displeasure! How you hate to wait, plump, spoiled, bejeweled queen of the glass castle. I apologize.

I won't make you wait any longer, darling, dear, sweet-smelling co-conspirator of mine. Here is my gift.

Come closer....

I am gone.

Don't be angry. Since that first too-hot morning, I am your laughing puppet, your dance floor caddy, and my heart leaps only for you.

Soon, you will wake up from a well-deserved afternoon nap. For one moment, you experience that wonder of not knowing who you are or where you are, or if it's day or night. You could be, and are, anyone.

Then: the lake out the window, the newspaper beside you on the bed, the glasses in your hand, your daughter's laughter swirling up up up through the pines.

And you remember, *I am Violet Parry*.

But this time: you rejoice. Throw your basket in the air! Know I am by your side. See, I am branded, my arm forever abloom in your name.

I know you're scared, so am I.

I have stumbled enough. I am forgiven. I am abundant. I am certainly insouciant. I'm not your tar baby. You're the star, baby. Love the lucky well.

READING GROUP NOTES

THIS ONE IS MINE

Maria Semple

This One Is Mine is your first novel. What was your path to becoming a writer?

My father created the sixties TV series *Batman* and went on to write a bunch of movies. When you're a kid, and your dad's job consists of walking around the house in socks all day, then having barbecues with Archie Bunker, Major Anthony Nelson, and Sebastian Howell III, you decide, I want *that* job.

I was an English major at Barnard. I could have happily spent my life as an English major—reading books, writing papers, maybe teaching, eventually writing a novel—but I wrote a spec screenplay that sold to Fox (and never got made). It was the late eighties, when basically anyone could get a development deal. The stuff I wrote was terrible. I was too young.

Around that time, I met Darren Star, and he gave me my first TV job, on *Beverly Hills, 90210*. That led to about fifteen years of TV writing. I was good enough at it, but I secretly knew it was too hard. Not old-fashioned-hard-work hard, but sweaty-something's-wrong-here hard. For the life of me, I couldn't come up with sitcomy joke-jokes, which mainly consist of a person walking into a friend's house without knocking, insulting them, then helping himself to a bottle of water from the fridge. If, in real life, I was even once on the receiving end of such behavior, I'd probably burst into tears.

The last show I worked on was *Arrested Development*—a brilliant show I'm humbled and a little embarrassed to have my name on because it's all Mitch Hurwitz. (Mitch, if you're reading this, BIG KISS.) After that, I thought, hey, I'm going to try writing that novel.

How was writing a novel different from writing for television?

Television is collaborative. I was in a room with ten fabulously talented writers, all working together, with an infernal machine bearing down on us. We answered to actors and network executives. Plus, we were sleep-deprived, behind schedule, and lucky to pull it all together for show night. Multiply that by twenty-two episodes, add a couple of pant sizes, and you get a year in the life of a TV writer.

Writing *This One Is Mine,* I was very much alone. I wrote it with no agent, no publisher, no deadline, no concept that it would make the least bit of sense, let alone get published.

But, really, the biggest and scariest difference is that in TV, if the work wasn't great, I could always blame someone else. With my novel, it feels like I'm handing out something and saying, "Here's the best I can do."

Where did you get your inspiration for this book?

When I decided to write a novel, I had just finished rereading *The House of Mirth* and was in the middle of rereading *Anna Karenina*. I realized my favorite kind of story involves strong, singular women who set out to destroy themselves. Especially if the women are living in fancy houses, have lots of help, and commit adultery. Sorry, but I just love that. I decided simply to write what I liked to read. So I cobbled together a story.

Tell us about the title.

This One Is Mine comes from the poem in the front of book by the Sufi poet Hafiz. I love it because it's deeply passionate. Yet at the same time, it's impersonal and a little frantic, like, "You—you over there! I don't even know your name, but you're mine!" It fits with the theme of the book, in that at the beginning every character confuses love with possession. David sees Violet as *his wife*. Violet tries to buy Teddy's love and is wildly jealous of Coco. Sally feels as though she has more right to David than Violet. During the course of the story, all that changes.

How did you approach writing these decidedly flawed characters?

When I was writing the book, I'd ask myself, "If I was reading this in bed, what would keep me from turning off the light?" Which is asking a lot because, man, I love to sleep. So I made sure my characters threw themselves headlong into their pursuits. You might not sympathize with Violet risking a life of luxury, and even her child, for a shifty dirtbag like Teddy, but hopefully it's compelling reading. And if I've deprived my reader of precious sleep, I consider my job well done.

Do you see yourself in any of your characters? Which ones were the easiest or most difficult to write?

I knew the basic story I wanted to tell—woman having an affair; sister-in-law envying her. Constructing the characters, I tapped into aspects of myself and greatly exaggerated them. For Violet, it was the deadening effect of too much time in L.A. For Sally, it was self-will born out of anxiety. At the risk of being an author who claims my characters "wrote themselves," I will say that if you have your characters want something really badly, it makes life a lot easier.

What are you working on next?

Another novel. My big idea is for it to be fast-paced, surprising, psychologically astute, gorgeously written, and deeply, deeply moving. Pray for me.

QUESTIONS AND TOPICS FOR DISCUSSION

1. Why do you think Violet is drawn to Teddy? What makes her risk "losing everything," as David puts it?

2. How does the novel's title, *This One Is Mine*, relate to the story? The book's epigraph opens with the image of a slave block. Are any of the characters in the book "enslaved" in a way?

3. In the first chapter, David is upset with Violet for what he perceives to be her lack of interest in maintaining the household. Is his anger justified?

4. What does Violet find sad about Los Angeles? Where do you think this sadness stems from?

5. What do you think about Sally's friendship with Maryam? Why does Maryam put up with her?

6. Los Angeles could be said to be a city of ambition. How do the characters' ambitions relate to one another's? What fuels those ambitions, and when do they get out of control?

7. In some ways, Sally seems to want everything that Violet has: a successful husband, financial security, a nice house, and stylish friends. Do you think Sally would be happy if she suddenly

had everything she wanted? What similarities to you see in Sally and Violet?

8. Do you see any similarities between David and Jeremy?

9. Teddy seems to have a set of problems that make Violet's (and everyone else's) pale in comparison. Do you think Violet is drawn to him because of or in spite of these traits?

10. What do you make of Sally and Jeremy's relationship? Do you think there is a way that it could ever have worked out?

11. Why is Violet happy when Sally tells her that she never really liked her?

12. In many ways, this is a very "L.A." story. To what extent do you think the characters' attitudes and actions are shaped by Los Angeles? Could you see this story taking place anywhere else?

13. At the end of the book, Violet, Sally, and David all visit Teddy in the hospital. In what ways did Teddy's arrival in their lives bring them all together? How might this story have turned out differently if Violet had never met Teddy at the health fair?

14. In Leo Tolstoy's *Anna Karenina,* Anna is miserable in a loveless marriage and recklessly succumbs to her desire for the dashing Vronsky. What similarities do you see between Tolstoy's novel and *This One Is Mine*?

15. What other books did *This One Is Mine* remind you of? What was similar or different about them?

BOOKS I LOVE: A LIST COMPILED BY MARIA SEMPLE

Henderson the Rain King by Saul Bellow

The Selfish Gene by Richard Dawkins

Ablutions by Patrick deWitt

Middlemarch by George Elliot

All About Lulu by Jonathan Evison

The Good Soldier by Ford Maddox Ford

The Corrections by Jonathan Franzen

Headlong by Michael Frayn

The Art of Fiction by John Gardner

On Becoming a Novelist by John Gardner

What I'd Say to the Martians by Jack Handey

The Portrait of a Lady by Henry James

English Passengers by Matthew Kneale

When We Were Romans by Matthew Kneale

Lolita by Vladimir Nabokov

Pale Fire by Vladimir Nabokov

True Grit by Charles Portis

American Pastoral by Philip Roth

Operation Shylock by Philip Roth

Last Night by James Salter

Anna Karenina by Leo Tolstoy

Everything Ravaged, Everything Burned by Wells Tower

The Travelling Hornplayer by Barbara Trapido

I'm Losing You by Bruce Wagner

The House of Mirth by Edith Wharton

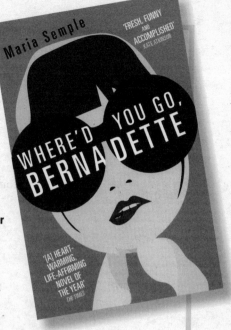